Th_____ade Chuck's heart skip several beats.

Chuck glanced at PJ standing _____ to him. "How was it? Y_____ want to know."

"I did fine."

"I would have _____"

"I know you w_____. If you could have."

"Why didn't you tell me?" Chuck tipped Charlie into the crook of his arm and stared down into her little face.

"Your focus needed to be on staying alive," PJ said. "What was the point in telling you?"

His anger stirred again. "The point is, I'm Charlie's father."

"And if there had been complications, what could you have done from Afghanistan?"

Chuck sighed. "Nothing."

A long silence stretched between them.

"I won't try to keep you from seeing Charlie," PJ said.

Chuck liked the strong, determined woman she'd grown into in the year he'd been away, and found himself even more attracted to her than before. But he wasn't as sure about where they stood, or if he trusted her with his heart.

BODYGUARD
UNDER FIRE

BY
ELLE JAMES

First published in Great Britain 2013
by Mills & Boon, an imprint of Harlequin (UK) Limited,
Eton House, 18-24 Paradise Road, Richmond, Surrey TW9 1SR

© Mary Jernigan 2013

ISBN: 978 0 263 90374 4
ebook ISBN: 978 1 472 00745 2

46-0913

Harlequin (UK) policy is to use papers that are natural, renewable and recyclable products and made from wood grown in sustainable forests. The logging and manufacturing processes conform to the legal environmental regulations of the country of origin.

Printed and bound in Spain
by Blackprint CPI, Barcelona

A Golden Heart Award winner for Best Paranormal Romance in 2004, **Elle James** started writing when her sister issued a Y2K challenge to write a romance novel. She has managed a full-time job and raised three wonderful children, and she and her husband even tried their hands at ranching exotic birds (ostriches, emus and rheas) in the Texas Hill Country. Ask her, and she'll tell you what it's like to go toe-to-toe with an angry three-hundred-and-fifty-pound bird! After leaving her successful career in information technology management, Elle is now pursuing her writing full-time. Elle loves to hear from fans. You can contact her at ellejames@earthlink.net or visit her website at www. ellejames.com.

This book is dedicated to my father who sacrificed a lot for his country and his family. He's the rock in my life and I love him so much.

Chapter One

Chuck Bolton walked to the edge of town, working the kinks out of his bum leg, his limp more pronounced after his two-hour ride on one of the resort nags, housed in the old-fashioned livery stable.

He hadn't had much call to ride in the military, spending most of his time on foot or in an armor-plated vehicle, patrolling the villages and Taliban-riddled hillsides of Afghanistan.

He'd still be there had he not turned all Rambo and gone off the deep end. Some called him a hero. His commander called him an idiot for risking his life. But other than ending his military career, he couldn't regret his vigilante justice on the Taliban stronghold he'd leveled to the ground single-handed.

After what they'd done to that kid…

Chuck shook his head to clear the images. That was the past. Wild Oak Canyon and Covert Cowboys, Inc. were his future.

On the edge of town, looking south, he drew in a deep breath of hot, dry air and let it out. Not many understood the lure of this parched desert or chose to live here. Outsiders didn't last long, not with miles and miles of flat, unchanging terrain, with the Davis Mountains rising in the distance, appearing closer than they actually were.

Hell, Chuck might not have come back had he not been invited to join CCI, the secret organization billionaire ranch owner Hank Derringer had started recently. Wild Oak Canyon held too many memories, both good and bad.

Everywhere he turned he ran into mental images of PJ.

PJ riding a horse across the desert landscape, PJ smiling up at him from their favorite swimming hole, begging him to join her, PJ telling him she'd love him forever…

Forever had been all too short. She'd begged him not to volunteer for the rotation to Afghanistan, wanting him to wait until his unit was called up, giving them a little more time together before he was put into harm's way. His Army National Guard unit hadn't been due for rotation for another twelve months when a call went out for volunteers.

Chuck had insisted on going, telling her duty called and he had to go.

They'd argued, Chuck had said things he wished he hadn't, his temper getting the better of him. Looking back, he could see that PJ had been scared, afraid of losing him. And he'd pushed her away so effectively she'd ended their engagement, throwing the ring in his face shortly before he'd left for predeployment training at Fort Hood.

God, he'd been so stubborn. If only he'd said he was sorry, they might be married by now. He wouldn't be wandering the streets of Wild Oak Canyon in search of what he'd lost.

Yeah, and if wishes were horses, he probably would have been bucked off on his butt anyway.

Bottom line was that he was back. He hadn't had the nerve to look up PJ yet and wouldn't. That didn't stop his gaze from searching every face passing by on foot or in cars and trucks.

So far, he hadn't seen her. For all he knew, she might not be here at all. The last correspondence he'd had from her was a letter asking where she could send the things he'd accumulated at her house. The address had been the same house she'd lived in with her mother in Wild Oak Canyon, but that had been a year ago. A lot changed in a year. He'd driven by that address when he'd gotten to town. A Hispanic family with two small children lived there now.

Chuck performed a clumsy about-face and headed back to the Wild Oak Canyon Resort staff quarters, his temporary lodging for the assignment Hank had given him.

His cover was as a handyman, fixing things around the resort and Cara Jo's Diner, adjacent to the resort compound. Cara Jo Smithson, the most recent owner of the diner and the new property manager for the resort, would give him the particulars about the real assignment. He was to be a bodyguard for one of her employees. No one was to know that but Hank, Cara Jo and Chuck. Not even the employee. What was so special about that person that he needed protecting? Chuck wouldn't know until Cara Jo returned from her supply run to Fort Stockton. She'd fill him in with all the particulars of the case then.

Hank had given him a key to one of the rooms in the resort staff quarters. The room was at the back of the resort closest to the diner. From what he could tell, there were only two staff rooms in this wing of the resort, and they shared a bathroom down the hall.

After settling his duffle bag in the room, Chuck had examined the exterior of the diner and the resort compound. Wild Oak Canyon's Main Street and the resort had a quaint Wild West theme with weathered-wood storefronts, an old-style barbershop, a general store and a saloon with a hitching post out front. Cara Jo's Diner was just like the rest of the town, only some of the weathered wood needed repair before someone got hurt or the building suffered further damage from wind and the elements.

Chuck noted weatherworn boards peeling up on the porch, along with a splintered railing and loose shingles on the roof. One of the eaves had rotted through and would need replacing. As soon as he had sufficient supplies, he'd go to work on those little fix-it items. They wouldn't keep him busy for long. He hoped there was more work to be done on the inside of the resort or maybe the old livery stable. He preferred working outside, especially around animals. They weren't as judgmental as people.

Until he had the supplies and his marching orders, he was at loose ends with energy to burn. Thus the ride, followed by a walk to the end of town and back.

Temperatures hovered close to ninety, even after the sun set and the stars came out to fill the night sky with their brilliance.

Chuck headed to the resort. The back door to the office remained locked, no light inside indicating Ms. Smithson's return.

Sweaty and smelling of horse, Chuck decided on a shower before his meeting with the boss lady and clumped up the stairs to his room. After gathering soap, shaving gear and a towel, he slipped off his boots and socks and headed down the hallway.

A noise in the room beside his had him leaning in toward the door. A baby cried, and a woman's voice talked softly, soothing it.

Chuck knocked on the door. Was Ms. Smithson younger than he'd thought? Did she have a baby?

After a long moment the door opened to a slim, pale-skinned young woman with dark hair piled in a messy bun on the back of her head. She clutched a baby in her arms, balancing a bottle under her chin as she juggled the door handle and tried to look up at him. "Yes?" she managed without dropping her chin-hold on the bottle.

"Are you Cara Jo?" Chuck asked.

She let go of the door and gripped the bottle, holding it for the baby to feed. "Oh, no, I'm Dana. Cara Jo is the owner of the diner. She lives above it."

"Sorry, I'm supposed to meet with her about a job. I'm your new neighbor." He jerked his head to the left toward his apartment door.

"Oh, you must be the handyman." She balanced the bottle with her chin again and held out her hand. "I'm Dana. Cara Jo should be back any minute. She left early this morning for Fort Stockton to get supplies for the resort and diner. They said they'd be back by nine tonight. It's almost nine now."

"I'm Chuck Bolton. Nice to meet you, Dana."

"Good to have a handyman around again. My, but you are very tall."

He smiled. He got that a lot. At six feet five inches, he tended to be taller than most men. "I can see that you're busy. I won't bother you." He glanced down at the baby, a bubbly, milky smile spreading across her face. Her brown hair curled across her forehead, and the big brown eyes were in sharp contrast to Dana's cornflower-blue eyes. "Cute baby."

Dana smiled down at the child in her arms. "Hear that, Charlie? He thinks you're cute. Me, too, my sweet little baby girl."

"I guess I'll be seeing you around." He chucked the baby under the chin and she reached out, snagging his finger in her tight little grip. "A little tiger, aren't you?" He smiled down at the baby, his heart squeezing in his chest. He'd had dreams of him and PJ raising a family together. A strapping brown-haired, brown-eyed boy like him, and an angelic blond-haired, green-eyed girl the spitting image of her mother.

The phone rang in the apartment behind Dana. "Excuse me. Nice to meet you."

Chuck turned away as Dana shut the door.

Yet another reminder of PJ and the family they should have had. He needed to get over her and get on with his life.

It just wasn't that easy.

CARA JO DROVE the truck behind the resort and backed up close to the rear entrance of the diner. "I don't know about you, but I'm past exhausted. What say we leave most of this stuff in the back until tomorrow, when we can get some help unloading?"

Peggy Jane Franks dropped down out of the truck and stretched. "Agreed. We can grab the perishables and store them in the walk-in refrigerator and call it a night. I want to see Charlie."

Mentioning her daughter made PJ smile. An entire day away from her baby made PJ miss her so much it hurt.

Cara Jo dropped the tailgate and slid the ice chests full of everything from butter to frozen yogurt to the edge. The normal delivery truck had broken down in Fort Stockton, and they were running low on supplies. Otherwise they wouldn't have made the long drive themselves.

Once they had the food stored in the freezer and refrigerator in the restaurant, PJ hurried up the back stairs of the resort, hoping to catch Charlie awake. They'd arrived later than she'd expected, and Dana would be tired and ready to go home.

PJ fit her key in the lock of her small apartment and pushed the door open. "Hey, Dana, I'm home."

Dana looked up from bending over the crib, situated just inside the bedroom door. "Oh, it's you."

PJ laughed. "Yeah, it's me. Expecting anyone else?"

Dana smiled. "No, no. I just met the new handyman Cara Jo hired out in the hallway a few minutes ago. I thought maybe he got lost on his way back to his room."

"How's my sweet Charlie?" PJ crossed the room, anxious to hold her daughter.

Dana lifted the baby out of her crib and handed her to PJ. "She was just about to nod off, but when she heard your voice, her eyes popped wide open."

PJ smiled down at Charlie and hugged her against her. "Hey, sweetie, did you miss your mommy?"

Charlie cooed up at her, a toothless smile spreading across her face.

"Of course she did. The sun rises and sets on you, in Miss Charlie's eyes." Dana stared down at the child in PJ's arms. "You're so very lucky."

"I know." PJ kissed Charlie's cheek. Charlie was a perfect baby, full of joy and so easy to take care of. Everyone loved her.

Dana touched PJ's shoulder. "I gotta run. Tommy will be yowling for dinner."

PJ glanced up. "This late?"

"You'd think the man didn't know what a microwave oven was. I bet he didn't bother to get the plate I left for him this morning out of the refrigerator." Dana laughed and smiled at Charlie. "She was an angel."

"Ha. I'll bet she wore you out."

"Not at all. I didn't mind watching her a bit." Dana's eyes glistened.

"You're a natural, Dana. Have you talked to the doctor again? Is there anything you can do?"

"It's in God's hands." Dana smiled through unshed tears. "Two miscarriages must be a sign it isn't meant to be."

"Don't talk like that. It'll happen when you least expect it." As it had happened for PJ.

"I'm not getting my hopes up. Been there too many times and cried buckets of tears." Dana hugged PJ. "Take care of my baby. I think I could love her as much as you do." Dana left, closing the door behind her.

Alone at last with Charlie, PJ dropped into her rocking chair. It wouldn't take much for Charlie to fall asleep, but PJ wanted to hold her a little longer. The sweet scent of baby shampoo and powder filled her senses and gave her a feeling of home.

After a few minutes Charlie slept, her mouth working a sucking motion, the fingers of one hand bunched into a tiny fist. She looked so much like her father—brown hair, brown eyes and ready for a fight.

PJ chuckled, her laughter catching on a sob. She missed Chuck so much she thought she might die sometimes. If not for sweet Charlie, she might have lost the will to live altogether.

Still wearing the clothes she'd traveled in, PJ felt wrinkled, covered in road grime and in need of a shower to wash away the stress of the long drive.

She laid Charlie in her crib and gathered clothing, a bathrobe and toiletries. Switching on the baby monitor, PJ tucked the receiver in her pocket and headed for the door to her suite. She exited and turned to lock the door behind her.

The bathroom was between her suite and the only other staff apartment in this section of the building. When she opened the door, a waft of warm, moist air and a scent she could never forget enveloped her.

Someone had used the shower. Must be the new handyman Cara Jo had spoken of on their trip to Fort Stockton.

PJ's stomach clenched, and her fingers tightened around the doorknob. The new guy would have to use the same soap Chuck had, and damned if he didn't also use the same cologne. As tired as she was, PJ could barely hold it together as the aromas washed over her, bringing back memories best left in the back of her mind.

She had to have a shower and didn't have another option close enough to her room that the monitor would carry to, so PJ closed the door behind her. Her hands shook as she set the monitor on the sink and turned it up loud enough that she could hear it over the water's spray.

With quick, efficient movements, she flung off her clothes and stepped beneath the cool spray. She was fast about her showers, concerned about leaving Charlie alone too long.

After a quick shampoo and rinse, she ducked her head around the curtain and listened to the monitor. A reassuring staticky silence was all she heard. As she closed the shower curtain, a different sound carried over the speaker.

Click.

PJ strained her ears.

Click.

She shut off the water and listened more intently.

Click.

Then a sharp sound, like something falling, echoed through the monitor.

What the hell?

PJ pulled on her pajama bottoms and top, grabbed her key and flung the bathroom door open.

The door to her apartment stood open.

PJ's heart slammed to a halt and then kicked into high gear. She had been careful to close and lock the door when she'd left. As she stared into her dark apartment, fear rooted her to the floor for only a moment.

Her baby daughter was in that room. Cold dread filled her and she shot forward, ready to take down anyone who threatened to harm…

"Charlie," she said and launched forward.

When she stepped through the open door, a dark figure wearing a black ski mask grabbed her and flung her inside.

PJ screamed and scurried backward and then turned to run. She made it only one step before a hand latched onto her hair and yanked her backward.

PJ screamed again, her cry cut off by a large gloved hand clamping down over her mouth. She bit into it, her teeth barely making a dent in the thick leather glove.

She kicked and slammed her elbow into his gut, but he wouldn't release her hair, the pressure on the roots pulling her skin tight over her forehead, pain radiating through her scalp.

All PJ could think about was Charlie. She had to protect her from this madman. Giving up was not an option. She stomped hard on the man's instep and he yelled, let go of her hair and backhanded her so hard she flew across the room, tripped over the couch and fell against an end table. The lamp on the table teetered. PJ grabbed it and swung it at the man's head. The ceramic base hit him in the ear and shattered.

He grabbed the electric cord, ripped it from the wall and wrapped it around PJ's neck, pulling it tight.

PJ's fingers fumbled for the cord, panic setting in as her vision blurred, her air cut off. No. She couldn't die. Charlie needed her. She kicked and twisted, managing only to tighten the cord around her throat. It couldn't end this way. She wouldn't let it happen.

The man lifted her to her feet and dragged her backward toward the door.

PJ's feet flailed beneath her, her strength fading with lack of oxygen. She focused on the crib in the bedroom and gave new effort to saving her own skin. With all the force she could muster, she brought her heel up hard between her attacker's legs.

The man grunted and slumped forward, jerking harder on the cord around her neck.

Her world faded and her strength drained. She couldn't give up.

A loud crash sounded behind her as her apartment door slammed inward, bouncing off the wall. PJ heard it but couldn't see who'd entered. All she could hope was that the cavalry had arrived to save her and Charlie.

Her attacker jerked, releasing his hold on the cord around PJ's neck.

PJ pitched forward to her hands and knees and crawled away, dragging in huge gulps of air. When she turned, the man in black sailed through the air toward her.

She threw herself to the side in time to avoid the collision.

The man hit the ground hard, rolled to his feet and dived for the sliding glass door leading onto the balcony, slamming it open.

Her savior charged after him, naked to the waist, his body glistening with droplets of water.

It all happened so fast, PJ didn't see his face, only his hulking size and rippling, well-toned muscles flashing past.

The attacker in black launched himself over the balcony and dropped to the pavement below, disappearing out of sight. The bare-chested man braced his hands on the rail, his muscles bunched, ready to follow, and then he hesitated.

He stood with his back to PJ for a long, agonizing moment. Would he jump?

PJ prayed he wouldn't. She didn't wish for her hero to be hurt in the fall. At long last, he turned to face her.

Ready to thank her rescuer, PJ's breath left her lungs in a rush.

"Oh, dear God." She pressed her fist to her mouth, her eyes filling with tears, all her hopes and fears of ever seeing this man again wrapped up in one word. "Chuck."

PJ's world faded into black.

Chapter Two

Chuck's instinct had been to leap over the railing and chase after the black-clad attacker and pummel him into a bloody pulp for terrorizing his neighbor. As he'd bent his knees to do just that, pain ripped through his bad leg, reminding him that he couldn't and shouldn't drop fifteen feet to the ground if he wanted to keep the leg to walk on. Even if his leg survived the landing, he wasn't up to running full speed yet.

Defeat rode heavily on his shoulders as he swung back to the woman pulling herself to her feet in the doorway.

She shifted in the shadows, and the overhead light illuminated her sandy-blond hair.

Chuck's heart burst into a gallop, pounding against his ribs. The throbbing pain in his bum leg faded to the back of his mind as joy filled him at the sight of her. He stepped forward.

Her eyes widened and she stepped back. "Chuck?"

"PJ?"

And she crumpled to the floor.

Had he been able, he'd have caught her before she landed. His injury-induced limitations hampered him in his rush to get to her.

Chuck gathered PJ into his arms, his heart plummeting to the bottom of his belly at her reaction when she'd recognized him.

The entire time he'd been in the oppressive heat and constant dust of Afghanistan, he'd pictured her coming to greet him upon his return, arms wide, a smile of happiness lighting her eyes. In the back of his mind, he'd known it was only a dream.

The stark reality of her standing in front of him, her hands clenching and unclenching at her sides, her face blanching before she passed out, shattered those silly dreams.

She was no happier to see him return than she had been to see him leave. Shock best described her response.

Crushed, Chuck held her, cherishing every second he could feel her against him. He examined the bruising around her throat, anger firming his spine, pushing aside his deep disappointment. Who would attack a lone woman like that? Why would anyone want to hurt PJ? Since he hadn't spoken to Cara Jo yet, he couldn't be certain, but he'd bet his right arm that this was the employee Hank wanted protected.

Chuck had walked into this assignment blind. Hank had assured him Cara Jo would fill him in on what his duties were and, when he had met the employee, he could go to Hank with any unanswered questions.

Chuck had a few, and the sooner he got his answers the better.

After only a moment, PJ's face stirred against his chest and her eyes blinked open. "Chuck, what are you doing here? I thought you were still in Afghanistan." She pushed to a sitting position.

His lips tightened. Had he not been a loose cannon and acted on his own, he would still be in Afghanistan for another two months, fighting with his unit. Instead he'd gotten himself shot in the leg and medically discharged out of the army. "The army didn't need me there after all." It wasn't a lie. The army didn't need broken soldiers.

"Oh." Her gaze traveled across his naked chest, her cheeks reddening. "Why are you half-naked?"

His lips twisted into a wry grin. "I just hired on with the

resort as the handyman. I live down the hall." He frowned. "Why are you in this apartment? I met a woman here a little while ago named Donna or Dana or something like that. She had a baby."

The baby whimpered from inside the bedroom as if emphasizing Chuck's question.

PJ's face paled at the sound, her gaze shifting to the crib against the wall inside the next room. She pushed his hands aside and rose to her feet. "I live here."

Chuck straightened, heat rushing up his neck into his head. Like a zombie, he trudged toward the bedroom, his fists tightening, a sharp pain pinching his chest. "Then who is…?" In the dimly lit room, Chuck peered down at the baby with a tuft of silky dark hair, and his world crashed in around him as he remembered what Dana had said. "She called her Charlie," he said, his voice raspy, uneven.

PJ entered the room, switched on a lamp and leaned over the crib, running her fingers over the baby's face and body. "She seems to be okay."

The baby slept through PJ's touch, a soft smile curling her little lips, as if she knew she was safe and in good hands. "I named her after her father," PJ whispered.

"Charlie." Chuck's fingers curled around the crib rail so tightly his knuckles turned white. "Why didn't you tell me?"

PJ sighed. "You were in Afghanistan. What could you have done? From what I know, the army doesn't grant leave from a war zone just so a man can be there when his baby is born, unless under dire circumstances."

"I had a right to know." His words came out sharper than he intended, but hell, what did she expect? A man didn't learn he had a daughter every day. The news had his belly flipping into knots.

"So, now you know." PJ brushed her fingers over her daughter's hair and stepped back. "You have a right to be angry. But I didn't know what else to do. We didn't part on the best of terms."

A muscle jerked in his jaw, and he had to breathe several calming breaths before he could speak again. "Call the police."

PJ passed through the small living area and into the kitchen. Her purse lay strewn across the counter. She dug her cell phone out of a side pocket, hit three buttons and then walked back to the threshold of the bedroom, her gaze on the baby in the crib. "This is PJ Franks at the Wild Oak Canyon Resort. I need to report an intruder attack."

When she'd given details to the dispatcher, she hung up and glanced at Chuck. "They're sending a unit."

Chuck straightened and crossed to her, his fingers reaching out to touch her throat. "We should have asked for an ambulance, as well."

Her eyes filled, but she shook her head. "No. I'm fine." She raised her hands to the bruising around her neck and gulped. "I was so afraid." PJ's head dipped.

Chuck pulled her into his arms. No matter how mad he was, he never could stand to see PJ cry, and after seeing a man choking the life out of her, now was no different. "He's gone."

"Yeah, but why was he here in the first place?" She pushed away from him and wandered back into the living room.

Chuck followed. "Is anything missing?"

She checked her purse, thumbing through her wallet. What few bills she'd had were still there, along with her credit card and identification. "The items were scattered across the counter, but nothing seems to be missing."

"What about the rest of the apartment?"

"I don't have anything of value. Just a few keepsakes and used furniture. As a waitress, I can't afford much." PJ continued around the room, her fingers skimming across the top of the old couch Cara Jo had given her. She ducked into her bedroom and came back out, holding a photo frame, a frown denting her forehead. "This photo is the only thing out of place. It was standing on my nightstand when I left for my shower. I just found it lying on its face."

"The intruder could have knocked it over." Chuck reached for the frame.

PJ handed it over. "It's a picture of me and my birth mother."

A woman looking remarkably like PJ held a child in her arms and was smiling for the photographer. Her eyes were shadowed, but the love for her little girl was clear in her expression.

"She died when you were little, didn't she?"

PJ nodded. "I was six. My adoptive mother, Terri Franks, pretty much raised me. We moved to Wild Oak Canyon before I started high school."

Chuck remembered the pretty young PJ hanging out around the stables, talking to the horses. She'd been more comfortable with the animals than with people.

A knock on the door was followed by a man's voice. "PJ Franks? Sheriff's Deputy Johnny Owen. You called?"

PJ hurried to open the door for the officer.

He took her statement, in which she described the attacker, what he wore and which direction he'd gone.

Chuck searched the apartment, analyzing everything he saw for clues as to who had broken into PJ's apartment and why. All the while he fought to process the miracle of the baby in the next room. His child.

When Owen finished with PJ, the deputy asked Chuck a few questions and then tucked the pad of paper into his pocket and sighed. "Since the man was wearing gloves, I don't see a need to dust for prints. I'll have a look around outside to see if there are any footprints on the ground, but—"

"It's been dry, and the chance of a footprint showing up is slim to none," Chuck finished. "Thanks for trying."

After the deputy left, Chuck made a round of the apartment, checking the windows and sliding glass door locks.

When he'd deemed them secure, he met PJ at her open apartment door.

"It's getting late," she said. "I need to get some sleep before I hit the day shift at the diner."

"Will you be all right?" Chuck stepped into the door frame and gripped PJ's arms, his gaze capturing hers.

"I'll be fine." The shadows beneath her eyes spoke of her exhaustion and the lingering fear.

Fine, humph. Chuck wanted to hold her so badly, it hurt to drop his grip from her arms and walk out into the hallway. "If you need me…"

"You're just a yell away." She gave him a half smile.

Chuck nodded toward the interior of her apartment. "She's beautiful."

PJ's face reddened, and she nodded. "We'll discuss Charlie tomorrow."

"Yes, we will." Now that Chuck knew he had a daughter, he was determined to be a part of her life, whether PJ wanted him in *her* life or not.

PJ closed the door behind him.

Chuck waited until he heard the click of the lock being engaged. Then he hurried down the hallway to his room, grabbed a sleeping bag and a pillow and returned to bed down in front of PJ's door. As he stretched out on the floor and worked the kink out of his leg, he reminded himself that it beat sleeping in a foxhole. And he refused to let anything happen to PJ and his precious baby daughter, Charlie.

Once he was settled, he grabbed his cell phone and hit the speed dial number for Hank Derringer.

The older man answered on the third ring. "Derringer," he said, his voice scratchy and slurred with sleep.

"Hank, Chuck here. Tell me my assignment was just some sick joke on your part."

Hank sighed. "I take it you met PJ?"

"I did. You didn't tell me I'd be protecting my ex-fiancée."

"If I had, would you have taken the job?"

Chuck wanted to tell the man he would have, but truth was, he probably would have told Hank where to go with his job and assignment. "No."

"And now?" Hank asked.

With a sigh, Chuck answered. "You know damn well I can't walk away."

"I take it you met your daughter, Charlie?"

Chuck swallowed the lump forming in his throat. "Yes."

"Beautiful baby girl, isn't she?" Hank chuckled. "Looks like her father."

"How did you know?" Chuck asked.

"Let's just say I make it my business to know as much as I can about the people I hire. And I have a special interest in PJ that I won't go into at this time."

"Now that I'm here and know who I'm supposed to protect, maybe you can tell me why someone tried to kill PJ tonight."

AFTER PJ LOCKED the door behind Chuck, she'd leaned her head against the cool, wooden panel, telling herself to breathe.

Chuck still had too much of a hold on her, even after almost a year's separation. She thought pushing him out of her life had been the best decision at the time. Now she wasn't quite as convinced. Breaking their engagement had been only a part of it.

Even if Chuck hadn't insisted on volunteering, PJ suspected she'd have found another way to push him away. They'd gotten too close. She'd fallen too hard, and it scared her.

What was she afraid of? Why had she been so hesitant to allow him past the barriers she'd built around herself and her heart?

All her life, her adoptive mother had kept her from playing with others, refusing to let her out of her sight for long. She'd instilled in PJ a lack of trust in people and a determination to live a life independent of others. PJ had found companionship in the horses she loved at the resort stables, volunteering to muck out stalls and exercise the animals.

Chuck had been there, working quietly around her, his love of the animals equal to her own. Over time, he'd overcome her shyness and they'd gone riding together and talked. He'd taught her how to laugh again, something she thought she'd never do. And PJ had fallen in love with the big ex-football jock cowboy, breaking her self-imposed rule not to invest her heart in anyone but to rely solely on herself.

She'd gone so far as to accept his proposal of marriage and actually started dreaming of a wedding and happily ever after.

Until Chuck's National Guard unit had asked for volunteers to deploy and Chuck had raised his hand.

PJ's world had caved in around her. She'd been heartbroken that Chuck would want to leave her and go to war. All she could see in her future was how alone she'd be. Her adoptive mother wouldn't be around forever, her health having deteriorated over the past several years.

She'd been so upset, she'd thrown his ring in his face and told him she never wanted to see him again. Looking back, she realized how childish she'd been.

She hadn't been there to see him off when he'd left for predeployment training. Hadn't told him that she'd missed her period and suspected she was pregnant.

For a short time, PJ thought she could handle being a part of another person's life. But then Chuck had left. Not long afterward, Terri Franks died of a heart attack, leaving her alone in the world, without money or a home to live in. She'd been saving money for years so that someday she could afford to start college online and study animal husbandry. When Terri died, all the money had gone to pay for Terri's funeral.

Terri had been renting the house they lived in. When she'd passed, PJ had gone to work instead of college in order to pay the rent. But the rent had been too much for the meager earnings she'd gotten from the odd jobs she was able to get around town. Without family or a degree and any formal experience, she was destitute and alone. Everyone she'd ever loved was gone, making her promise herself never to get too close to anyone, lest they die and leave her.

Then Charlie came along....

A voice outside her door brought her out of her sad memories and across the room to press her ear to the door. From the deep timbre and pitch, PJ could tell it was Chuck. She peered through the peephole but couldn't see him.

Something shuffled against the outside of the door. What was he doing?

She pressed her ear harder against the door and listened.

"She had a scare, but she's all right," Chuck was saying to someone.

Who was he talking to?

"Whoever broke in tonight won't try again. He'll have to go through me to get to her."

PJ smiled, feeling better about going to sleep now than she had a few moments before.

Apparently Chuck planned to sleep in front of her door.

"We'll talk tomorrow."

Something bumped softly against the door, and all went silent.

PJ pressed a hand to the door. Chuck was on the other side. So close, and yet a huge chasm stretched between them. She'd kept knowledge of his daughter from him.

Even if he forgave her, she wasn't sure she could let him back in her life.

Chapter Three

PJ rose early the next morning, fed Charlie, dressed and loaded the diaper bag with frozen breast milk and diapers for the day care. She had to be at the diner for the first shift.

She dreaded opening the door and waking Chuck after he'd spent the night sleeping in the hall. A twinge of guilt pinched her chest at the thought of him lying on a hard vinyl-tile floor all night, while she'd had a soft mattress and pillows to cushion her.

With the words to thank him poised on her lips, she hooked the infant carrier with Charlie in it on one arm and the diaper bag on the other and eased open the door.

The hallway was empty. Chuck's door was closed. Had he slept outside all night or just part of it?

PJ let go of the breath she'd been holding, relieved she wouldn't have to confront him yet. She'd spent the better part of the rest of her night tossing and turning, thinking about the man who'd attacked her, and more so, the one sleeping on the other side of her door.

She'd known that one day she'd have to tell Chuck about Charlie, and she'd been fully intending to tell him upon his return from his deployment. She thought she had two more months. The day had come sooner than she'd anticipated, and she hadn't been ready.

PJ exited the building and hurried toward her car, hoping she wouldn't run into Chuck outside. Charlie had fallen asleep in her infant carrier even before they'd left the apartment. Her little eyes scrunched as the full force of the morning sunlight shone down on her tiny face.

PJ juggled the carrier to unlock the car. Charlie whimpered but remained asleep.

As she settled the carrier into the car, PJ's skin prickled and the hairs on the back of her neck stood on end. She cast a glance over her shoulder.

No one was there, although she could have sworn a shadow shifted at the corner of the building. Snapping the seat into place, PJ straightened and faced the back of the resort building.

"Anyone there?" she called out, her voice shaky, her knees even shakier.

No answer. A curtain was pushed aside in a window above and Chuck peered down, half of his face covered in shaving cream.

Warmth filled PJ's neck and cheeks. The man was ageless and looked as good today as he had a year ago when she'd been young and stupid in love. Seeing him standing there with his razor in his hand made PJ's heart turn cartwheels against her ribs.

Chuck disappeared and reappeared at the sliding glass door on the balcony of his room, bare-chested, a towel slung over one shoulder. "Are you okay?" he called out.

The heat built in her cheeks as she nodded. "I'm fine."

"I thought I heard you call out."

"I talk to myself sometimes." Feeling foolish and paranoid, she gave him half a smile. "Gotta go." PJ slipped behind the wheel of her beat-up car and closed the door to avoid further conversation with the father of her child. What else could she say while standing in the parking lot and him hanging over the balcony? *Welcome back? Sorry I didn't tell you about your baby? Or, damn, you look good?*

She shifted into Reverse, backed out of the parking space and pulled out onto the road. A glance in her rearview mirror confirmed that Chuck was still standing on the balcony, watching her. Below, at the corner of the building, something moved. PJ frowned, slowed the vehicle and shot a quick glance over her shoulder at the resort.

Nothing.

She supposed paranoia was bound to be a result of post-attack jitters. With a shrug, she turned the corner and drove to the church day care on the other side of town where Charlie spent her days with Dana, who worked there part-time, and the other ladies who ran the child care program. She'd been going there since PJ started to work for Cara Jo at the diner two months prior.

PJ worked mornings, lunch and early afternoon. Late afternoon, she spent either at her computer or in the library taking college courses online.

Dana met her at the door to the infant room. "Running a little late, aren't you?"

PJ dropped the diaper bag on the floor and slid the infant carrier off her arm. Dana took the carrier and set it on a counter, unbuckling Charlie from the restraints. "Hey, sweetie, come see Auntie Dana."

Charlie's eyes blinked open, and she stared up at Dana.

Regret tugged at PJ's heart that she had to spend so much time away from her daughter. But she'd made a commitment to build a better life for herself and Charlie, and the only way she could do that was to get a degree. And she wouldn't have been able to do that if not for the scholarship she'd received from an anonymous benefactor.

Dana lifted Charlie into her arms and stared across her downy hair to PJ. "So, did you meet him?"

"Meet who?" PJ pulled the bottles of breast milk from the diaper bag and settled them into the refrigerator, determined to ignore Dana's questions. Unfortunately, she couldn't stop the slow burn rising in her cheeks at the mere mention of her new neighbor in the resort apartments.

A smile spread across Dana's face. "You did. Isn't he hunky?"

"Dana, you're married. What would Tommy say?"

She shrugged. "I'm married, not dead. And I'm only thinking of you, not myself."

PJ's lips twisted into a half smile. "I know him."

"You do?"

"Yes, we dated for a while."

"Shut up. You're kidding, right? That gorgeous hunk?"

Knowing it would be out before long, PJ kissed Charlie, her heart pinching tight. Then she crossed to the door, her hand resting on the knob, ready to yank and run. "Look, I have to get to work. But you should know that the man you met last night is Charlie's father." She opened the door.

"Oh, no you didn't." Dana advanced on her, carrying Charlie. "You didn't just hit-and-run. You have to stay and tell me everything."

"I can't. I'm already late for work. I promise we'll talk this afternoon when I pick up Charlie."

"Darn right you will." Dana smiled down at Charlie. "And we'll spend all day talking about your daddy, won't we, sweet baby?"

PJ slipped out before she broke down in front of Dana. After the attack last night, the intense joy of seeing Chuck for the first time in almost a year and then breaking the news of Charlie to him, PJ was emotionally wrung out. And she hadn't even pulled her eight-hour shift yet.

She trudged to her car and hurried back the way she'd come, anxious to dive into work so that she could forget everything else.

Ha. As if that would happen. With Chuck hired on as the handyman, she didn't have a chance.

Cara Jo cornered her as soon as she entered the diner

with its black and white tiled floor and fifties-style tables and chairs. "I can't believe I slept right through everything."

PJ shook her head. "I take it you heard about the incident last night." She stepped around the counter and tucked her purse behind the stash of paper towels.

"I didn't hear anything. No sirens, no screaming, nothing. I had to hear it from a deputy who'd stopped in for coffee this morning." Cara Jo grabbed PJ's arms. "Are you okay?"

PJ smiled. "I'm here, aren't I?"

"That bastard didn't hurt you?"

A chill rippled across PJ's skin, and she touched the base of her throat where the lamp cord had almost been the death of her. "Not much. Just scared the fool out of me." PJ grabbed a full coffeepot and struck out across the diner, determined to end the conversation. After refilling several empty mugs and taking orders for breakfast, she returned to the counter and Cara Jo, a little more in control of her emotions and ready to launch her own attack. "Why didn't you tell me about Chuck?"

Cara Jo's brows rose innocently. "Chuck?"

"The handyman you hired for the resort?" PJ's brows rose to match Cara Jo's.

"Oh, yeah, him." Cara Jo's cheeks reddened. She rested a hand on PJ's arm. "When Hank told me he'd hired a handyman, I didn't know it was Chuck at first. Hank's my new boss. I didn't have a say. He hired him and told me he'd be starting today. It wasn't until we were on the way to Fort Stockton that Hank let me know who he really was. I swear." She held up her hand, her expression too solemn to be a hoax. Cara Jo had never lied to PJ. Why would she start now?

"Why didn't you warn me then?"

"I was trying to find the words, but for some reason, I never could come up with the right ones." She shrugged. "Are you mad at me?"

PJ sighed. "No. I can't stay mad at you." She set the coffeepot on the burner. "Do you have any say in who works as the handyman?"

"Not yet. I just accepted the position of resort manager. I haven't even had a chance to move my stuff into the office."

PJ sighed. Chuck would be around for a while. "I guess we won't be seeing much of you around the diner once you get oriented with your new duties."

"My first responsibility is to the diner. It's my baby. I won't desert you and the staff here." Cara Jo hugged PJ. "And you'll always be my friend, so don't think you're getting out of this relationship without an argument from me."

Her heart warming at Cara Jo's display of affection, PJ reminded herself how lucky she was to have Cara Jo in her life. When her adoptive mother had died of a heart attack, PJ had felt more alone than she had since she'd come to Wild Oak Canyon. If not for Cara Jo giving her a job and arranging with the resort for a place to live, she and Charlie would have been destitute. Then out of the blue, the scholarship had landed in her lap and PJ felt she was finally on her way to a new and better life for her and her daughter.

The bell over the diner door jingled and PJ glanced up, her heart flipping over.

Chuck entered, his gaze crossing the room to clash with PJ's. Hank Derringer entered behind Chuck and then smiled and nodded toward Cara Jo and PJ. The two settled in the farthest corner in a booth.

"Want me to get them?" Cara Jo asked.

"No. I can do this." PJ stiffened her spine.

"Does Chuck know about Charlie?" Cara Jo whispered.

PJ nodded, gathering two menus and two coffee mugs, her hands shaking. "He found out last night after he chased the attacker out of my apartment."

Cara Jo whistled softly. "Wow, what a way to learn you have a baby daughter."

A stab of guilt twisted in PJ's gut. "Yeah. But what's done is done. I have to live with the choice I made."

"Any chance you two will get back together?" Cara Jo asked.

Her chest tightening so much she could barely breathe, PJ shrugged. She was afraid if she spoke, her voice would crack along with her composure.

"I get it. It's too soon to talk about it." Cara Jo gave her a pat on the back. "Go on. You're tough—you can handle this."

PJ wasn't so sure, but she didn't plan on hiding every time she ran into Chuck. Wild Oak Canyon was too small to think she could avoid him forever.

"ANY OTHER PROBLEMS after last night's initial incident?" Hank asked.

Chuck dragged his gaze away from PJ as she strode across the black and white linoleum tiles of the diner toward them. He had a hard time focusing on Hank with PJ nearby. "What? Oh, no. I checked her balcony door locks and each of the windows and then bedded down in the hallway to make sure no one bothered her again."

Hank sighed. "I figured something might happen, but I wasn't sure what or when."

PJ stopped at their table and set the menus and the empty coffee mugs in front of them. "Coffee?"

"Yes, please." Hank frowned. "Are you all right, my dear?"

PJ smiled down at the older man. "I'm fine, thanks to Chuck. I understand you hired him as the handyman for the resort."

"I did. Thought we could use someone with carpentry skills who could also work with the horses since Juan is no longer with us."

She nodded curtly. "I'll be right back with the coffee."

As soon as PJ was out of earshot, Hank leaned closer. "I

don't want anyone to know I hired you to protect PJ. The less connection she has to me, the less chance of her being hurt."

"What's going on? All you told me was that I needed to provide protection to an employee of the resort. What made you think PJ needed protecting?"

"I got a call from an adoption agency in Flagstaff, Arizona. They noted that their computer system had been hacked, and PJ's files had been the target."

"And why would they call you?"

Hank glanced around the diner, his blue eyes darkening. "I knew PJ's birth mother, Alana Rodriguez. She made sure that if anything happened to PJ's adoptive mother, all correspondence or concerns should be directed to me."

"Why you?"

"I helped her escape her abusive fiancé twenty-six years ago in Cozumel, Mexico. It was easy for her to fit into a new life in the United States. She spoke fluent English and had sandy-blond hair and green eyes just like PJ. I suspect her coloring was a throwback from her European Spanish heritage."

Chuck's eyes narrowed. "Something tells me there's more to this story."

Hank sighed. "I told her if she ever needed me for anything to let me know." He stared across the table at Chuck. "When she disappeared, her fiancé had the Mexican police arrest me, claiming I'd murdered Alana."

"What happened to her?"

"I arranged for her to get to the States, gave her a new identity and she disappeared. I didn't see her again."

"How did you get the Mexican government to drop the charges?"

"With no body and no evidence of foul play, they couldn't keep me. Although I barely got out of Mexico."

"So why is this all surfacing again?"

"Her fiancé, Emilio Montalvo," Hank slid a blurry picture

of a Hispanic man in front of Hank, "had connections deep in the Mexican Mafia. He swore when he found Alana, he'd make us both pay. I stayed away from her, sure that any contact with her would put her at risk of him finding her. I didn't know she'd had a child and the child was PJ until last year."

"How did you find out?"

Hank's gaze dropped to the empty coffee mug in his hand. "I found out when Terri Franks, a woman I barely knew who'd worked at the resort for the past eight years, died."

"PJ's adoptive mother." Chuck's gaze slipped from Hank to PJ, headed their way with a carafe of coffee.

Hank turned a smile toward PJ as she stopped to fill his cup.

"Ready to order?" PJ directed her question to Hank, refusing to lock gazes with Chuck.

They had a lot to discuss, but Chuck didn't want to do it in public. It would wait until that evening when he could get her alone.

Hank and Chuck ordered breakfast, and PJ walked away.

"How did you find out PJ was Alana's daughter, not Terri's?"

"I received a package in the mail from Terri Franks's attorney. In it was a letter from Alana, asking me to look out for her daughter should anything happen to Terri. In the letter Terri left with her lawyer, she explained how she'd been PJ's nanny when they lived out in Arizona. Alana had arranged to have Terri adopt PJ if something should happen to her. I only wish I'd known then."

"Why do you think the hacking into the adoption agency's files points to you and PJ?"

"My corporate and personal computer systems were also maliciously hacked. All the data was downloaded to some site in Mexico."

"Was your letter from Alana in those files?"

"No."

"Then how would the hacker connect you to PJ?"

"PJ doesn't know it, but the scholarship she's going to school on comes from one of my corporations. The bank statements and money trail were part of the system hacked."

"Any leads on who might be hacking into your system, or who might want to hurt PJ?"

"Anyone could be getting to me by targeting PJ."

Chuck drummed his fingers on the table. "But hacking into the adoption files…that makes it a little more personal."

Hank nodded. "Exactly."

"You think Alana's ex-fiancé might have traced PJ through the adoption agency?"

"It's a possibility."

"How long ago did you say it was when you helped this woman, Alana?"

Hank stared across the table at Chuck. "Twenty-six years ago."

Chuck did the math in his head. PJ had turned twenty-five while he'd been in Afghanistan. His gut tightened. "The next question—and I wouldn't ask if I didn't think it might be important—but just who is PJ's father?"

The older man opened his mouth and then closed it and smiled, his head turning toward the woman in question.

"Your breakfast." PJ set a steaming plate of eggs, sunny-side up, in front of Hank and one in front of Chuck, her arm brushing against his, sending sensual shock waves across his senses.

Chuck's fingers tightened on the napkin in his lap to keep from reaching out and pulling PJ into his arms.

PJ jerked her arm back, her eyes flaring wide for a moment. Her chest rose and fell on a deep breath. "Is there anything else I can get you?" she asked, her voice shaking.

"No, thank you," Hank answered for them both.

Chuck couldn't speak, his throat tight around his vocal cords. He wanted to hold PJ so badly, he had to remain completely still or risk leaping from his seat and taking her into his arms.

When PJ turned and hurried away, Chuck let go of the breath he'd been holding and faced Hank. "Were you and Alana more than just acquaintances?"

Hank nodded.

"So PJ could be your and Alana's daughter."

The older man lifted his fork and put it down again. "I don't know. Without informing PJ of our connection, I don't know how to get a sample for DNA testing. If she's my daughter, she runs the risk of kidnapping attempts."

"Like your wife and son…" Chuck had heard about Hank's family before he'd deployed. Everyone in Wild Oak Canyon knew they'd disappeared two years ago and Hank had been looking for them ever since.

Hank stared across the table at Chuck, his face haggard, older than his fifty-something years. "I couldn't bear for her to be hurt because of me."

"You need to tell her," Chuck said.

"When I know for sure."

"The only way you'll know for sure is to do DNA testing. You'd have to tell her something to get the sample you need."

Hank threw his napkin on the table, his brows furrowed. "I couldn't bear it if someone targeted another person because of me."

"She might not be yours at all. Alana could have had another relationship with someone else shortly after disappearing."

Hank's eyes narrowed. "Then why leave the letter for me?"

"She counted on you to help." Chuck stared across the room at PJ, leaning close to an elderly woman, taking her order. "What if PJ is the ex-fiancé's daughter?"

"Things might get even worse." Hank's lips tightened. "He'll want what is his and will stop at nothing to take her and the child."

Chapter Four

PJ felt as if she was walking on eggshells the entire time Chuck and Hank were eating their breakfast. Several times she fumbled coffee mugs, almost dropping them.

"Hey, it's okay." Cara Jo rested a hand on her arm. "The world will not come to an end because the old fiancé is back in town."

"I know. But we haven't had *the talk* yet. I don't know what he's going to want in the way of visitation with Charlie." PJ wrung her hands, staring at Chuck's back. "He might sue for custody, for all I know."

Cara Jo clucked her tongue. "Don't borrow trouble, sweetie. He doesn't strike me as the vindictive type."

"No, but he's always wanted children. He'll want to be a part of Charlie's life."

"And that's a problem?" Cara Jo's brows rose. "Honey, a girl needs a daddy in her life. Not that you wouldn't do a good job of raising her. But having a good male role model sets her up for future relationships and expectations of the kind of men she should date."

"Charlie's only three months old, for God's sake." PJ flung her hands in the air. "I'm not ready for my baby to start dating."

Cara Jo chuckled. "I know. But having a good role model

early in her life gives her a firm foundation when it comes to the kind of guy she might one day marry."

PJ pinched the bridge of her nose, a headache forming at the thought of Charlie as a teen. "I don't want to think about Charlie dating or marrying until at least after the terrible twos."

"Order up!" Mrs. Kinsley yelled through the window from the kitchen.

Cara Jo handed her two plates of biscuits and gravy. "Sadly, it'll be here before you know it. Take these to table nine, while I see if I can help Mrs. Kinsley catch up."

PJ threw herself into taking orders and delivering food, busing tables in between. The hectic pace kept her too busy for her eyes to stray to the corner where Chuck and Hank sat, taking their sweet time over coffee. Still, her gaze found its way there every time she turned around.

Chuck's broad shoulders and the high-and-tight military haircut made butterflies swarm in her belly and stirred the longing she'd thought was buried with the letters from Chuck she'd kept in a box beneath her bed.

She hadn't opened them for fear she'd lose her determination and conviction that she was doing the right thing by moving on. Yet she hadn't returned them or thrown them away. At first, he'd sent a letter every other day after he'd deployed to Afghanistan. When she refused to respond, the letters slowed to a trickle until about a month before Charlie was born, when they'd stopped altogether.

In her eighth month of pregnancy, PJ had never felt more alone. Sure, Cara Jo had been beside her, had gone to prenatal classes with her and coached her through the actual delivery, but it wasn't the same.

The guilt of not having told Chuck of the baby and her continued longing gnawed at her heart. She hadn't wanted to give her heart to him, knowing he'd leave her and possibly never come back. With her luck, he'd die just like every other presumably permanent person in her life. Her mother, what little she remembered of her, and her adoptive mother. Hell, she had never known her father.

Now she had Charlie in her life, and every day she worried that something horrible would happen to her. And it almost had the night before.

On her break PJ retreated to the diner office to use the telephone and dialed the number for the day care.

"Heavenly Hope Day Care, this is Dana."

"Oh, good," PJ breathed. "Just the person I wanted to talk to."

"PJ?"

"I know it's overprotective of me, but I had to call and check on Charlie."

"I'm holding her in my arms as we speak. She's just fine." Dana paused. "How about you? You sound a bit shaken."

"I guess I am after last night's attack."

The phone clattered and Dana muttered an expletive before saying, "Sorry, dropped the phone. Now, what do you mean *attack*? You didn't say anything about it when you dropped Charlie off. Did Chuck attack you?"

PJ shoved a hand through her hair and sighed. "Sorry, Dana. I must have forgotten, what with Chuck being there and all."

"Did he hurt you?"

"No. Chuck came in and saved the day." PJ glanced around the office. "I have to get back to work. I just wanted to know Charlie was okay."

"I'll keep an extra special eye on her and let you know of anything out of the ordinary. Sheesh. Attacked? You better fill me in on *all* the details this afternoon."

"I will."

"That's something a girl doesn't forget. I guess having Chuck around has you completely rattled."

"You don't know the half of it." PJ said her goodbyes and

hung up. When she returned to the dining room, her gaze went straight to the empty corner booth.

The tension eased from her shoulders, and she let go of the breath she'd been holding for what felt like the entire morning.

The sooner she got used to having Chuck around, the better. No doubt, knowing he had a child, the big cowboy wasn't going anywhere for a while.

The rest of the morning passed quickly with customers straggling in for late breakfast and then into the lunch hours. PJ glanced toward the door every time the bell above it jingled, half expecting Chuck to stride through.

Her nerves were shot by the time the lunch crowd thinned and she hung up her apron. "If you don't mind, I have to leave early to get some errands done and study before I pick up Charlie at the day care."

Cara Jo smiled. "No problem. I can handle the cleanup. Go on. And PJ…"

PJ slipped her purse strap over her shoulder and faced Cara Jo.

"Things will turn out for the best. Just you wait and see." Cara Jo hugged her.

PJ returned the hug, her vision blurred with ready tears. "I hope so." She left the diner and climbed the back stairs to her apartment over the resort. The shadowy hallway made her hurry along, her key at the ready.

When she stepped into the apartment, her gaze darted all around the postage stamp-size living-room-and-kitchen combo. The normal scents of talcum powder and baby shampoo held a hint of aftershave.

PJ shivered and wondered when that smell would dissipate. She vowed to throw open the windows when she got home that evening to air it out.

As she grabbed her notebook and papers from her corner desk, she paused. The photo album she kept on the shelf above her ancient computer stuck out a little more than usual. It hadn't been that way that morning when she'd straightened her desk before heading for work.

Her chest tightened as a chill slipped across the back of her neck, making the tiny hairs stand on end. How long would it take to erase the memory of a man breaking and entering her home? Not only had her apartment been breached, but her safe haven had also been compromised.

Every little thing that seemed out of place would get more scrutiny. PJ shoved aside her paranoia and left, carefully locking the door. As a second thought, she tore off a corner of one of her papers and slipped it between the door and jamb above the lock. If someone broke in, the paper would be displaced. Call her crazy, but she needed some measure of security, and though minuscule, the little trick left her feeling a little more in control.

Her apartment behind her, PJ climbed into her car and headed for the law offices of Hanes and Taylor. She had to know what her rights were and what she might face if Chuck decided he wanted custody of Charlie.

Even the slimmest chance of losing custody of her baby had PJ's gut so knotted she could hardly breathe.

THROUGHOUT THE DAY, Chuck worked on projects ranging from replacing rotted eaves to mucking stalls. In between tasks, he made it a habit to swing by the diner's wide windows to peek in at PJ.

So many times during his tour in Afghanistan he'd dreamed of seeing PJ again, of holding her in his arms. In his imagination, he could hear her voice telling him she'd been wrong, that she wanted him in her life no matter what profession he chose.

Those dreams had helped him hold it together during the dangerous missions. The thought of coming back to Wild

Oak Canyon to salvage his relationship with the woman he loved ended in a hero's welcome. Such were his dreams.

The reality was, PJ had lied to him by withholding information about Charlie. If Chuck hadn't returned to Wild Oak Canyon, he'd never have known he had a daughter.

His chest swelled as he thought of the tiny baby, lying in her crib, her soft tuft of hair like silk against his fingers.

He'd smashed his fingers with a hammer more than once, losing his focus over little Charlie. And the more he saw PJ through the window, the more he alternated between wanting to hold her and wanting to shake her.

Around noon, he ducked into the resort office.

The young woman manning the counter, barely out of her teens, smiled. "May I help you?"

Chuck read the name tag. "Hi, Alicia. I'm Chuck, the new handyman."

Alicia reached across the counter and shook Chuck's hand. "Welcome to Wild Oak Canyon Resort."

"Do you know of any repairs that need to be made in any of the rooms?"

The young woman behind the counter smiled and shrugged. "I only work part-time in the afternoons after my classes get out at the community college, so I don't always get the 4-1-1. You'll have to ask the new manager."

"Ms. Smithson?" Chuck asked.

"Yes, sir. You can find her at the diner until about two. Then she'll be back in her office at the resort."

Chuck glanced at the old-fashioned guest register on the counter, committing the names on the list to memory. Perhaps one of the guests was PJ's attacker. "Are there many guests this time of year?"

"It's a slow season, from what they tell me. Only about twenty-five people are here for the week. Many are planning to attend the rodeo in the neighboring town. We get the overflow."

Chuck made a note to work with Cara Jo to review the list of guests and to get Hank to run a background check on any who might be questionable. Since the attack had just happened only the night before, whoever did it could be new in town, thus needing a place to stay. One close enough where he could study PJ's every move. Chuck's fists tightened. The sooner he discovered the culprit and put him in jail— or out of his misery—the better. "I guess I'll be seeing you around, Alicia."

"Nice to meet you."

Chuck went back to work in the stable. By early afternoon, he'd finished mucking stalls and was just emptying a wheelbarrow full of manure in the pile behind the stables when he saw PJ's car pull out of the rear parking lot of the resort. Even if he hadn't been tasked with protecting the confounded woman, curiosity got the better of him.

Chuck dusted off his jeans, climbed into his truck and followed. Wild Oak Canyon wasn't a big enough town to boast a single stoplight. A couple of dozen streets crisscrossed in straight lines on the flat terrain.

PJ pulled into a building a few blocks from the diner.

Chuck waited at a stop sign until PJ went inside before he passed. His heart skipped several beats when he read the sign in front of the neat little house, converted into a business. Hanes and Taylor, Attorneys at Law.

Was that the way she'd play this? Anger spiked as he turned the corner and circled the block. Most likely she was getting legal advice about child custody.

As Chuck rounded the block and came back out on Main, PJ's car was pulling away from the curb. She hadn't had time to consult with anyone. She had probably only set up an appointment.

Chuck's jaw tightened. Tonight, he and PJ would have a talk about Charlie's future. A future that would include Chuck, by God.

Feeling a bit guilty over stalking PJ, Chuck left a big gap between his truck and her car.

PJ's next stop was on the other side of town at a quaint little church with a fenced playground out back and a sign out front with the words painted in block letters, Heavenly Hope Day Care.

Chuck kept his distance, parking in an abandoned gas station until PJ came out.

Twenty minutes later, he'd about given up when PJ emerged carrying an infant car seat, Charlie's little head barely visible over the sides. Her tiny hand waved at the sky, bringing a smile to Chuck's face.

He wanted to hold his little girl, to get to know her and watch her grow.

Had PJ not shut him out of her life, Chuck would have moved heaven and earth to be there when Charlie came into the world. He sighed. Then again, the army didn't always let soldiers out of their deployments for the births of their children. Even had PJ told him he was going to be a father, he probably wouldn't have gotten a furlough to return home for the event.

He could understand some of the reasoning behind PJ keeping the birth of his child from him. But Charlie was three months old. Chuck had been back in the States for a month of that, in the hospital for rehab and then processing out of the military.

After almost a year's separation, he'd thought he'd be over PJ, but that was as far from the truth as he could get.

The woman had never been far from his mind, and his job of protecting her would only put them closer still.

Chuck considered asking Hank to pull him from this case. But who did he know he could trust to guarantee PJ's safety? And who had as much at stake when it came to Charlie?

If the Mexican Mafia was after PJ and Charlie, he'd need a friggin' army to surround her, especially in this part of south Texas where drugs traveled across the border seemingly unconstrained. There were enough Mafia members on both sides of the border that if they wanted PJ and Charlie, one cowboy wasn't going to stop them. Chuck wondered if the four cowboys Hank had hired made up the entirety of Covert Cowboys, Inc., or if Hank had additional help he hadn't met yet.

Chuck stayed behind PJ as she drove back to her apartment. He gave her five minutes to unload and get into her room before he parked and climbed out.

The more he thought about PJ and Charlie being at risk with the Mexican Mafia, the more he needed to know about those he might be up against. A visit with Hank's computer guru who had access to just about anything that had a computer footprint was in order. But first, he had to make sure PJ and Charlie would be okay.

Chuck scanned the parking lot, noting all the shadowy areas a person could hide to ambush an unsuspecting mother. He made notes to himself to trim back bushes and install motion-sensor lighting to ward off surprise attacks. Since he, PJ and Cara Jo were the only people who should be parking behind the buildings, safety in numbers wasn't really an option.

At the top of the staircase leading to the pair of apartments he and PJ occupied, Chuck paused and surveyed the hallway. The light overhead gave a dingy glow. He'd clean the globe and change the bulbs.

He paused with his fist hovering over PJ's door and got a good whiff of his own stench. After mucking horse manure for part of the day, he probably smelled like the stuff.

Chuck turned back toward his apartment when PJ's door jerked open.

"I knew it."

Chuck spun to face her.

She had Charlie in her arms and a scowl on her face. "You were following me, weren't you?"

Chuck couldn't lie to her. "Yes."

"I don't need a keeper, so back off."

"Are you mad because I followed you or because I saw that you stopped at an attorney's office?" he threw back at her.

Charlie batted at her mother's face, blowing bubbles with her spit.

Chuck had a hard time staying mad when the baby drew his attention out of the fight.

"I only made an appointment. I figured we'd have to have some kind of agreement written up over visitation with Charlie."

"We still need to have that talk."

PJ sighed. "I know."

"But let me get a shower first. I smell like hell."

PJ's nose twitched, the hint of a smile tugging at her lips. "You really do."

Chuck's heart flipped. He'd missed her smile. "Five minutes."

"Just knock."

Chuck hurriedly collected his toiletries and ducked beneath the hot spray, scrubbing away a day of hard work. It had been a long time since he'd worked with horses and barnyards. His muscles were stiff from shoveling. Other than digging foxholes, he hadn't had to shovel much in the army, and he could tell the muscles had been neglected. And his bum leg ached like hell.

He let the warm water pepper his muscles as he collected his thoughts for the coming confrontation with PJ.

Showered and dressed in clean clothes, he knocked on PJ's door.

"Just a minute," she called out.

A moment later, she opened the door, again holding Charlie. "Sorry. We were in the middle of Charlie's supper." PJ tugged her T-shirt down over her hip.

It took a moment for Chuck to digest her meaning. When it hit him that she had been breastfeeding Charlie, his face heated.

PJ folded a cloth over his shoulder and held Charlie out. "Here, you can burp her while I fix something to eat." Once he'd taken the baby, she performed an about-face and hurried toward the kitchenette in the corner. "I hope you like spaghetti. It's cheap and easy to fix."

"I didn't expect you to cook for me."

She shrugged. "It's just as easy to cook spaghetti for two as for one person."

Chuck still held Charlie out at arm's length. "How do I burp her?"

PJ chuckled. "Lay her over your shoulder and pat her back. She'll do the rest."

No sooner had Chuck laid her over his shoulder than Charlie burped.

"See?" PJ turned with a wooden spoon in her hand. "Easy."

"All I did was put her on my shoulder."

"Sometimes that's all it takes." She waved the spoon. "Pat her back anyway. She probably has another one in there."

In awe and a little afraid of the tiny bundle of baby, Chuck patted her back gently, afraid he'd break her little body with his big hand.

"Oh, come on, she won't break. Give her a firm pat."

Chuck patted her back again, this time a little harder. Nothing happened.

"Don't stop. She likes it."

As he patted her back, Chuck paced across the small room and back, sure he was doing it wrong. Finally Charlie burped again and cooed.

The sound made Chuck's heart skip several beats. "Is that normal?"

"That's her way of saying thank you. I told you, she likes it."

Chuck glanced at PJ standing with her back to him. She seemed to be thinner than he remembered. "How was it?"

"What?"

"Your pregnancy, the delivery? I want to know."

"I did fine. I guess my body is built for bearing children. No health issues and a natural delivery."

He wanted to know more, but he clamped down on his tongue to keep from asking too many personal questions. "I would have been there…"

"I know you would have. If you could have."

"Why didn't you tell me?" He tipped Charlie into the crook of his arm and stared down into her little face.

"You weren't here. You wouldn't have been here even had you known." Her hand stopped stirring the sauce, and she stood for a long moment, unmoving. "Your focus needed to be on staying alive. What was the point in telling you?"

His anger stirred again. "The point is, I'm Charlie's father."

"And if there had been complications, what could you have done from Afghanistan?"

Chuck sighed. "Nothing."

A long silence stretched between them.

"I won't try to keep you from seeing Charlie," PJ said.

Chuck stared up at PJ. She'd lied by omission about Charlie. Would she lie about trying to keep him from seeing his daughter? What about the visit to the attorney? Was she only trying to set an agreement in place, or was she preparing to cut him out of Charlie's life?

At this point, Hank didn't want her to know Chuck had been hired as her bodyguard, not as a handyman as he'd told PJ.

PJ glanced at him and sighed. Then she held her hand up, spoon and all. "I swear on my mothers' graves I won't keep you from Charlie. There. Are you satisfied?"

Chuck nodded. He liked the strong, determined woman she'd grown into in the year he'd been away, and found himself even more attracted to her than before. "Okay. I trust you." He might trust her about visitation with Charlie, but he wasn't as sure about where they stood, or if he trusted her with his heart. Was attraction enough?

"Trust or not, it's the truth." She turned back to the stove. "You about ready for dinner?"

Chuck gazed down at the baby sleeping in his arms. He didn't want to let go of her even to eat supper. "I guess."

PJ chuckled. "Does my cooking reputation precede me? I'm not Cara Jo, but I can—"

Footsteps pounded on the staircase and then in the hallway outside PJ's apartment door.

PJ turned to Chuck. "Give me Charlie." She held out her hands for the baby.

Chuck handed her over and motioned for her to get behind him. "Go into the bedroom and close the door."

PJ did as she was told, her eyes wide, her face pale. As she closed the bedroom door, someone pounded on the door to the apartment.

"Help! Please, help!" a female voice called out, followed by loud sobs.

Chuck peered through the peephole and then yanked the door open.

The young woman from the resort front desk fell against his chest, her face streaked with tears. "Please help him."

Chapter Five

Chuck caught the woman and held her as she sobbed into his chest. "Help who?"

"Danny, my boyfriend. He's hurt." She sniffed and pushed her hair out of her face. "He's at the bottom of the stairs. I don't know if he's breathing."

Chuck shoved the woman into the apartment. "Stay here and call 9-1-1, and lock the door behind me."

The woman nodded, her hands shaking.

PJ, still carrying Charlie, flung her bedroom door open. "What's wrong? What's happening?"

"I don't know. I'll be right back." Without waiting for her response, Chuck slipped past the distraught woman and lumbered down the stairs two at a time, jolting his bad leg with each step. He almost fell over the crumpled body at the bottom.

The light over the stairs wasn't working, but the glow from the security light in the rear parking lot shone enough on the inert form that Chuck could see a pool of blood.

As he felt for a pulse, Chuck glanced around to ensure whoever had done this wasn't waiting to do it again.

After several long seconds, he could detect the weak beat of the young man's heart. Rather than hurt him further, he carefully checked for injuries without moving him.

The blood appeared to be coming from a wound to the forehead, which would explain why he was unconscious.

Within minutes, sirens wailed from the direction of Wild Oak Canyon's small hospital. A sheriff's vehicle whipped into the parking lot before the ambulance, lights blazing.

A man in uniform leaped out, gun drawn. "Step away from the body," he called out.

"I'm the one who had you called." Chuck didn't recognize the man from the previous night's call.

"Still, step away from the body until we secure the area."

Chuck held up his hands and stepped out into the parking lot. "He's alive, seems to be breathing on his own, but he appears to have suffered a blow to the head."

The ambulance bumped over the rough pavement and came to a halt. Two emergency medical technicians jumped out. One opened a side panel and extracted a medical kit while the other unloaded a backboard.

Cara Jo rounded the corner of the building, her eyes wide. When she spotted Chuck, she hurried to his side. "What the hell's going on?"

"I'm not sure. You know almost as much as I do. The young man's name is Danny. His girlfriend, Alicia, the young woman who works part-time at the front desk of the resort, found him and let us know he'd been hurt."

"I know Danny. He's a nice kid. Who'd want to hurt him?" Cara Jo shook her head.

"Good question."

"Holy hell." Cara Jo shoved her hand through her hair. "Two attacks in as many days. I don't get it."

"Me, either. But tomorrow, this handyman is putting in some additional security measures."

"Glad to hear it. I'm sure the boss won't mind footing that bill. Especially when his employees are being mauled." Cara Jo laid a hand on Chuck's arm. "PJ and Charlie are okay, aren't they?"

"Yes. I was with them when Alicia showed up at the door. Alicia and PJ are upstairs now, if you want to check on them. The deputy will want to speak with the one who found Danny. Maybe you could bring Alicia down as soon as the EMTs get him loaded into the ambulance."

"I'll do that." Cara Jo waited while the EMTs checked vitals and carefully maneuvered the injured man onto the backboard, stabilized his neck and lifted him onto a gurney.

Once the stairway was cleared, the diner owner sprinted up the stairs.

Chuck and the deputy followed the injured man as he was rolled across the rough pavement. Danny's eyes blinked open as they neared the ambulance.

"Wait." The deputy touched the arm of one of the medical technicians. The gurney came to a smooth halt, and the officer leaned over the gurney. "Son, can you describe the man who attacked you?"

The young man blinked again, and then his eyes rolled upward and he slipped into unconsciousness.

The emergency personnel loaded Danny into the back of the ambulance and climbed in beside him.

Cara Jo was leading a distraught Alicia down the steps.

When Alicia reached the bottom, she ran toward the ambulance. "Is he going to be okay? Can I ride with him?"

"Are you a member of his family, ma'am?" the attendant asked.

She shook her head, wringing her hands. "No, but he's my boyfriend."

"I'm sorry, only family members." The technician closed the door.

Cara Jo slipped an arm around Alicia's shoulders. "Don't worry. I'll give you a ride to the hospital."

The deputy shook his head. "I'll need to ask her a few questions first."

The ambulance pulled away, and tears fell anew from Alicia's eyes.

"I'm Deputy Farnam. I'm sorry about your boyfriend," the policeman offered. "He's in good hands. Can you tell me what happened here?"

"Danny and I were supposed to meet back here after I got off work this evening. Only I was a little late because I had to check in a new guest as I was about to close the office.

"I was in a hurry, afraid Danny would think I'd stood him up. When I came around the side of the building, at first I didn't see anyone. Then I heard Danny shout. He was standing in the shadows by the stairs. Someone dressed in dark clothes and a ski mask was halfway up the stairs. He came down and hit Danny with what looked like a stick." Alicia shook her head, tears making rivulets across her smooth cheeks. "I screamed. The man turned on me. I couldn't move." She shook her head, her eyes wide. "My feet wouldn't budge. The man practically ran over me."

"Did he hurt you?" the officer asked.

"No." Alicia stared at the officer, her face pale, her eyes glassy. "His shoulder bumped me and spun me around. By the time I regained my balance, the man was gone. And Danny…that's when I ran up the stairs to get help." Alicia's voice caught on a sob. "Danny's going to be okay, isn't he?"

"Officer, do you need anything else from Alicia?" Cara Jo hugged the young woman. "I'd like to take her to the hospital."

"Will you be available to sign a statement tomorrow?" he asked.

"Sure." Alicia wiped the tears from her face, her lips thinning. "Anything to catch the bastard who did this to Danny."

Cara Jo led Alicia around the side of the building.

"Chuck?" PJ touched his arm.

He spun to face her. She held Charlie in her arms. The

baby's eyes blinked at the bright lights spinning on the police car.

Chuck wanted to pull PJ and Charlie into his arms and hold them. After listening to Alicia's account, Chuck had no doubt that the attacker was headed up the stairs to get to PJ's apartment, his intentions obviously nefarious.

"Are you okay?" PJ asked, her brows furrowed, her arms tightening around Charlie.

"I'm fine. Although I'm not sure how Alicia's boyfriend will be."

A shout went up from another officer who'd arrived after the first. He held something up in the air.

Deputy Farnam shook his head. "I think we found the weapon our perp used."

The other deputy closed the distance between them, carrying a tire iron. It caught the light where wet blood still clung to the metal.

PJ gasped. "He hit Danny with a tire iron?"

"That's what it looks like." The other deputy held the tire iron with gloved hands. "I hope we can lift prints. I found it in the dust."

PJ stroked Charlie's downy head and pressed a kiss to her chubby cheek.

"You'd better get her inside. I can't believe we didn't hear the attack while it was happening."

"We had the fan over the stove going. You can't hear anything outside over that."

"True. Go on. I'll be up in a minute," Chuck promised. He wanted to talk to the sheriff's deputy before he left.

PJ climbed the stairs, her gaze sweeping the parking lot as she disappeared into the building.

After explaining to the deputies that this had been the second attack in as many days, he asked if they would provide more surveillance in the area until they found the culprit.

"I don't think Danny was the intended victim," he told Farnam.

"I can have a unit come by once every hour until daylight."

Chuck thanked him and then returned to PJ's apartment.

He wouldn't take any more chances. He'd be staying with them tonight.

PJ LAID CHARLIE in her crib and tucked a blanket around her, and then she paced.

When Alicia had told her the same story she'd told the sheriff's deputy, a solid, heavy weight settled in the pit of PJ's gut. The attacker had been headed up the steps. The only people living at the top were Chuck, PJ and Charlie.

She rubbed the gooseflesh rising on her arms. Since her apartment had been the one broken into the night before, it stood to reason her apartment was once again the target.

Why? Who would want to hurt her or Charlie? She didn't owe anyone money. She hadn't made anyone mad at the diner—at least not mad enough to take a tire iron to her. Had Danny not stopped him…

Chuck had been there. But who was to say the attacker wouldn't have surprised him, armed with a pretty convincing weapon?

PJ stopped in the middle of the floor, hugging her arms around herself, wishing Chuck would finish his business with the cops and come back up the stairs. Not that she expected him to stay in her apartment, but having him nearby gave her more of a sense of safety than if she lived alone in this isolated part of the resort.

Footsteps sounded in the hallway outside, and a light knock sent PJ scooting across the floor. Her hand braced on the doorknob, she hesitated and then looked through the peephole.

Chuck's handsome face filled PJ's view, and she ripped open the door and threw herself into his arms. "Thank God."

He held her, stroking her hair for a moment, and then edged her through the door and closed it behind them.

"What's happening?" she whispered, her fingers clutching at his shirt, refusing to let go.

"I don't know," Chuck said, his voice rumbling against PJ's ear. "But whatever it is, I don't like it."

A tiny whimper sounded from the bedroom.

Chuck gripped PJ's shoulders. "I'll get her."

PJ unwound her fingers from his shirt, pulled herself upright and stepped out of the warmth and safety of Chuck's arms.

The big cowboy filled the doorway to PJ's bedroom as he entered to collect the baby, who had started crying softly.

"Hey, didn't anyone ever tell you that cowgirls don't cry?" He lifted her as if she were a fragile doll, afraid his big old hands would somehow break her. Just as carefully, he tucked her into the crook of his arm, her body so tiny next to his hulk.

She turned her face into his shirt, making sucking motions and then jamming her fist into her mouth.

Chuck grinned. "I think she's hungry."

PJ hurried toward them. "I'll feed her. You don't have to stay."

"I'll just wait in the other room." His face heated. He wasn't a prude, and he'd seen PJ's breasts before. Hell, he'd touched them and nibbled on the tips, making love to her. But they weren't together anymore, and watching her breastfeed Charlie, well, just wouldn't be right. He handed Charlie to her mother and left the bedroom.

PJ closed the door, leaving a little bit of a gap, and settled on the bed.

Chuck wandered around the little living room, checking the doors and windows, even though he'd done the same the night before. He couldn't rest until he knew PJ and Charlie were safe.

He pulled back the curtains over the sliding glass door and tested the latch by pulling on the handle. The door shimmied and held, but with a little muscle behind it, it would give. He made a note to install a new latch. In the meantime, he found a broom in the miniature pantry and broke off the bristled end.

"Did you just break my broom?"

"Yes." He glanced toward the bedroom.

The light in the room cast a soft glow over PJ as Charlie lay clutched to her breast. PJ pressed her fingers against her skin and pulled Charlie off, and then she moved her around to the other side and lifted her shirt.

The baby latched on.

Chuck sucked in a breath, the miracle of a woman's body—of PJ's body—rocking him to the core.

"That's the only broom I had." She glanced up, her gaze capturing Chuck's.

He spun away, blood burning in his cheeks. "I'll buy you another." He jammed the pole between the door frame and the sliding door. Again he tested the sliding door. This time it didn't budge at all. If someone wanted to come in, he'd have to break the glass.

Movement behind him made him turn.

PJ stood with Charlie cradled in her arms. "Could you watch her while I shower?"

Chuck took the baby, his knuckles brushing against PJ's, sending bursts of awareness through his system like tiny electric shocks. "Leave the apartment door open."

PJ GATHERED A TOWEL, toiletries, clean pajamas and the baby monitor, out of habit, and stepped out into the hallway. She turned, her brow furrowing, and stared back into her apartment, which was quickly being taken over by Chuck and his overwhelmingly large presence.

The cowboy settled into her favorite rocking chair, laying Charlie over his shoulder. He glanced at her. "What are you waiting for? Charlie and I will be fine."

"Are you sure I should leave the door open? Won't that put Charlie at risk?"

"I'll take care of Charlie, but I can't take care of you if I don't know whether or not you're in trouble."

"I don't need you to take care of me," she said, a mutinous frown settling on her face. Then it slid away. "But thanks."

She hurried from the apartment, but she couldn't walk away from how she was starting to feel about the big galoot. Starting…no, she'd never stopped having feelings for Chuck. All through the long year of separation, her pregnancy and the first few months of Charlie's life, she'd thought about Chuck and how it could have been. So many times she'd pulled the box of letters he'd written out from under her bed, only to push them back. What was done was done. Her total focus had to be on Charlie.

As she stepped beneath the shower's spray, a little voice in the back of her head kept telling her that Chuck was back, and he wasn't in the military.

Or was he still in the Guard, subject to call-up? She wouldn't know if she didn't ask. If he was still part of the military, nothing had changed. He could be deployed again, this time leaving her *and* Charlie.

The more Charlie grew and got to know her daddy, the more difficult it would be when Chuck left. And PJ would be the one to pick up the pieces and explain to her daughter why her father couldn't be with her.

The image of Chuck sitting in the rocking chair, holding Charlie as if he had been born to be a father, had left an indelible mark on PJ's memories.

PJ didn't have the right to keep Charlie from her father.

The stress of the past twenty-four hours had taken its toll, giving her a stiff neck and a headache. She stood for a long time under the hot spray of the showerhead, until the muscles loosened and the pounding against her temple reduced to a throb.

When the water turned cold, she flipped the shower off and toweled dry. As she stepped out of the tub, a crackling sound made her jump.

The light glowed red on the monitor. She'd forgotten to turn it off. Now she smiled, imagining she'd heard the creak of the rocking chair.

Then static blasted her again, followed by heavy breathing.

PJ froze, clutching the towel to her chest.

Then in a low, whispered monotone, a voice said, "Who's your daddy, little girl?"

PJ screamed and ran for the door. Whoever had spoken was in the apartment with the base unit and Charlie, and it didn't sound like Chuck.

Without thinking, she flung open the shared bathroom door and ran into a solid wall of muscles.

Terror seized her, and she fought to get past the barrier.

"Charlie."

"Is asleep in her crib." Chuck lifted the edges of the towel she still clutched and wrapped them around her naked body. "Calm down and tell me what happened."

"Was it you?" PJ gripped his shirt. "Tell me it was you."

Chuck shook his head. "I'm sorry, PJ. I don't know what you're talking about."

"The monitor. Did you speak into the baby monitor? Did you say 'Who's your daddy, little girl?'"

He captured her hands in his. "What monitor? What are you talking about?"

"Oh, dear God, let me by. Charlie's in there with him."

Chuck's brows dipped. "What do you mean? I just laid

her down in her crib, checked all the windows, closets and under the bed. She's okay."

Tears dribbled from the corners of PJ's eyes. "Please. I have to know for sure."

"Come on." Chuck turned and led the way into the tiny bedroom crowded with a double bed and a baby crib.

PJ leaned over the crib, bumping into the musical mobile, making it play several notes before it stopped.

Charlie's eyes blinked open and she whimpered.

Her heart still hammering, PJ reached into the crib and gathered her daughter into her arms. "Oh, baby. It's okay. Mommy won't let that ol' bad man get you."

Chuck stood in the doorway, his eyes narrowed. "You mind telling me what all that was about?"

Holding Charlie close, still wearing nothing but a towel, PJ stared over her head at Chuck. "Someone spoke into the baby monitor." She closed her eyes for a moment and let go of the breath trapped in her lungs since hearing that terrifying voice. She opened them and stared at the dresser beside the crib. Blood rushed from PJ's head, and she swayed.

"PJ?" Chuck slipped an arm around her waist to steady her. "Are you okay?"

She pointed to the dresser. "The base unit is gone."

"The intruder could have taken it last night."

Before he finished talking, PJ was shaking her head. "No, it was there this morning."

Chapter Six

Chuck checked behind the dresser and under the crib. "Are you sure?"

"Yes. I'd knocked it off the dresser with the diaper bag when I was getting ready this morning. I set it upright before I left." She pointed to the dresser. "It was there. I know it."

"Baby monitors probably don't have much of a range." Chuck's muscles bunched. "Wait here." He spun and raced for the door.

"Where are you going?" she called after him.

"To find the base unit and the guy playing with it."

"Are you crazy?"

Chuck didn't respond. He ducked into his apartment, grabbed a flashlight and his Glock from on top of his dresser, removed the trigger guard and then raced down the stairs, jumping the last four to the bottom. In the parking lot, he spun in a 360-degree circle, searching for movement. When nothing, not even a stray cat, budged in the darkness, Chuck headed for the scrub brush on the edges of the pavement. Whoever was tormenting PJ had probably taken off. After a few minutes, Chuck had checked behind every cactus and yucca plant and found nothing. Then his flashlight beam glanced off something white, half-hidden beneath a squat saw palmetto. He kicked it with his boot.

Lying at his feet was the battery-powered base unit for the baby monitor.

Chuck removed his T-shirt, wrapped it around the monitor and carried it back up the steps, stashing it in his apartment. He'd have Hank run a check for fingerprints. If the guy was the same one who'd hurt Danny, he had a lot of nerve coming back so soon. Unless he'd been among the onlookers gathered around the ambulance and police cars. He double-checked the Glock Hank had assigned him from Covert Cowboy, Inc.'s arsenal of weapons. He ejected the clip, checked that it was fully loaded and then slid it back into the handle and checked the safety. He stuffed it into the back of his jeans, pulled his T-shirt over it and left his apartment.

He knocked on PJ's door.

She yanked it open, her eyes wide, her gaze going past him to the empty hallway beyond. Her body wilted, and her brow furrowed. "I take it you didn't find him?"

"No, but I found the base unit. I'll have it checked for fingerprints tomorrow. It's in my apartment for now."

"Well, I'm glad you didn't find him." She held the door open and stepped to the side. "He could have hurt you like he hurt Danny."

Chuck's lips quirked upward in the corners. "I'm a little bigger than Danny. I think I can handle this guy."

"As long as he's not carrying a gun. Who's to say he won't attack again?"

Chuck shook his head. "After two incidents in one night, I doubt he'll be back again tonight." He pulled the gun from his waistband and laid it on the counter in the kitchen. "And if he comes with a gun, I'll be ready."

Her eyes rounding like saucers, PJ held up her hands. "You can't leave that there. What if it goes off? It could hit Charlie."

"I know how to use the gun, and it's safe as long as you treat it with respect." Chuck lifted the weapon and turned it over. "This is the safety switch to keep you from firing it accidentally. When you have to shoot, you flip it like this, point the gun at your target and pull the trigger. It's simple. Get familiar with it, in case you have to use it. And always be prepared to kill whatever you're aiming at."

"I know how to shoot a gun." PJ's face paled and her hands shook as Chuck laid the Glock in her palms. She knew how to use it, but she wasn't sure she could. PJ had the gun she'd found in her adoptive mother's nightstand. It remained in a box on a shelf, high in PJ's closet, away from Charlie.

"Just hold it for now. I'll take you out to Hank's for target practice soon."

"I told you, I know how to shoot. I just don't like to." PJ weighed the weapon in her palms and shook her head again. "Take it."

Chuck relieved her of the weapon and returned it to his back waistband.

"This is all too much." PJ walked back to the bedroom and stared down at the crib.

Chuck locked the apartment door behind him, making another note to himself to have the locks changed on the apartment and shared bathroom, and to install dead bolts.

"This is insane. Wild Oak Canyon is a tiny little town in the middle of nowhere. It's supposed to be a safe place to raise kids. Now—" she glanced across at Chuck "—I don't feel safe in this apartment, outside…anywhere…" PJ rubbed her arms. "And to think whoever broke into my apartment was in here with Charlie." Her voice cracked. "I can't let anything happen to Charlie. She's everything to me."

The band around Chuck's heart tightened. At one time, he'd thought he was everything to PJ. But that had changed. She'd pushed him away when he'd needed her most. Deployment had been hard enough as it was. But he had felt strongly about giving back to his country, and going to Afghanistan was his way of demonstrating his love for the United States.

He had no regrets, other than having been medically discharged when the men he'd fought with remained behind.

He followed PJ into the little bedroom and stood behind her as she stared down at the defenseless baby who couldn't even crawl yet. He knew a feeling of such longing, his chest hurt from it. The tiny baby girl with the short tuft of dark brown hair so like his lay curled on her side, her fist tucked beneath her cheek.

Chuck rested a hand on PJ's shoulder. "I won't let anything happen to Charlie."

PJ leaned into him. "What if you're not here? What if you deploy again? What if an attacker gets to her first?"

"I'm done with the army." The familiar stab of pain in his leg seemed less important than the thought of something awful happening to his baby girl.

PJ stared up at him, her eyes widening. "You're not in the Guard?"

He shook his head, glad for the first time he wasn't deployable. "I'm here now, and I want to be a part of Charlie's life."

PJ leaned her forehead into his chest. "I want to believe you."

"Why shouldn't you?"

"Everyone I ever loved has either died or left me. My mother, my adoptive mother, *you*."

"Me?" He shook his head. "You ended it between us."

"You left for the war."

"I didn't have a choice."

"Point is," her fingers curled into his shirt, "I couldn't take it if something were to happen to Charlie."

"I'd take a bullet for that kid. No one is going to hurt her as long as I'm alive." He wrapped his arms around PJ and added, "And no one is going to hurt you, either. Not if I have anything to do with it."

"Thank you."

Not exactly the response he would have chosen, but it was a start in regaining PJ's trust, as well as learning to trust her. She said she would make sure Charlie was a part of his life. And yet she'd promised to be a part of his. She'd ended their engagement, not the other way around. "You should get some rest."

She leaned away from him and snorted. "Like that's going to happen."

"Do you work tomorrow?"

"Of course."

"Then you need rest so that you don't fall flat on your face waiting tables."

She gave him a weak smile. "I can go without a little sleep. Babies don't always sleep through the night. I had to get used to it."

Guilt ate at Chuck. PJ had been on her own throughout her pregnancy and the first three months of Charlie's life. No one to help her, to let her rest. "I'm here now. You don't need to go two nights in a row without sleep." He rubbed her arms and let his hands fall to his sides. "I'll stay in the living room, in case someone tries to break in again." Chuck backed toward the door. "You'll be okay."

PJ glanced down at Charlie again and then toward her bed. "I can't get over the feeling that my personal space has been violated, that someone is targeting me for some reason." She shivered. "It gives me the creeps. Should I get the sheriff involved?"

"Absolutely."

"In the meantime, I have to live here and I don't feel safe."

"Let me put your mind at rest." He went to the small closet and threw open the door. Inside hung the little bit of clothing that comprised PJ's wardrobe, along with shoes neatly lined up along the floor. "No one hiding in the closet."

PJ's lips quirked. "Scaring away the boogeyman?"

"You bet. Gotta take care of my girls." Chuck bent to

look beneath the bed. "Nothing under there but a couple of dust bunnies." He pulled back the clean floral comforter that had seen better days and many washings. "All clear here, as well." He jerked his head to the side. "Get in."

She gave him a lopsided frown. "I'm not a child to be tucked in."

His gaze swept over her from the top of her drying hair to her bare feet, and his groin tightened. "No, you're not. But you've been through a pretty frightening ordeal. It's okay to be scared."

PJ moved toward the bed. "For Charlie."

"For Charlie." With a nod, Chuck shook the comforter, encouraging her to take him up on his offer.

PJ climbed into the bed and pulled the sheets up to her chin. "You'll be in the living room?"

"Unless you want me to stay with you until you go to sleep?" He tucked the comforter around her, his breath held in wait for her answer.

"No," she said, her eyes wide, her fingers clenched around the blanket.

He let go of the breath. What did he expect? She wasn't going to invite him into her bed after one night back. Chuck straightened, fighting back his disappointment and the heat growing inside at the image of PJ's long, silky legs sliding beneath the sheets. He cleared his throat. "Close your eyes and sleep." Then he left, his hand reaching for the doorknob to pull it closed.

"Wait." PJ's voice arrested him in midstep, a hint of fear making it tight.

He didn't turn, afraid he wouldn't be able to leave again if he did. "I'll only be in the living room. Just yell if you need anything."

"I was wrong," she whispered.

Hope blossomed, filling Chuck's chest and lodging with

the lump in his throat. Still he refused to face her. "About what?"

"I want you…to stay until I go to sleep." Her voice was little more than a soft sigh. "Please?"

Chuck sucked in a deep breath and slowly turned.

PJ lay against the sheets, her eyes wide, the dark circles beneath them giving her a vulnerable look.

He wanted to tell her no. That he had been wrong to think he could stay with her in her bedroom without holding her, touching her, wanting to kiss her. Inwardly he groaned. "Okay."

She smiled. "Thank you." PJ turned on her side, facing him and the baby crib. "You can sit here." She patted the mattress beside her. "I won't bite."

His teeth grinding in the back of his head, Chuck closed the short distance to her bedside and hesitated. "I'll just stand here."

"I'd never fall asleep with you hovering over me like a vulture." She patted the mattress, her mouth a firm line. "Sit."

Chuck obeyed, sure he was in for the toughest hour of his life. This felt even more dangerous than stalking the streets of an Afghan village searching for insurgents. He settled on the bed, kicked off his boots. Then, resting his back against the headboard, he gave up the fight. "Come here."

PJ scooted closer.

Chuck pulled her into his arms and let her rest her face against his T-shirt. His entire body begged for more. "Go to sleep," he said, his voice gruff.

"You don't have to be grumpy."

"Yes, I do. If I'm not, then I might be tempted to do this." He leaned over and claimed her lips, his own pressing down hard, all the pent-up frustration of having her so close over the past twenty-four hours and not being able to hold her exploding into that one kiss.

Her lips opened on a sigh, her teeth parting, letting his tongue slide in to caress hers in a long, sensuous stroke.

Her fingers climbed up his chest and locked behind his neck, dragging him closer, her breasts pressing against his chest, their bodies melting together.

Chuck's hands slid down her shoulders to the small of her back, pulling her over to lie across him.

His groin tightened, his member pressing into her belly. Nothing but the soft cotton of her nightshirt and shorts between him and…

Who was he kidding? Nothing had changed between them. PJ was working off fear. She didn't want to be alone, and holding him was her only way of feeling safe. He couldn't take advantage of her in her current state.

Chuck gripped PJ's arms and laid her back against her own pillow. "Sleep."

She stared up at him, eyes dark gray-green pools, her lips swollen from his kiss. "What just happened…"

"Shouldn't have. Rest assured, it won't happen again." He tucked the blanket around her and crossed his arms over his chest to keep his hands from straying back toward her.

"Chuck…" PJ cleared her throat.

"Just go to sleep, damn it." He closed his eyes to the vulnerable look in hers. "I'll stay until you do."

She lay still for a long moment, and then the sheets rustled and she shifted.

When Chuck dared to look again, PJ lay on her side, facing away from him, her body rigid. He didn't try to comfort her. Instead he focused on remaining as still as possible.

Before long, her muscles loosened and her breathing grew deeper and steady.

When he was sure she was asleep, he climbed out of the bed. As he passed the crib, Charlie whimpered and rolled to her back, her eyes blinking open.

"Go to sleep, sweetheart," he whispered, smoothing a finger across her velvety cheek.

Her eyes opened wider, and she batted the air with her tiny fists.

Afraid she'd cry, Chuck lifted her into his arms and carried her out into the living room. As soon as he laid her over his shoulder, she gnawed on her fist and settled against him, falling back to sleep.

He gave her a few minutes and then walked back into the bedroom to lay her in the crib. As soon as he tilted her onto her back, her eyes opened and she whimpered again.

Chuck sighed, gathered her in his arms and took her back into the living room. He eased into the rocker recliner and set the chair in motion.

Charlie lay still against his chest. The scent of baby shampoo filled his senses with a new memory he'd never forget.

This was his little girl, so defenseless and dependent on her parents to protect her from harm. After a while, Chuck stopped rocking and leaned back, lifting the footrest.

Charlie slept on, and before long, so did Chuck.

PJ WOKE IN the darkness, her breasts tight, knowing she needed to rise and feed Charlie. She lay for a moment, listening. Usually Charlie alerted her to the need to eat by crying out. The room was eerily quiet. Too quiet. She tossed the comforter aside and pushed to her feet, crossing to the baby crib.

As she leaned over to check on Charlie, her heart stopped and she almost cried out.

Charlie was gone!

PJ raced out into the living room and almost fell across the outstretched footrest of the recliner.

Chuck's big form lay sprawled across the chair. In his arms Charlie lay sleeping, her cheek resting against his broad chest, a little spot of drool darkening his T-shirt.

PJ froze, her heart seizing, a sob rising to close off her throat.

The big man and the tiny baby looked so right together.

Chuck stirred, his hand touching the baby as if, even in his sleep, he was checking on her to make sure he didn't drop the precious child.

For a long moment, PJ stared, filling her senses with all of what could have been among her, Chuck and Charlie. With all that had happened, the months of living without him, not telling him about his child and what he'd surely suffered in Afghanistan, PJ didn't know what was best for any of them.

All she knew was what she witnessed. Chuck would make a great father to Charlie. No matter what she'd done in the past, PJ wouldn't stand in the way of Chuck and Charlie's relationship and time together.

Trouble was, where did she fit into the picture? Could she let Chuck back into her life? Would he want to come back? And in what capacity? As the father who has joint custody of his little girl? Or the husband who loves and takes care of his family?

PJ knew very little about Chuck's family. He'd mentioned his parents once to say he was estranged from them, but he hadn't given a reason. What had his childhood been like?

If she and Chuck were to get back together—not that she was leaning in that direction, but if they were—she'd want to know everything. Having Charlie made her even more aware of the importance of family and maintaining that connection.

So many questions were left unanswered and would have to remain unanswered, at least until morning. PJ glanced at the clock on the wall and sighed. She had to be up in three hours to get ready for work.

She gently lifted Charlie from Chuck's chest.

His eyes shot open and he grabbed her wrist, his grip tight enough to bruise. "What are you doing?"

"I'm taking Charlie to feed her." PJ fought not to drop the baby. "You're hurting my wrist."

For a moment, the pressure increased, and then Chuck blinked and looked at her as if for the first time. "PJ?"

"Yes, of course." She glanced at where his hand still held her. "You can let go. I'm one of the good guys."

He jerked back his hand and sat up in the chair. "I'm sorry." Chuck stared at her reddened wrist where he'd held her, his brow furrowing. "Did I do that?"

PJ shifted Charlie into the crook of one arm and shrugged. "It'll be okay."

"No, it won't." He reached out and then stopped, his hand falling to his side. "Maybe it's not such a good idea for me to be here."

"Why?"

"I sometimes have nightmares."

"Post-traumatic stress kind of nightmares?"

He nodded and pushed a hand through his hair. "Yeah."

"I'll take my chances. I'd rather have your nightmares than that nightmare stalking me."

Charlie turned her face into PJ's chest, nuzzling for food. Her fist found its way into her mouth, and she sucked on it with a loud smacking sound.

PJ smiled. "I need to feed Charlie."

Chuck stood and stretched. "Right. I'll just check the doors and windows."

"You've done that already."

"Then I'll do it again." He nodded toward Charlie, sucking PJ's shirt into her mouth. "You better get busy before that one rips a hole in your shirt."

"She's a determined little girl." PJ entered her bedroom, leaving the door open slightly, and turned her back to it before lifting her shirt.

Charlie latched on and settled against her, a hand on her breast, her fingers curling into the skin.

The world stood still while she fed Charlie, leaving PJ with nothing else to do but think. About Charlie, about Chuck, about the way Chuck had kissed her and held her in his arms.

She had no idea what to do next, but she knew she hadn't stopped loving the big man.

Her cell phone vibrated on the nightstand beside her bed, indicating a text message. Who would text her at three-thirty in the morning?

PJ leaned over, careful not to disturb Charlie, and grabbed the phone with her free hand. She clicked on the message from a sender with a blocked number.

The message was long, and for a moment PJ didn't understand. When the words sank in, she dropped the phone and yelled, "Chuck!"

Chapter Seven

When the wind blows, the cradle will rock
When the bow breaks, the cradle will fall
and down will come baby, family and all.

The short bit of a twisted child's lullaby roiled through Chuck's head for the rest of the night, keeping him awake until the gray streaks of dawn crept in around the edges of the curtained windows.

He'd given up on sleep long before dawn and moved around the kitchen, quietly setting out pans and plates for breakfast.

Why would someone target PJ and Charlie and then threaten their family, unless they knew Hank's secret? As soon as he could, Chuck planned to talk to Hank. PJ had a right to know what was going on. Her connection to Hank or to her mother's former fiancé had to be the reason for the threats and attacks.

PJ had to know everything in order to protect herself. And a DNA test would help to prove her lineage and give them a better understanding of what they would be up against.

PJ emerged from the bedroom fully clothed at five-thirty.

Chuck had just cracked an egg into the skillet. "One egg or two?"

"I'm not hungry."

"You, better than anyone else, know that you have to eat." He nodded toward the bedroom. "Charlie's counting on you."

Her shoulders sagged. "I know. One egg."

"Scrambled, right?" He cracked an egg into a coffee mug and stirred it with a fork.

"You remembered."

"There's not much I don't remember about you." He didn't glance up when he spoke. He didn't want to spook her with too much intimacy too soon. Not when he'd almost lost control the night before and kissed her. He'd wanted so much more than just a kiss.

"You like yours sunny-side up." PJ slipped behind him and reached for the glasses in the cabinet next to the sink. She filled them with the last of the orange juice and tossed the jug into the recycle bin.

Hyperaware of her every move, Chuck almost dropped the spatula when PJ pulled open the drawer beside him, her hip rubbing against his.

She grabbed utensils from a drawer, rounded to the other side of the bar and laid them in front of the two bar stools. "Sorry, the apartment isn't big enough for a dining table."

He grinned. "Anything beats eating MREs in the sand."

"How was it…you know…over there?" PJ asked.

Chuck's lips turned downward as a flashback blinded him as effectively as the desert sun. Sand all around, dull, beige-colored hulls of bombed-out buildings in mountain towns. Being alert at all times, never knowing who was friend or foe. Watching every step you took, to avoid improvised explosive devices. Not knowing if a gun would go off in your face around every corner. "Harsh."

PJ swallowed hard. "Why did you come back early?"

He slid the eggs onto the plate so fast, they slipped over the edge and landed on the counter. Chuck slammed the skillet onto the stove and glared across at PJ. "I don't want to talk about it."

PJ held up her hands, her brows rising into her hair. "I'm sorry. But maybe talking about it will help. When you're ready, I'll listen."

Bread popped up in the toaster and Chuck jumped and spun toward the appliance, his fists clenched. When he realized he'd overreacted toward PJ and the toast, he closed his eyes and willed his muscles to relax. "I'm sorry." He turned to face her, plates in hand.

"No problem." PJ's voice was casual, but one hand rubbed the wrist of the other where light purple bruises were beginning to show.

Chuck set the plates on the bar and took PJ's injured wrist in his hand. "I did that?" He skimmed his thumb over the mark and shook his head. "I'll bed down in the hallway tonight."

"No." Her hands closed around his.

When he tried to pull free, she held on.

"Look at me." PJ squeezed gently.

Chuck gazed into her beautiful gray-green eyes. "I never want to hurt you."

"You didn't. I'm okay, and I want you to stay in the apartment." She sucked in a deep breath and let it out. "I'm afraid for Charlie…and myself. Having you there until this nutcase is caught would help me sleep better."

"Even when I'm capable of this?" He held up her wrist, his jaw tight, lips pressed together.

"Especially because of this. I know you can take care of us better than we could take care of ourselves." She carried his hand to her cheek. "Please. Let it go."

"For now." He pulled his hands free, wanting to take her into his arms and hold her more than he wanted to breathe, but afraid he'd hold her too tight or lose himself again to the images seared into his mind from his deployment.

PJ slipped onto the bar stool and patted the one beside

her. "I have to eat in a hurry. Charlie will be awake any moment and demand her breakfast."

Glad for the change of subject, Chuck sat beside PJ as if nothing was wrong. "She seems healthy and happy."

PJ smiled. "Charlie's been an ideal baby from the moment I brought her home from the hospital. Other than the late-night feedings, which is natural for breast-fed babies, she sleeps the rest of the night."

"I want you to put me on the emergency contact list for the day care, in case something comes up and you're not able to pick her up on time."

"I'll do that when I drop her off today."

"And warn the caregivers to keep a close eye on her and keep you informed of any strangers coming in or out of the building for any reason."

PJ set her fork down. "Do you think someone would try to take Charlie?"

"We don't know what the text message meant, but we can't take chances." He would talk with Hank that day and find out if there was anything else he could do to protect Charlie and PJ.

PJ stared at her uneaten egg. "Should I even take her to day care today? I have to work. I can't afford to take time off."

"No. For now, go on, business as usual. Just let the staff know to be aware."

A cry from the other room made PJ jump. "That's my cue." She set her plate in the sink, having taken only one bite of egg and toast.

Chuck didn't like that PJ was so on edge she didn't eat. He'd put security measures in place around the resort and the parking lot where PJ entered and exited the building. And later that day, if they had time, he'd take her out to Hank's and teach her how to fire the Glock.

PJ left at six-thirty. Chuck walked with her to her little

car and helped her settle Charlie into the backseat. "I'll follow you to the day care."

"No. It's daylight. I'll be okay for a few blocks. I'm sure Cara Jo has a long list of things for you to do around here today."

"What time will you be done at work?"

"Around three, then I head to the library to use the computer for my online classes."

"Classes?"

She smiled. "Yeah. I started college."

He'd known she'd been saving for it when they'd gotten engaged. "What are you studying?"

"Animal husbandry and business management." Her shoulders straightened, and her eyes glowed with excitement. "I want to work with animals on a ranch or a farm someday."

"I'm happy for you, PJ." His chest swelled. She'd chosen the same field he'd studied. "I'm glad you're getting to realize your dream." And he was. "What time do you pick up Charlie from the day care?"

"Around five. Still daylight. We'll be okay." PJ stood beside her car door, staring up into Chuck's face. "Thanks for being here for us." She leaned up and brushed her lips against his, and then she slid into the driver's seat and pulled away.

Warmth filled Chuck's chest, edging out the cold hollowness he'd experienced in Afghanistan.

PJ had turned onto the main road and disappeared around the edge of the diner, yanking Chuck back to the present. He pulled out his cell phone and hit the speed dial for Hank Derringer.

"Hey, Chuck, I'm glad you called. We need to meet."

Chuck's jaw tightened. "Damn right we do."

"I'm headed into town in about an hour. I'll see you at the diner?"

"Stop by my apartment first. I want to talk to you in private."

"Will do."

Chuck went to work making PJ's home a safer place to live. He installed fresh, brighter light bulbs over the staircase and landing, cleaning the globes of bugs and Texas dust. As soon as he was certain the hardware store would be open, he headed there. On his way past the diner, he slowed long enough to catch a glimpse of PJ through the large windows.

She was busy serving to the morning crowd of cowboys and businessmen and women, her hair pulled back in a ponytail, her face flushed.

Chuck's belly tightened. If anything happened to her…

He mashed his boot to the accelerator and hurried toward the only hardware store in town, hoping it also sold more advanced electronics.

Inside the store, he noted everything a man could want in the way of nails, screws, plumbing and building supplies. He located new doorknobs with matching locks and keys. Then he went in search of motion-sensing lights.

"May I help you?" An older gentleman stepped up beside him and did a double take. "Chuck?" His eyes widened and he grinned. "Chuck Bolton? Boy, how've you been?" He stuck out his hand and shook Chuck's.

Chuck smiled at the old man. "How are you, Mr. Bergman?"

"Other than rheumatism in my joints and a bum knee, I'm still kickin'. Missed seeing you come in here for supplies for the resort and the stables. Thought you'd left this hole-in-the-wall behind to go into the army?"

"I did for a while when my Guard unit deployed." Chuck clenched his teeth. "Now that I'm back, I'm working for the Wild Oak Canyon Resort again."

It reminded him of his years growing up. When he hadn't been at school, he'd spent all his time outside from the crack of dawn until after sunset, riding, fencing, hauling hay and caring for the animals his father had accumulated over the years.

He could still remember the first horse he'd purchased with the money he'd made helping a neighbor haul hay. There had been some good times, before his falling-out with his father had driven him away and ultimately to this small town.

"Always liked you around here," Mr. Bergman was saying. "You worked hard and set a good example for the young folk." He clapped Chuck on the back and looked around. "What can I help you find?"

"I need motion-sensing exterior lighting."

"Got some of those in just yesterday and hadn't had time to put 'em on the shelf."

"Grandpa, this cash register is giving me fits." The pretty blonde at the counter slapped the side of an antique register older than her—and probably her parents, too.

"Let me get Ross to help you. He's good with all the electronics and computer gizmos." Mr. Bergman turned toward the back stockroom. "Ross!"

A tall, bulky younger man with a sulky scowl on his forehead appeared in the doorway leading to the rear of the building. "What?"

Mr. Bergman's brow furrowed at the abrupt response. "Chuck here needs some of those motion-sensing lights that came in the shipment yesterday. Help him out while I fix the confounded register."

Ross glared toward Chuck and then turned back into the rear of the building.

"You can go on back and see if they're what you want," Mr. Bergman offered, steering Chuck with a hand on his back. "I'll help as soon as I can."

Chuck followed the surly Ross into the back stockroom.

Stacks of boxes stood in lines, some open, some half-empty and many needing to be unpacked.

"Here." Ross unearthed a black package from inside a cardboard box and tossed it to Chuck.

Chuck caught it, wondering how this boy kept his job. With such a poor attitude and disposition, he would be more of a liability to Mr. Bergman than an asset.

"Well?" Ross stood with his hand on the box full of lighting supplies.

Chuck inspected the outside writing and opened the box to peer inside. "I can use them. I need six."

Ross's eyes narrowed, and a snarl lifted his lip. He grumbled as he dug into the box. "Only have four."

"I'll take them all."

Ross dug the others out, handing them all to Chuck, rather than offering to take them out to the counter.

"Finding what you need?" Mr. Bergman appeared in the doorway.

"Got it," Chuck answered.

"Let me help you with those." Mr. Bergman reached for the black boxes.

"Thanks, but I got 'em."

Ross shuffled around in the back of the storeroom, knocking a box over. "Damn!" The young man shot a killer look at the store owner.

Mr. Bergman led the way out of the stockroom. "That boy has a chip on his shoulder. Would fire him, but he's my only grandson. His mother's divorced and working at the truck stop. She's got enough on her mind without having to worry about her boy."

That explained why the kind old gentleman kept a surly employee on the books.

"I keep hoping he'll find another job. He's been applying, but no takers so far. Ross is a wizard at computers, but he's terrible with people." Mr. Bergman shook his head.

Skills only got you so far, as Chuck had learned. The ability to work with others was vital, a lesson he'd learned the hard way himself. "I'll need new locks and keys, as well."

Mr. Bergman nodded. "I can help you with that."

Chuck paid for the lights and new door locks and left the store. Having been to war with young people who would give their lives for their brothers in arms, he didn't have much patience for people like Ross. He hoped like hell Charlie didn't grow up to marry someone like him.

The thought of Charlie growing up hit him again with the weight of his commitment to the tiny baby. He hurried back to the resort to install the four motion-sensing lights on the corners of the building. Each light and position had its own challenge—from finding electrical wires hidden in the eaves to running the wire out to the corners. Like a puzzle. He'd always enjoyed a good puzzle that he could work out with his brain and his hands. Once he had the wiring in place, he began mounting the lights, aiming the globes at the ground where he knew PJ would be walking.

Now that he was back in Wild Oak Canyon, he had more reason than ever to want to be with PJ. But would it work? She'd ditched him when he'd told her he was deploying. How would she feel about his work for Covert Cowboys, Inc.? The job could prove equally dangerous. With Charlie in the picture, should he give it up and find safer employment? Thoughts whirled around his mind. The clearest one was of Charlie. She needed a father.

While standing at the top of the extension ladder, holding the last light fixture in place with one hand and a screw and screwdriver in the other hand, he fumbled the screw and dropped it.

"Need this?" a deep, accented voice called out from below.

Chuck shot a glance to the bottom of the ladder.

An older, Hispanic man, probably in his sixties, with deeply salted hair, stood on the sidewalk below, holding the screw.

"Yes, I do." Chuck descended until he stood beside the stranger.

The man placed the screw in his hand.

"Thanks."

The man tipped his head. *"De nada."*

"If you will excuse me, I'll finish." A little hesitant to turn his back on anyone, including a mild-mannered older man, Chuck eased up the ladder and twisted the screw in place.

When he glanced down, the man still stared up at him, this time holding the ladder steady.

Chuck descended. "Thank you."

"You're very, how do you say, handy?"

"Comes with the job." He stuck out his hand. "I'm Chuck, the handyman."

The man took his hand in a firm grip. "Ricardo Iglesias. Pleasure."

"Are you a guest here at the resort?"

"Sí."

"From around here?"

"Vacationing from Belize."

Chuck's brows rose. "Vacationing here?" He glanced around at the flat, dry countryside extending out from the back of the resort, more desert than anything else.

The man shrugged. "It has its own beauty and interests."

Chuck understood the man's reasoning. "But isn't Belize a lush tropical paradise?"

"Some would say so. But I believe happiness is derived from closeness to one's *familia.* Regrettably, I don't live close to *mi familia.*"

A regret Chuck was all too familiar with. "We all make choices." He'd made his seven years ago.

"Some are made for us, and we must, unfortunately, live with the outcome."

An image of his father rose to Chuck's mind, of the day he'd kicked him out of the house and told him to make his own way in the world. He'd been eighteen. And he hadn't talked to his father since. Nor had he had contact with anyone from his family, including his mother, younger brother and sister, in the seven years since he'd left home.

The older man tipped his head. "Señor Bolton, do you live close to your family?"

"I don't remember giving you my name."

The man shrugged. "I asked in the cafe. Are you close to your family?" he repeated.

The question caught Chuck off guard. His first instinct was to say no, even though his father, mother, sister and brother were less than a hundred miles away. Then he recalled he wasn't alone in Wild Oak Canyon. He had PJ and Charlie. "As a matter of fact, I am." At least Charlie was family. And by default PJ was part of it. Even if she'd chosen to push him away. She couldn't escape the fact that she was Charlie's mother and Charlie was his daughter.

"When you get to be my age, you learn wealth and fame are nothing without family."

"I know that." One look from his baby girl's brown eyes had taught him that.

"You have *niños*—children?" Ricardo asked.

His chest swelled with the love already firmly rooted in his heart for Charlie. "I do."

"Guard them well. Never let them know a day without your love."

"I plan on loving her every day of her life." Chuck glanced at the man, noting the deep lines of sorrow written in his face. "What about you? Do you have children?"

"I do." The older man gave him a sad kind of smile. "And I made many mistakes."

"Is any parent perfect?" Not for the first time, Chuck wondered if he'd be a good father. If the mistakes he made would drive Charlie away as his father's had driven him away.

"Teach your children love and humility through your own example. It's all we can do."

"I'll keep that in mind." Chuck glanced up at the ladder. "If you'll excuse me…"

"*Sí,* of course." Ricardo backed away. "I have kept you from your work long enough."

"I hope you enjoy your vacation at Wild Oak Canyon." Chuck collected the empty boxes. When he straightened, Ricardo was gone.

Another glance at the motion-sensing lights had Chuck convinced.

It wasn't enough.

Hank pulled into the parking lot in an older four-wheel drive pickup. The fact that the man had millions, probably billions, hadn't changed what he liked to drive. He parked and climbed down, staring up at the extension ladder still leaning against the side of the two-story resort building.

"Motion-activated?" he asked.

Chuck nodded.

"I take it the attack last night on Danny Reynolds got to you?"

"That and other things."

"Let's go inside, and you can fill me in."

Inside Chuck's apartment, Hank pulled out his cell phone and handed it to Chuck. "Got this text message early this morning."

Chuck read the message, a sick feeling washing over him. "Around three-thirty this morning?"

Hank frowned. "As a matter of fact, yes."

"PJ got the same message."

"Then that's it." Hank dragged in a deep breath, the lines in his forehead deepening. "Whoever is after PJ is probably doing it to get to me. You say he specifically mentioned PJ's father?"

"He said, 'Who's your daddy, little girl?'"

"He has to be someone who knows PJ's lineage."

"Whoever it is has been in her apartment more than once." He told him about the missing monitor and the voice PJ heard. "I'm installing new locks and dead bolts today."

"Good. I'll get my computer guru to set her up with a security system, as well. But it will take time."

"The way things are going, I'm not sure she has time." Chuck stared into Hank's face. "You have to tell her what you know. She deserves to know what she could be up against."

"That puts you in the middle of it. How do you feel about revealing that you've been lying to her about your position here?"

"She won't be happy." She'd probably feel betrayed. Chuck clenched his fist. "What's important at this point is to keep them safe. If telling them about my role in this helps, then so be it."

"When shall we tell her?"

"The sooner the better."

"Bring her and Charlie out to the ranch this evening. We can break it to her then."

"Hank?"

"There's more?"

Chuck handed him the baby monitor he'd wrapped in a brown paper bag. "I need you to use your connections and have the fingerprints lifted off this baby monitor and run it against the Integrated Automated Fingerprint Identification System's database."

"I'll get right on it."

"One other thing." Chuck's jaw firmed. "We need to get PJ's DNA tested."

Hank nodded. "I figured it would come to that."

"Why wait?"

The older man stared out the small window at the sky. "I've already lost one family. If PJ really is my daughter, I couldn't stand to lose her, too."

"And you'd feel differently if she isn't your daughter?"

With a chuckle and wry twist of his lips, Hank answered. "No. I love PJ as if she were my own. But if she's not, some-one knows she's connected to me in some way. She could be a target for kidnapping and ransom, either way."

"Or, if her mother's ex-fiancé knows of her existence," Chuck noted, "he could be at the bottom of this and might take her life in revenge for you taking his fiancée."

Hank ran his hand through his shock of gray hair. "And equally as frightening...if he finds out she's his daughter—"

"PJ and Charlie will be in grave danger of kidnapping."

"And taken to Mexico where she might never be found."

Chuck slammed his fist into his palm. "We can't let any of that happen."

"No," Hank agreed. "We can't."

BUSINESS AT THE diner was brisk that morning and stretched right into lunch, giving PJ no time for a break. She wanted to check on where Chuck was. Having him so close and yet not being able to see him...well, it was distracting, tummy-knotting and plain frustrating. Twice she'd ducked into the kitchen to phone the day care. Both times, Dana assured her that Charlie was fine and no strangers had been in or around the facility.

After the attack, the voice on the monitor and the threatening text, PJ couldn't dispel a sense of impending doom, making her twitchy and tightly strung.

Someone dropped a pan in the kitchen and PJ jumped, emitting a tiny scream.

Cara Jo leaned close to her as she passed by with a heavy tray. "Honey, you're about as nervous as a cat in a room full of rockin' chairs."

PJ pressed a hand to her chest, willing her pulse to slow to normal. "I'm fine."

"Thinking about the attack on Danny last night?"

"Yeah." And the other incidents. And Charlie. And the way she'd felt when Chuck had kissed her.

"I called the hospital this morning. He's going to be fine. They're monitoring him for a concussion one more day, and then they'll release him."

"I'm glad he'll be okay." To think, if Danny hadn't been there, the attacker might have gotten to Chuck or Charlie.

"Why don't you take a break? I'll cover your tables."

"No, but thanks. I need to work. It keeps me from think-ing about everything else."

"Including the handsome Chuck Bolton?"

"Is he here?" PJ spun toward the door.

Cara Jo chuckled. "No, but your reaction to his name told me all I needed to know."

Heat burned its way up PJ's neck and into her cheeks. "We're not back together, if that's what you're thinking."

"No?" She raised her brows and smiled. "If the look on your face is any indication, and if the man's still willin', it won't be long."

PJ pressed her palms to her cheeks and made a dash for the ladies' room. Cara Jo was right. She was flushed, her eyes shining and far more animated than they'd been in a long time.

Damn.

She couldn't fall in love with Chuck all over again. She had Charlie, and that was all she needed. Chuck would be like every other adult in her life and either leave her or die. Why get attached only to be left once again?

After a stern jerk on her own bootstraps, PJ washed her hands and emerged from the ladies' room with purpose. A new customer sat at one of her tables, looking around ex-pectantly.

PJ grabbed a menu and went to work. "New to town?" she asked politely.

"*Sí, señorita.* I am staying at the resort for the week."

The gray-haired man spoke with a thick Spanish accent, the sound melodic and comforting.

PJ smiled. "You'll like the resort. It's laid-back, and the rooms are all comfortable. Can I get you something to drink?"

"Coffee, *por favor.*"

PJ headed for the coffeepot, snagged a mug and the coffee carafe and returned.

"Gracias." He had a noble air to the way he held his head high, and his piercing brown-black eyes seemed to look right through PJ into her soul.

She shook her head, reminding herself of how little sleep she'd gotten the night before. "What can I get you to eat?"

As she hung the man's order in the window to the kitchen, a younger man wearing a ball cap entered the diner and sat at the bar, tapping his fingers on the counter until PJ stopped in front of him. "Can I get you something to drink?"

"Coke," he said, his answer so abrupt as to be almost rude.

PJ set the glass in front of him and handed him a menu. "Cara Jo will take your order. She'll only be a moment."

She returned to the Hispanic gentleman, setting out a bundle of cutlery wrapped in a napkin. "Is there anything else I can get you while you're waiting for your order?"

"Señorita, are you from around here?"

"Pretty much."

"Can you tell me where I might hire a horse?"

"You said you're staying at the resort?"

"Sí."

"They can arrange for you to ride. They have a stable with several decent riding horses."

"Gracias."

When PJ turned to leave, the man captured her hand. "Pardon me, but you remind me of someone I once knew." He let go.

PJ snorted.

"Do you look like your mother?"

"I don't know. All I have is a faded picture of her. Hard to tell."

The man nodded. "Family means a lot to you?"

Not before. Not when she'd lost everyone she'd loved. But since Charlie had come into her life… "It does now."

"As it should."

"Order up!" the cook in the kitchen called out.

When PJ turned to collect the plate, she could see in her peripheral the man at the counter watching her as she crossed the room to the kitchen window.

A chill slipped across her skin.

She had to get a grip. Her paranoia was affecting her work.

If she wasn't mistaken, the young man in the ball cap worked at the hardware store, and he normally walked around with a sullen expression. PJ shrugged and concentrated on her job.

Forty-five minutes later, she grabbed her purse and headed for the library. She'd barely have enough time to finish her homework, load up her new assignments and get across town to pick up Charlie.

While she pulled up her college assignments account on the computer, she checked her email on her smartphone, paging through the spam to get to her instructor's responses to her homework assignments. One email caught her eye, the title blurring as she clicked to open it.

In the subject line, written all in caps, were the words *Rock-a-bye Baby.*

Chapter Eight

Chuck hit the talk button on his cell phone before the first ring ended. "PJ?"

"Meet me at the day care." PJ's voice came across in labored bursts, as if she was running.

"When?"

"Now."

Before he could ask why, the line clicked off. Chuck dropped the ladder he'd been carrying and ran for his truck, leaving a trail of burned rubber on the pavement of the resort parking lot. In less than five minutes, he skidded into the lot in front of the church where PJ had dropped Charlie off the day before.

PJ pulled in behind him.

Chuck leaped out of his truck and joined PJ on the stairs leading up to the door. "What's wrong?"

"Charlie," she said. Without slowing, PJ charged into the church. "We have to get to our baby."

They ran down the long hallway to the entrance and burst through the door.

A woman's scream brought them to a screeching halt.

Dana stood with her hand pressed against her chest and laughed shakily. "You two scared me half to death. What's wrong?"

"Where's Charlie?" PJ demanded, pushing past Dana to

move into the room beyond where cribs lined one wall and playpens another. She went straight for the first crib and peered into the bed. "Dear God, where is she?"

"Looking for Charlie?" Another woman's voice called out from the floor at the end of the room, on the other side of a playpen.

"Charlie?" PJ rushed forward.

Chuck followed, his pulse hammering against his ribs.

Lying on her back on a colorful blanket, Charlie stared up at the playset dangling over her. She smiled and kicked her feet.

"Charlie." PJ's voice caught on a sob. "Oh, thank God."

When the baby heard her mother's voice, she turned her head toward her and cooed.

PJ lifted the child into her arms and held her close, tears trickling down her cheeks to splash onto Charlie's silky hair.

"Charlie's okay." Chuck steadied his hand against PJ's back and pulled her into his arms, shocked that he was shaking.

"I was so scared," PJ whispered.

"Do you mind telling me what got you so upset?" Chuck asked.

She pulled her cell phone from the back pocket of her jeans and handed it to him. "Click the link on that email." PJ turned away from him and paced across the room, giving him time to digest what had scared her so badly.

"PJ, what's going on?" Dana stood in the doorway, her face creased in a frown. "Debbie, is everything okay in here?"

The woman who'd been beside Charlie on the floor stood out of range of PJ's pacing. She shrugged. "As far as I know."

Chuck clicked the link and a video came into view, featuring Charlie lying in her crib in the apartment. The video switched to PJ carrying Charlie into the day care. Then another shot showed Charlie sleeping in the day care crib.

As the video ended, dread settled over Chuck's heart like a cold hand. "Which crib is Charlie's?" he demanded.

Dana pointed. "The first one."

Chuck spun and walked to the end of the crib. With his back to the bed, he glanced toward the ceiling at a light fixture, the only object affixed to the textured drywall ceiling. He grabbed a chair, stood on it and unscrewed the glass fixture.

As he pulled it from the ceiling, a tiny black object fell to the ground.

Chuck checked the inside of the globe for any other foreign objects and then replaced it in the fixture and locked it down with the screw.

Careful not to step on the black device, Chuck dropped out of the chair, yanked a tissue from a nearby box and scooped the object from the floor. "It's a remote camera."

PJ, still carrying Charlie close to her chest, appeared at Chuck's side. "Who would do this?"

Chuck faced Dana. "Have any repairmen been in the facility over the past couple days?"

She shook her head. "No one. Everything has been working fine, for once."

"Who has keys to the building besides you ladies?" he asked.

"The preacher and his wife are the only others I know who have keys to this section of the church." Dana glanced at PJ. "I can't believe someone is trying to kidnap my sweet Charlie."

PJ shook her head. "I don't know if someone is planning to take her or if they're just playing some sick joke on me." Her tears had dried, and her gray eyes held a steely glint. "Whoever it is will have to kill me to get to Charlie."

Chuck almost smiled at PJ's determination. If he hadn't been so shaken by the intimacy of the video, he would have. "Come on."

PJ grabbed Charlie's diaper bag and followed Chuck. "Are we going back to the apartment?"

"Only for a moment." Chuck walked toward the infant carriers against the wall and grabbed the one he'd seen PJ carrying earlier. "I'm betting there's another camera just like this in your bedroom."

A shiver shook PJ's body. "Nice to know. Not only is my attacker a child stalker, he's a pervert, as well."

Chuck followed PJ to the apartment and then transferred the infant car seat base to the backseat of his truck. He lifted Charlie out of her carrier and handed her to PJ. "Maybe you should stay in the car."

"If it's all the same to you, I feel safer close to you."

Chuck's chest warmed. Even if PJ couldn't find it in her heart to love him again, at least she felt safe with him. And he felt better knowing where she and Charlie were.

Once inside her apartment, Chuck made a thorough scan of all light fixtures, starting in PJ's bedroom. He found a similar camera mounted to the globe of the ceiling fan aimed at the baby's crib.

"Is this something?" PJ called out from the living room. She'd laid Charlie in her crib and gone back to the living room to help in the search. She squatted on the floor, staring up at the bottom of an end table.

Chuck dropped to his back and stared at the spot she pointed to. A small metal object was stuck under the table with a wad of chewing gum. "Good catch. Got any paper or plastic bags?"

PJ scrambled to her feet and returned a few seconds later with a paper towel and several small paper bags.

Chuck scraped the gum and device from the bottom of the table and into the bag, closing it. "Mark it with the location you found it."

"Gotcha." PJ grabbed a pen from a can on the counter and scribbled on the bag.

After searching every surface, nook and cranny in the small apartment, they concluded they'd found the only devices set.

Chuck left PJ in the apartment and scoured the hallway and the shared bathroom, both efforts revealing nothing more.

When he returned to PJ's apartment, PJ stood with her arms crossed, her face set in tight lines. "What now? Go to the police?"

"We go to Hank Derringer's place."

PJ's arms fell to her sides, her brow furrowing. "Why?"

"He'll explain when we get there."

"Explain what?" She shook her head. "Do you know something I don't?"

Chuck's gut tightened. This was the part he didn't look forward to. "Please, just come with me. Hank can help us with what's going on."

PJ's brows remained dented, her eyes narrowed. "I'll go, but I sense you're not telling me everything. And frankly I don't like it."

Chuck bit hard on his tongue to keep from retorting.

Before he could say anything, PJ's shoulders slumped and she sighed. "I guess I deserve that, considering I didn't tell you everything about our daughter. I'll get Charlie."

Chuck let go of the air he'd held in his lungs and helped gather Charlie's things.

PJ SAT SIDEWAYS in the front seat of Chuck's pickup, straining at the seat belt to check on Charlie in the back. She seemed so far away.

"Have you ever been out to Hank's place, the Raging Bull Ranch?" Chuck asked.

PJ shook her head. "No. Hank's a nice man and all, but we haven't grown close enough to visit each other's homes."

Chuck nodded. "He's a pretty private man."

"I'd say so. I have the occasional conversation with him at the diner and he seems interested in what goes on around Wild Oak Canyon." PJ stared at Chuck. "How can he help with the situation with Charlie? And why should he?"

"He has resources."

"That's it? That's all you're going to give me?" PJ rolled her eyes and sat back against her seat, crossing her arms over her chest.

When they pulled up to the gate at Raging Bull Ranch, Chuck stopped to press a button.

The speaker above the keypad crackled. "State name and purpose."

"Chuck Bolton. I'm here at Mr. Derringer's request."

In the long pause, PJ noted, "I didn't realize Hank was so well-to-do."

"Not many know." Chuck glanced her way. "He likes it that way."

"Thus the security?"

"Exactly."

The speaker crackled. "Proceed." The gate panels parted at the center, swinging inward toward the ranch driveway.

Chuck shifted into Drive and eased forward.

Halfway open, the gate jerked to a stop. Chuck hit the brake.

PJ pitched forward, caught by her shoulder strap. "What the heck?"

"Probably just a malfunction." Chuck waited, his hand on the gearshift.

The gate lurched and swung toward the truck.

Chuck whipped into Reverse and hit the gas, shooting the truck back as the gate closed completely.

PJ chuckled. "Are you sure Mr. Derringer wants to see us?"

Chuck frowned and punched the button on the keypad.

"State your name and purpose."

"Still Chuck Bolton, and Hank still wants to see us."

"Hmm. Seems to be a malfunction with the gate system. Hold on just a minute, please."

"Can't do much else," Chuck grumbled and glanced across at PJ.

Her brows rose, and she stared at him pointedly. "Since we're delayed indefinitely, why don't you just tell me what's going on?"

"It's not for me to tell." Chuck nodded as the gate swung open again.

"Proceed."

Once again, Chuck eased forward. And again, the gate stopped halfway, lurched and then swung toward them.

A computerized voice blasted over the speaker. *"Ha, ha, ha. Open, close, open, close. Which will it be? Ha, ha, ha."*

PJ gasped. The voice sounded like the mystery voice on the baby monitor when she'd been in the bathroom at her apartment.

"What the hell?" Chuck reversed out of the way of the gate and checked all directions.

"Feeling safe now?" the voice on the speaker wailed.

A black SUV sped toward them from the other side of the fence.

Chuck eased his Glock out of the side pocket of the truck door. "Be ready to duck."

"Why? What's going on?"

"I don't know, but it's never a bad thing to be too cautious."

"I don't like this. Can't we just leave?"

"We need to talk to Hank." Chuck shifted the gun to his left hand and aimed it out the window at the approaching vehicle. "We'll leave if this situation doesn't get better in the next two seconds."

The SUV skidded to a stop. Two men in black jumpsuits

leaped from the front, brandishing what looked to PJ like military rifles.

The back door burst open and Hank Derringer dropped to the ground, a frown marring his usually kind face.

From the other side of the vehicle a young, pale-faced man wearing skinny jeans and high-top sneakers jumped down, carrying a pair of wire cutters. "If all else fails, disconnect." He opened a box on the other side of the gate, reached in and snipped wires. He nodded toward the men in black, who pulled the gate open.

Hank walked through and leaned into the driver's window. "Sorry about that. We've been hacked."

"How bad?"

"All the systems have been compromised." He nodded to the man piecing the wiring back together. "Brandon Pendley is my tech support. He'll have us up and running soon. Mind if I ride back to the house with you?"

"I'll ride in back with Charlie." PJ slipped out of the front seat and dropped to the ground before Chuck could protest.

"Thanks." Hank held the door for PJ and then climbed into the front passenger seat with Chuck.

Chuck pulled through the open gate and along the winding, paved road through a stand of scrub oak trees.

"PJ, has Chuck told you anything about what's going on?" Hank asked.

PJ's lips tightened. "Not a thing. And frankly, it's pissing me off."

Hank chuckled, cleared his throat and shot a glance over the back of the seat. "Blame me. I asked him not to."

"Why would you ask him not to tell me anything? What would a handyman know that's so all-fired important?" PJ shook her head, and then her heart skittered a few beats, anger shoving her pulse into high gear. "Unless Chuck isn't really a handyman at all. What the hell's going on?"

The truck burst through the last stand of oaks into a clearing graced by a large, sprawling ranch house built of white limestone and cedar.

"Come in out of the heat, and I'll tell you everything." Hank hopped down and opened PJ's door for her.

"Darn right you will. Then Chuck and I are going to have words." She glared at Chuck's reflection in the rear-view mirror.

Chuck unlatched the infant carrier from the base and carried it, Charlie and all, into Hank's house.

PJ followed, stepping into the wide foyer with its high ceilings and smooth, Saltillo tiles. Though large and sprawling, there was nothing ostentatious about the beautiful home.

The warm terra-cotta-colored walls and Mexican tile floors invited her in. Had she visited under any other circumstances, PJ would have enjoyed exploring the rooms with the Southwestern decor and sturdy leather furniture capturing both the grace and beauty of the desert view through the windows.

"Come into my study." Hank led the way.

PJ followed the older man into a large room with floor-to-ceiling bookcases filled with leather-bound volumes, hardback fiction and well-worn paperback novels.

A large desk sat in the middle of the room, the wood an unusual light shade and pattern. She'd seen a table like it in the antique shop in town. Mr. White, the owner, had told her it was mesquite and handcrafted in a small town in Texas.

Hank strode to the desk and stood there, leaning back against the fine wood. He waved to the bomber-jacket brown leather couch. "Please, have a seat."

Chuck set the infant carrier on a cushion in the middle of the sofa.

PJ perched on the edge and peered down at her daughter, still a little shaky after the scare of the video.

Charlie stirred, her eyes blinking open.

PJ unbuckled the restraints and lifted the baby into her arms, and then glanced at Chuck.

Chuck remained standing near the end of the couch, his feet spread, his arms crossed over his chest, his gaze on Hank.

Dragging in a deep, fortifying breath, PJ turned and gave Hank her full attention. "What's going on?"

Hank sighed. "We're not exactly sure. But I think someone might be targeting you and Charlie to get to me."

PJ's arms tightened around her baby. "Why?"

"It's a long story." Hank shoved a hand through his shock of graying hair.

PJ leveled her gaze on the man. "I'm listening."

Hank told her a story about Alana Rodriguez, a beautiful woman he'd met in Cozumel, Mexico, and how she'd been on the run from her abusive fiancé. He went on to tell PJ about how he'd helped her hide until he could arrange for her to relocate to the United States. He gave her the money, the tickets and a new identity so that she could start fresh, free from fear of her fiancé ever finding her.

"What happened to her?" PJ asked.

"She made me promise not to contact her when I returned to the States. She said her fiancé had many connections on both sides of the border and they were dangerous. And it was just as well I didn't contact her." Hank turned toward the window. "As she'd suspected, Alana's fiancé learned of my connection to her and sent his thugs to…extract her whereabouts from me. I told them I didn't know what they were talking about." Hank snorted. "That didn't stop them from breaking my nose and two ribs. When they couldn't get anything out of me, her fiancé paid off the local Mexican police and had them arrest me for her murder."

PJ's heart hurt for the older man standing in front of her. She could almost feel the pain of his injuries, the fear of giving up even a shred of information that would seal the beautiful Alana's fate. "But you didn't kill her."

He turned to face PJ. "If I told the officials that she was still alive, her fiancé would have continued looking for her."

PJ leaned forward. "What did you do?"

"Spent time in a Mexican jail, hired half a dozen attorneys and finally was released six months later."

"How did you get off the charges?"

"They never found any concrete evidence a murder had been committed. No body. No blood. No crime." He laughed, the sound anything but amused. "I hopped a plane for Houston and never returned to Cozumel. I didn't dare contact Alana in case her fiancé traced her through me. He had connections."

"I don't understand." PJ shook her head. "What does that have to do with me?"

"I didn't know when I sent her away that she was pregnant, and I couldn't contact her to let her know what had happened. I'd made a promise. Based on what happened in Cozumel, I couldn't contact her without risking her life. I didn't hear from Alana again. I didn't even know she'd died until years after her death."

"How did you find out she'd died?"

"I received a letter from an attorney upon the death of the woman who'd adopted Alana's baby."

PJ's gut wrenched, and tears slipped from the corners of her eyes. A knot the size of a baseball lodged in her throat. She couldn't say anything, couldn't tell Hank not to tell the rest of the story. As if standing in the path of a train, PJ couldn't move, couldn't leap to safety.

"Alana had left a letter to be delivered to me should anything ever happen to Terri Franks—"

"My adoptive mother." The tears fell, dripping onto the baby in PJ's arms. "I'm Alana's daughter."

Chapter Nine

Chuck leaned forward and touched PJ's arm. He wanted to hold her, make the hurt and uncertainty go away, but she needed to hear Hank out. "Let me take Charlie." He smiled, aiming for reassurance. "Please, before you soak her."

PJ stared down at Charlie as if seeing her for the first time. Teardrops stained the baby's outfit, and a few had landed on her face. "I'm sorry, sweetheart." She brushed them away and gave up, handing her to Chuck. She turned back to Hank. "Is that the meaning of the voice on the monitor? When he asked…*who's your daddy?*" Her voice dropped to a whisper. "Do you know who my father is? Is he Alana's abusive fiancé?" Her gaze went to Charlie. "I'll kill anyone who tries to hurt my baby."

Hank shook his head. "That's just it—we don't know who your father is without a DNA paternity test."

Chuck braced himself for the next revelation.

PJ frowned. "Is there any doubt the monster is my father?" When Hank didn't answer immediately, PJ's eyes widened. "Did you have an affair with Alana?"

Hank nodded. "She hid in my bungalow for days. She was beautiful, I was young…I fell in love with her."

"And you sent her away." PJ stood and paced across the room, her gaze shooting to Charlie. "How could you love her and never contact her again?"

"I made a promise to Alana."

"All this time I wondered what my father was like. My mother told me he'd died before I was born. I imagined him to be a kind man and that he'd have been a good daddy, had he lived." PJ stared across at Hank. "I never dreamed he could have been a killer, a member of the Mexican Mafia." Her eyes were narrowed, and her jaw tightened. "Or potentially a deadbeat who didn't even bother to check on the woman he professed to love."

Chuck winced at PJ's attack on his boss.

Hank nodded. "I deserved that."

PJ faced Chuck, her frown deepening. "And you."

Chuck stiffened.

"How long have you known all this?" PJ demanded.

"Not much longer than you."

"You knew when you moved into the apartment next to mine, didn't you?"

"Not until the next day. I only knew I had a job to protect one of Cara Jo's employees. Not who, or why."

PJ stared at him as if he'd grown two heads.

Chuck's heart twisted. This was not how he'd hoped the meeting with Hank would go. But PJ had to know.

"You weren't hired to be a handyman?"

He shook his head, absorbing her glare and wishing he could ease the blows PJ was taking.

She held out her hands, her lips pressed together. "Let me have my baby."

Chuck laid Charlie in her arms, wondering if he'd ever be allowed to see his daughter again.

Anger sparked from PJ's moist eyes. "I feel like I've been living in lies of other people's making. No one is who they said they were. Even my mother lied to me." She turned to Hank. "The least you can do is give me a ride back to my apartment."

Hank's brows dipped. "It's not a good idea."

"And it's a good idea to stay here with a man who abandoned the woman he loved and didn't even bother to know she had a child?" PJ shook her head. "I could be your daughter." She tipped her head back and closed her eyes. "God, I've been a fool. You're the unknown benefactor. You gave me the scholarship to go to college."

"PJ, I'm sorry." Hank walked toward her, hands outstretched. "I should have told you. I don't know why I didn't. I guess I was afraid if I did, it would put you at risk of Alana's fiancé coming back to find you. I've kept tabs on his movements over the years. His power within the cartel has grown. He's been responsible for hundreds of murders and kidnappings." Hank stopped in front of her, his hands falling to his sides. "I've lost one family. Now that I've found you, I couldn't lose you, too."

"Hank." She said his name like a curse. "You never had me. You don't even know if I'm your daughter without a DNA test." PJ turned toward Chuck. "Please. Take me home."

Chuck shook his head. "Not until Hank sends a team in to check for more bugs. I'm not sure it's safe for you and Charlie to stay there anymore."

"I'm not staying here. Not with a man who professes to care about family, but only a select few. And another who's been lying to me since he returned. I've had it. The only person who hasn't lied to me is Charlie."

The baby stirred in her arms as if sensing her mother's unhappiness.

PJ pressed a kiss to her daughter's forehead. "Take me back to Wild Oak Canyon. I'll go to the sheriff. Let them protect me. I don't need you or your bodyguards."

"PJ, the sheriff's department wouldn't know what they're up against. They barely have enough resources to handle local crime." Hank sighed. "Let me send a team in. I promise I'll get you home once they've cleared the apartment. In the meantime, my housekeeper has prepared a meal for us."

"I'm not hungry." PJ's stomach rumbled, belying her statement.

Chuck hated seeing PJ so hurt. The woman had gone through so much, and there wasn't an end in sight. But they both had someone else to keep in mind. "Eat for Charlie."

PJ bit down on her lip.

Chuck could tell she wanted to tell them both where to go. His lips twitched at the stubborn set to her jaw. PJ was a strong woman, and she'd do what was right by her daughter.

Finally she sighed. "For Charlie."

THE MEAL STARTED off in silence. Which was just fine by PJ. Enough had been said for a lifetime. And the sooner she left this house the better. Her heart felt bruised, and she was tired beyond her usual exhaustion from working at the diner. The roller coaster of emotions she'd experienced over the past forty-eight hours had taken their toll, and she didn't know how much more she could bear.

Hank sat at the head of the table with PJ on one side, Chuck on the other and Charlie in her infant seat, balanced on a chair beside PJ.

The housekeeper had prepared a roasted chicken so tender the meat practically fell off the bone. Hank passed the different dishes to her and Chuck, playing the gracious host. Genetically, they could all be related. By outward appearances, they were one big happy family.

PJ almost laughed out loud at the word *family*. Did anyone know what a family was anymore?

For that matter, she'd known Chuck for three years and he'd rarely mentioned his family. PJ assumed his parents were dead. But then what did she know? Apparently not much. Everyone who'd ever professed to love her had kept her in the dark about all the important stuff. She didn't know who to believe anymore.

After choking down several bites of the savory meal, PJ

decided she'd go for more answers. "Chuck, in all the time we've known each other, you've never mentioned your family." She stared across the table at him. "Are they still alive?"

Chuck sat for a long time, his fork poised over his plate, his gaze on the food.

He paused so long, PJ thought he'd either forgotten the question or had chosen to ignore it.

Finally, he spoke. "They're alive."

PJ sucked in a breath, feeling as if she'd been punched in the gut yet again. She nodded. "And here I thought Charlie had no other relatives in the world." The lid burst on PJ's emotions, and she shoved back from the table so fast, her chair toppled over backward. "Please excuse me. I need to go throw up." She grabbed Charlie's carrier and darted from the room.

Not knowing where to go, she ran to the opposite end of the house, ducking into an open door and finding a beautiful sitting room with an antique Victorian sofa, a dainty rocking chair and a fireplace with a beautifully carved mahogany mantel. The room was so different from the rest of the house, PJ had to wonder who it belonged to until she noticed the portrait over the mantel.

Hank Derringer, with silver-streaked hair, sat beside a beautiful, raven-haired woman who held a baby in her arms. Hank and the woman smiled, appearing to be happy.

She remembered seeing them at the diner, looking happy and in love. When news got out that she and the toddler had disappeared, she'd volunteered to help search for them. Her heart pinched at the devastation she'd witnessed in Hank's face back then. Having her own baby to protect, PJ couldn't imagine the grief Hank had lived with.

PJ set the carrier on the floor and sank to her knees, the pain in her chest so great, she found it difficult to breathe.

Charlie whimpered.

"I know, baby. Grown-ups are so messed up." PJ lifted her

daughter into her arms and the baby nuzzled her, searching for the comfort of her mother's breast.

PJ lifted her shirt, shifting Charlie close.

The baby latched on, making smacking, sucking noises as she settled in.

The love she had for her daughter swelled in her heart, overwhelming her with emotion. For so long, PJ thought she and Charlie were alone in the world. In the past few hours, she had learned that not only were they not alone, but they had extended family, the grandparents PJ missed growing up. And no one had bothered telling her until now, when their whole world had gone to hell.

A movement at the door jerked PJ out of her musings, and she glared at the intruder.

Chuck leaned against the door frame, a scowl etched into his brow and his mouth pressed into a thin line.

"If you don't mind, I'm feeding Charlie." PJ shifted so that her bared breast was out of view of the big man. "Is a little privacy too much to ask for?"

Chuck shook his head. "We need to talk."

"Can't it wait?" PJ shut her eyes, blocking out the way the light caught the highlights in Chuck's hair and emphasized the dark circles beneath his eyes. He'd aged in the time he'd been away. What had happened to him in Afghanistan?

PJ told herself not to care, but damn it, she did. "So is the only reason you're hanging around us because you're being paid to by Hank?"

"No." He entered the room and pulled up a wing-backed chair to sit across from PJ. "After I discovered it was you, I thought about going to Hank and telling him I didn't want the job. But knowing you and Charlie were in danger, I couldn't."

"Nice to know you had a moment of hesitation." PJ hated that her voice sounded waspish. She wanted to be the one to rise above the craziness with grace and dignity, to set a good example for her daughter. Yet anger still burned in her belly, along with the desire she couldn't force away.

Sex had never been an issue between the two of them. Honesty and trust had. The way things were going more recently proved nothing had changed.

"Since I'm pretty much a captive audience and you don't appear to be taking my plea of privacy seriously…" PJ glared at Chuck. "What do you want?"

"I want you to understand."

"That you lied to me?"

Chuck's brows rose, his gaze slipping to the baby contentedly nursing.

PJ sighed. "Okay, I guess we're even."

"Not by far." A muscle in Chuck's jaw twitched. "I've missed three months of my daughter's life."

With a nod, PJ gave it to him. "Touché." She glanced up at him. "Why have you never mentioned your family until now?"

"I don't talk to them. Haven't for seven years."

"Why?"

"It doesn't matter." He stood and paced away from her, stopping to stare out the window.

"If you ever want me to trust you again, you can start by trusting me with whatever deep, dark secret you're holding on to regarding your family." She tipped her head. "Is one of them a murderer?"

Chuck shook his head. "No."

"Then how bad can it be?"

"Let's just say I refused to live up to my father's expectations." He stood with his back to her, his body rigid.

PJ wanted to go to him, but she had to remain still while Charlie nursed. She decided it was just as well. Being mad at Chuck had easier consequences to deal with than falling in love with him all over again.

"My father was a colonel in the army. He retired when I

was ten and moved to West Texas, bought a ranch and raised us to take care of the animals, like were our troops."

"That doesn't sound so bad."

"The man never forgot his military connections and wanted his sons to follow in his footsteps."

"You went into the army. Isn't that following in his footsteps?"

"He doesn't know that."

PJ frowned. "Why?"

"My father wanted me to accept a football scholarship to West Point."

"And you didn't?"

Chuck shook his head. "I accepted a scholarship to Texas Tech, no ROTC, no military."

"Your father wasn't happy, I take it."

Chuck faced PJ. "My father was so angry, he called me a coward. He told me to get the hell out of his house and don't bother coming back. That was seven years ago."

"We met three years ago."

"I'd finished college, got a degree in animal husbandry with a minor in financial planning. When I graduated, I didn't know what I wanted to do. I got a job as an assistant manager of the resort here in Wild Oak Canyon because it was close to the area I'd been raised, and I could be around the animals."

He dropped into a chair and ran a hand through his hair. "One day I met a man who was vacationing in the area. He'd been to Afghanistan. He told me stories about his platoon, about the tough living conditions and the dangers they faced on a daily basis."

PJ snorted. "So you signed up for the army?"

"Not then. It wasn't until he told me how he wished he could go back and help. He'd give his life for his brothers in arms." Chuck looked up at PJ. "I wanted to feel that commitment. I wanted to know what it was like to care that much about the people around you. To love them like family should love each other.

"Before we met, I'd joined the Army National Guard unit he'd been attached to and went to basic training. When I got back I was in a holding pattern until the unit came back in rotation to deploy. I picked up where I'd left off here in Wild Oak Canyon, but with the training I'd received, I didn't feel like I belonged. I felt like I still hadn't done my part, shown my patriotism."

"But then you met me." The pain etched in his face made PJ's chest tighten. "Were your father's words still playing in the back of your mind?"

"Yes." Chuck dragged in a deep breath and let it out. "I wanted to know what it was like to face death and want to charge right back into it."

"You wanted to prove to yourself you weren't a coward."

"In Afghanistan, I saw things…faced death…" He bowed his head. "I know now. Family is everything."

"Then why haven't you reconciled with them?"

He glanced away. "I got kicked out of the army."

"Why? What happened?"

"I lost it."

PJ sat up, switched Charlie to the other breast and asked, "What do you mean?"

"There was a kid who hung around outside the wire. Whenever we left the compound to go out on patrol, he was there. He always had a smile for us, and we brought him candy and gum."

Chuck's voice thickened. "One day when we left on patrol, he wasn't standing by the gate waiting for us. Instead, there had been a pile of rags where he usually waited."

PJ closed her eyes to the immediate flood of tears. "The boy?"

"The Taliban had beaten him to death and thrown his

body out there for us to find and to serve as a reminder to the other children of the village not to side with the Americans."

"What happened?"

"I'd never felt such rage. When people talk about seeing red, that's what I saw. The red of the boy's blood smeared over his ragged clothing. The red of all the bloodshed that continued in a region that had never known a time of peace." Chuck stared across the room, his gaze far away. "I wanted to crush the people who'd done that to the boy, to their country, to the innocent lives they took on a daily basis."

PJ breathed in and out, and then asked in a whisper, "What did you do?"

"I went into the village against my CO's orders." Chuck's face hardened, and his eyes narrowed. "I went alone to where I'd heard the Taliban had been hiding out." Chuck's fists clenched so tightly, his knuckles turned white.

PJ's heart pounded as she waited for him to continue.

"I killed them. Every last one of them."

She touched his arm, her chest hurting, feeling some of the pain Chuck must have felt to have placed his own life at risk to seek revenge for an innocent boy's death.

Chuck stood, shrugged and walked away. "I went against orders. They were planning to stage an attack later that night. I didn't know about it. I went ahead of their plans. I could have ruined the mission."

"Instead, you risked one man's life over your unit's lives." PJ shook her head. "You could have been killed."

"What they did to that kid…" He stopped again at the window. "I couldn't get the image out of my head. I got shot in the leg and barely made it back to camp."

PJ gasped. "I didn't know you'd been injured. Is that why you limp?"

Chuck nodded. "My CO was pissed. Because of my wound, I was evacuated from Afghanistan. The doctor wouldn't allow me to return. It didn't matter. Even if I could have, my CO probably wouldn't have let me."

PJ ached for Chuck, for the horrors he'd seen and endured. "You lived."

Chuck snorted. "Some life. I barely slept, and when I did, I woke up fighting. The psych doc called it PTSD. With my leg messed up and a lousy psych eval, the doctor recommended a medical discharge. My CO agreed."

"Did you *want* to come home?" PJ asked, bracing herself for the answer.

Chuck shook his head. "Even though I knew you were back here, I didn't want to leave my buddies behind to fight on without me." Chuck stared down at his hands. "I wasn't given a choice." He squared his shoulders and faced her. "Now you know all my darkest secrets."

PJ stared at the man, so hardened, a little lost—so different from the one who'd left a year ago. Yet he was still the same man she'd fallen in love with, the man who was kind to animals and little children. "Why haven't you been back to see your parents?"

"I lived up to my father's expectations. Having failed the military, I've failed him. I couldn't go back."

"Seven years is a long time to go without speaking to your parents."

"It doesn't matter." He straightened. "The important thing to consider is how to keep you and Charlie safe from whoever is stalking you."

PJ couldn't let it go. "You have a daughter, Chuck. Doesn't she deserve to know who her grandparents are?"

"If they refuse to accept her because of me, she's better off not knowing."

"A lot of time has passed. Don't you think your father will have changed his mind? What about your mother?" PJ glanced down at Charlie, her heart squeezing as she imagined a child of hers never coming back to visit. "Don't you think she should have a say in this? What about siblings? Does Charlie have aunts and uncles?"

For a moment Chuck was silent, his eyes sadder than she'd ever known them to be. "Yes, an uncle and an aunt."

Charlie finished feeding. PJ straightened her shirt and lifted the baby to her shoulder, patting her back gently. Over her daughter's little form she stared at Chuck.

"Personally, I think you're being selfish." She stood so that she could look at him, eye to eye.

"It's been too long." Chuck's face steeled. "Let it lie."

The past few days had brought it home to PJ that it wasn't right to hold back. Not when it came to family.

"No." PJ walked right up to him. "I barely knew my mother. Never had a father, grandparents or siblings. If Charlie has a chance at family, by God, I'm going to see that she gets it."

"And I'm here to see that you live long enough to stand on your damned soapbox. Then you can have what you wanted, and I'll get the hell out of your life. But I'll always be a part of Charlie's." Chuck stormed from the room.

"You may be out of my life, Chuck Bolton, but you'll never be out of my heart," PJ whispered.

Chapter Ten

Dusk had settled into darkness as Chuck marched through Hank's house. When Hank waved him into the study, he almost told him to go to hell.

Then he reminded himself he wasn't mad at Hank. He was mad at himself for letting PJ's words get to him. For letting his father's rejection taint his life for seven long years. And for the painful reminder of the family he missed so much it hurt.

Some of the tension seeped out as he entered Hank's private domain.

The older man didn't waste time. "Just heard from the guys checking out PJ's apartment."

A lump of cold, hard lead settled into Chuck's gut. "What did they find?"

Hank stopped behind his desk. "You don't want PJ to go back tonight."

"That bad?"

"Someone broke into her apartment and tossed it." Hank pulled a bottle of whiskey off the counter behind his desk, grabbed a couple of shot glasses and held them up. "Care for some?"

Chuck shook his head. He hadn't had a drink since he'd returned to Wild Oak Canyon. As much as he craved one to steady his nerves, he had to keep a clear head. Charlie and PJ needed that much from him. "I had just changed the locks on the doors."

Hank's eyes narrowed. "As far as the guys reported, it didn't look like forced entry. Whoever got in picked the lock or had a key."

"Why would they toss the place?"

"I don't know. There weren't any messages left behind. PJ would have to tell us if anything was missing." Hank set the bottle back on the counter unopened. "Point is, it's not safe for her to return to the apartment."

Chuck dragged in a deep breath and let it out slowly. "And you want me to break it to her?"

Hank shook his head. "I'll do it."

"You might want to." A wry smile tugged at Chuck's lips. "She's not too happy with me right now."

"I'll see what I can do to smooth her feathers."

"Good luck. She doesn't take kindly to feather-smoothing." Chuck nodded toward the computer on Hank's desk. "Your guy Pendley find the hacker yet?"

"He's still working on it. He has to go back to a week-old recovery backup. Once he has it installed and the new firewall program in place, he'll work on finding the hacker. Right now he's just trying to keep the bastard out of my bank accounts."

"Seems like he has a bone to pick with you. Doesn't sound like the work of a Mexican Mafia man. Don't they usually go for more guerrilla tactics like chopping off heads and drive-by shootings?"

"I have to admit, these attacks don't make much sense. The only connection they have to me is PJ and Charlie."

"Your Achilles' heel?" Chuck offered. "They were an easy target as long as they were outside your perimeter."

"My perimeter has been breached via the computer. I don't know what help I'm going to be other than providing firepower to a game of cat and mouse."

"Think back. Have you made anyone angry lately? Anyone who might have the ability to hack into a computer system as effectively as he has?"

Hank's eyes narrowed. "Not recently. Brandon's been working for me for the past eight months. He's been busy putting firewalls in place and beefing up the equipment and software it takes to run this place and my financial holdings. He also helped me set up the database for the Covert Cowboys, Inc. Thank goodness the hacker hasn't broken into that one."

"Brandon's done all that in only eight months?"

Hank smiled. "The kid's amazing. Possibly the best technical support a man could hire."

"Did you interview other candidates before you hired him?"

"We're talking eight months ago. Surely whoever is causing trouble now hasn't been stewing for eight months."

"Some people carry grudges a long time." Chuck didn't add, *like my father.* For that matter, Chuck had been carrying one around since the day he'd left home and never looked back.

He could still see an image of his mother through his rearview mirror as he'd driven away in his beat-up truck. She'd been standing on the porch, his teenage brother Jake's arm around her shoulders, his ten-year-old sister, Katie, running after his truck, crying.

Not a day went by that he didn't think of them. And his father hadn't even stepped out of the house—refusing to see his son off as he left home for the last time.

Katie would be seventeen now. Chuck wondered if Jake had gone to West Point as his father had wanted his boys to do.

Chuck had to get outside. He needed to burn off steam and memories before he exploded.

"Chuck?" Hank's voice cut into Chuck's musings. "You still with me?"

"Not really." He scrubbed a hand across his face. "I have too much on my mind. Is it possible for me to borrow a horse?"

"Going for a ride this late?"

"If I can. I have to get some air."

Hank nodded. "Supposed to be a clear night with a full moon. Should be bright enough to see most anything. My foreman can fix you up."

"Thanks." Chuck headed for the door.

"In the meantime, I'll inform PJ of the break-in. And Chuck, what are the chances of getting PJ to agree to a DNA test?"

Chuck paused at the door. "Somewhere between hell freezing over and a snowball's chance in hell."

Hank sighed. "Either way the test turns out, I feel like she's part of my family, and I wouldn't want anything bad to happen to her or Charlie."

"You and me both."

"Again, no matter what, it puts her at risk for kidnapping. If she's Alana's ex-fiancé's daughter, he's possessive. He'll want her and Charlie with him in Mexico. If she's mine, he might still want me to suffer for taking Alana away from him, and pay me back in kind by taking PJ and Charlie away from me."

"I understand." Chuck's shoulders straightened. "No one's taking PJ or Charlie away. They'll have to go through me first."

"And me."

Chuck nodded. "Then we're in agreement."

"One hundred percent." Hank's lips lifted in a hint of a smile. "Go ride. I'll keep an eye out for PJ and Charlie."

Chuck left the house and strode to the barn.

A light shone inside. Apparently, true to his word, Hank

had called his foreman, giving him the heads-up. The man had led a black gelding out of a stall and was settling a saddle blanket on his back.

The smell of hay, sweet feed and the earthy scent of horse manure filled Chuck's head with memories. "I can do that," he offered.

"Been around horses much?" the foreman asked.

"Since I was ten."

The older man tipped his head in the direction of a door. "Bridles are in the tack room. Saddles are on the rack."

Chuck saddled the horse, adjusted the stirrups for his long legs and led the animal out of the barn into the big, Texas night sky.

Already he could feel the worries melting away from his shoulders. Not that he'd forget about Charlie and PJ. Not when they weighed heavily on his mind. But the other stuff he'd revealed to PJ could blow away with a strong Southern breeze for all he cared.

For seven years, he'd pushed his family to the back of his mind. Seven years he'd tried to forget the look in his mother's eyes and the way Katie ran after him. It all came crashing back on him with the harsh look on his father's face as he'd told him to leave.

Chuck led the gelding to the nearest gate, which opened into the huge pastures stretching out and away from the ranch house. Once through, he latched the gate and stepped up into the stirrup, swinging his leg over the saddle.

The gelding didn't need any encouragement. As if he, too, had a few cobwebs to clear, he lurched into a gallop, flying across the flat land, dodging sage and prickly pear cactus.

Chuck bent low over the gelding's neck, the wind in his face fresh, scented with yucca and dust.

For a long stretch, he gave the horse his head, letting the animal set the pace. When he finally settled into a steady trot, Chuck reined him to the west, riding toward the property line that bordered the highway. If he kept going, they'd run into the fence. He wanted to check the front gate to see if they'd fixed it or if it was still jerking open and closed.

The huge, arched gate rose out of the darkness, standing higher than any scrub brush in the pasture.

Chuck slowed the gelding to a stop, tied him to a fence post and walked the rest of the way to the rock and wrought-iron gate. When he reached it, he breathed a sigh. The gate was closed. Whether or not the mechanics worked was another question. At least he could rest a little more easily knowing someone wasn't just going to drive right in and wreak havoc on the ranch house and its occupants.

He'd turned and was headed back to the horse when the gelding whinnied.

An engine sound buzzed along the highway at a distance, moving closer, coming from the direction of Wild Oak Canyon.

Chuck glanced over his shoulder toward the sound, but he didn't see any headlights. The noise grew louder, and still no headlights appeared in the distance.

He untied the gelding and led him into the moon shadows beside the rock gate and stroked his nose.

After a moment, a motorcycle pulled up to the gate, lights out. The rider, dressed in black, wore a black helmet with a dark visor pulled down over his face. He stared at the closed gate for a minute and then laughed, spun the bike around and raced back the way he'd come, lights still off.

Chuck jumped out into the road, hoping to read the license plate numbers on the back of the bike. The rider had obviously disengaged the taillights and he'd removed the license, if there'd ever been one.

A mile down the road, the headlights blinked on.

If there hadn't been a fence in the way, Chuck might have followed on horseback, but the motorcycle would have quickly outpaced the already tired gelding.

Chuck rode back to the barn, eager to check on PJ and Charlie. But first he had to report what he'd seen at the front gate.

Hank wasn't in his study. Chuck found one of the bodyguards.

"Where's Hank?"

"Follow me." The bodyguard led the way to a door that opened to a staircase, leading into a basement below the house.

The walls were solid concrete, as was the ceiling overhead. For all intents and purposes, it was a bunker.

The bodyguard stopped at a steel door and bent to a machine next to it, pressing his thumb on a pad and then leaning close.

A retinal scanner scanned his eye, and a lock clicked. The door opened and they entered.

"Ah, Chuck, back so soon from your ride?" Hank stood next to the young man who'd dismantled the gate earlier.

The man sat hunched over a computer keyboard, his gaze intent on the screen where page after page of numbers and letters scrolled by in rapid succession.

"Chuck, I don't believe you've been properly introduced to our computer expert, Brandon Pendley."

The man at the keyboard raised his hand without turning around. "Nice to meet you," he said.

"Likewise."

"You'll have to excuse Brandon. He's in the process of reloading a backup of our system software. Ever since the computer was compromised, he's been fighting to get us back online."

"Any luck isolating the hacker?"

"Not yet," Brandon said. "I made a ghost copy of the system on a separate backup server, hoping to fool the hacker into thinking we're still infected. When I get us back up and running, I'll go after him and nail the guy."

Hank crossed his arms. "Brandon has taken this attack personally."

"He hacked the corporate computer," Brandon said. "How could I not?"

"Hank, do you know anyone who rides a black motorcycle?" Chuck asked.

"I have one, not that I ride often. Otherwise I can't think of anyone I know personally. Why?"

Chuck told him of the rider who'd stopped at the gate and drove off without headlights.

"Think he's our hacker or maybe the man who attacked PJ?" Hank asked.

"Maybe. We don't even know if they're one and the same." Chuck didn't like not knowing. "Any word on the baby monitor?"

Hank nodded. "We were able to lift prints, but so far my contact in Austin says there are no matches in the IAFIS system."

"So maybe this is our guy's first crime," Chuck suggested.

"Or he's never been caught."

"Tomorrow I'll escort PJ to the apartment and have her look around for anything that might be missing."

"Good idea."

Chuck glanced around at the concrete walls. "Quite a place you got here."

Hank shrugged. "A man never knows when he might need a bomb shelter. I can't say that I've led a pristine life, and my wealth makes me a target."

"Any news on your wife and son?"

Hank shook his head. "Nothing over the past two years except a cryptic hint from that corrupt FBI agent who died in the operation Zach Adams handled for us."

"Any clues as to who in the FBI he was talking about?"

"No. And no leads on my family."

"I won't let anyone take PJ and Charlie."

"What scares me is that I had security in place and he managed to get to them."

Chuck's fists tightened. "I'm not going to let that happen again."

"How did your talk with her go?"

"Great." He glanced away.

"I guess you don't want to talk about it." Hank yawned and stretched. "Better get some rest. I have a feeling things are going to get worse before they get better."

Chuck nodded and headed for the door leading out of the bunkerlike basement. Once in the main part of the house, he went in search of PJ, anxious to make certain she was still there. With all that had happened, he didn't trust anyone else with her safety.

Chuck paused outside the door to the bedroom Hank had assigned to her. He'd even brought his son's crib in for Charlie.

He tapped softly but got no response. When he pressed his ear to the door, he couldn't hear movement inside. Chuck tried the handle, but the door was locked.

While frustrated that he couldn't get a visual on the two women in his life, he understood PJ's wariness. She had to be scared to death for Charlie.

Chuck moved on to the room Hank had offered to him next door to PJ and Charlie. At least he was close enough to help if the need arose.

Still too wound up to sleep, Chuck opened the French doors and stepped out on the porch, inhaling the warm, dry night air. Insect songs filled the sky with a constant hum. The temperature had fallen at least twenty degrees since sunset to a comfortable low seventies. A full moon outshone the stars, creating an almost dusky glow.

A movement caught his attention, and he turned.

PJ leaned against the rock exterior of the house, wearing a soft white nightgown. On PJ it was loose and flowing with the little bit of night breeze lifting the hem to expose her long, lithe legs.

Chuck's pulse increased. God, she was beautiful. The moon, still low on the horizon, bathed her half in light and half in the shadows of the house, giving her an ethereal blue glow.

"Can't sleep?" she asked, her voice little more than a whisper.

Chuck heard her over the sound of the cicadas. "Sleep is overrated."

PJ chuckled. "I try to tell myself that, but it doesn't help when I'm in the seventh hour of my shift at the diner." She stepped toward the porch railing and tipped her head back, closing her eyes. "I love the night in the country. It seems so peaceful, like nothing bad could happen when the stars are twinkling and the land is at peace."

When she'd moved forward, the moonlight shone through the nightgown, silhouetting her body through the sheer white fabric.

Chuck's breath caught and held.

"Didn't you grow up on a ranch?" she asked.

Swallowing hard past his rising desire, Chuck answered, "We didn't move out onto the ranch until I was about ten, when my father retired from the army."

"Do you miss it?"

He stared out at the night, the shape of the barn and the outlying pastures bathed in a gentle glow. "Yes." He'd loved the life of a rancher from the moment they'd moved into the old ranch house.

His mother had made the house a home, filling it with colorful curtains and pillows and the smell of fresh bread baking in the oven.

He turned away from the scene in front of him. "That's no longer my life."

"But it could be…if you wanted it."

"Can't really make a living ranching unless you have a spread as big as the Raging Bull Ranch and money to seed the livestock."

PJ nodded. She'd served enough ranchers at the diner to know ranching was a hard way to make a living. Many had gone under and sold their spreads to commercial ranchers or big game outfitters. Still, if someone had a dream… "Everyone has to start somewhere."

"And where is that starting point for you?" Chuck moved closer and leaned against the railing. "What do you want out of life, Peggy?"

PJ sucked in a breath, remembering how she'd loved it when he'd used her full name. Chuck had been the only person to call her Peggy since her mother had died. Even her adoptive mother hadn't called her Peggy except on the few occasions she'd been angry. PJ shook herself and tried to focus on Chuck's question, not her heart beating out of control at his nearness. "I'm past my starting point." She lifted her chin and gazed up at him. "I'm well on my way to the life I want."

"Are you?" He cupped her cheek, smoothing a strand of hair behind her ear. "Just you and Charlie?"

"We're the only people I can count on." She hated that her voice quavered or that she liked the feel of his work-roughened fingers on her skin. Despite her vow not to, she leaned into his palm.

"What about me?" he asked.

She swallowed hard. "You left."

"I'm back." His lips descended, hovering over hers, his breath warm against her mouth.

"How do I know you won't leave again?"

"The only guarantee in life is death." He brushed his thumb over her lips. "Is that what you want? A guarantee?"

"Yes," she said, tears pooling in her eyes.

"You will never get those. And in the meantime, you'll

miss out on all life has to offer, risks included." His mouth swept across hers, his tongue pressing between her teeth to find hers.

PJ melted against him, too tired to resist, too emotionally drained by all that had happened to care about the consequences or to rouse her earlier anger. She needed his kiss, his embrace, like a drooping flower needed rain.

His tongue stroked hers in a long, sensual glide as his hands smoothed down her back. His fingers slid over her buttocks and cupped the back of her thighs, and he lifted her, wrapping her legs around his waist.

Her sex pressed against the ridge beneath his jeans, sending sparks of awareness racing across her nerves. PJ laced her fingers behind his neck and dragged him closer still, the tips of her breasts rubbing against the cotton fabric of her nightgown, the friction making her nipples bud and tighten.

Chuck leaned her against the limestone wall of the house, the warm ridges pressing into her back.

When one of his big hands slid beneath the hem of her gown, PJ was powerless to resist. She wanted to be naked with him, to feel his skin against hers.

Her fingers slipped between their bodies, attacking the buttons on his denim shirt, flicking them free in rapid succession.

Chuck lifted her and carried her through the open French doors into her room, kicking the door shut behind him. He sat her on the edge of the bed, grabbed the hem of the gown and whipped it up over her head.

Her arms free, PJ pushed the shirt over his shoulders and down his back. She tugged the tails from his waistband, and the shirt fell to the floor.

Chuck's fingers went to his belt.

PJ stopped him with a hand over his and a short shake of her head. "Let me."

He lifted his hands to her face, cupping them around her

cheeks. "You're even more beautiful than the day I left for deployment."

She snorted softly, unbuckled his belt and slid it through his belt loops. Then she pushed the rivet through the button-hole on his jeans and slipped the zipper down, freeing his member into her hands. "Remember the last time we vis-ited the swimming hole at Sandy Creek?" PJ wrapped her hands around his shaft.

His sucked in a breath, his head tipping back. "All too well."

"That was the day Charlie was conceived."

"You know that for sure?" he said, his voice more strained with each stroke of her fingers.

She had always liked that power over him. She had him in the palm of her hand with a few simple strokes. Too bad it hadn't changed his mind about going to war. Now that he was back, she could barely remember why she'd been so angry. "Don't you remember what you said?" She glanced up, her gaze meeting his in the light from the moon shining through the window. "I was trying to convince you not to leave."

"I had to. I had a commitment."

"After we made love, you said it was magic and that you'd never forget."

"I never did." His fingers threaded through her hair. "And that magic conceived Charlie?"

She smiled and shrugged. "I like to think so." Then she let go of a low chuckle. "That, and I counted the days from my last period. I would have been ovulating at that time." She rubbed her cheek against the velvety skin of his mem-ber. "I like the other story better."

Chuck's fingers slipped lower, and he hooked her beneath her arms and laid her back against the quilted comforter. Then he shucked his jeans and lay down beside her in all his naked, masculine glory. "Every time with you was magic."

For a moment PJ pushed aside all the old hurt, the fear and

the sorrow of losing him. She wanted to feel the power of their connection, to put aside the hollowness of her existence since he'd been gone. "Show me some of that magic tonight."

"Are you sure?" His brows furrowed. "What about tomorrow?"

"You said it yourself." She touched her hand to his face. "No guarantees."

"That's not what I meant." His lips brushed across her eyelids, one then the other. He held her face with his hand as he bent to kiss her, taking her lips with such gentle firmness.

PJ shifted his hand from her face down her throat to her breast and lower. "This is what I have to offer." She guided him to the apex of her thighs. "Tonight."

"Does this mean you're not mad at me anymore?"

"I was afraid of losing you." PJ kissed him, her knees parting, allowing his hand to cup her.

He parted her folds, his finger finding the tender nubbin between and flicking it until she gasped. He slipped a finger into her, swirling around her moist channel, and then another, stretching her entrance.

PJ dug her heels into the mattress, her hips rising to meet his thrusts, a moan rising up her throat.

"Please," she begged, urging his body over hers.

He slipped between her legs, his member pressing into her, filling her.

PJ closed her eyes and gave herself up to his magic.

Lost in the beauty of the moment, she didn't stop to think about tomorrow. She lived for the moment, every muscle, nerve and blood cell reveling in the present, the bombardment of sensations and the explosion of her senses.

When she finally fell back to earth, she lay spent in his arms, a happy glow warming her from the inside.

Chuck gathered her into his arms and pressed a soft kiss to her forehead. "You know, this changes everything."

PJ rolled into his side, pressing her face against his chest, refusing to acknowledge anything past the moment. There would be time later to sort through her feelings. Tomorrow would come all too soon.

Chapter Eleven

Something moved in the darkness, jerking Chuck out of the first deep, dreamless sleep he'd had in a long time. He sat up straight, straining to find the source of the noise.

A silhouette disengaged from the corner shadow and stepped into the predawn light edging through the windows of the French doors.

Chuck slipped silently from the bed and moved toward the form, grabbing it around the middle and clamping an arm around its throat. "What the hell are you doing?" he demanded.

"Trying to breathe," said a raspy female voice.

It was then that Chuck's mind cleared the remainders of sleep and he realized just who was sneaking around the interior of the bedroom. His arm loosened. "PJ?"

"Yes, you idiot. Who else would it be?" She rubbed at her throat and faced him, fully dressed in the clothes she'd worn the day before. "I have to go to work in an hour, and I need to stop by my apartment for a change of clothes."

Chuck stood in front of her, naked, shoving a hand through his hair and trying to focus on what she'd said when all he wanted was to toss her back in the bed and make love all over again. "You can't go to work. It's too dangerous."

She planted a fist on one hip. "I have to go to work. It's how I make money to pay for Charlie's diapers."

"I'll buy her diapers."

PJ's eyes narrowed. "I'd rather do it. Besides, it takes more than diapers to raise a child. I can't stop working or quit school because one person is making my life hell."

"The contacts are becoming more frequent and personal. Who knows what this lunatic will do next?"

"Last night you said life isn't full of guarantees. I can't put my life on hold waiting for something that may never happen."

"What about Charlie?"

"I'm going to set up a playpen in the office at the diner so that I can keep an eye on her. Between me, Cara Jo and the cook, we'll all keep her safe."

"I don't like it."

"You don't have to. It's my life."

Her words hit him square in the gut. "And I'm not a part of it? Is that what you're saying?"

"I didn't say that. I just don't know how you fit in it yet." She slipped into her shoes and stared across at him. "I can get one of Hank's bodyguards to take me to town."

"Like hell you will."

"Then you'll have to put some clothes on. I don't think the Wild Oak Canyon police would condone public indecency."

"Give me a minute to shower and dress."

"I'll give you ten. It'll take at least that long to feed Charlie."

As if aware she was being talked about, the baby squirmed in her crib and let out a pathetic cry.

"That's my cue." PJ scooped Charlie up in her arms and sat on the side of the bed, pulled up her shirt and guided the baby to her nipple.

No matter how many times Chuck witnessed this natural connection between PJ and Charlie, he couldn't help but marvel at the miracle of life.

"Nine minutes," PJ stated, her brows raised.

Chuck gathered his clothing from the floor and hurried into the bathroom connected to PJ's bedroom.

He shot a glance over his shoulder as he stepped through.

PJ was watching his every step.

A smile curled his lips as he twisted the handles on the water faucet and stepped beneath the spray. The cooler the water the better, if he planned to wear jeans in five minutes or less.

A quick shower cleared the remaining vestiges of sleep from his head and chilled the lingering desire from his body. He dressed quickly and ran a hand over his stubbled chin. Shaving would have to wait until he could get back to his gear in his apartment. He feared if he took too long in the bathroom, PJ would pull a dumb stunt like finding someone else to take her into town.

When he emerged into the bedroom, PJ and Charlie were gone.

"Damn woman," Chuck muttered. "Couldn't wait a lousy ten minutes." He dragged his boots on and hurried down the hall to the front of the big house. But when he heard voices in the kitchen, he made a sharp left.

Standing at the counter, stirring a spoon in a mug, PJ was smiling and talking to an older woman Chuck recognized as Hank's housekeeper.

"You can pour that into this insulated cup if you like and take it with you," she was saying. She set a disposable cup on the counter beside PJ.

"Thanks, I will." PJ tipped what smelled like hot tea into the white cup and set the mug in the sink. When she turned and spotted Chuck, a smile lifted the corners of her lips. "Want a cup of coffee to go?"

"That would be great."

"I'll fix it if you'll change the baby's diaper. Or vice versa."

"I'll take a chance on changing Charlie, if she'll take a

chance on me." He lifted Charlie from her carrier and blew a raspberry against her belly.

Charlie giggled and grabbed a fistful of hair.

"Hey, slugger, I believe that belongs to me." He pried her fingers loose and settled her in his arms.

"I think there's a diaper left in the bag, and a changing mat, as well." As she pulled a mug from a cabinet, PJ nodded over her shoulder toward the bag on the chair beside Charlie. "You can take her into the sitting room."

Chuck hadn't changed a diaper since his baby sister had come home from the hospital when he'd been eight years old. Surely it couldn't be any harder now than it had been then. With the improvements they'd made to disposable diapers, how could he go wrong?

Five minutes later, with the diaper tape stuck to his fingers and a squirming Charlie refusing to lie still, Chuck was about to give up and call for reinforcements.

"Here, let me help." PJ knelt on the carpet beside them and held on to Charlie's ankles while Chuck repositioned the diaper beneath her bottom. Before PJ could settle her daughter against the diaper, it curled upward, as it had a dozen times before.

"I don't get it."

"The trick is not to worry." She laid the baby down on the curled diaper and pulled the edges out to the side, straightening it before tugging the tapes across the middle. "See? Nothing to it."

"I'd have gotten it sooner or later." Chuck didn't like that he'd failed at his first attempt at changing Charlie's diaper, but he was a quick learner and he'd get it right the next time. Right then all he could think about was how good PJ smelled beside him. Her hair held the scent of honeysuckle on a warm summer day, and her cheeks glowed a soft pink this morning, the glow that had been missing the day before.

Before she could scoop Charlie up and stand, Chuck captured her face in his hands and kissed her soundly, and then he let her go.

She laughed. "What was that for?"

"Rescuing me and Charlie from a fate worse than death."

"A little melodramatic, maybe?"

"A twisted diaper is nothing to laugh about." He lifted Charlie into the crook of his arm and pushed to his feet, a stab of pain reminding him of his injured leg. He offered his free hand to PJ.

She took it and let him pull her to her feet. "Ready?"

He winked. "For anything you have in mind."

Her brow furrowed. "Work. I'm going to be late if we don't get going."

"Hear that, Charlie? We're making your mama late." Chuck carried her to the truck. After PJ settled the infant carrier into the base, Chuck buckled Charlie in.

The drive to town went by in comfortable silence, with the sun rising to the east, spreading a warm, golden glow across the horizon. The weatherman had promised a scorcher that day, but for now, it was tolerable and pretty outside.

If they could nab their troublemaker, all would be pretty darn right with the world.

Chuck parked in back of the resort. "Wait for me and we'll go up together."

PJ stood beside the truck as Chuck retrieved Charlie. He handed her to PJ and led the way up to PJ's apartment.

"Let me go first." Chuck moved ahead, testing the door-knob. It was locked. Hank's men who'd checked it out the night before must have locked it behind them. Chuck fit PJ's key into the lock. It turned easily, and he pushed the door open.

PJ leaned around him and gasped, her face pale. "Wow."

The place was in shambles. Whoever had been inside had turned every drawer upside down, emptying the contents onto the floor. Sofa cushions had been tossed, and clothing was strewn about the bedroom.

"I'd have no idea what was taken, if anything, until I set the place to rights." PJ tried to step around Chuck.

He held his hand out. "Let me." Picking his way across the floor, he inspected the little apartment, looking for anyone still lurking in the closet or under the bed. Then he searched for hidden cameras in case whoever had been inside had hidden fresh devices throughout. When he was as satisfied as he could be without picking everything apart, he nodded to PJ. "You can come in."

PJ handed Charlie to Chuck and moved about the apartment setting chairs on their feet, putting drawers back in the kitchen cabinets and finally making her way into the bedroom for clothing.

She picked up a pair of jeans and dropped them into a basket. "I don't even want to wear any of these clothes until they've been washed." For a long moment she stared at the mess, her face tight and bleak. "I'll wear what I have on until after work when I can get this stuff to a Laundromat. At least I have a clean uniform waiting for me at work."

"Off the top of your head, is anything missing?"

PJ stood in one spot in her bedroom and turned in a 360-degree circle. Facing the bed, she stopped. "The photograph that was on my nightstand." She darted forward and checked the ground beside and under the bed, tossing clothing to the side as she searched. "It's not here." She stood and worked her way through the living room, tossing pillows, sheets, towels and anything else in the way of her search. On her hands and knees, she crawled around the room until she stopped in front of the bookshelf. "Oh, my God." She knelt beside the case and stared at the books scattered across the floor.

"What?" Chuck moved forward with Charlie, whose eyes were wide and curious.

"My photo album. The picture in the frame and the photo album were all I had left of my mother. All the photos are gone." She pressed her fist to her mouth, blinking back tears.

Chuck held out his hand.

She stared at it for a moment, swallowing convulsively. "That's it. I have nothing left of her."

"You have Charlie." He bent and took her hand, pulling her to her feet and into the curve of his arm, opposite Charlie.

When Charlie saw her mother, she smiled and leaned toward her, arms outstretched.

PJ took her, rested her cheek against the baby's and leaned into Chuck's chest. "Those things were all I had of my childhood with my mother."

"We'll make new memories. You can fill albums full of pictures of Charlie growing up."

"Why is this happening to me?" She let Chuck hold her for a long time.

He wanted to beat to a pulp whoever had been in PJ's apartment and taken the things she'd held dear. For now all he could do was hold PJ and let her grieve again for the mother she'd lost. The more he thought about PJ and her mother, the more it reminded him of his own mother, and he missed her more than ever.

After a few moments, PJ straightened and wiped the moisture from her eyes with the back of her hand. "I have to go to work."

"Cara Jo would understand if you called in sick."

"I need to stay busy. If I sat around and thought about everything, I'd go crazy."

"What can I help you do?"

"Carry the playpen to the office in the diner." She glanced around at the box of diapers. "At least he didn't destroy Charlie's things."

While Chuck folded the portable playpen, PJ gathered diapers and a change of clothing for Charlie. When she started awkwardly picking up the scattered clothing while holding Charlie, Chuck caught her hand.

"I'll come back in a little while and do that. You worry about Charlie."

He'd return as soon as PJ was settled in at the diner. "Are you sure you don't want me to take care of Charlie today? You'll be busy waiting tables."

"Cara Jo won't mind. She usually spends part of the day going through paperwork in the office. She'll keep an eye on Charlie and let me know if she needs anything."

"I don't like the idea that you might have to leave her un-attended. Leave her with me. I promise to take good care of her."

PJ glanced up at Chuck, her brows pulled low. "Are you sure you can handle her? I could take her to the day care…"

"No, I'd feel better knowing exactly where she is. Until this insanity is over, I'd feel better if she's with either you or me at all times."

"Okay." She sucked in a deep breath. "I guess we won't need to move the playpen downstairs."

"No, I'll need it here, while I gather your clothes for the Laundromat."

"Maybe I should call in sick. You shouldn't have to pick up my clothes and things."

"Stop worrying." Chuck gripped her arms and stared down into her eyes. "I wouldn't offer if I didn't want to help. Besides, it gives me some one-on-one time with my girl." He held out his hands.

Charlie leaned into them, and PJ let her go to Chuck.

"See?" Chuck grinned. "She agrees. We'll have fun hang-ing out in the apartment and running errands."

"You'll let me know where you're going?" PJ leaned for-ward and kissed Charlie.

"Charlie might not, but I will." His eyes narrowed. "Now get to work, woman."

"I'm going." PJ gave one last glance around the room. "I'll be glad when life gets back to normal."

"I've been waiting for that for a long time." Chuck tilted his head. "Sometimes we just have to adjust to a new normal."

"Well, if you're taking care of Charlie today, you'll need to know a few things." PJ showed him where the frozen breast milk was and how to defrost it without making it too hot for the baby to drink.

"Does Charlie eat solid foods yet?" Chuck asked.

"Not yet. I'm still nursing, and she gets all the nutrients she needs for now. I'll start introducing cereals soon."

Chuck had forgotten how complicated raising a baby was. His mother had handled most of that for his sister. He'd just been responsible for an occasional feeding and diaper change. But how hard could it be? Charlie wasn't even mobile yet.

"Okay, then. I'm off." PJ headed for the door.

Chuck followed. "We'll walk you over. I can get breakfast there, and then we'll come back and tackle the apartment."

"Thanks, Chuck." PJ leaned up on her toes and pressed a kiss to his cheek.

He turned at the last minute, capturing her lips with his own. Unwilling to end the brief exchange, he wrapped his free hand around her waist and pulled her closer.

Charlie cooed and fisted a hand in PJ's hair.

When she pulled back, PJ winced. "Hey, that's mine." She pried Charlie's fingers loose, kissed them and descended the stairs.

Chuck locked the door behind him and pocketed the key.

In the diner, PJ went right to work, slipping into her uniform and apron. Then she grabbed a pot of coffee and started her rounds of filling cups.

The diner was busy with the early morning customers stopping for a quick bite before heading off to work.

"Thank goodness you're here." Cara Jo swished by, carrying a tray filled with steaming plates of eggs and pancakes. "I thought I could handle them all without your help if you didn't make it in, but I was wrong."

"I didn't stay in the apartment last night."

"Oh?" Cara Jo's brows rose, and her gaze shifted to where Chuck and Charlie were sliding into a booth.

PJ wished she could take back her words. She'd rather have stayed silent than to have stirred up a barrage of questions. "Forget I said anything."

"Hardly." Cara Jo winked. "You can fill me in after the rush."

"Or I can just work and keep my mouth shut," PJ muttered as she hurried forward to take Chuck's order.

"I heard that," Cara Jo said. "You're not getting off that easy."

As busy as they were at the diner, PJ didn't have time to dwell on the fact that Chuck seemed to be handling Charlie just fine. Seeing him with her daughter made her only more aware of him as a man, as a father and as someone who would be a permanent part of Charlie's life.

How that would work out in the long run, PJ had no idea. With an attacker on the loose wreaking havoc in her life, she didn't want to look past the current situation to think about what might lie in her and Charlie's future.

When Chuck finished breakfast and left with Charlie, PJ found herself wishing she could have gone with them. Instead she threw herself into her work, waiting tables and cleaning up after customers.

By the time two o'clock rolled around, she was tired and thankfully had worked off the worry of the night before.

"I have some things to check on at the resort office. I'll be right back. Don't go anywhere until we've had a chance to talk." Cara Jo left through the front door of the diner.

Seeing a chance to escape before Cara Jo returned, PJ

slipped off her apron, ran for the back room and changed into her street clothes. On her way out the back door of the kitchen, she remembered she hadn't taken out the trash, her last task of each day. PJ grabbed the two large garbage bags and hauled them toward the back door.

"Leave those, and I'll get them when I'm done cleaning the kitchen." Mrs. Kinsley stood with her hands up to the elbows in sudsy sink water.

"It's okay, Mrs. K. I'm on my way out anyway." PJ left the diner through the back door, weighed down by the two bags. She stopped several times to reposition her hands on the bags before she made it to the Dumpster. Once she had the bags dealt with, she'd round the side of the building and make a quick stop in her apartment to check on Charlie and Chuck before going to the library to do her homework.

PJ practically fell backward lifting the first bag up over the edge, but she finally managed to roll it into the bin. When she had the second bag perched on the edge and ready for a final push in, black plastic slipped down over her head, obliterating the bright sunlight.

At first she thought she'd dropped the trash bag on her face. But when she breathed in to cry out, the bag filled her mouth, cutting off any chance of air.

PJ let go of the trash bag she'd been balancing and it slipped away, crashing in front of the bin. Before she could pull the plastic bag off her face, her hands were captured, wrenched behind her back and tied together with a hard plastic tie.

She struggled, fighting with all her might as someone dragged her by her arms several feet and dumped her on the ground, and then tied her ankles together with the same hard plastic line.

The more she fought for air, the deeper the loose plastic filled her mouth—until the world faded and she could struggle no more.

In the haze of semiconsciousness, PJ lay on her side, wrists and ankles bound. The heavy weight of a knee pressed into her side and kept her pinned to the gravel. The bag was pulled from her mouth but tied tightly over her eyes before she could catch a glimpse of sunshine.

With her mouth wide open, PJ sucked in a deep breath.

Hands pulled her head back and jerked her jaw downward. A stick was jammed into her mouth, and something cottony scraped across the inside of her cheek. Then the stick was removed and the weight lifted from her side, the hands let go of her face and footsteps pounded away from her.

For a long moment PJ lay on the ground, breathing to desperately fill her starved lungs. The only sound she could hear was the rustle of the plastic bag over her eyes and ears and the rattle of her breaths. The sun beat down on her, so hot she could feel her skin beginning to burn. She knew she should shout to let someone know she was there, but she just didn't have the strength.

"Help," she cried, her mouth dry, her voice croaking. "Please."

Chapter Twelve

Chuck and Charlie had spent the morning talking to the Wild Oak Canyon police about the break-in. They'd come, taken pictures and promised to catch PJ when she got off work for additional comments to add to their report.

After they'd done what they could, Chuck and Charlie spent the rest of the morning rearranging PJ's apartment. Or at least Chuck had done the work—Charlie had lain in the playpen, watching his every move until her eyes drifted closed and she napped.

Besides the missing photos and a few broken mugs tossed from the cabinet, there had been little damage. Chuck gathered the clothing strewn across the floor and dumped it into a pillowcase and the laundry basket. He'd hauled it down to his truck, fitted Charlie in her carrier, left a message at the diner for PJ that he was leaving with the baby and where he was going, and made the short drive to the only Laundromat in town. There he'd spent a couple of hours feeding quarters into the machines and sorting darks and lights.

Charlie talked to him with little cooing sounds, smiled and batted at him with her little fists, keeping him thoroughly entertained. The more he was around his tiny daughter, the more she wrapped him around her little finger. Chuck couldn't imagine another day in his life without Charlie in it. He was falling in love with her so fast it scared him. He prayed PJ wouldn't change her mind about letting him see his little girl, that she wouldn't sue for sole custody, thus taking away both of the girls he loved.

After folding the laundry, Chuck piled it all into his truck. On the way back to the apartment, Chuck stopped at Wild Oak Canyon Hospital to check on Danny's status.

The nurse said he was awake, preparing to leave as soon as the doctor released him. Chuck and Charlie could go in for a visit.

Chuck knocked on Danny's door.

"Come in," a voice called out.

Danny sat on the edge of the hospital bed, a big white swath of bandage wrapped around his forehead. He wore jeans, a T-shirt and tennis shoes and appeared to be anxious to leave as soon as the doctor gave him the go-ahead.

Alicia stood beside the bed, her purse slung over her shoulder, her hand in his. They both turned toward the door as Chuck entered carrying Charlie.

"Hey, baby girl." Alicia smiled at the baby and then turned a more serious expression toward Chuck. "Mr. Bolton, thanks for stopping by to check on Danny. I don't know what I would have done the other night if you and PJ hadn't been home."

Danny held out his hand. "I hear I owe you a thank-you."

Chuck took his hand and shook it. "I didn't do much. Just stood by your side until the real heroes showed up. The med techs did all the work."

"Well, thanks for being there for me and Alicia." Danny shook his head. "I hate to think what might have happened if I hadn't been meeting Alicia that night. That guy was on his way to Ms. PJ's apartment."

"Do you remember anything about the guy?"

"I gave the police my statement. I didn't see anything. The man was wearing a ski mask. As soon as he saw me, he came after me with the tire iron. I didn't have a chance to get away."

"Can you remember if he was tall, short, fat or thin?"

Danny closed his eyes. "When he was standing on the stairs above me, he seemed taller, but as he got to the bottom, he wasn't quite as tall as I'd originally thought." Danny shrugged and opened his eyes. "Not much to go on."

"Any distinguishing features? Tattoos, rings, voice?"

"No rings that I remember, or tattoos for that matter. And he didn't say anything. Sorry, I'm not much help."

"Thanks anyway. If you think of anything later, don't hesitate to let me know. Sometimes even the smallest detail can be important."

"I'll let you know."

"In the meantime, meet your girlfriend in a well-lit area from now on." Chuck smiled at them and left. Without a description, Chuck had nothing to go on. He returned to the apartment and unloaded Charlie and the laundry.

PJ usually got off work at two o'clock. As the hour came and went, Charlie fell asleep and Chuck paced.

By two-thirty, he'd waited all he could stand. As much as he hated waking Charlie, he needed to check on PJ. She'd said something about going to the library but had promised to stop by the apartment before she left.

Charlie stirred a little when he lifted her out of the playpen and onto his shoulder, where she fell back to sleep with little effort.

He locked the door and descended the steps. PJ's car sat in the parking lot where they'd left it the night before. Chuck figured she was working late to make up the time she'd missed earlier.

Chuck and Charlie rounded the front of the resort complex to enter the diner.

Cara Jo met him at the door. "Hi, Chuck. The diner's closed until four. Can I do something for you?"

"I was looking for PJ."

"Mrs. K says she left thirty minutes ago."

Chuck frowned. "She didn't stop by the apartment like she said she would, and her car is still here."

"Maybe she was late for her class and got a ride with someone."

"It's online. I didn't think she had to be there at a certain time. And she promised to stop by the apartment before she went to the library."

Cara Jo's brows dipped. "That's not like her to ditch someone." She strode to the kitchen door. "Mrs. K, what time did you say PJ left?"

"Right after two." Mrs. K wiped her hands on her apron and rounded the big butcher block in the middle of the kitchen, where she'd been rolling out dough for biscuits. "She took the trash as she left through the back door. I told her I would, but she insisted."

"Can you hold Charlie?" Chuck shoved the baby at Cara Jo.

"Sure." Cara Jo took Charlie and laid her over her shoulder.

Chuck ran out the back door and stood in the gravel, his gaze panning the lot behind the diner. No sign of PJ, but a bag of trash lay on the ground in front of the bin, split open with the contents spilling out onto the ground.

Chuck's heart leaped to his throat. He sprinted to the trash container and peered inside, half expecting to see PJ's crumpled body lying among the cardboard boxes and bags of trash. He breathed a sigh when all he saw was more trash and no PJ. Had someone kidnapped her without leaving a trace?

Chuck spun, his pulse racing, his hands clenched into tight fists. He didn't have a clue where to look. "PJ?" he called out, desperate.

A low moan sounded from behind the trash container.

Hope surged, sending Chuck flying around the side of the big metal Dumpster.

Lying on her side, her wrists and ankles bound with zip ties, her head half covered in a black trash bag, lay PJ.

Rage and worry blasted through him as Chuck dropped to his knees beside PJ and yanked the bag from her head.

She cringed, her eyes closing tightly and then opening in short blinks. "Chuck?"

"It's me, baby."

"Where's Charlie? Is she all right?" Her voice was raspy.

"She's fine, sweetheart." He pulled his knife from his pocket and sliced through the bindings at her wrist. "Cara Jo is holding her."

Her hands free, PJ rolled to her back and rubbed at the raw stripes on her wrists. "How long have I been out here?"

"About thirty minutes." He sliced through the zip tie on her ankles and folded his knife, shoving it into his pocket. "Did your attacker hit you?"

"No, but he almost smothered me with the bag." PJ touched her throat and closed her eyes.

Anger burned in Chuck. This was the second time PJ had almost been killed and he hadn't been there to stop it. "The bastard."

A tear slipped from the corner of her eye and trailed across her cheekbone into her hair as she lay on the ground. "All I could think of was you and Charlie."

Chuck could barely contain the anger he felt at whoever was doing this to PJ. He couldn't lash out, not knowing who it was and with PJ lying in front of him so helpless. He had to take care of her first.

"After he stuck the stick in my mouth, I must have passed out." PJ sat up, swayed and would have lay back except that Chuck slipped an arm around her shoulders.

"What do you mean, stuck a stick in your mouth?" Chuck asked.

"I don't know. I was half out of it, too busy breathing air after almost suffocating. He held my head back and jaw down and scraped something around the inside of my mouth." She pressed a hand to her cheek. "At least I think. It's all a bit fuzzy." She stared up at him. "I'm so glad you found me. Much longer, and I'd have had a helluva sunburn." She laughed shakily.

Chuck pulled her against his chest and held her tight.

"Easy. I'm feeling a little guarded about my breathing." She laid a hand on his chest.

Chuck swallowed hard to chase back the lump in his throat. She could have died, and he had been so close and known nothing about it.

"PJ? Chuck?" Cara Jo's voice called out from the door of the diner.

"We're behind the Dumpster," Chuck called out. He scooped PJ up from the ground and stood, ignoring the pain in his leg.

"I can walk." PJ slipped an arm around his shoulder. "But this is nice."

"Let's get you hydrated." He stepped out from behind the trash container, forcing himself not to limp.

Cara Jo and Mrs. K rushed forward.

"Oh, my God." Cara Jo, her eyes wide, touched PJ's arm. She carried Charlie on her hip. "Are you all right?"

"I'm fine. Chuck's just playing the he-man." She frowned up at him. "Really, I can walk."

"Let him carry you," Mrs. K said. "If you age like I did, someday you'll wish he still could." She patted PJ's hand, her eyes tearing. "Honey, I'm so sorry. I should have taken that darned trash out."

"Mrs. K, I'm fine. I wasn't going to let you do my job for me. Besides, you couldn't have known. And what if he'd attacked you?"

"He wasn't after Mrs. K." Chuck's arms tightened around

her. "Whoever did this was waiting for you. He knew you
took the trash out at two and that you'd be alone." Chuck
knew this without a doubt. "And I know what he was after."

"DNA?" PJ asked.

PJ SAT ON a gurney in one of the examination rooms in the
emergency room of Wild Oak Canyon Hospital, swinging
her leg, ready to get the heck out of there. "Why are we still
here? The doctor told me I'm fine—no lasting damage, and
the bruises will heal in a couple weeks."

"Hank's on his way. He wanted you to stay put until he
got here."

PJ's eyes narrowed. "Why?"

Chuck didn't want to get into an argument. Not now. Not
when he'd almost lost her. "You can guess why."

"He wants to do that DNA sample thing?" PJ shook her
head. "Why the heck didn't you say so in the first place?"

"You'll do it?"

PJ nodded. "After what happened a little while ago, I'm
feeling the need to know what everyone else is eager to attack me to find out. If it will help us catch the jerk terrorizing us, I'm all for it."

Chuck smiled at her and caressed her cheek. "That's my
girl."

"In the meantime, do you think Cara Jo's okay with Charlie?"

"She and Mrs. K are out in the waiting room providing
her entertainment."

PJ frowned. "You don't think Charlie will catch anything
here, do you?"

"Hopefully not. I don't want her too far out of our sight.
I think she'll be safe here in the hospital until we can take
her back to Hank's."

A nurse entered the examination room carrying two packages and two vials. "You have a visitor."

Hank Derringer followed her in.

"Normally, I don't let anyone back here but family." The nurse smiled. "Mr. Derringer says he might be just that." She ripped open one of the packages containing a stick with a swab at the end. "Ms. Franks, just to be certain, do you agree to this DNA paternity test?"

PJ drew in a long breath. "For my entire life, I'd believed my father was dead." She laughed, a short, not very amused sound. "And this test might prove that he isn't, and that my mother lied to me."

"To protect you, dear," Hank interjected. He reached out and patted her hand. "Whether or not we are blood related, I'll always consider you family."

She looked up into Hank's kind face. This was the type of man she'd always pictured her father would look like. A man she wished he'd been. "I always thought family never lied to each other."

"I'm sorry, my dear. Had I known Alana was pregnant when I sent her away…"

PJ raised her hand. "It doesn't matter now. I remember my mother saying, *'Don't borrow trouble, Peggy.'*" PJ's lips twisted. "For all we know you aren't my father. And I still won't know who he is."

"PJ, we need to narrow it down. Whoever stole your sample earlier today will know something soon. We need to know what we're up against." Chuck took her hand and squeezed it. "But it's totally up to you. It's your choice, and I'll stand behind whatever you decide."

PJ's glance shifted to Hank. "And you, Mr. Derringer? If I decide not to do this, will you respect my wishes?"

"My dear PJ, you make the decision. I'll stand behind you either way. You and Charlie mean more to me than a test result."

PJ turned to the nurse. "Let's do this." She opened her mouth.

The nurse swabbed the inside of her cheek and stuck the swab into a tube. She performed the same procedure on Hank. Then she put both vials into a padded envelope and sealed it. "Do you want to do the honors of placing this in the mail?"

"Yes." PJ took the package from her. "Can we leave now? I want to see Charlie."

"Yes, my dear." Hank helped her off the gurney. "She was giggling with Cara Jo and Mrs. Kinsley in the lobby when I came through."

"Good. She's happy. And if we hurry, we can get to the post office before it closes." Now that she had the samples, she was more eager to get the results than she wanted to admit to Hank or Chuck.

"PJ, you have the choice of what lab to send the DNA samples to." Hank followed her out of the room. "And they will do a fine job, no doubt. But I'd feel a lot better if the samples were hand-delivered to a lab in San Antonio that performs these kinds of tests by the hundreds. I could have it hand-delivered and put an expedite on it, and we could get the results back in two days."

PJ stopped and faced Hank. "And how long will it take if I send it to the lab indicated on the package?"

"It can take anywhere between five days and a week, depending on how soon the samples are delivered and how big a backlog the lab has." Hank's lips pressed together. "If we send it to San Antonio, it requires that you trust me to handle it."

She raised her brows. "No more lies?"

Hank nodded. "My dear, I've never lied to you."

Her eyes narrowed. "No more lying by omission?"

"Agreed."

She handed him the package. "I trust you, Hank."

Hank hugged her. "Thank you for that." Then he chucked

Charlie beneath the chin and left them standing in the lobby to hurry out to the parking lot.

PJ took Charlie from Cara Jo and hugged her close. "It's been a crazy day, hasn't it, sweetie?"

"Glad you came out when you did." Cara Jo shifted the diaper bag to her shoulder. "Charlie's getting hungry, and there wasn't a bottle in the bag."

Chuck pressed a hand to PJ's back and guided her toward the exit. "Let's get you out to the truck."

Charlie leaned into PJ's neck, found her fist and made loud sucking noises.

PJ laughed. "Yeah, Charlie, I know it's time for supper."

Cara Jo and Mrs. Kinsley drove off in Cara Jo's car.

Chuck helped PJ into the truck and handed Charlie into her lap. "Want me to wait outside?" he asked.

PJ shrugged, pulling her blouse out of her waistband. "It's up to you. I'm perfectly comfortable nursing her in front of you. Question is, are you comfortable around a woman nursing?"

"I'm fine. Let me get the AC going for you and Charlie." Chuck rounded to the driver's side and slid in. He inserted the key and cranked the engine, setting the AC on cool. With dusk settling in on the little town, the temperature had begun to drop, but not enough to keep them from sweating in the closed confines of the cab.

Despite his best efforts to keep his eyes averted to give PJ some privacy, Chuck's gaze strayed more than once to the baby suckling at her mother's breast. Each time a sense of warmth spread through him, filling him with a sense of something he couldn't quite put his finger on.

All he knew was this felt right. Being with PJ and Charlie. PJ trusting him enough to nurse their baby in front of him, and no words needed to fill a comfortable silence.

"She's so tired, she's falling asleep." PJ shifted Charlie and dropped her shirt over her bare breast. "We can go home now."

"Don't you mean back to Hank's?"

"No. I want to be at my own place with my own stuff."

"I don't know. With all that's been happening, I don't feel like I can keep you safe enough."

PJ reached out and touched his arm. "You're doing a pretty darned good job so far. I trust that you'll continue."

He nodded and climbed down from his seat, rounding to her side of the truck. PJ handed a sleeping Charlie to him, and he carefully buckled her into her car seat in the back, pressing a kiss to her milky cheek.

Charlie smelled of baby powder and soft-scented shampoo. He could get used to having that smell around. He tucked a light blanket around her and closed the door.

As he got back into the truck, he glanced toward PJ.

She stared out the window, a frown on her face.

"What's wrong?" he asked.

"That SUV." She pointed. "It's been sitting there for a long time."

"Might be someone visiting a relative in the hospital."

"No. It's not empty. Every once in a while, I see the silhouette of someone's head through the tinted glass." PJ shrugged and sat back against the seat. "I'm getting paranoid."

"You have a right to be." Chuck shifted into Drive and eased toward the SUV. "Wouldn't hurt to run the license plate. Got a pen?"

"Hold on." PJ dived for her purse, rummaging through until she pulled an old receipt and a pen from the depths. "Got it."

Before Chuck could move toward the SUV, the vehicle pulled out of the parking lot and turned right.

"Did you catch the license plate?"

"No, it was too far away and obscured by a frame around it."

"I'm going to follow." Chuck punched the accelerator with his foot and tore across the parking lot to the street.

PJ touched his arm. "No, Chuck, not this time. We have Charlie with us. I don't want her in the line of fire. Not that I think they'll shoot at us."

"But why take the chance?" Chuck hesitated before pulling out onto the street in the opposite direction the SUV had taken. "I'll call the police and have them keep a look out for it."

"I like that idea better." PJ glanced over her shoulder at Charlie. "I need to get Charlie home. She needs a bath, and I need something to eat." As if to emphasize her words, her stomach growled.

Chuck grinned. "How about we eat at the diner tonight?"

"I'd love that. I'm too tired to think about fixing a meal."

"Then it's a date. You, me and Charlie."

PJ settled back in her seat, a slight smile tugging at her lips. She could get used to having Chuck around. He made her feel safe. Not for the first time, she questioned her decision to push him away a year ago. The only conclusion she'd come to was that she'd been afraid. Afraid to love him too much and lose him, like every other important person in her life.

PJ's gaze shifted to the baby sleeping in the backseat. She loved Charlie more than she loved her own life. If anything were to happen to her baby daughter, she didn't know how she'd cope. But as Chuck said, there were no guarantees.

Would PJ give up the time she had with Charlie now, banking on the possibility of losing her in the future?

No.

So what was the difference?

She glanced at Chuck from beneath her lashes. He'd aged

in the year he'd been gone. The lines around his eyes were more pronounced, and the shadows beneath them spoke of the sorrow and tragedy of the war he'd fought.

PJ wanted to hold him and wipe away the terrible images he must have stored in his memories. He'd been angry with her for keeping news of his daughter's birth from him. Would he ever forgive her for that? Would he ever learn to trust her again?

The drive ended at the back of the resort.

PJ jumped down from her seat before Chuck could get around to her side and hold her door. She didn't want him to do nice things for her. Not when she was so confused by the blossoming feelings she harbored and the wrongs that stood between them.

Chuck unbuckled Charlie and lifted her, seat and all, carrying her as if she weighed less than a kitten.

Thankful for Chuck to help out, PJ followed him up the steps. "I'd like to shower and change before dinner. I still feel like I have gravel and dirt in my hair and skin."

"Take your time. I'll keep an eye on Charlie. And leave the apartment door open so that I can keep an eye on the hallway, as well."

PJ grabbed her bathrobe, brush and soaps and hurried toward the bathroom, leaving the door to the apartment open.

At her last glance, Chuck had scooted the recliner to a position from which he could see the outer hallway and the baby crib. He stood with Charlie in his arms. "Go on, we'll be okay."

She hesitated, taking in the picture of the big cowboy holding the tiny baby in the crook of his arm.

Chuck winked.

PJ scooted into the bathroom, her face and body burning with something far different from embarrassment. A chilly shower did nothing to cool the fire building at her core. After scrubbing the dirt and grime off her body, she hopped out of the bathtub and ran a towel across her sensitized skin, imagining a pair of work-roughened hands skimming over her instead.

Still burning, with no relief in sight, PJ pulled jeans over her hips, snapped a bra in place and dragged a T-shirt over her head. A quick brush through her hair, and she stood with her hand hovering over the doorknob, her breathing faster than usual and her heart thumping against her ribs.

Maybe Charlie will sleep a little longer while Chuck and I...

PJ sucked in a deep breath and stepped out into the hall, fully expecting to see Chuck sitting in the chair, Charlie in his arms.

The chair was empty.

PJ frowned and hurried toward the apartment, every bad scenario her fevered mind could think of running through her head.

"Chuck?" she said as she stepped into the apartment.

"Hey, where's the fire?" He snagged her arm and pulled her into his embrace. "Did you miss me?" He pushed the door closed behind her.

"Don't scare me like that."

"I was just straightening the picture on the wall. It's okay."

"I didn't see you and Charlie." She closed her eyes and let go of a long, steadying breath. "This situation is making me crazy."

"Not nearly as crazy as it's making me." He pushed a damp strand of hair behind her ear. "Being this close to you..." Chuck bent, his lips claiming hers.

The kiss started out soft, gentle, almost a brush of two mouths.

PJ's hands slid around Chuck's neck and she deepened the contact, dragging him closer, her hips pressing against his. Her tongue pushed past his teeth and stroked his in long, sensual thrusts. All the pent-up emotions of the past couple of days erupted inside, and she couldn't hold back.

Chuck backed her against the wall and lifted her, wrapping her legs around his waist, never taking his mouth from hers.

The heat intensified, the need to be naked flaming the inferno until the sound of a baby crying pulled PJ back to earth.

Chuck let her legs drop to the floor. "We need to talk."

"Yes, we do." PJ disengaged her arms from around his neck and stepped around him, pressing her hands to her burning cheeks. "Later. Charlie needs me."

A diaper change and a few minutes of nursing later, the fires had cooled but weren't forgotten. PJ carried Charlie out to the living room, ready to have that conversation.

Chuck had his back to her, his cell phone to his ear. "We figured as much. It has to be someone nearby. Can he narrow it down to an address?"

PJ frowned and circled around Chuck, studying his face as he spoke on the phone.

"We will. No, we'll be staying in town tonight. Thanks, Hank."

Chuck clicked the off button and met PJ's eyes. "Brandon, the computer guru, has the IP address of the hacker."

Chapter Thirteen

Chuck wished he hadn't told PJ about the IP address as soon as the words were out of his mouth.

"Where is it?" PJ grabbed the diaper bag and crammed diapers into it, and then she snatched a bottle of breast milk out of the freezer and stuffed it into the side pocket. "What are you waiting for? Let's get there. I have a few choice words for the guy who has been making my life miserable."

Chuck shook his head. "We can't go."

PJ stood at the door to the apartment, diaper bag slung over one shoulder, Charlie on her opposite hip. "Why?"

"I want to nail the guy as badly as you do, but Brandon only has the IP address. He's still tracing it to a physical address."

The light in PJ's eyes faded, and her shoulders sagged. "Well, darn. And here I was getting all hopeful."

"Come on, we'll get that dinner I promised and maybe by the time we've eaten, Brandon will have performed his miracle and found the address." Chuck led the way down the steps, careful to scan the parking lot in the dull light emitted from the one security light. As he stepped away from the building, the motion-sensing lights blinked on, illuminating the corners halfway down the building, making it a lot easier to see someone who might be coming to attack them.

Throughout dinner, Chuck and PJ sat in strained silence,

both listening for Chuck's cell phone to ring. It didn't happen. By the time they'd eaten, Charlie had fallen asleep, and PJ yawned so wide Chuck was afraid she might break her jaw.

"We might as well call it a night," Chuck finally announced. He'd wanted to hear from Brandon as badly as PJ had. "Brandon will call when he has it."

"What's taking him so long?" PJ stifled yet another yawn.

"These things take time." Chuck gathered the infant carrier with Charlie in it and carried her up the stairs to the apartment. Once inside, he laid her in her crib.

PJ stripped the baby's clothes, changed her diaper and slipped her pajamas on.

Charlie stirred but didn't awaken. Apparently the excitement of being at the hospital and then the diner had taken its toll on the baby. She was out for the night.

Which left Chuck relatively alone with PJ.

"If you think you and Charlie will be all right, I'll hit the shower."

"Are you staying here or in your apartment?"

He couldn't tell if she wanted him there or if she was trying to get rid of him, but he wasn't going to give her a choice. Not after all that had happened. "I'm staying here."

She nodded, her gaze sliding away from his. "Good. I'll get you a blanket and pillow."

Chuck suppressed a groan. Another night on the couch or in the lounge chair so close to where PJ would be sleeping. He should have expected that, but deep down, he'd hoped their previous night's sleeping arrangements had meant something more than a blanket and pillow on the couch tonight.

Just as well. Without the protection of Hank's security system and additional firepower, Chuck was on his own to protect PJ and Charlie. He'd have to focus his thoughts out of the bedroom in order to keep them safe.

He hurried through a lukewarm shower, frustrated that

he couldn't make the water any colder or that he had to get out so soon. The longer he stayed away from his girls, the more likely someone else could get to them.

Several times he'd shut off the shower to listen for footsteps on the landing. Each time, he shook his head, thinking he'd grown more paranoid than ever.

After barely five minutes, he jammed his feet into clean jeans and padded barefoot back to the apartment, carrying his shirt. He entered using a key PJ had loaned him, careful not to wake the baby, and then he closed the door behind him and locked the dead bolt.

PJ stood in the bedroom, pulling her T-shirt over her head.

Chuck stood transfixed, unable to look away.

When she'd tossed the shirt aside, she glanced up, her gaze capturing his. A soft pink blush rose up her neck, filling her cheeks, and her mouth rounded into a pretty O shape.

She didn't try to cover herself, nor did she flash an angry look his way. Instead, PJ reached behind her and flicked the catch on her bra, releasing it. The straps loosened, and she let them slide down her arms to drop to the floor.

"Peggy Jane," Chuck moaned. "You sure you want to do that?"

She braced one hand on her jeans-clad hip and raised her brows. "Would I be standing here half-naked if I wasn't sure?" she challenged. A quick glance at the crib and she strode out of the bedroom into the living room, stopping directly in front of him. "Are you going to stand there and stare, or do something?"

He chuckled. "What did you have in mind?"

"This." She lifted his hand and placed it on her breast. "And this." PJ plucked the T-shirt he'd been holding out of his hand and tossed it onto the couch, and then she guided his fingers to her face, pressing her cheek into his palm. "Do I have to do it all?"

"So far, I have no complaints. Except one..." He tipped

her head back. "We're both overdressed." Past the point of teasing, Chuck pulled her into his arms and crushed her lips with his.

PJ worked the button loose on his jeans, slid the zipper down and shoved his pants over his hips.

Chuck did the same, going a step further by sliding the denim down her long, slender legs until she stepped free. God, she had great legs, and when they wrapped around him...

He lifted her off her feet.

PJ locked her ankles behind him, pressing her warm wetness down over his straining member.

He thrust up into her, her tight channel taking his full length, encasing him in delicious heat.

PJ's head dropped back, her hair falling down to brush against his knuckles.

He lifted her and thrust into her again.

She moaned. "Faster."

He backed her against the wall, held her hips and pounded into her again and again until she writhed, her fingers gripping his arms.

The tension built, the fierce longing he'd carried for this woman for such a long time exploding in his veins, sending him catapulting over the edge of reason.

As he neared the peak, PJ's heels dug into his buttocks, her fingernails clawed his shoulders and her body grew rigid.

One final thrust, and his insides detonated in a burst of sensations so powerful he thought he might have died.

He held her hips, reveling in the wonder that was their most intimate connection.

When he finally came back to himself, he buried his face in her neck.

Her fingers combed through his hair. "Chuck?"

"Hmm?"

"My legs are cramping."

Chuck carried her to the bedroom and laid her on the bed. Then he crawled in beside her and spooned her body against his, burying his face in the side of her neck. The herbal scent of her hair surrounded him, reminding him of the days before he'd deployed, when they'd been carefree and in love.

"Remember that night at the swimming hole in Willow Creek?"

"Uh-huh." He nuzzled her throat, pressing kisses against her soft skin. "You almost stepped on a snake."

She batted at his hands. "Is that all you remember?"

"No. I remember it was the first time we'd made love."

"I was afraid you didn't really like me."

"I was afraid I liked you too much, and would scare you away." And he had. "Do you ever wish we could go back?"

"No," PJ stated with a certain conviction in the one-syllable word. "I wouldn't change anything, because if I did, we wouldn't have Charlie. And I can't imagine life without my sweet baby."

"Agreed." Chuck stroked the length of her arm and down across the curve of her hip. She felt like heaven to him.

"What are we going to do about us?" PJ whispered.

"I suggest we take it one day at a time."

"What if we don't have another day? What if this maniac gets to me when you're not there? What will happen to Charlie?"

"I'm not going to let anything happen to either one of you."

She rolled over and stared up into his eyes. "Promise?"

He cupped her cheek, and with his lips hovering over hers, he said, "I'll do my best." And prayed his best was good enough. A little Afghan boy had died because Chuck hadn't been able to protect him from his own village. What made him think he could protect PJ and Charlie from a man they couldn't seem to locate?

PJ drifted to sleep, her body warm and soft against Chuck.

He lay for a long time, fighting a rising sense of panic, telling himself that losing focus now would do neither one of them any good. Afraid to go to sleep, he lay awake, remembering all the good times he and PJ had before he deployed, hoping that when he went to sleep, he wouldn't go back to that place that haunted him since he'd stormed into a Taliban stronghold and wrought his revenge on the killers of children.

He must have drifted to sleep sometime during the night despite all his efforts not to. The next conscious thought was of a buzzing vibration sound on the nightstand beside him.

When he opened his eyes, he noted the gray, predawn light filtering through the edges of the blinds, and the irritating, vibrating buzzing started again.

Chuck reached for the telephone before it rattled against the wood of the nightstand again. He hit the talk button but didn't say anything until he'd rolled out of bed and strode into the living room. "Bolton here," he said softly.

"Chuck, we have an address." Hank's voice cleared the remaining haze of sleep from Chuck's brain.

"Where is it?"

Hank gave him the details. "I'm going to call the police with it, as well."

"Give me a few minutes before you do. I want to be there when they arrest the guy."

"I'm on my way in from the ranch. I want to be there, as well."

Chuck clicked the phone off, grabbed his clothes from the floor where he'd left them the night before and dressed. When he sat to pull his boots on, a noise made him turn.

PJ stood with a sheet wrapped around her naked body, her hair tousled and her face still flushed from sleep. "Are you leaving?"

"Hank called."

She blinked and took another step into the room. "They have the address?"

He nodded.

"I'm coming with you." She turned toward the bedroom.

Chuck pulled his second boot on, stood and crossed the room. He rubbed his hands down her arms. "The police will be handling the arrest, and we don't know if it'll be dangerous. I'd rather you and Charlie stayed away from it all."

PJ's gaze shifted to the crib, where Charlie was just beginning to stir. "I guess we wouldn't have time to get ready, anyway." She glanced up at him, her brows lowered. "You'll be careful?"

He brushed his lips across hers. "You bet."

Gripping the sheet with one hand, PJ raised the other and pulled him back, deepening the kiss. "Come by the diner when it's over. I want a full report."

"Yes, ma'am." He swatted her bottom and headed out the door. "Lock it behind me." He left, praying this would be the arrest to end the troubles. Then he and PJ could sort things out.

PJ SHOT THE bolt on the door, returned to the bedroom, fed Charlie and dressed for work. Still not feeling comfortable about leaving Charlie at the day care, PJ called Dana, hoping she was off that day since she worked at the day care only three days a week.

"As a matter of fact, today is my day off," Dana said.

"Do you already have plans? I'll understand if you do."

"Relax, PJ. I'd be happy to stay with Charlie while you work. Then maybe you can fill me in on all that's been happening with you. I can't believe someone actually bugged the day care."

"Honey, that's not all."

"Hold that thought," Dana said. "I can be there in ten minutes."

PJ hung up and made a mad dash through the apartment, picking up the discarded clothing from her crazy hot sex with Chuck in the living room. Her cheeks burned at the image etched permanently in her mind of making love with Chuck against the wall.

She'd never look at that wall the same. PJ's pulse pounded with the same intensity of the night before. Forcing herself to look away, she hurried to the bedroom to make the bed, smoothing the sheets that still smelled of Chuck.

A knock on the door startled her back to reality and set her pulse racing.

"PJ, it's me, Dana." Her friend's voice came through the door.

PJ took several deep, steadying breaths and forced herself to look normal when she opened the door for Dana.

Dana stepped in, her gaze on PJ's face, her eyes narrowing. "Wow, PJ, you look different."

PJ pressed a hand to her cheeks as they burned hotter.

Her friend's eyes widened, and a grin spread across her face. "You did it with Chuck, didn't you?"

"I d-don't know what you're talking about," PJ stammered.

"I knew it! You and Chuck are back together, aren't you?" She grabbed PJ's hand. "That has to be the reason for the glow."

"I'm glowing?" PJ laughed. "Now you're just being silly."

"No, my dear, you are most certainly glowing." Still holding PJ's hand, she marched her into the bedroom and made her stand in front of the mirror over the dresser. "See?"

PJ stared at the stranger in the mirror. Her cheeks were flushed, and her eyes sparkled.

Dana grinned beside her. "That's love, sweetie."

PJ's heart stopped and then skipped into gear again, pounding against her ribs.

"I take it you two have figured everything out," Dana was saying. "It's about time."

PJ shook her head. "No, no, we haven't." Her brows dipped, and the flush paled in her cheeks. She turned away from the mirror and stared at the floor. "We keep saying we have to talk, but we end up making love instead."

Dana gripped her arms and forced her to look at her. "Hey, that's a good start."

"But nothing's resolved." PJ stared into her friend's eyes, tears welling in her own. She pulled away and walked across the room. "I don't know where this is going or if he'll stick around once they arrest the man harassing me."

"They found him? Oh, thank God." Dana lifted Charlie from her crib and held her in her arms.

"If all goes well…" PJ stopped at the window, staring out into the parking lot. "They'll be arresting someone any minute now."

"You hear that, Charlie?" Dana kissed the baby's cheek. "We're going to have a great day."

"I have to go to work."

Dana leaned over and kissed PJ's cheek. "You and Chuck were meant for each other. It'll work out, just you wait and see."

PJ ducked her face and swung away, afraid Dana might see the sudden rush of tears in her eyes. "Thanks for coming on such short notice, Dana. We'll talk later."

"We'll be here, waiting for Mommy and Daddy to come home." Dana held up one of Charlie's hands and waved. "Bye-bye, Mommy."

PJ waved at the two and then left the apartment, locking the door behind her and running down the stairs and around the building to the diner.

If the police arrested the man responsible for the attacks, then for all intents and purposes, Chuck would be done with his assignment to protect her and Charlie. Hank would send him on another job, possibly more dangerous than this one had turned out.

Where would that leave her and Charlie?

For the next hour, PJ could barely focus on waiting tables. Every time someone stepped in the door, she spun to see if it was Chuck.

The kind, older Hispanic gentleman, Señor Iglesias, caught her arm as she tried to pour ice water into his coffee mug. "Señorita Franks, that is not necessary."

"I'm so sorry. Let me get you a fresh cup."

"No need. I sense you are disturbed. Is there anything I can do to help?"

"No, I'm just a bit distracted. I'm sorry I ruined your coffee."

"You are much too pretty to be so worried."

"It's just that…" She shook her head. "Never mind."

"I am your only customer at this moment, so *por favor,* sit. Maybe talking will help."

PJ sank into the seat across from the man. His kind eyes and the sincere look on his face made her want to spill her guts to this stranger. "So much has happened in the past few days."

"I heard there have been some attacks on you as well as another young man." Señor Iglesias frowned. "Have the police found the person responsible?"

"I hope so. I would hate for anything to happen to my little girl."

"Ah, a sweet bambina." Señor Iglesias smiled. "Does she look like her beautiful mother?"

"No, she's more like her father than me. She's everything to me. If anything were to happen to Charlie…I couldn't live without her."

"I know what you mean. A mother's love for her child is strong. A father's love isn't always as deep as it should be.

His expectations can be too high, and he can be too stubborn to see. Mother and child have a special bond."

"You have children, don't you, Señor Iglesias? You must know how heartbroken a parent would feel to lose one."

His dark eyes clouded. "I have lost a child."

When PJ's brows furrowed, the older man raised a hand. "Not to death, but to a life I could not approve of. He turned his back on his *familia*. I truly believe his mother died of a broken heart."

"I'm sorry." PJ reached across the table and touched the old man's arm. "She must have loved him dearly."

"Sí." Señor Iglesias covered her hand with his. "You remind me of her."

"Thank you."

"If ever you need anything, *por favor,* call on me. I will help you in any way possible." He handed her a business card. "My apologies, *está en Español.*"

"Numbers are easily translated. Thank you." PJ patted the man's arm and tucked the card into her apron pocket. "Now I'd better get back to work so that I can pay rent." She smiled and pushed to her feet. "Enjoy the rest of your stay in Wild Oak Canyon. Despite the trouble lately, it's a wonderful place to live."

He nodded. "Thank you for entertaining an old man."

PJ slipped out of the diner and back up to her apartment, anxious to see Charlie.

The lock clicked, and she pushed the door open.

"Oh, PJ." Dana stared across at her. "I'm so glad you're here."

"Where's Charlie?"

Dana smiled. "Relax. She's in her crib, and she's hungry."

PJ sucked in air and let it out. Thank God, Charlie was all right.

IT TOOK FORTY-FIVE minutes for the sheriff to arrange for assistance from the Texas state troopers and get them in place before making a move on the street location of the IP address. Chuck stood by with Hank outside the perimeter of the police-barricaded streets. Chuck wanted to be in on the action, to come face-to-face with PJ's attacker.

Hank touched his arm. "I know you want to be in there."

"I'm not good at waiting." It was the primary reason he'd been booted from the army. He'd disobeyed orders and gone off in a fit of rage to find and kill the people responsible for torturing a small boy, and he'd gotten himself shot in the process.

"They'll let us know soon enough."

"Not soon enough for me." Chuck paced back and forth beside a sheriff's cruiser, parked sideways across the road.

The neighborhood was barely awake, and most people had yet to leave for work. One by one, lights blinked on inside the homes as alarms woke residents.

Hank's eyes narrowed as he stared at the house the state police were targeting. "Looks like they're moving in."

Chuck stopped pacing and squinted into the eastern sunrise. "Finally."

The house was surrounded by armed men. The Wild Oak Canyon temporary sheriff, Deputy Johnny Owen, stepped up to the door, weapon drawn and pounded. "This is the sheriff's department. Open up."

Several long seconds passed before the door opened and a man wearing a bathrobe peered out, blinking sleepily. He spoke to the deputy, his eyes wide, hands raised.

"I can't hear what he's saying." Chuck leaned forward, as if that would help.

"Me, either."

The man in the bathrobe was led outside by a deputy. A woman, also wearing a robe, stepped outside carrying a little boy.

"The deputy's going in," Hank said.

The deputy and several other uniformed men entered the house. After a few minutes they emerged and spoke with the homeowner again.

The man pointed to the house next door. A For Sale sign leaned crookedly in the overgrown yard. The blinds in the windows were closed, and the house appeared vacant.

"What do you suppose is going on?" Hank asked.

"I don't know." Chuck could barely stand still. He wanted to be close enough to hear what the man in the bathrobe was saying.

The deputy and two more uniforms crossed to the empty house and tried the knob on the front door. When it didn't open, they rounded the side to the back.

Several minutes later, they emerged from the front door.

Deputy Owen pointed to the houses surrounding the empty one and the deputies took off, knocking on those doors, waking residents. Dogs barked and children peeked around parents' legs.

"They're canvassing the neighborhood," Hank said.

"Why aren't they arresting the man in the bathrobe?" Chuck's fists clenched and unclenched.

"Maybe he's not the person they're after."

"Holy hell." Chuck jammed his hands into his pockets. "This can't be a dead end."

Deputy Owen broke away from the man in the bathrobe and strode toward Hank.

Hank straightened. "What's going on?"

"The address you gave us is the right one."

"Then why no arrest?" Chuck demanded.

The deputy frowned at Chuck and then addressed Hank. "He has a Wi-Fi network set up without a password. Apparently someone tapped into it. I suspect it was the person using the vacant house next door. We found candy wrappers and soda bottles inside. My team is collecting evidence and fingerprints now, and we're asking neighbors if they've seen anyone going into or around the house in the past few days."

Chuck closed his eyes. "What you're saying is, you still have no idea who's tapping into Mr. Derringer's computers or who attacked PJ and Danny?"

Deputy Owen shrugged. "We don't even know for certain the events are connected."

"They are," Hank said.

"We'll let you know if we learn anything from the neighbors. Other than that, we can't arrest a man for having an unsecured router." The deputy shook his head. "In the meantime, we try to fit the pieces together."

"Damn." Chuck turned away from the scene.

Hank rested a hand on his shoulder. "The police will find out who was in the house."

"When? Today? Tomorrow? After something happens to PJ?"

"We're doing the best with the resources we have."

"Excuse me." A woman walked up to Deputy Owen.

"Yes, ma'am." The deputy faced the woman.

"A deputy asked my husband if he'd seen anyone coming through here in the past few days. He hadn't, but I remember seeing someone. I'm not sure it means anything, but you never know."

"Who?" Chuck asked before the deputy could.

The woman's gaze shifted from Chuck back to Deputy Owen. "Mr. Bergman's grandson walks through here every day going to and from work at the hardware store. I'm sure it's nothing, but I thought you'd like to know." She wrung her hands. "Are you looking for someone dangerous? Should we, as residents, be scared?"

The deputy frowned. "We're not sure. Lock your doors at night, and you should be all right."

"I told my husband we should lock our doors." The

woman walked away, shaking her head and muttering about her spouse.

"I'll send someone over to the hardware store. Mr. Bergman opens pretty early."

"Mind if we come along?"

"No." The deputy held up a finger. "As long as you let me do all the talking."

"Absolutely," Hank agreed.

Chuck clamped his lips shut and nodded.

Rather than walking the two blocks to the hardware store, Hank and Chuck drove over in Chuck's pickup.

The acting sheriff and a couple of his deputies had pulled into the space in front of the store. Hank and Chuck entered behind them.

Mr. Bergman was wiping his hands on a rag. "Good morning, deputies, Mr. Johnson, Hank. What brings you here so early?"

"We'd like to speak to your grandson, Ross Felton," the deputy said.

The store owner frowned. "Ross doesn't usually come in until around ten."

"Do you know where we can find him?"

"He lives in the apartment above Mrs. Grissom's garage on Fifth Street. Why? What's he done?"

"We don't know. We just want to ask him some questions." The deputy nodded toward Mr. Bergman. "Is your grandson familiar with computers?"

Bergman snorted. "That's all the boy did when he lived with his mother. He played games and sat behind his computer rather than get outside and do a decent day's work."

"Has he said anything to you about Hank Derringer or PJ Franks?"

Mr. Bergman's glance strayed to Hank. "Not that I've heard. Isn't Miss Franks the waitress at the diner?"

"Yes," Hank answered.

"Other than waiting on his table, I can't imagine he even knows who she is. He doesn't socialize much." Mr. Bergman shook his head. "He doesn't do much of anything, from what I can see. I can barely get him to show up for work."

"Thank you, Mr. Bergman." Deputy Owen led the other deputies out to the sidewalk.

Hank hurried after the deputy, questioning him as they walked.

Mr. Bergman caught Chuck's arm as he turned to follow Hank out the door. "Is Ross in trouble?"

"I really can't say."

"He's always been a challenge to his mother, and he's been a pain in the butt working here, but I like to think he's got a heart in there somewhere behind all that attitude."

"I'm sure he does."

"His mother has gone through a lot already. Ross's father was abusive. He used to hit my daughter and the boy when they lived with him. Whatever happens, please give him the benefit of the doubt. If not for Ross, then for his mother." Mr. Bergman let go of Chuck's arm.

Chuck nodded and left the store. His desire to choke the life out of the man responsible for attacking PJ warred with the old man's desire to give his grandson a break to spare his daughter.

Why did the world have to be so messed up? Abusive fathers, delinquent sons, computer hackers and Taliban retribution. It all made Chuck's own falling-out with his father seem insignificant.

Hank met him on the sidewalk. "The sheriff is on his way to Felton's apartment. In the meantime, we have bigger trouble coming."

"What do you mean?"

Hank held out his cell phone with a photo on it.

It was a picture of PJ in her waitress uniform. Beneath it was a text message.

Chuck grabbed the phone and read: If you don't want the Mexican drug lords to know who the waitress really is, bring one million dollars to the abandoned Ferguson barn tonight at midnight. Alone. Don't be late. You don't have much time.

Chapter Fourteen

PJ checked on Charlie several times during the day, and everything seemed all right. After a slow morning at the diner, Cara Jo told her to take off before lunch and get some rest.

Chuck and Hank had yet to call with an update on the arrest, and the waiting was killing PJ.

She stopped by her apartment prior to heading for the sheriff's office.

"Heard anything?" Dana asked as PJ stepped through the door.

PJ sighed, dumping her purse on the counter. "Nothing."

"I would have thought Chuck and Hank would have stopped at the diner by now."

"All I can think is that the arrest didn't go as planned."

"Are you going to wait here for news? Charlie will be happy, won't you, baby?" Dana tickled Charlie's belly.

The baby giggled and batted her hands at Dana's face.

PJ lifted her daughter into her arms and kissed her soft cheek. "I'm behind on a couple of assignments for school. If you don't mind staying a few more hours, I'm going to run by the sheriff's department and then the library. I'll be home before five." She hugged Charlie and kissed her again before handing her back to Dana.

"Take your time." Dana perched Charlie on her hip and smiled at PJ. "Charlie and I have been having a great time, and I'm catching up on my television programs." Dana waved her toward the door. "Go on. I've got you on speed dial, and I'll keep the doors locked."

"Thanks, Dana. I won't be any longer than I have to."

"Be careful out there."

"Will do."

PJ peered through the peephole before opening the apartment door. When she closed it behind her, she waited to hear the click of the dead bolt Chuck had installed before she headed to the parking lot and her car.

As she scanned the area all around her, she was hyper-aware of her surroundings, determined not to be a victim again. Before she climbed into her car, she checked the backseat in case someone was hiding on the floor, waiting for his chance to nab her.

PJ laughed shakily as she climbed into her car, locked the doors and took off across town to the sheriff's office. When she arrived she parked in front, next to a cruiser.

Deputy Owen stepped out of the building at the same time PJ got out of her car.

She hurried forward. "Sir, can you tell me how the arrest went this morning?"

Deputy Owen frowned. "It didn't." He moved to go around her.

PJ's heart plummeted, and she refused to be sidestepped until she got answers. "What do you mean, it didn't?"

"The computer at the address had an unsecured router with Wi-Fi capability."

"I'm sorry, I don't understand."

"Anyone could have used the man's IP address to hack into Mr. Derringer's system and send you the messages you've received."

"Oh." PJ stood still as Deputy Owen went around her to his vehicle. So much for feeling safer in Wild Oak Canyon.

Basically, they were right back at square one. Then why the heck hadn't she heard anything from Chuck or Hank?

PJ climbed back into her car and drove to the library on autopilot, her mind miles away from homework. As she passed the street Hank had indicated as the one on which the arrest was to have been made that morning, PJ decided to drive down it.

What she hoped to accomplish, she didn't know.

Someone had tapped into another person's personal router to conduct the hacking. That someone would have had to be close enough for the connection to work.

As she neared the end of the street, she slowed to turn onto the next one, glancing in her rearview mirror to make sure no one was following her, paranoia a given since the attack in her apartment.

A movement near the corner of a house caught PJ's eye and she inched onto the next street, her gaze flipping between the road in front of her and the street behind.

A young man in a T-shirt and baggy jeans slipped between houses, crossed the street and passed by the house with the stolen bandwidth.

The person was headed the same direction as PJ, so she slowed more, thankful traffic was so light in the small town during the middle of the day. As she neared the turn for the next street, the man crossed that road and walked between two more houses, head down, hands jammed into his pockets.

PJ turned and hurried toward the spot where the man had disappeared. She noted a fence blocking access to the backs of the houses. A driveway led to a garage with what appeared to be an apartment over the top.

Thinking she'd lost him, PJ rolled down her window and listened while she scanned the area. She almost missed the soft click of a door closing at the top of the stairs leading into the garage apartment.

She drove by and rounded the corner to the next street, parking in the driveway of a vacant house with a For Sale sign jammed into the dry grass.

Her heart hammering, PJ checked all around for anyone following her before she opened her door and got out. Not a single vehicle passed on the street. The sun beat down on her, making her glad she'd opted for a ribbed knit T-shirt and khaki shorts. She grabbed a ball cap from the backseat, shoved her hair up into it and slid her sunglasses over her eyes. Then she took off along the sidewalk leading to the house with the garage apartment, stopping at the front door of the main house and quickly making up a story before she knocked.

An old woman answered, squinting through the screen door. PJ recognized her as one of the ladies who came into the diner maybe once every six months—Mrs. Grissom, if she recalled.

"Hello, I'm PJ Franks. I work at Cara Jo's Diner. I notice you have a garage apartment. Is it for rent?"

The woman's hand shook as she pushed the screen open to get a better look at PJ. "You're the waitress from the diner. I remember you."

"Yes, ma'am." PJ smiled.

"I'm sorry, but the apartment is already rented out to Bergman's grandson."

"Mr. Bergman, the hardware store owner?"

"That's him." The woman snorted. "Wouldn't have rented it to Ross, except I like his grandfather. Been wonderin' what he's been up to, but I don't get up those stairs often. The man has a bad attitude, and he's rude. Sheriff was by earlier lookin' for him. Probably up to no good."

"The sheriff?" PJ forced a smile, while her insides churned.

"Asked if I knew anything about Ross using computers or some such." The woman waved her hand. "I don't know anything about computers and, like I said, I haven't been up those stairs in a couple months."

All PJ heard was that the sheriff had been there looking for Ross with questions about computers. She sucked in a steadying breath and gave the old woman another smile to say that the world didn't hinge on Ross's computer abilities. "Oh, well, I hope it all works out with Mr. Bergman's grandson. And let me know if the apartment becomes available anytime soon. You know where to find me—at the diner."

"I sure do. Don't get there often, but I'll let you know." The old woman closed the screen door and the front door before PJ left the stoop.

Instead of going back to her car, PJ walked farther along the street until she was out of view of the windows from the upstairs apartment. Then she ducked between houses into the alleyway behind the buildings. A gate stood ajar, leading to the back of the garage apartment. Just inside the gate, a trash can stood against the fence. It was overflowing with garbage, and the lid was half-open.

With a quick glance at the staircase leading up the side of the garage, PJ carefully lifted the lid and poked around.

If Ross made a daily trek through the neighborhoods, maybe he had something to do with hijacking the Wi-Fi capability. He could be the one hacking into Hank's computers. Who would have thought a small-town kid would know so much about computers? But was he also the man who'd broken into her apartment, attacked her and scared her by stealing her baby monitor? He was the right size and build.

Maybe there was a clue in his trash. PJ dug around an old pizza box and several soda bottles. When she encountered a cardboard box with a picture of a video camera on it, just like the miniature cameras they'd found in the day care and in her apartment, her hand shook and she almost dropped the evidence.

"Oh, my God." Her gaze shot to the door above. Nothing moved. PJ flattened the cardboard box and slid it under her shirt, and then she lowered the trash can lid and stepped toward the gate.

As she slipped through, she cast a glance back at the apartment in time to see the door opening.

Her heart in her throat, PJ ducked behind the fence and crouched in case Ross could see over the top of the wooden slats. If she kept still, he wouldn't know she was there.

Footsteps sounded on the steps and crunched across the gravel toward her. This guy who'd potentially hacked Hank's database might also be the guy who'd attacked her in her apartment, plus the other time to get a cheek swab. He was strong enough to easily overpower her and finish her off.

PJ debated making a run for it but decided to stay put. What reason would Ross have to go out the back gate?

The lid to the trash can opened, and the sound of cardboard hitting gravel gave PJ a start.

A man's muttered curse sounded as if next to her.

PJ held her breath and prayed he'd leave soon so she could get the hell out of there without being spotted.

The gravel crunched on the other side of the fence, and footsteps moved away from her.

About to let go of the breath she'd been holding, PJ stopped dead still when the cell phone she'd jammed into her back pocket rang.

Without waiting to see if Ross had heard and come looking for the source, PJ made a run for it, away from her car.

"Hey!" someone shouted behind her.

She ducked between two houses. A dog barked, racing along the side of a chain-link fence as she ran by.

Her lungs burned with each breath she inhaled, and she thought she might pass out before she circled back to her car. PJ held on to the tattered remains of the video camera box and ran as fast as she could, telling herself she'd been a fool to risk her life when she had a baby at home to protect.

After rounding the corner by the next house, she dared to look back over her shoulder.

Nothing moved except the dog, still running back and forth along the fence.

PJ couldn't have heard pounding footsteps over the animal's barking and her own pulse in her ears. She dived behind a bush and squatted low to the ground, trying to catch her breath. After a while, the dog stopped barking and PJ dared to part the branches to peer out.

She couldn't see past the driveway, but she heard footsteps on pavement, running toward her from the other end of the house.

PJ cowered lower, her ragged breaths caught in her throat. Through the tiny window through the leaves, she saw Ross Felton running by.

He stopped in the middle of the street and spun in a 360-degree circle before jogging within a foot of the spot where she crouched, hidden by the bush.

The dog commenced barking, the sound moving away from her, back in the direction she'd just come from.

PJ crawled from behind the bush and edged close to the house. The dog was at the corner of his yard farthest away from PJ. Ross Felton was nowhere to be seen.

She inched back around the house and stood, brushed herself off and jogged back to her car, glancing over her shoulder every step of the way. Once she got into her car, cranked the engine and shifted into Drive, PJ finally allowed herself to breathe.

She wasn't cut out to be a spy, and she vowed never to do that again. After the scare with Ross, all she wanted to do was get home to Charlie.

When she pulled into the parking lot behind the resort, Chuck's truck was there and Dana's car was gone.

Great. Chuck would be mad she'd left the diner and even madder when he found out what she'd been doing. But damn it, he hadn't bothered to come fill her in on what was going on. He might be angry, but she had a bone to pick with him, as well.

Straightening her shoulders, she got out of the car and climbed the steps to her apartment.

Chuck opened the door before she could get her key in the lock.

With an excuse poised on her lips, she didn't get a chance to say anything before Chuck pulled her through the door and into his arms.

"Thank God you're home. I was worried when you didn't answer your phone."

Too late, PJ remembered the call that had triggered her headlong rush to get the hell away from Ross Felton's apartment. She would have laughed if she wasn't so busy kissing Chuck.

Her hands wound around the back of his neck, and she gave him her lips, hungry for contact with this big man who'd managed to turn her world inside out every time they were together.

When he finally set her at arm's length, he demanded, "Where have you been?"

PJ pulled the cardboard box out from beneath her shirt and handed it to Chuck. "Is this the same kind of video camera you found in the day care and here in my apartment?"

He took the box from her and frowned down at it. "Yes, it is. Where did you get it?"

"I found it in Ross Felton's trash can."

Chuck closed his eyes and drew in a deep breath. "How did you find out about Ross?"

PJ stepped out of his embrace. "Since no one bothered to call or let me know what was going on, I stopped by the sheriff's office. They told me someone had hacked the IP address. I just happened to drive down that street when I saw Ross Felton ducking through the houses."

Chuck gripped her arm with his empty hand. "Please tell me you didn't go to his apartment."

PJ shrugged. "Okay, I won't. But then I'd have a tough time explaining how I got this." She tapped the box he still held. "Don't worry. It wasn't in his apartment. I found it in his trash outside." She didn't tell him that Ross had almost caught her, or that she'd had to run from him to get away. Since the incident had ended well, that little bit of information was not necessary.

Chuck let go of her and ran his hand through his hair. "Woman, you have no idea how badly I want to shake you."

PJ grinned. "Don't worry. That's not something I'll ever do again. I'll leave spying up to the professionals." She looked around him. "Where's Charlie?"

"Napping in her crib. Dana left fifteen minutes ago. I need you to pack a bag."

"Why?" PJ stared up into his face.

The lines across his forehead and around his eyes seemed deeper.

"I'll explain when we're safely on the road to Hank's."

"I take it we're staying the night there," she stated.

"Right." Chuck refused to tell her anything more until they were in his truck and on their way out to the Raging Bull Ranch.

When he did fill her in on the blackmail note, PJ sat back against her seat and shook her head. "You think it's Ross who sent that note?"

"I'd say whoever it is might be getting desperate. With the sheriff looking for him and Hank's computer guy getting closer to tracking his hacking trail, he's running out of options."

"Why not just ignore the threat? So what if he tells the drug lords anything? Hell, we still don't know who my father is. Why would they care? How could his threat make things any worse than they already are?"

Chuck's fingers tightened on the steering wheel. "Because they can. The Mexican cartels have a far-reaching influence. If they decide you're a worthy target…"

"Great." PJ stared out the window at the road in front of her. The sun shone through the side window on its slow descent to the horizon. "Chuck, I don't know about you, but I'm tired of this."

AFTER A DELICIOUS dinner Hank's housekeeper had prepared but that PJ had barely touched, she fed Charlie and rocked her to sleep.

When she had Charlie settled in the crib in the bedroom she'd used the last time she'd stayed at Hank's, PJ headed back to the living room for answers.

Chuck and Hank stood by the window, staring out at the stars.

"Now that Charlie is asleep, perhaps you two could tell me why someone thinks he can blackmail Hank to keep from telling the drug lords who I am? Why is it a big deal? I'm just PJ Franks, not a celebrity, secret princess or someone special."

Hank faced her, a hint of a smile turning his lips upward. "You're special to me."

"No offense, Hank. But we barely know each other." PJ shoved her hands into her jeans pockets. "Does your blackmailer think this Mexican Mafia man will come after me? After all these years?" She shook her head. "It's hardly likely."

"Are you so confident that you'd stake Charlie's life on that?"

PJ's lips clamped shut, and she fought the urge to run to the bedroom where Charlie was sleeping, just to verify the baby was still there. "No. But it's insane to think a man can carry a grudge for that long." Her gaze slipped to Chuck in time to see him flinch. Perhaps her statement had hit too close to home in the case of his grudge with his own father.

"Still, PJ," Hank said, "I feel better knowing you're safe under my roof for the time being."

"I can't live here forever." PJ sighed. "I have a job and school."

"You have Charlie's safety and well-being to consider," Chuck argued.

"And I want to be able to support her and set a good example for her to follow by holding down a job and furthering my education. I can't run scared for an extended period of time. If we think Ross was the hacker, why hasn't the sheriff hauled him in for questioning?"

Hank shook his head. "They haven't caught up to him yet."

PJ's jaw tightened. "I should have called the sheriff instead of running," she muttered.

Chuck frowned. "What was that?"

She glanced up with a fake smile. "Nothing."

His frown deepened, but he didn't dig further.

PJ blew out a breath, thankful for the reprieve. She'd had enough drama for the day without explaining the wild chase scene to Chuck and Hank.

Running footsteps sounded on the Saltillo tiles. Brandon skidded around the door frame into the living room, waving a computer tablet. "Got something you might be interested in," he said, breathing hard.

Hank frowned. "What is it?"

Brandon pressed the screen and handed the tablet to Hank. "Emilio Montalvo was spotted going through a border checkpoint under an assumed name and passport."

Chuck and PJ crossed the floor to where Hank stood and leaned over his shoulder, studying the photo. It was a grainy likeness of a Hispanic man wearing a business suit.

A twinge of recognition flitted across PJ's consciousness,

but she couldn't put her finger on who Emilio reminded her of. "I take it Montalvo means bad news."

"The worst. Emilio Montalvo is a Mafia drug lord." Hank sucked in a breath. "He's my nemesis, and the man I mentioned who'd obsessed over PJ's mother."

The blood rushed from PJ's head, and she swayed where she was standing. "This Montalvo guy...could he be my father?"

Chapter Fifteen

Chuck stared across at PJ, whose face had gone completely white. He hurried over to her and slipped his arm around her waist, steadying her.

"Are you sure?" PJ shook her head. "Can't tell much from that photo."

Brandon reached between PJ and Chuck. "May I?"

Hank handed him the tablet, and Brandon tapped the screen several times and then handed it back to Hank. "That's the most current photo the DEA has on Montalvo."

The photo displayed a dark-haired, even darker-eyed Hispanic man, perhaps in his late forties or early fifties, with gray peppering his hair in natural streaks. He wore a light gray business suit and was standing in front of a building in what looked like a crowded business section of a city.

"That photo was taken two years ago in Mexico City," Brandon said. "Montalvo is influential in the government, having paid off every top official, and he has command of the largest cartel in all of Mexico. He's said to have amassed a fortune to rival Gates."

"That's my legacy?" PJ snorted. "A rich thug?" She shoved a hand through her hair, a smile hovering on her lips. "I don't know whether to laugh or cry."

"I wouldn't laugh." Hank stared across at PJ. "With that

kind of money at his disposal, he can do just about anything he pleases or hire someone who can."

"You're not saying it, but I take it he could hire men to kill or kidnap me or Charlie."

"That and more. He can afford to hire an entire army if he wanted to."

"And he has. He funds the cartel activities along the border, and he has links in Puerto Rico, Dominican Republic, Cuba and along the entire East Coast of the U.S. He can smuggle any amount of drugs through his fronts, and all the government organizations in the U.S. arsenal haven't been able to stop him."

PJ leaned closer. "He looks familiar."

"If he is your father, you look nothing like him," Chuck said.

Where Montalvo had bushy black eyebrows and thick wavy black hair turning gray around the temples, PJ's was a light, sandy blond, straight and fine.

PJ touched her hair. "I look like my mother." She cast a glance at Chuck. "You saw the photo before it was stolen."

Chuck nodded. "You're as beautiful as she was."

PJ's gaze locked with his.

For a long moment, they might as well have been the only two people in the room. Chuck could practically feel the strength of PJ's emotions at the mention of her mother and the lost photo. He wanted to take her into his arms and hold her until that hurt look disappeared from her face.

"Any news on which way Montalvo is headed?" Chuck asked, knowing the answer but hopeful that he was wrong.

Brandon shook his head. "No, but we do have an image taken at the border of the vehicle he's traveling in. It's a full-size black SUV with heavily tinted windows and a Mexican license plate."

Hank handed the tablet to PJ and turned to Brandon. "Send that information to the sheriff's department. Ask Deputy Owen to put out a general alert to be on the lookout for the vehicle and to notify me if they spot it in or around Wild Oak Canyon."

PJ stared at the man in the photograph.

Chuck pulled her against him. "Don't worry. I'm here for you and Charlie."

She leaned into his body, resting her head against his chest. "Thanks." PJ continued to stare at the picture as if memorizing the man's features. "I can see how my mother might have fallen for him. He's not bad-looking. In fact, he's rather handsome. I could swear I've seen him before."

Chuck's hand tightened around her hip. "I had the same feeling."

She laughed. "To think, I always wanted a father. And now I might actually come face-to-face with him." She glanced across at Hank.

Hank stood with his hands in his pockets. "Not the best introduction to a man you didn't even know existed. Either way the DNA falls, huh?" He sighed. "I'm sorry, PJ. If I could undo the past, I would."

PJ smiled at him. "It's not your fault. Look how much you've done already, and I might not even be your daughter." She rubbed her arms. "I'll be glad to get the DNA results to settle the matter once and for all."

"I almost don't want to know." Hank sighed. "I like thinking you're my daughter. If the results come back that you aren't…"

Chuck could only imagine what it was like to be PJ, torn between wanting to know who her father was and fear of disappointment if he turned out to be a murdering drug lord.

Chuck's father hadn't been around much, but he'd made his mark on Chuck and his brother by his example. If not for the disagreement over Chuck's school choice, he could have claimed a normal childhood, filled with good moments as well as some not so good. He could still remember playing catch with the football when his father was home from deployments or overseas temporary-duty assignments.

On rare occasions, they'd gone camping as a family, his father teaching him and his brother how to start a fire without matches, how to make a shelter from limbs and branches and how to fish in a creek without a pole or hook. He'd treasured those moments. They'd made him the self-reliant man he was today.

PJ didn't have memories of her father and barely any of her mother.

Chuck's jaw tightened with his resolve to give Charlie memories she'd cherish. To be around for all those moments when a young girl needs a man to lean on.

"Any word on Ross Felton?" PJ asked. "Did the sheriff pull him in for questioning?"

Hank shook his head. "I called half an hour ago. Still nothing. They obtained a search warrant on his apartment. Apparently, he got wind of it and cleaned out his computers and files and ran with them."

"I guess there's not much more we can do then." PJ stepped away.

Chuck already missed the warmth of her body against his. "Might as well get some rest."

PJ nodded, her gaze locking with his.

Chuck couldn't read into her thoughts, whether she wanted him with her that night or not. He let her go to her room without him.

"She's very brave to have gone to Ross's apartment alone," Hank commented after PJ left.

"I can't believe she did. Alone." Chuck shoved a hand through his hair and paced the length of the living room. "I don't know if I can provide the protection she needs. The woman has a mind of her own."

Hank chuckled. "That she does. Much like her mother.

Leaving a man of such influence in her country had to take a will of iron. To this day, I don't know how I let Alana go."

Chuck's gaze strayed to the hallway PJ had disappeared down. "I don't know how you let her go, either." He straightened his shoulders and steeled his resolve. "I'm not going to let go of PJ without a fight."

"I'm glad to hear that. You two belong together."

"I agree." Chuck cast a glance at Hank. "If you'll excuse me, I need to go convince *her*."

Hank's chuckle echoed behind him as Chuck strode down the hallway to PJ's room. He knocked and then pushed the door open. "PJ, we need to talk—"

"Okay, close the door and we'll talk." PJ stood by the bed, stripped her clothes off and held a soft white T-shirt against her front, covering little of her nakedness. "Well?"

"Sorry." Heat burned a path from Chuck's groin up his body into his cheeks. "I could just wait outside until you're finished."

PJ shook her head, tossed the T-shirt onto the bed and advanced across the floor. "Don't go."

Chuck couldn't move. His feet felt glued to the floor, his gaze on the woman who'd stolen his heart more than three years ago.

Her body glowed in the soft light from the bedside lamp, her skin like pale cream, her curves fuller than before she'd had Charlie.

Chuck's gut clenched, his groin tightened and he finally stepped out of the doorway, closed it firmly behind him and twisted the lock. Then he gathered PJ in his arms, his hands sliding over her shoulders and along her sides, skimming the narrow arch of her waist to the flare of her hips. When he reached her thighs, he scooped her up, wrapping her legs around his waist.

"What was it you were saying about talking?" She cupped his face and lowered her lips to his.

"We need to…" Chuck couldn't wrap his mind around coherent thoughts when she was naked, her bare breasts pressing against his chest.

"Yes." Her lips claimed his in an urgent summons. "We do."

He carried her to the bed and laid her among the sheets, and then he straightened to feast his senses on PJ, his heart pounding against his ribs, his blood burning like fire through his veins.

Her long sandy-blond hair splayed out in a fan around her head. Her cheeks flushed a rosy pink, and she reached out. "Hurry."

Chuck ripped his shirt over his head, shucked his boots and jeans and moved between her legs. "You're even more beautiful than I remembered."

"Enough talk. I want you inside me. Now."

When he didn't move immediately, she frowned and sat up, her legs dangling over the side of the mattress. PJ wrapped her arms around his waist, and she kissed his belly. "Don't you want me?"

"You have no idea how badly I want you." Chuck disengaged her arms from around his waist and dropped to his knees in front of her. "But I want you to want me as badly."

"I don't think that will be a problem." She feathered her fingers through his hair and sighed. "What are we going to do about us?"

"This, for starters." He pressed his lips to the inside of her thigh.

"Mmm." PJ's fingers tugged at his hair. "Good start, cowboy."

"That's just the beginning." He licked and nipped a path, slowly moving toward her core.

As he touched his tongue to her center, PJ fell back against the bed, her fingers convulsing in the sheets, her back arching off the mattress. "Oh, please," she begged.

Chuck's chest rumbled with a chuckle he couldn't contain. His mouth left her briefly as a surge of passion fueled the joy he felt in that moment.

She half rose from the bed. "For Pete's sake, don't stop now," she moaned.

Bending to the task, he parted her folds and flicked that nubbin in the middle.

Her body grew rigid with each touch.

Lust powered through him, urging him to rise and take her, to drive deep inside her warm, wet channel. Chuck resisted, knowing PJ was close. He wanted her to feel everything as intensely as he did when he finally thrust into her. With a tenuous grip on his own excitement, he stroked and coaxed until her body grew rigid and her heels dug into his shoulders.

Chuck pushed to his feet and wrapped PJ's legs around his waist, thrusting deeply into her warmth.

Rocked by the force of their passion, PJ tightened her legs around Chuck, urging him to pump faster, to drive deeper and fill all the emptiness she'd endured for the past year. As they catapulted over the edge together, she knew in that startlingly clear instant that she could not send this man away ever again. She needed him in her life. He made her feel complete.

As she drifted back to earth in a warm haze of contentment, she guided him up beside her on the bed, refusing to lose their intimate connection.

With so many thoughts in her head swirling around, needing to be voiced, she couldn't think past Chuck's arms around her, holding her close, or his body enveloping hers in his strength.

The craziness of the day faded in the security of Chuck's arms, and PJ slipped into a deep sleep, nestled against the broad expanse of his chest. They could talk in the morning. First thing.

In the darkness of the night, Chuck stirred beside her, slipping from the bed. He drew the blanket up around her shoulders and pressed a kiss to her forehead.

PJ's eyes opened. "Where are you going?"

"I need to check on something."

"I'll come with you."

"I shouldn't be long. You need your sleep. Charlie will be waking early and needing her mother."

"Don't go far. I need you, too." PJ drifted back into a deep sleep, dreaming of a house with a picket fence and a yard that Charlie could play in.

Chuck strode through the gate, a cowboy hat tipped forward, that sexy swagger making PJ's heart stutter.

CHUCK STEPPED INTO his jeans and slipped into the hallway, carrying his shirt and boots. He met Hank in the living room.

"I'm sorry to wake you at this hour, but the sheriff's department called. They spotted two dark SUVs meeting the description Brandon sent them."

"Did they stop them?"

"They don't have any probable cause."

Frustration burned in Chuck's gut. "What can we do?"

"Nothing for now. I thought you'd want to know."

Chuck nodded. "All the more reason to stay close to PJ."

"Right. I've notified my security team, as well."

"Sheriff have anything on Ross?"

"Nothing. He seems to have made a clean getaway. Oh, and Mrs. Grissom told them Ross owns a black motorcycle."

Chuck's lips tightened. He hated inaction.

Hank tipped his head toward the door. "You might as well get some sleep. The night shift is competent, and the security cameras are back online."

"Thanks for letting me know."

"Just take care of PJ and Charlie."

Chuck returned to the bedroom, removed his boots and shirt and lay down on top of the covers beside PJ.

She turned toward him and snuggled against him, her hand resting on his chest, her eyes closed in sleep.

What Chuck wouldn't give to freeze this moment in time, to always be with PJ and Charlie. They had so much to talk about.

He lay for a long time staring up at the ceiling, planning what he'd say to PJ when she woke. He'd tell her he never stopped loving her and that they belonged together. Whatever she wanted from him, he'd give. If she wanted him to stay in Wild Oak Canyon and take a job that kept him close to home, so be it. He wanted to be a husband and father, to build a life for the three of them.

And after seven long years, he'd do something about the rift in his own family. Seven years was a long time to hold a grudge. He and his father had had more good times than bad. That should count for something. All that was needed was someone to take the first step.

The more he thought about it, the more excited he became about seeing his brother, sister, mother and even his dad.

Morning couldn't come soon enough.

He must have drifted off to sleep somewhere around two in the morning.

The next thing he knew, an enormous boom rocked the bed and threw him onto the floor.

with one of Hank's security guards. Who he trusts outside the bedroom door. He's going to watch out for you two while I'm gone. Will it make you feel any better to have him in the hallway when I leave?" he murmured into her hair. He inhaled the scent of her freshly washed hair and the French milled soap.

She nodded into his chest.

PJ hugged Charlie and kissed the top of her sleepy head. She'd kiss the tar out of her mom and let Charlie sleep all while trusting in the world to do anything.

Chapter Sixteen

Her ears ringing, PJ jerked upright in the bed. "Chuck?"

A groan sounded from the other side, and she heard a muttered, "What the hell?"

"Chuck?" PJ scrambled to her feet, wrapping a sheet around her naked body. She swayed, blinking the sleep from her eyes. "What was that?"

"I don't know." He rose to his feet. "Stay put until I figure it out." Chuck jammed his boots on his feet and threw open the French doors.

Charlie whimpered in her crib. PJ gathered her in her arms and followed Chuck to the door.

Outside, the night sky was lit up like daylight, a two-story blaze ripping toward the sky from where one of the outbuildings had once stood.

"Damn." Chuck faced PJ. "You should be all right in the house, but that fire is getting really close to the barn and horses."

"Go. Get those horses out before they burn." She glanced at Charlie and back to Chuck. "We'll be okay. I'll keep watch in case the fire spreads."

Chuck cupped her cheeks between his palms and kissed her. "I'll be back as soon as possible."

She smiled and kissed him back. "I know."

Before he left, he ran down the hallway and returned

with one of Hank's security guards, who he posted outside the bedroom door. "He's going to watch out for you two while I'm outside. Yell if you need him. And try not to give him any trouble." Chuck winked, kissed her again and took off toward the barn, where several more of Hank's security guards and his foreman had converged.

Charlie turned her face toward PJ.

PJ laughed. "The world's on fire and you're hungry." She pulled the sheet off her breast and let Charlie nurse, all the while feeling as if she could be doing more.

PJ reminded herself that Charlie's well-being was her sole responsibility.

When Charlie had nursed for several minutes, she slipped back into a deep sleep, tummy full, cheeks still moving in a sucking motion.

PJ leaned her over her shoulder and patted a burp out of her before laying her back in her crib and hurrying to dress in case they had to leave quickly. She flipped the light switch on the wall, and nothing happened.

Apparently the explosion had knocked the electricity out. PJ moved around in the dark, rescuing her clothes from the floor where they'd fallen earlier that night.

After dressing, she stood staring out the windows of the French door, the scent of smoke seeping through the cracks every time the wind shifted. If it got much worse, she'd have to move Charlie deeper into the house.

A shout rose from one of the men racing around the barnyard. Flames rose from his arm where his shirt had caught fire.

PJ's breath caught. She pushed the French door open and stepped out onto the porch, debating whether she should help or stay put. Silhouetted against the inferno of the burning outbuilding, the man's face was hidden in dark shadows.

For all PJ knew, it could be Chuck.

She ran along the porch and down the steps toward the

barnyard. Before she reached the bottom, another man emerged from the smoke, tackled the burning man and smothered the flames.

PJ waited until the men on the ground both stood, and then she released the breath she'd been holding.

When she turned back toward the house, she frowned.

She could have sworn she'd left the French door to her bedroom open.

Perhaps the wind had blown it closed. Only the wind wasn't blowing at that moment.

PJ hurried back to the door and reached for the knob.

It wouldn't turn.

She twisted it harder. Still it wouldn't open. Her heart hammering against her chest, the flames rising higher behind her, PJ panicked and ran for the front of the ranch house.

The enormous double doors stood open, the interior cast in shadows. With the electricity out, PJ could only feel her way across the foyer, dependent on the light edging through some of the windows from the fire outside.

Her pulse pounding against her eardrums, she fought to remember how many doors had been before hers on the long, dark hallway. She counted two and flung open the third. The fire's blaze lit up the room through the open curtains. It wasn't the right one.

She backed into the hallway and moved to the next room. When she tried the door, it was locked. Too late, she remembered Chuck locking it the night before. Back down the hallway, she ran out onto the deck. Charlie was alone in the locked room. If the fire spread to the house…

PJ couldn't bear thinking about the consequences. She might not have the strength to open a locked wooden door, but she sure as hell could break a window in the French door.

Back around the side of the house, she ran, arriving in front of the French door. She leaned back and jammed her heel into the glass near the door handle.

It cracked but held.

Again, she kicked the glass. This time it broke, the shards falling inside. Careful not to cut herself, she stuck her hand through the broken glass, unlocked the French door and ran inside. "Charlie, baby, Mommy's back."

She hurried to the crib and bent over to gather her daughter into her arms.

Only Charlie wasn't there.

A plain white envelope lay against the crib sheet, barely visible in the light streaming through the open French door.

Her heart thudding against her ribs, PJ snatched the envelope from the sheet and ripped it open. She read the words by the light of the fire's blaze:

If you want to see your baby again, be at the barn on the old Frisco Ranch at 3:00 a.m. Come alone and tell no one. If you bring anyone with you, your baby will disappear forever.

Tears spilled onto the paper, blurring the ink. PJ's first instinct was to run to Chuck and beg him to help her get her daughter back.

How could she get to the barn when her car was back at her apartment? She didn't have Chuck's truck keys, and she couldn't ask Hank's employees to give her a lift without raising questions.

She grabbed her purse, pulled out her cell phone and clicked it on. The clock indicated she had less than an hour to get where she needed to be. She was vaguely familiar with the location of the Frisco Ranch. It had been abandoned three years earlier when the old man who'd owned it died and his relatives had put it up for sale. No one had lived there since, as far as PJ knew.

If she could get to her apartment, she had the nine-millimeter pistol in her closet, the one she'd inherited from her adoptive mother when she'd passed.

She could call Dana for a ride, but Dana would ask too many questions PJ couldn't answer. And Dana wouldn't let her go alone to find Charlie. PJ wouldn't want her to follow because that would place her in danger, as well. No, she needed a taxi, someone who wouldn't ask questions, just pick her up and take her back to her apartment. Unfortunately, Wild Oak Canyon was fresh out of taxis, and her time was running out with each passing minute.

Then she remembered the card Señor Iglesias had insisted she take should she ever need anything. PJ had slipped it into her wallet and forgotten about it until now. Was he still at the resort? Would he pick up a call at this hour and take her back to the resort where she could collect her car?

PJ yanked her wallet from her purse, found the card and, using the light from the display screen of her phone, keyed in the number. She held her breath, praying for enough reception for the call to go through.

After a long, agonizing few seconds, the phone rang. And rang again.

After the fifth ring, PJ's hands trembled and she was on the verge of tears.

"Hola," a gravelly voice said.

"Oh, thank God," PJ breathed into the phone. "Mr. Iglesias, this is PJ Franks."

"Señorita Franks, *por favor,* what is wrong?"

Her voice shook. "I need a huge favor."

"Anything. You have but to ask."

Minutes later, PJ was racing down the long driveway toward the highway.

Sirens screamed in the distance, headed toward the Raging Bull Ranch.

PJ reached the highway and turned toward town, running until she got a stitch in her side.

The sirens were getting closer. PJ couldn't risk someone noticing her and trying to stop her from getting to her rendezvous. She ducked into the ditch and lay flat on the ground until first a paramedic truck raced by, and then a fire engine. All the while she lay against the dry Texas soil, she prayed for Charlie and Chuck and that there weren't any snakes or scorpions on the ground around her.

Once the rescue vehicles sped by, PJ was up and running again toward town. A lone set of headlights blinked into view. By the time the vehicle pulled up next to her on the highway, PJ couldn't take another step.

The window slid down and Señor Iglesias's kind face gazed out in concern. "Señorita Franks." He shifted into Park.

"Don't get out," PJ gasped between breaths. She ran around to the passenger seat and climbed in. "I need to get to my apartment as fast as you can go."

"What is going on?" His gaze rose to the sky lit up by the raging fire.

"A building exploded. Please, I need you to take me back to my apartment at the resort. Now."

"Sí." He turned the sleek black sedan in the middle of the road, bumping along the shoulder until he was aimed in the opposite direction. Once he had the vehicle straight, he pressed his foot to the floorboard, shooting them forward.

His hands gripped the steering wheel in a knuckle-white grip. "Perhaps you can tell me why we must break the speed laws?"

"I'm sorry, but no." She sat against the other side of the car, her thoughts on Charlie and what her baby was going through. She wouldn't understand what was happening. She wouldn't recognize her abductor. If she cried, would the kidnapper hurt her? PJ's heart squeezed so hard she could barely breathe. Now that she wasn't running, she had too much time to think.

"You are obviously distressed." The old man shot several glances at her, quick to return his attention to the road, which was speeding by at an alarming rate. "Is there any-thing I can do to help?"

"No." Her voice caught on a sob. She swallowed hard. "I just need to get to my apartment."

He sat quietly, concentrating on the road. When they neared town, he slowed.

PJ chewed the inside of her mouth to keep from urging him to go faster. They couldn't afford to be stopped by the law. She didn't have time to waste. She checked her cell phone. Less than thirty minutes remained.

Her stomach clenched as they neared the resort. "Please, drop me here."

Before he pulled to a complete stop at the corner of the diner, PJ flung open her door and jumped out. "Thank you, Señor Iglesias," she called out as she sprinted for the back of the building, clutching her keys in her hand. The motion-sensing lights blinked on, illuminating her way to the stairs. She ran up them two at a time, jamming the key into the lock when she reached the door.

She headed for the closet, pulling the ladies' shoe box down from the top shelf. The nine-millimeter pistol lay wrapped in a baby-blue winter scarf with a box of bullets beside it. She grabbed both, expelled the clip onto her bed and loaded it with bullets, fumbling twice, dropping ammu-nition on the coverlet.

When she had the clip full, she jammed it into the weapon, grabbed her keys and ran for the door.

Once in her car, she checked the time on her dash. Fif-teen minutes to get there. She didn't have time for stop signs or speed limits. PJ flew through town, heading north on a farm-to-market road. She knew where the Frisco Ranch was only because she and her adopted mother, Terri Franks, had visited the old man when he'd been sick. That had been years ago. In the dark, with only the stars and a general idea to guide her, PJ was at a disadvantage. Several times she screeched to a halt—to peer through the gloom at a rickety gate, to read the name on an old mailbox and to hesitate at a faded dirt road leading off the highway. When she'd about given up hope, her headlights glanced off a wooden gate with the faded lettering written across the arch listing to the east: Frisco Ranch.

PJ swallowed the sob rising up her throat and turned onto the rutted road. Tire tracks pressed into the dust, indicating someone else had arrived before her.

"Charlie."

PJ pressed the accelerator, shooting the vehicle forward. Her little car bumped along, spewing a cloud of dust behind it, hitting bottom several times on the high center between the ruts.

Finally the old cabin came into view. PJ passed it by, heading straight for the rustic barn behind.

She almost cried when she didn't see any vehicles in front of the weathered building. PJ jammed the gun into the back of her pants and climbed out of the car, leaving the engine running and the headlights shining at the building.

"I'm here and I'm alone," she called out. "Where's my baby?"

Her voice echoed in the night sky.

For a long moment, nothing stirred and no one moved or came out from the shadows.

"Please," PJ sobbed. "Please don't hurt her."

"Shut up. No one's gonna hurt anyone." Ross Felton pushed the barn door open and stepped out, carrying a gun.

PJ peered around him, trying to see into the barn. She stepped forward.

Ross raised the pistol. "Stay where you are."

"Where's Charlie?"

"In the barn. She'll be fine as long as you do exactly as I say."

"Anything, just don't hurt my baby." PJ wrung her hands,

wanting to pull out the gun and shoot the bastard for taking her baby, but afraid he'd do something to hurt Charlie if PJ missed. "What do you want?"

"I want you to shut up." He glanced over her shoulder. "Good, their timing is right on."

PJ looked behind her to see two pairs of headlights pulling into the barnyard.

Black SUVs parked beside her little car, and rough-looking men in dark clothing stepped down. One of them came forward. He had a scar across his face and tattoos across his arms and neck. He grabbed her from behind and pulled the gun from her waistband, and then he spun her away. He laughed and waved the gun at the others, speaking in rapid-fire Spanish.

The other men laughed.

PJ straightened, pushing back her fear. Charlie needed her to keep a level head and get the two of them out of this mess. "What do you want with me?"

The laughter died away, and another man stepped out from behind one of the SUVs.

PJ's breath caught. It was the man from the picture Brandon had shown her earlier. Emilio Montalvo.

"I wish to know my daughter and granddaughter," he said in heavily accented English.

With her heart plummeting, PJ held her head high. "And who might that be?" she stalled, afraid he knew more than she did about her lineage. Dear Lord, she wasn't ready to accept the truth.

His brows rose, and the corners of his mouth turned up. "You, *hija.*"

Lead hit the pit of her belly, and she fought to keep a poker face. "I don't know what you're talking about."

Emilio nodded to Ross. "Tell her."

Ross licked his lips, his gaze darting between Emilio and PJ. "Your DNA results came back a match with his."

PJ's eyes narrowed, and she focused her anger on Ross. "You're the bastard who tied me up and left me behind the trash can."

Ross shrugged. "I needed the sample and didn't figure you'd give it willingly."

"So you've established who my biological father is. So what?" PJ crossed her arms over her chest to keep her hands from visibly shaking. "That means nothing to me."

"On the contrary. It means you are a Montalvo. You belong in Mexico with your family."

"My family is here. I'm not going anywhere."

"Oh, we will take your baby, as well. After all, she is a Montalvo, as well."

PJ was already shaking her head. "No."

Emilio's eyes darkened, and his brows dipped low. He stepped up to her and stared down his nose at her. "You deny your heritage?"

"I told you, my home is here. I'm not going anywhere with you."

His hand shot out, and he slapped her face so hard, she fell to the ground.

PJ's hand rose to her mouth where warm, red blood trickled from her lip onto her fingers. She pushed to her feet. "This is how you treat family? I understand why my mother ran away from you."

"Madre de Dios," he gritted out. He raised his hand to strike again.

PJ held her ground, refusing to back down from the man.

"No mas!" a voice cried out behind Emilio.

PJ glanced over Emilio's shoulder to the man standing at the edge of the shadows, holding a gun pointed at her biological father.

"Señor Iglesias?" PJ shook her head, regret burning a hole in her gut. The man had followed her and now faced a firing squad of cartel members.

"Hit her again," Iglesias said in English, "and I will kill you."

Emilio laughed. "You do not have the stomach to kill your own son."

PJ stared at the older man, her jaw slack. "Son?"

Emilio turned back to PJ. "Ah, I see you have already met your grandfather."

ONCE THE FIRE trucks arrived, Chuck pulled away from the blaze and trudged back to the house to check on PJ and Charlie.

Before he reached the porch, Brandon raced up beside him. "Where's Hank?"

"With the fire chief." Chuck stopped in front of the younger man. "Why?"

"I know who did it. I know who set the explosion."

"Who?" He gripped Brandon's arms. "Who did this?"

"Ross Felton." He grinned. "Once I got the electricity on and the video monitoring system back online, I checked the last feed before the system went down to see if I could track what had happened. I noticed someone sneaking up on the corner of the outbuilding that exploded."

Chuck climbed the steps, pushing past Brandon. If Ross Felton had been on the Raging Bull Ranch…

As he crossed the decking, all the air left Chuck's lungs.

The glass in the French doors to the bedroom he'd shared with PJ was broken, and the door stood open.

Brandon followed. "Why is the door broken?"

Only half listening, Chuck entered the bedroom, crunching across shards of glass. "PJ?" The lights were on, but no one stirred in the room.

He hurried across to the crib and stared down, knowing before he saw it with his own eyes that Charlie wouldn't be there. Instinct told him they were gone, but he had to know for sure. "PJ?" he yelled, throwing open the door to the rest of the house. The guard he'd posted lay crumpled against the wall, a knot forming on his head. He checked for a pulse. "Call 9-1-1 and get this man some help."

"Will do," Brandon said.

Chuck raced along the corridors, searching each bedroom, the living room and the kitchen on the off chance she'd gone for a bite to eat, even though it didn't explain the broken glass or the unconscious guard.

"Mr. Bolton." Brandon emerged from the bedroom. "I found this." He held out a crumpled note. "It was on the floor beside the crib."

Chuck snatched the paper from his hands and read, the blood rushing out of his head, his hand tightening on the note until his knuckles turned white. Then he fisted the paper and threw it. "Get Hank. Now!"

Brandon ran for the door. He was back in less than a minute.

Chuck had returned to the bedroom to gather his gun and ammo. "I'm going after them."

"I'm coming with you," Hank said. "I've already put a call out for the other agents. They will meet us there. If we leave now, we can be there in thirty minutes."

"Thirty minutes is fifteen minutes after PJ was supposed to meet Felton at the barn. We might be too late."

"I'd suggest taking the helicopter, but we don't know if it was damaged in the explosion."

"We're wasting time." Chuck charged for the door.

Hank followed, shouting orders to his security guards. "In twenty minutes, notify the police. No sooner. If they get there before us, no telling what Felton will do. We can't risk PJ and Charlie's lives."

"Assuming Felton's our only problem." Chuck reached his truck first, leaping into the driver's seat. He shifted into Reverse a little harder than he should have, jamming his foot to the accelerator.

Hank pulled his seat belt across his chest and snapped it in place. "They'll be okay."

Chuck's jaw tightened. "I promised I'd take care of them."

"And you will," Hank reassured him.

Yeah, Chuck thought. *If we aren't already too late.*

Chapter Seventeen

PJ inched to the side, hoping to get out of the line of fire from Señor Iglesias's gun. If Emilio refused to back down, it would get ugly.

As soon as she moved, Emilio reached out and snagged her arm, yanking her in front of him. He jammed the barrel of a pistol into her temple. "You will have to shoot us both."

"Let her go, Emilio." Señor Iglesias stared from Emilio to PJ and back. "I am an excellent marksman."

"Por favor." Emilio stood still, calling the old man's bluff. "Gamble on your skills."

"Why would you kill her?"

"He took my Alana. Hank Derringer stole her from me. I will finally make him pay."

PJ's gaze caught a movement to her right. One of Emilio's goons had raised his weapon and was aiming it at Señor Iglesias. If PJ didn't do something quickly, he'd be shot.

She sucked in a breath, pulled her arm up to her chest and jammed it backward into Emilio's gut, ducking as soon as his arm loosened around her. "Run, Señor Iglesias!" she cried out and threw herself to the ground.

A shot rang out.

PJ scrambled to get her feet under her, but not fast enough.

Emilio grabbed her hair and dragged PJ to her knees. "You should not have done that, *hija*. Look what you have done." He jerked her head around. "You cost my father his life."

A sob rose up PJ's throat.

Lying on the ground in a pool of blood was Señor Iglesias.

"And so that you know, his name was Ricardo Iglesias *Montalvo*." Emilio flung her away from him. He nodded toward his men and spoke in Spanish.

With PJ's limited understanding of the language, she caught only a word or two. Something about *child* and *woman*. Two men moved toward the barn.

Ross Felton stood at the door. "You don't get the baby until I get my money."

Emilio snorted. "I will pay you when I get both the woman and the child."

"And I told you I wouldn't let you have both until I get paid."

Emilio's lip curled into a snarl, the look so evil it made PJ's gut clench and a chill slither down her spine.

In the blink of an eye, Emilio raised his gun and shot Ross through the heart.

The stunned look on Ross's face would have been comical had he not dropped to his knees in the next second, falling to his face in the dirt.

"No!" PJ lurched to her feet and ran for the barn. "Leave my baby alone!" she cried.

One man grabbed her as she tried to duck past him.

PJ was no match for his size and strength.

He jerked her arms behind her and held her effortlessly at arm's length while the other man entered the barn.

A few seconds later, PJ heard a curse.

The man emerged with a baby blanket and a child's doll. He threw them to the ground at Emilio's feet.

Emilio spoke to him in Spanish. Three men entered the barn.

PJ held her breath. Where was Charlie? Ross was the

only one who had that answer, and he was dead. Her heart skipped several beats as a dozen different scenarios flitted through her head, each with a worse outcome than the last.

When the men emerged empty-handed, Emilio roared, crossed to Ross and kicked his lifeless body. He yelled at the men, "Look again!"

PJ positioned herself to run. If the men were occupied searching for Charlie, she could escape and come back to find the baby with some help. Assuming she could get back to town on foot without being spotted by Emilio and his gang. In the meantime, anything could happen to Charlie. If she was lying somewhere in the dark, an animal could hurt her; a snakebite would kill her.

She couldn't leave, not without Charlie.

Emilio returned to PJ and jerked her to her feet. "Where is the baby?"

PJ shook her head, convinced Charlie was better off lost than in the hands of these terrorists. "I don't know."

Emilio backhanded her.

This time PJ was ready. She ducked, the blow glancing off the side of her head. Just as quickly as he hit her, PJ kicked him hard in the groin.

The man doubled over and fell to the ground, his hand angling upward, the gun pointed at PJ.

PJ kicked again, sending the gun flying into the brush. Then she ran, knowing if she stayed, Emilio would kill her, daughter or not.

She made it two steps before Emilio grabbed her ankle.

PJ toppled to the ground, hitting her head so hard that her vision blurred and she teetered on the edge of passing out, gray fog creeping in around her.

Emilio crawled up her body, grabbed her hair and jerked her head back. "You will pay for that, *hija*."

A shot pierced the night.

Emilio jerked backward, his hand still wrapped around PJ's hair, flinging her with him.

PJ landed on her side, pain shooting through her temples. Blackness engulfed her, pulling her down into an abyss so deep, she could no longer resist.

"Charlie," she whispered as the darkness claimed her.

"I THINK SHE'S coming around." Katie's voice made Chuck raise his head from the back of the uncomfortable hospital chair where he'd fallen asleep holding Charlie. It had been two days since he'd found PJ at the Frisco Ranch. Two long days where she'd lain in the hospital bed, pale, listless and unconscious.

The doctor said she had a concussion but couldn't predict when she'd wake up. The stress of all she'd gone through plus the trauma to her head had done a number on her.

"Look, her eyes are twitching." Katie leaned over PJ's face.

Chuck couldn't get over how Katie had grown in the past seven years. At seventeen, she was a beautiful young woman with all the joy and exuberance of youth.

She glanced at him, a frown pulling her pretty brows together. "You're looking at me that way again. Stop."

"What way?"

"Like you're gonna hug me again." She grinned. "Not that I mind. It isn't every day your long-lost brother calls in the middle of the night." Her eyes welled. "You should have seen Mom's face."

Chuck stared down at the baby in his arms, imagining her refusing to return home because of something he'd said. He vowed never to say anything to drive her away. And he vowed never to let words drive a wedge between himself and his family again.

"Any change?" A woman's voice at the door brought Chuck's head up.

His mother smiled at him and entered, followed by his father.

His parents looked so much older than when he'd left. His father's hair, which had just a hint of gray seven years ago, had turned solid gray. The crow's feet around his mother's eyes had deepened, and the worry lines across her forehead were permanently etched into her skin. "Can I?" She reached for Charlie.

Chuck let her take the baby, and then he stood and stretched. "How long was I asleep?"

"All of twenty minutes. Mom said I couldn't wake you."

"We should go out to the waiting room." Sylvia Bolton hugged Charlie to her. "PJ needs her rest to get better."

Katie rolled her eyes. "She's unconscious, Mom. How much more restful can you be?"

Chuck snagged her around the waist and pulled her into his arms. "I missed you and your smart mouth."

"Yeah, I know." She hugged him back. "Don't ever ditch me again, you hear?"

"Yes, ma'am." He rubbed his knuckles across the top of her head as he had when she was ten.

"Hey, you're messin' up my hair."

"Then stop getting so pretty." Chuck patted her hair into place. "I bet Dad's been beating the boys off with a stick."

"No, but he polishes his rifle on the porch every time a date comes to pick me up. Talk to him, will ya? It's cramping my style." Katie headed for the door. "Come on, Mom, we can play with Charlie in the waiting room. It's crowded in here."

The two women exited, leaving Chuck alone with his father for the first time in seven years.

Daniel Bolton stood with his hands in his pockets, his gaze on PJ. "She must be something special."

"She is." At a loss for how to bridge the gap between himself and his father, Chuck stood on the other side of the bed, staring at the woman who'd changed his life forever. "I'd give my life for her and Charlie."

"I hear you almost did."

Chuck shrugged. "It could have gone bad just as easily." He and Hank had arrived at the Frisco Ranch a lot later than he'd wanted to, but driving with the lights out to keep from being detected too soon had been difficult with scattered clouds limiting the light from the moon and stars.

He and Hank had ditched his truck on the highway and gone on foot, in a parallel path to the driveway leading in. When they heard gunfire, they'd thrown caution to the wind and ran the remaining yards to the house.

The second shot rang out as they peered around the corner of the house. Ross Felton had toppled to the ground.

When Chuck saw Emilio yank PJ up by the hair, blood flushed over his eyes and the same feeling he'd gotten when he'd found the dead Afghan boy outside the compound almost took over.

But he'd learned his lesson. He couldn't go off half-cocked. He had to think, to plan, to make his next move count, or he could lose PJ forever.

He raised his pistol and aimed, his eyes lining up his sights. Then he'd fired, all in the space of a second. Emilio lay dead. PJ lay beside him in the dirt, unmoving.

Hank picked off the first of Emilio's men to emerge from the barn.

Chuck focused enough to take out the second. The third man came out with his hands up, tossing his weapon to the dirt.

The sheriff arrived within minutes, calling for the ambulance.

Then the desperate hunt began. It took every able-bodied person searching the entire ranch compound to locate Charlie. Just when they were about to give up, Hank found her.

Ross Felton had stashed her in a closet in the abandoned

house. When he'd emerged from the house carrying a softly crying Charlie, Chuck had gathered his tiny daughter in his arms and cried with her.

They rode in the back of the ambulance to the hospital with PJ and had been there since.

"Thank you for calling when you did." Chuck's father broke through Chuck's thoughts, bringing him back to the hospital room and PJ's still body.

"I waited too long." Chuck shook his head. "I was too stubborn."

"No, I waited too long." His father sighed. "As soon as you left, I knew I was wrong. I wanted to call you back, but I was so angry. I wanted the world for you."

"I didn't want your world."

"I know that now." His father stared down at PJ. "I'm sorry."

Chuck nodded. "Me, too."

They stood silently on opposite sides of PJ's bed, the chasm between them narrowing.

Chuck felt as if a great weight had lifted from his heart. He couldn't wait for PJ to wake and share the joy with him.

"Hey." The soft sound of PJ's whisper tugged at Chuck's consciousness. At first he thought he'd imagined it.

Then PJ's eyes blinked open. She stared up at him and raised her hand to shield her eyes. "Charlie?"

"Is fine. She's with my mother and sister in the waiting room."

She turned to the other man smiling down at her. "You must be Chuck's dad."

He chuckled. "How'd you guess?"

"You look so much alike."

Chuck stared at his father, and his father stared back.

"It's been said we're a lot alike," the older Bolton said.

"Then we'll get along just fine, seeing as I love your son." Her voice trailed off, and her eyes closed.

Chuck clutched her hand, his throat tight, his eyes stinging with unshed tears. "PJ?"

"I'm here," she said. "I'd open my eyes, but that light is really bright."

Chuck's dad crossed to the light switch and flipped it off. "I'll let the doc know she's awake." He slipped from the room, leaving them alone.

Chuck pressed his lips to PJ's forehead. "You had me scared."

"Think I'd go off and leave you to take care of Charlie on your own?"

He chuckled. "Something like that."

"Don't worry. I'm not going anywhere."

"And neither am I. If you'll have me."

"Chuck?"

"Yeah, baby?"

"I meant what I said to your father."

"That we look alike?"

"Not that." She opened her eyes and stared up into his, her hand tightening around his. "I love you. There, I said it. I can't take it back and wouldn't if I could."

"I've always loved you, PJ. You're what kept me sane in the sandbox. The thought of seeing you again made me want to go on living."

"I was wrong to push you away. You have to take love any way you can get it." She pressed his hand to her cheek. "If you want to go off to war and defend our country, I'll be here when you get back. I'll take any time you give me. Just come back when you're done. Charlie and I will be waiting."

"I'm done with the army."

"What about Hank's team?"

"I like what he stands for. I want to continue working for him. But if it makes you uncomfortable, I'll go to work at the local feed store or hire on as the stable hand at the resort. I hear they need a permanent replacement for the one who quit." He smiled.

"No. Work for Hank. He's a good man. I'll take whatever love I can get for as long as I have it." She pulled him close and brushed her lips across his, wincing. "Ouch."

Chuck frowned, touching her cheek with his thumb. "You have a bruised lip."

"Emilio." Her eyes widened. "Is he—"

Chuck nodded. "Dead."

"Ricardo?"

A smile tilted the corners of his lips. "He was air-lifted to the hospital in El Paso and is in intensive care, but the prognosis is good."

"I'm glad." PJ sighed. "He tried to save me. How did he know where to find me?"

"He said he'd had a team of computer hackers following Emilio's communications. He intercepted the emails from Ross and wanted to see for himself the granddaughter he'd never known. And never will."

Chuck was about to kiss PJ again, but a soft tap on the door interrupted.

Hank Derringer poked his head inside. "I hear she's—" His gaze landed on PJ. "Hey, you're awake."

"I am." She held up a hand.

Hank crossed the room and took her hand in his. "I'm glad you're doing better. You had us all worried."

"Thanks for hiring Chuck to protect me."

"Only the best for my girl." He leaned over and kissed her forehead.

PJ blinked up at him, her eyes clouding. "Only I'm not your daughter. Ross and Emilio told me." She smiled, her bottom lip trembling. "Guess it wasn't meant to be."

Hank frowned. "What are you talking about?" He laid his hand on her forehead. "Is she still hallucinating?"

Chuck laughed. "She better not be. She told me she loved me."

Hank grinned and pulled a sheet of paper from his pocket. "In that case, I'll leave this with you."

Chuck took the paper and spread it out on the bed beside PJ.

"It's the results of the DNA test." Hank's smile broadened. "I'm afraid you're stuck with me, PJ."

"But Ross said—"

"He lied. Brandon hacked his computer and found out what Ross had been up to through a series of emails he'd sent to Emilio. When Ross broke into Hank's computer, he discovered Hank's ongoing investigation of Emilio, as well as PJ's connection. He sold the information to Emilio, making him believe PJ was his daughter and Charlie was his granddaughter. Emilio demanded a DNA test to prove it."

"And?"

"Brandon found the email with the DNA results of the test he conducted on you and Emilio. You weren't a match."

"You're my father?" Her lips spread, followed quickly by a grimace. "I have a father." She looked up at him. "I'd smile, but it hurts."

Hank patted her hand. "Don't worry. You'll have plenty of opportunities to smile. And if you can stand being around an old guy, I want you and Charlie to come live with me."

PJ glanced from Hank to Chuck.

Chuck shook his head. "Sorry, Hank. PJ's all grown up and getting married soon."

Her eyes widened. "I am?"

He kissed her fingertips. "If you'll say yes."

She smiled, winced and smiled again. "Yes!"

Hank chuckled. "I'll leave you to it, but I want you to visit often. Chuck will take good care of you." The older man left the room, a smile on his face.

"I can't believe it." PJ shook her head. "I woke up this

morning with Charlie as my only family. Now I have a father, and a stepmother and brother when they find them and bring them home."

"Hey, don't forget me and my family."

"I saved the best for last." She cupped his cheeks and pulled his mouth close to hers. "I have a fantastic cowboy for a fiancé, and his wonderful family. Now shut up and kiss me like you mean it."

* * * * *

**She looked up and found him look-
ing down at her. Even in the semi-
darkness, she could see the heat in
his eyes.**

He offered nothing but comfort, but the heat was
there between them anyway.

She didn't look away.

And then, in the blink of an eye, somehow
everything changed. Slowly, giving her plenty of
time to protest, he lowered his lips and brushed
them over hers.

Oh, wow. Was this really happening?

That Moses Mann would be kissing her seemed
surreal on some level. He was so...strong and
brave and a millionaire and worldly—everything
she wasn't. She was just a plain country girl.

They were so completely wrong for each other.
Unfortunately, her hormones didn't give a
damn. Need punched into her like never before,
something big and scary and overpowering and
completely unexpected.

MOST ELIGIBLE SPY

BY
DANA MARTON

MILLS &
BOON

First published in Great Britain 2013
by Mills & Boon, an imprint of Harlequin (UK) Limited,
Eton House, 18-24 Paradise Road, Richmond, Surrey TW9 1SR

© Dana Marton 2013

ISBN: 978 0 263 90374 4
ebook ISBN: 978 1 472 00746 9

46-0913

Harlequin (UK) policy is to use papers that are natural, renewable and recyclable products and made from wood grown in sustainable forests. The logging and manufacturing processes conform to the legal environmental regulations of the country of origin.

Printed and bound in Spain
by Blackprint CPI, Barcelona

Dana Marton is the author of more than a dozen fast-paced, action adventure, romantic-suspense novels and a winner of a Daphne du Maurier Award of Excellence. She loves writing books of international intrigue, filled with dangerous plots that try her tough-as-nails heroes and the special women they fall in love with. Her books have been published in seven languages in eleven countries around the world. When not writing or reading, she loves to browse antiques shops and enjoys working in her sizable flower garden, where she searches for "bad" bugs with the skills of a superspy and vanquishes them with the agility of a commando soldier. Every day in her garden is a thriller. To find more information on her books, please visit www.danamarton.com. She loves to hear from her readers and can be reached via email at danamarton@danamarton.com.

With many thanks to my wonderful editor, Allison Lyons. Thank you so much Deb Posey Chudzinski, Lisa Boggs, Amanda Scott, Maureen Miller, Valerie Earnshaw and all my wonderful friends who support me online.

Chapter One

She had that Earth Mother kind of natural feminine beauty, the type of woman who belonged at a bake sale or a PTA meeting, not in an interrogation room on the Texas border. Then again, smugglers came in all shapes and sizes.

Dressed in mom jeans and a simple T-shirt—a crew neck, so there wasn't even a hint of cleavage—she wore precious little makeup. Her chestnut hair hung in a simple ponytail, no highlights, nothing fancy. She did her best to look and sound innocent.

Moses Mann, undercover special commando, did his best not to fall for the act. "Let's try it again, and go for the truth this time."

If all her wholesome goodness swayed him, he was professional enough not to show it as he questioned her. He wasn't in the small, airless interrogation room in the back of an office trailer to appreciate Molly Rogers's curves. He was here to pry into her deepest secrets.

"When did you first suspect that your brother, Dylan Rogers, was involved in illegal activities?"

The smell of her shampoo, something old-fashioned like lemon verbena, filled the air and tickled Mo's nose. He kept his face impassive as he leaned back in his metal folding chair and looked across the desk at her.

Anger flared in her green eyes. "My brother didn't do

anything illegal," she said in a measured tone. "Someone framed him."

Mo's gaze dropped to her round breasts that suddenly lifted toward him as she pulled her spine even straighter. He caught himself. Blinked. "Your brother was a cold-blooded killer."

He'd personally seen the carnage at the old cabin on the Texas–Mexico border not far from here, the blood-soaked floorboards and the pile of bodies. He'd been the one who'd taken to the hospital the two children Dylan had kidnapped to sell into the adoption black market. Dylan had ended up with a bullet in the head during the takedown—well deserved as far as Mo was concerned.

He didn't have much sympathy for the man's sister, either. "Have you ever helped him smuggle illegal immigrants into the country? Drugs? Weapons?"

Her jaw worked with restrained anger. She clutched her hands tightly in front of her. The nicks and red spots on her fingers said she saw her share of farm chores and house-work on a daily basis. Her full lips narrowed, but somehow remained sensuous.

"Let me tell you something about my brother. He stood by me all my life. By me and my son. I don't know if we'd be alive at this stage without him." She stuck out her chin. "He was a good man."

Her absolute loyalty to family was commendable, even if misguided. Mo waited a beat, giving her time to calm a little before he said, "People are multidimensional. The face he showed you might not be the face he showed to others."

For the four men he'd killed at the Cordero ranch, Dylan Rogers had been the face of death, in fact. And he would have killed Grace Cordero, his neighbor, too, if not for Ryder, Mo's teammate, who'd arrived just in time to save Grace and those two kids.

Dylan Rogers had been a dark-hearted criminal. And the crimes he was publicly accused of paled in comparison to the one Mo couldn't even mention. Dylan was likely connected to people who planned on smuggling terrorists into the country—the true target of Mo's six-man undercover team.

As far as the locals were concerned, the team—all seasoned commando—were working with CBP, Customs and Border Protection. They'd come to survey the smuggling situation and investigate recent cases so they could come up with budget recommendations for policy makers. A fairly decent cover while they did their counterterrorism work without anyone being the wiser.

Smuggling was big business in the borderlands, sometimes even with customs or police officers on the bad guys' payroll. His team gathered information from local law enforcement, but shared nothing. They trusted no one at this stage. They kept to themselves while gathering every clue, following every lead. And one of their best leads right now was Molly Rogers.

But instead of cooperating, she was looking at the time on her phone in front of her. She bit her bottom lip.

"In a hurry?"

She nodded.

Too damn bad. "If you want to leave, you need to start talking." Mo tapped his pen on the desk between them. "Are there any illegal activities going on at your ranch at this time, Miss Rogers?"

"No. I already told you." She glanced at the phone again. "How long are you going to keep me here? If you're not charging me with anything, you have to let me go. I know my rights."

He regarded her dispassionately.

She had no idea how quickly a "terror suspect" designation could strip away all her precious rights. He'd seen people go into the system with that tag and disappear for a good long time, sometimes forever. If her brother's smuggling career included terrorist contacts… If she knew about it…

Her brother was dead, beyond questioning. Without information from her, Mo's team sat without a paddle, trapped on the proverbial creek, with the rapids quickly approaching.

She squirmed in her seat. "I have to go home to meet the school bus."

Her weak point. He was about to get to that.

He patted his shirt pocket, pretending to look for something. "I can arrange for someone to pick up your son. I have a card here somewhere for Social Services."

All the blood ran out of her face as she caught the veiled threat. She was a single mother without family. If they took her into custody, her son would go to foster care.

"I don't know anything about any illegal business," she rushed to say. "I swear. Please."

He liked her pleading tone. Progress. He'd scared her at last. He'd done far worse before to gain usable intelligence from the enemy. He'd done things that would shock her.

He pushed his chair back and stood. "I'm going to step out for a minute. Why don't you give some thought to how you really want to play this? For your son's sake."

"I'm not playing."

He didn't respond. He didn't even turn. He simply walked out and closed the door behind him.

Jamie Cassidy, the operations coordinator, sat at his computer in the main part of the office the team shared. He looked up for a second. "Singing like a bird in there?"

"I wish. She says she doesn't know anything."

"Do you believe her?"

Mo considered that for a moment, recalling every word she'd said, adding to that her body language and all the visual clues, and the depth of his experience. He didn't like what he came up with. He wanted her to be guilty. It would have made everything much easier.

He shrugged. "Bottom line is, we have nothing to hold her on." Maybe her brother did keep her in the dark about his smuggling. Either that, or she was an award-worthy actress.

"You gonna push her harder?"

He could have. "Not today."

Not because he felt that stupid attraction, but because of her son. Whatever she did or didn't know about smuggling, her son was innocent, and Mo wasn't ready to turn the kid's life upside down until he had damned good reason.

The boy had just lost his uncle. He didn't need to come home from school and search through an empty house, wondering what happened to his mother.

"You got anything?"

Jamie shook his head. "Shep just checked in. Everything's quiet, he says."

Shep and Ray were patrolling the border, Ray's leg still in a cast, but well enough for a ride along. Ryder, the team leader, was off tying up loose ends with a human-smuggling ring the team had recently busted. With what stood at stake, the six-man team wasn't about to leave any stones unturned. They pushed and pushed, and then they pushed harder.

"Keith called in, too," Jamie said. "He's getting frustrated over there." Keith was across the border, doing undercover surveillance to identify the local players on that side.

"He's young. He'll learn patience." Not that Mo felt any

at the moment. "Once we have our third man, we'll have our link."

From what they'd gathered so far, three men coordinated most of the smuggling activities on this side of the border. They'd gotten two. Dylan Rogers had been shot, unfortunately, before he could be questioned. Mikey Metzner, a local business owner closely tied to human smuggling, was in custody, but seemed to be the lowest ranking of the three, and without any direct knowledge of the big boss in Mexico.

"The third guy is the key." Even if he hadn't been the link to the big boss before, he was now.

"We'll get him."

Mo nodded then turned and walked back into the interrogation room.

"I can't tell you something I don't know about," Molly Rogers said immediately. "Look, I think you're wrong about my brother. This is not fair. I—"

"We're done for today. I'll take you home." He'd picked her up earlier, so she didn't have her car.

He held the door open for her, and she gave him as wide a berth as possible as she passed by him, clutching her purse to her chest. The top of her head didn't quite reach his chin. About five-four, no taller than that, and curvy in just the right places and... Mo tried not to notice her enticing figure or the way her soft chestnut ponytail swung as she hurried ahead of him.

Jamie caught him looking and raised an eyebrow.

He ignored him as he led her through the office, then scanned his ID card and pushed the entry door open. Outside, the South Texas heat hit them like a punch in the face.

His black SUV waited up front on the gravel. "Better give it a minute to let the hot air out." He opened the doors, reached in and turned the air conditioner on the highest setting.

Renting office space in Hullett's business district would have been more comfortable, would have come with climate-controlled parking. But from a tactical standpoint, the trailer office by the side of the road in the middle of nowhere made more sense for his team.

They could see for miles without obstacles, had complete control over the premises. They didn't expect an attack, but if anything did happen, the Kevlar-reinforced trailer with its bulletproof windows was a hell of a lot more defensible than a run-of-the-mill rented office. In his job, practicalities always came before niceties.

He gave the AC another few seconds then slipped into his seat and waited until she did the same on the other side.

"Thank you for believing me," she said, her faint, citrusy scent filling his car.

He raised an eyebrow. "Don't get ahead of yourself. We're not done here. We're just taking a break."

He let her sit and stew for the first five minutes of the drive down the dusty country road before he started in on her again, gentling his voice, switching to the "good cop" part of the routine.

"Anything you tell me can only help your case. If you got dragged into something against your will… Things like that happen. The important thing now is to come clean. We need your help here."

Her posture stiffened. "Am I an official suspect?"

"A person of interest," he told her after a few seconds.

And when she paled, he found that he didn't like making her miserable. But he would, if the job called for it.

The op was too important to let something like basic attraction mess with his focus. She was the wrong woman at the wrong time for him to get interested in. Even beyond the op. He planned on this being his last job with the SDDU, Special Designation Defense Unit, an undercover commando team that did everything from intelligence gathering abroad to hostage rescue to counterterrorism work.

His focus was on his mission and nothing else. He could ignore the tingles he felt in the pit of his stomach every time he looked at the woman next to him. If he did well here, his CIA transfer was as good as approved. Molly Rogers wasn't going to mess that up for him.

THE CAR FLEW down the road, Molly's stomach still so clenched from the interrogation she thought she might throw up. She took in the fancy dashboard, covered with computer displays, radio units, radar and other things she'd never seen before. She so wasn't going to feel guilty if she ruined any of that.

"When do you think I can claim my brother's personal effects?"

All she wanted was to put all this behind her, for her brother's name to be cleared. And an official apology in the local paper. Dylan didn't deserve to be dragged through the mud like this.

But instead of law enforcement investigating how and why Dylan had been framed, they kept on with their idiotic suspicions about him, even dragging her into the mess.

The man next to her kept his eyes on the road. "For now your brother's personal possessions are evidence in a multiple murder case."

"The sheriff won't let me into Dylan's apartment in Hullett, either." Everyone seemed to be against her these days.

"They need to get everything processed."

She hated Moses Mann. He had zero sympathy for her or her situation. He was twice her size and had used that in the interrogation room to intimidate her. He was missing half an eyebrow, which made him look pretty fierce. His muscles were just on this side of truly scary. She had a feeling he knew how to use his strength and use it well.

If he had a softer—reasonable—side, she sure hadn't seen it. He'd called her brother a conscienceless criminal and pretty much accused her of being the same. He threatened her with Social Services.

Her stomach clenched.

The day she saw Moses Mann for the last time would be a good day. He made her nervous and scared and so self-aware it bordered on painful. She had to watch every move, every word, lest he read something criminal into it. She looked away from him.

The land stretched flat and dry all around them as far as the eye could see. He drove the dusty country road in silence for a while before he resumed questioning her, asking her some of the same questions he'd asked before. She gave him the same answers. He was still trying to trip her when they reached her road at last.

Thank God. Another ten minutes and she would have been ready to jump from the moving car.

He parked his SUV at the end of her driveway, and she was out before he shut the engine off. Her dogs charged from behind the house, Max and Cocoa in the lead, Skipper in the back, all three of them country mutts from the pound.

They greeted her first.

"No jumping." She pushed Max down then scratched behind his ear.

He kept jumping anyway. Skipper barked, running around her in circles. They were worked up over something.

They checked out the man by her side next, tails wagging. They were about the three friendliest, goofiest guard dogs in Texas, trained to be nice to everyone, since her son often had friends over.

"Be nice," she said anyway, even if she wouldn't have been too put out if one of them peed on Moses Mann's combat boots. Not that she was vengeful or anything.

But the dogs were doing their best to crowd each other out as the man gave them some ear scratching. They seemed to think they'd found a new best friend. Figured.

He looked as if he enjoyed the attention. "There you go. That's a good dog."

She hoped he'd at least get fleas.

He gave a few final pats as he looked at her.

She cleared her throat. "Thanks for the ride." *Hint, hint. Go away.*

She didn't like the relaxed smile he'd gotten from playing with her traitor dogs. It made him look more human than soldier machine. If she began to think of him as anything other than "the enemy," he'd try to trick her into a false confession or something. Since they couldn't do anything more to her brother now, he and his team would probably do anything to ruin her life instead. She couldn't afford to let her guard down for a minute.

She waited for him to get back into his car and drive away. She didn't want him following her into the house, so she went to check the mailbox, playing for time, and bit her lip as she opened the flap door, her hand hesitating.

"What's wrong?" he called over.

How on earth had he caught that half-second pause? "Nothing."

She thrust her hand forward and grabbed the stack of envelopes. *Everything.* Bills scared her these days. She'd received a mortgage check the day before, for the ranch that she'd thought had been long free and clear. Dylan had taken out a new mortgage, apparently.

Which didn't mean he was a bad brother. Or a murderer.

He'd worked so hard, had so much on his mind… He'd simply forgotten to tell her.

She kept her back to Moses Mann. "Just making sure there aren't any wasps in there. They keep trying to move in." Also true. She's had a lot of trouble with wasps this year.

She shuffled through the envelopes, then relaxed. No unexpected bills, thank God. The new mortgage was more than she could handle.

Her cell phone rang and she glanced at the display. The agent from Brandsom Mining. The man had a sixth sense for knowing when she felt desperate. But not that desperate yet. She pushed the off button.

"Who was that?"

She wasn't going to discuss her problems with Moses Mann. He would have no qualms about using any weakness against her. "Telemarketer," she said. Sounded better than *People who are trying to take the ranch away from me.*

The land had some collapsed mine shafts left over from its old coal mining days. The mine had run dry and had been abandoned in her grandfather's time. But Brandsom Mining wanted to buy the ranch for exploration, thought that with modern methods of surface mining they might be able to get something out of the place.

And ruin the land in the process, mess up the water tables, have heavy machinery tear up the earth. No thanks. Dylan and she had always been in full agreement about that. The ranch was her son's inheritance. The Rogers Ranch would stay in Rogers hands until there was no longer a Rogers left.

She glanced at her phone. "Bus should be coming in a minute." *Feel free to leave now.*

But the guy seemed impervious to hints.

Her heart lifted at the sight of the school bus coming

around the bend, its old engine laboring. She glanced at the major pain at her side, wishing he would disappear. If he stayed, Logan would be asking questions about him. But the man was looking at her pickup, his attention 100 percent focused there as the bus stopped and Logan ran down the steps.

For a second she forgot about Moses Mann as she caught her son up into her arms and held him tight. The dogs were jumping all over them, muscling their way in with enthusiasm.

Logan squirmed. "Mo-om, not in front of the other kids."

She let him go with a half smile. Right. He was a big kid now, supposedly, eight years old. She made sure not to take his hand, or offer to carry his bag as she turned toward the house. But she did say "I missed you, buddy" as the school bus pulled away.

Moses Mann was walking over, his cell phone in hand. "I need you to go sit in my car."

Her muscles clenched at the hard expression on his face and the silent warning in his eyes. "What's going on?"

"Just for a few minutes."

If she were alone, she would have demanded an explanation. But she didn't want to get into an argument with the man in front of Logan. Because he *could* make her sit in his car. He *could* take her right back with him. She didn't want things to get worse than they were. Which meant she'd do as he asked. For the time being.

She swallowed and reached for her son's hand, big kid or not. "This nice gentleman is Mr. Mann." She did her best to sound normal. "He has a really cool car. Want to check it out?"

"Hi, Mr. Mann. Can I sit in the front?"

He nodded with an encouraging smile, the first she'd seen on him. "Just don't turn on the siren."

Logan's eyes went wide, a big smile stretching his face. "You have a siren? Is it like an undercover police car?"

"Kind of."

"Are you going to find the bad men who hurt Uncle Dylan?"

He hesitated for a second, his gaze cutting to her, before he said, "I'm working on that situation."

Logan sprinted for the car and she walked after him, the streaks of dirt on his back catching her eye.

"What happened to your shirt?"

He froze and looked at his feet. "Nothing."

"Logan?"

He turned but wouldn't look at her. "It's no big deal, Mom."

Her heart sank. She didn't have to ask what the fight was about. He'd been teased again with what the papers said about his uncle. "What do we always say about fighting?"

He hung his head and mumbled, "The best way to win a fight is to walk away from it."

She caught Mo watching them. He didn't look like the type who walked away from a fight. Well, that was his problem. "All right. Let's get in the car. We'll talk about this later."

When she was behind the wheel, Mo started toward her house. But then he stopped and motioned her to roll the window down, tossed her his keys. "Lock yourselves in." He fixed her with a stern look. "And if there's any trouble, you drive away."

THE DOGS STAYED by the car, whining to get in. They wanted to play with the kid. Good. Better to have them out of his way. Mo dialed his phone, keeping his focus on the house's windows as he approached.

The two-story ranch house was well kept, had a new roof. A row of yellow roses trimmed the wraparound porch that held half a dozen rockers. He dashed across the distance to the steps just as Jamie picked up his call on the other end. "I'm at the Rogers ranch. I need a crime-scene kit."

"You better not be having fun out there while I'm filing reports at the office."

"Molly Rogers's tires were slashed. In the past three hours. Everything was fine when I picked her up earlier."

"You need backup? Ryder just came in."

Ryder had recently been appointed team leader when the powers that be made the SDDU's Texas headquarters permanent. The top secret commando unit mostly worked international missions, infiltration, hostage rescue, search and destroy, espionage and the like.

But when a terrorist threat had been indicated for this section of the border, the Colonel sent a small team in. They'd come for this specific mission, but there was enough going on in the border region that the Colonel decided to make the team here permanent.

"If you can bring the kit, that should be enough." Mo pushed the screen door open as he reached for his gun, then opened the entry door with a simple twist of his wrist and scowled. Hardly anyone kept their houses locked around here. He didn't understand that kind of blind faith in humanity, not after all he'd seen.

"I think whoever messed with the tires is gone." The dogs hadn't signaled an intruder. "But I'm going to check out the place anyway." He closed the phone and slipped it into his back pocket.

He started with the kitchen. He'd been in here before,

with a search warrant and his team, after Dylan's death. They'd found nothing usable then and he didn't bother to look for any incriminating evidence now, just for possible danger. He checked the gun cabinet in the hall closet—full of hunting rifles. Locked. Nothing seemed missing.

He moved through room by room. The bathroom at the top of the stairs still held the faint scent of Molly Rogers's shampoo, everything in its place, everything spotlessly clean.

A little more disorder in the boy's room, a dozen toy soldiers scattered on the floor. But the next room over, her bedroom, was immaculate. He scanned the old-fashioned antique four-poster bed, feminine and delicate.

Would probably break under his weight— He caught the thought. He didn't need to think about himself in Molly Rogers's bed.

But he couldn't help noticing the strappy nightgown that peeked from under the cover. He forced his gaze past the lavender silk after a long moment.

He checked the next two small rooms, including the closets, found no signs that anyone had been in the house. He put his gun away and plodded down the stairs. In the kitchen, he pulled out a business card with his cell-phone number and stuck it on the fridge with a magnet decorated with elbow macaroni, probably made by Logan. Then he strode down the driveway, told them to get out of the car.

He turned to the boy first. "I need to talk to your mom for a second."

Logan looked at his mother.

"Why don't you go play some video games?" she suggested.

He grinned as wide as a grin could go and ran up to the house, his backpack bobbing, the dogs following him. He glanced back and yelled, "Goodbye, Mr. Mann."

He lifted a hand in a wave. Seemed like a well-raised kid.

"What did he get into a fight over?" he asked when the boy had passed out of hearing distance.

"Kids have been picking on him this last couple of weeks because of what they'd heard about his uncle." She shot him a glare as if it was all his fault. "Usually he's pretty good at walking away, but he really idolized my brother."

Whatever Dylan Rogers had done, someone beating on the kid for it didn't sit well with Mo. "You can't always walk away from trouble. I could teach him how to defend himself."

"Absolutely not. I'll handle my son's problems." She crossed her arms. "What were you doing in my house?"

Mo rolled his shoulders. She was right. Her son was none of his business, had nothing whatsoever to do with his op. Getting personally involved would have been a bad idea. *Back to business.* He gestured her over to her pickup and pointed at the slashed tires, watching for her reaction.

She stared, her jaw tightening. For a second he thought he might have seen moisture in the corner of one eye as her gaze filled with misery. "I can't afford new tires."

Money was the least of her problems. "We'll be taking some fingerprints." He gave her a hard look. "I want you to keep your doors locked. Car doors, house doors, garage door, the works. Do you know how to shoot any of those guns in the gun cabinet?"

She drew her gaze from the tires at last. "I might be a pacifist, but I'm still a Texan."

He watched her, trying to puzzle her out. Back in the interrogation room, his threat of calling Social Services had scared her. The slashed tires hadn't, just annoyed her. He liked that she was brave, but he wanted her to be careful. "I left my number on your fridge. Call me if you need me for anything. Don't take this lightly."

She looked back at the tires. "Why would somebody do this to me?"

He had a fair idea. "Maybe one of your brother's friends saw me pick you up. This could be a warning to make sure you don't tell any secrets." He paused for emphasis. "We could protect you and your son. If you were to cooperate."

Instead of jumping on that offer, her muscles only tightened another notch, true anger coming into her eyes.

"Quit blackmailing me with my son. I don't know any secrets. Goodbye, Mr. Mann." Then she turned on her heels and marched up to the house, hips swinging. She let the screen door slam shut behind her.

He would have lied if he said all that fire didn't draw him in, at least a little.

To distract himself from that thought, he checked the outbuildings while he waited for Jamie. Not a single door locked, barn, stables, shed, all the outbuildings open. But he found no signs of damage inside any of them. If the tire slasher had gone through, he hadn't messed with anything else.

As he stepped back outside, he scanned the endless fields around the buildings, not another house in sight. He made a mental note to check on the status of Dylan Rogers's bachelor pad when he got back to the office. Molly and her son would be better off moving there, into town, for the time being.

Not that keeping her safe was his job. For all he knew, she was guilty as sin. But her kid didn't deserve to be in the middle of all this bad business.

There was an amazing connection between mother and son, love and affection, obvious from even their brief encounter. Had he ever had that? Not with his birth mother, for sure. And as his foster mother had died so early, he remembered very little of her.

"How is it that you get both the girl and the action, while I'm stuck in the office?" Jamie's arrival ended the trip down memory lane.

"You're here now."

He looked around. "Sounded more exciting over the phone. Didn't find anyone here?" He sounded disappointed at the missed opportunity for a scuffle.

His steps were sure as he brought the crime-scene kit over to the pickup, but he had a slightly uneven gait. Both of his legs were missing, courtesy of a rough overseas mission that had ended badly. He walked with the aid of two space-age technology prostheses, well hidden under his black cargo pants, originally developed for Olympic athletes.

He looked over the damage carefully. "Find anything else beyond the slashed tires?"

"Nothing."

While Jamie lifted prints, Mo dabbed the tires around the slashes with oversize cotton swabs and sealed those into evidence bags.

Jamie put away the prints he'd collected. "Could be a warning for her to keep quiet about her brother's dealings."

"That was my first thought."

She had no idea how out of her depth she was in all this. He looked toward the house, not liking that he was beginning to feel protective toward Molly Rogers and her son. That could become a problem.

"She's a person of interest in the investigation," he said out loud to remind himself of the exact nature of their relationship.

Maybe if he kept telling himself that was why he was so interested in her, eventually he'd believe it.

His phone rang at the same time as Jamie's. They clicked into a conference call with Ryder.

"Hey, Shep just called. He found some chopped-off fingers. No body to go with them," their team leader said on the other end.

"Where?" Mo tensed, pretty much expecting that he wasn't going to like the answer. He was right about that.

"Rogers land," Ryder said.

Chapter Two

"Anyone call from the lab?" Mo asked as he strode into the office, hating how the days ticked by without any serious progress. They needed a break and soon.

"None." Shep was busy at work at his desk. "Found the damn fingers four days ago. You'd think we'd have something by now." His face was stamped with frustration. "How was surveillance?"

"Hot." He wiped his forehead, enjoying the icy blast of air-conditioning after the hundred-degree heat out there on the border.

The terrain was rough enough so he couldn't drive his SUV up every ridge and down into every gully, which meant he spent half his time hiking, looking for footprints or any other sign of smuggling. He was hoping to catch some mules who could lead him to the man who handled all the dirty business on the U.S. side of the border. So far, he hadn't succeeded.

"Didn't see much. Busting Dylan Rogers slowed business to a trickle. I'm guessing his people are lying low. They figured out they're being watched."

"They'll start up again. They won't want to lose too much money."

"We'll be ready for them." Still, it didn't change the

fact that the team was having a spectacularly unproductive week, chasing down leads that all came to dead ends.

They hadn't been able to dig up anything new on Molly Rogers, either. They had no way to link the three chopped-off fingers to her. She claimed it had been months since she'd been out to the south border of her land. Mo hadn't told her about the fingers. The details of their investigation were strictly on a need-to-know basis.

His instincts said she was innocent. But since images of her wearing that lavender silk nightgown kept popping into his head at every unguarded moment, he wasn't about to trust his instincts on this one.

A small cardboard box sat on his desk. "What's this?"

"New batch of gadgets for testing. More sensitive sensors, longer-radius listening device, long-distance trackers. Pretty cool, actually."

He flipped open the box. Being able to test the latest spy gadgets was part of the perks of the job. But his phone rang before he could truly dig in. He picked it up as soon as he glanced at the display. He'd been waiting for this call all week.

"We have some matches for the prints you got off those slashed tires," Doug, a lab tech from the main office in Washington, said on the other end. "Dylan Rogers, Molly Rogers and a set of unidentified kid prints."

Logan's, he thought as frustration swept through him. "Nothing else?" All he wanted was one small lead, dammit.

"The tire swab samples had human blood in them. Preliminary DNA test links the blood to a murder victim in San Antonio. Garcia Cruz."

He shoved the box aside and sat up straighter. "Meaning the guy was killed with the same knife that slashed those tires?"

"Looks like it."

Garcia Cruz. The name sounded familiar. He brought up the law-enforcement database and did a quick search. The muscles in his jaw tightened as he read.

The Cruz murder had been a gang slaying.

Exactly the wrong type of people for Molly Rogers to get tangled up with.

"And the fingers?" he asked.

"I ran the fingerprints. Another gangbanger. He has a prior record and a long list of aliases. I'll write up a full report and send it over. Just thought I'd give you a heads-up."

"I appreciate that." Mo swore under his breath. Sounded as if it was time to visit Molly Rogers again.

THE DOGS WERE GOING MAD, barking and running around in the yard, then rushing up to her and pulling on her apron.

"I don't have time to play, sorry, guys. I'm way behind." Molly hustled on with her buckets.

Normally she fed the animals before she put Logan on the school bus in the morning, but they'd overslept. The power had gone out sometime in the night and reset the alarm clock. Thank God it was Friday. On Fridays she only had two deliveries, just a few boxes of produce to a local restaurant, and then the milk, both later in the day. She might catch up yet.

The horses were restless, too, snorting at her with reproach as she entered the stables.

"I know, I know. I'm late. Sorry." And she was, even if she *had* needed the sleep.

She'd been way too stressed since her encounter with Moses Mann at the beginning of the week. He didn't seem like the type of man who would just give up and go away.

Every time a car drove by, she expected it to be him, coming to arrest her on some trumped-up charge.

She doled out the feed, then the water to the impatient horses. She patted Paulie, an old gelding. "There. See? Nobody starved."

She moved on to her four cows next and milked them by hand before she let them out to pasture. She carried the five-gallon buckets into one of the outbuildings and got the milk ready for driving it into town. She milked morning and evening, sold the raw milk to an artisan cheese maker in Hullett.

Skipper, Max and Cocoa followed her everywhere, "helping." She took turns pushing the dogs out of the way. "Remind me to schedule your shots." Which brought Grace Cordero to mind. Her once best friend had recently left the army and opened up a vet practice down the road. The Cordero ranch was the closest house to her.

Except Molly hadn't talked to Grace since before Dylan's death.

Grace had been there when Dylan had been shot. She'd said Dylan had kidnapped her.... Why would she say that?

That terrible ache bubbled up in Molly's heart again, so she pushed those thoughts away and refocused on her chores. She let out the chickens from the coop and fed them. The dogs weren't allowed in the fenced-off area that protected her chickens from foxes and coyotes. She shooed them off. Dylan had some booby traps set up for anything that might go after her poultry. The dogs knew the traps and had been trained to stay away, but she didn't like them back here.

"Go play." She pushed them away, and they did run off.

Soon they were barking by the shed. What on earth was wrong with them today? Maybe they sensed a storm coming. She glanced up at the sky, but the clear blue dome stretched from horizon to horizon without a blemish. Looked as if the relentless heat would be staying. Wildfires were more of a threat than a storm at this point.

She collected the eggs into the empty bowl she'd brought the wheat in for the hens. Barely anything. The hens didn't lay much in this kind of heat. She took the eggs into the house, then went back out to look in on her sizable vegetable garden. Weeds never took a break. She didn't use pesticides or herbicides; all her fruits and vegetables were 100 percent organic, which got her top dollar at the local restaurants where she did weekly deliveries.

Since it hadn't rained in forever, watering came first. She decided to use some compost tea as well, so she headed to the shed. The dogs were still scratching at the door. She shooed them away, but when she stepped inside, they rushed past her, nearly pushing her over.

They were growling and sniffing at everything.

"What's up with you today?"

But then she caught it, too. Something was off. Okay, a lot of things were off, she realized suddenly, noticing that her buckets had been pushed around. A couple of the floorboards were damaged.

"All right. What got in this time?" She let the dogs investigate, stepping aside and leaving the door clear in case a wild animal was hiding in some corner and was about to make a dash for freedom.

Despite her best efforts and the dogs, wild critters had a way of getting into her garden and outbuildings from time to time. On the rare occasion, they'd done pretty spectacular damage in the past. Which didn't seem to be the case here. Unless…

Her gaze caught on the top of a large antique feed box in the corner, the lid askew.

"Oh, God, not the corn."

She kept her organic corn seeds in that box. She saved those seeds carefully year after year, since they were hard to come by. She always made sure the lid was closed tight so the occasional mouse couldn't get in. That corn was one of her most prized possessions. If something ate that...

She hurried closer, even as she thought, *A wild animal couldn't have opened the lid.* But she didn't relax when she found the corn still in place. The lid had definitely been moved. The short hairs stood up at the back of her neck. A wild animal couldn't lift the lid like that, she thought again.

A wild animal couldn't have gotten in here in the first place. The door hadn't been locked, but she did keep it barred. She turned in a slow circle, searching for holes in the floor and wall, the roof. She saw no hole that could have been an entry.

She squatted to examine the scratched floorboards, patting the dogs when they immediately came to lick her face. "I don't like the look of this."

The scratch marks were short and perfectly straight, not like what an animal would make.

"Crowbar," she muttered, and Skipper gave a sharp bark, as if agreeing.

"Oh, yeah? Where were you when this was happening?"

But she knew the answer. The dogs had been out here, barking. She'd heard them in the night. And she'd ignored them, thinking nothing of it. They had plenty of wildlife around; the dogs were always barking at something or other.

She stood and grabbed a rusty old screwdriver from the windowsill, then pried one of the floorboards up, then another and another, until she had a gap wide enough for a good look. Nothing under there but a foot-deep gap to the ground, filled with spiderwebs, then packed dirt. She set the boards back into place and looked around, trying to see the place through fresh eyes.

"Why would anyone break into the shed? Nothing's missing." She definitely didn't keep anything valuable here.

Had a drifter come by looking for food? Someone who'd come over the border in the night, stopping here for shelter? Maybe they'd tried to hide under the floor, then thought better of it on account of the rattlers that loved places like that. There was nobody down there now. She didn't stick her head all the way down to look, but the dogs would have let her know.

She mulled over the odd business while filling two dozen boxes from her garden, then she drove into town for groceries and to drop off her freshly picked vegetables at the Italian restaurant, and the milk at the cheese shop.

Running a fully working ranch of this size was too big of a task for her alone, so she made money any way she could, with her cows and her organic garden, with boarding horses or whatever opportunities came her way.

"Thanks," Ellie, the cheese maker, said. "I made this just for you." She handed over an herbed roll of soft cheese, Logan's favorite. "A gift. How are things at the ranch?"

What was she going to say? *I'm a person of interest in smuggling?* She forced a smile. "Everything is great." Then she hurried out before Ellie could think of any more questions.

The new, shiny black tires on her pickup—courtesy of her credit card—drew her eye. She hated the thought of how long it was going to take to pay them off. Great, now she was adding credit-card debt to the bills, on top of the mortgage.

Then an uncomfortable thought struck her and she stopped midstride. Were her slashed tires and last night's intruder connected? Could Moses Mann be right and some idiot was trying to send her a message?

On an impulse, she swung by the sheriff's office to ask him about the weird shed business.

"I normally wouldn't think anything of it, but someone slashed my tires in the driveway a couple of days ago," she told Shane as they stood by the reception desk, the small office buzzing with activity around them. They'd had layoffs recently, so everybody who remained had to double up on work.

He looked more annoyed than interested, probably figured he had bigger problems. "Maybe them tires just deflated."

"They had holes."

The sheriff shrugged. "Could have run over some nails in the road without noticing." He shuffled through a handful of pink phone-message slips.

"Will you come out to check the shed?"

He glanced up. The all-business look on his face was normally reserved for strangers. They'd known each other all their lives, but his features didn't soften any as he asked, "Anything missing?"

"No."

"You see anyone hanging around your place?"

"No."

"I have two dozen cases that take priority." He turned his back on her and walked away, toward his office.

"I wouldn't worry about it too much," Margie May, the receptionist, said, the only person at the station to show

Molly any sympathy. "Probably some illegals passing through in the night."

She nodded. That happened on occasion. She wasn't scared of them. They never went up to the houses. They didn't want trouble. All they wanted was to get up north unseen. One might have gone into the shed looking for food or water. But why would any of those people slash her tires? That didn't make any sense.

Margie May looked after the sheriff. "He'll come around. He's embarrassed over your brother. They hung out at the bar on game nights. He's gotten some flak for not realizing that one of his buddies was a criminal."

Molly stiffened as cold disappointment spread through her. "Dylan was *not* a criminal. He was framed." His exoneration could not come fast enough.

Margie May didn't comment, just went back to her typing.

Molly strode out and headed off to the grocery store. Dylan so did not deserve the way people treated him.

Her brother had always been the only one she could truly count on. She wasn't going to let him down. She was going to clear his name if it was the last thing she did.

She hurried through grocery shopping then went to the post office next. Missy Nasher, who'd always taken special pleasure in spreading rumors about her, stood at the end of the line.

If Missy saw her from the corner of her eye, she didn't acknowledge her. Instead, she backed right into Molly and knocked the package from her hand.

"Oh," she said as she turned around. Not *sorry*. Then put her nose in the air as she turned her back again, as if Molly was beneath her notice.

Missy struck up a conversation with the old woman in

front of her about what a shame it was that the sheriff's department was getting cut when crime was so obviously rampant in town. A direct dig at Dylan, no doubt.

Molly gritted her teeth, keeping her mouth shut. When the paper printed an apology, Missy and the rest of them would stand corrected.

Whatever people say about others, it always tells more about them than the person they're speaking about. Wasn't that what she always told Logan?

"How are you doing, Molly? I'm really sorry about your brother."

She turned to the man behind her, feeling ridiculously grateful for the kind words. Her muscles relaxed a little as she smiled her gratitude at Kenny Davis, the Pebble Creek sheriff. "Thank you, Kenny."

Kenny had gone to high school with Dylan. Good to see that he, at least, wasn't turning his back on that friendship.

He gave her a warm smile. "How are things at the ranch?"

"All right." She didn't want to discuss her latest troubles with half a dozen people listening in.

"Old Woodward still renting?"

She didn't work the whole ranch, couldn't have handled it on her own. She had her gardens and a handful of animals. Most of her income came from what Henry Woodward paid her for renting her land as additional grazing ground for his steers. "He doesn't get out much anymore. His sons have taken over," she said.

"Any trouble with rustlers?"

"Not that I heard of." With the economy being what it was, rustling was coming back, like in the old days.

Missy gave two letters to the postmaster, paid and left with head held at a haughty angle.

Molly stepped up to the window at last and handed over her package, returning a pair of boots she'd ordered online that turned out to be too large.

She said goodbye to Kenny on her way out, but he caught up with her again in the parking lot. His police cruiser stood next to her old pickup.

"I was heading over to grab some coffee." He gestured with his head toward the diner across the road. "How about it? I have a horse that needs to be boarded. I hoped we might be able to talk about that."

She hesitated for a moment. *The diner.* Did she want to put herself through that? The speculative glances... If someone said something nasty about her brother, God help her—

Oh, to hell with it. She wasn't going to run and hide. She had a life in this town. She was going to raise her son here. She had just as much right to be at the diner as anybody else did, regardless of what they all erroneously thought about her brother.

Nobody would accost her with the sheriff by her side, would they?

She forced a smile onto her face. "That would be nice." And she kept that smile as they walked across the road together.

Kenny wasn't overly tall, just a few inches taller than she. In high school, he'd been quite the heartthrob. He'd paid no attention to her back then, of course. None of her brother's friends on the football team had. They had their eyes on the cheerleaders. She'd been just a scrawny kid to them.

Despite the years that had passed since, he was still handsome, more handsome in the traditional sense than Moses Mann. Two of Kenny could have fitted into Mo, who was built like a tank and had a nose that looked as if it had been the landing place for a number of well-aimed punches. And with that half-missing left eyebrow, Mo had some sort of warrior vibe that Kenny lacked. It probably drew women in droves. Not that she cared. She pushed the thought away. Why was she comparing the two men, anyway?

"Booth or table?" the waitress asked as soon as they walked through the door.

"Booth," Kenny responded.

Molly ignored the curious looks as they were seated.

"Pie?" Kenny pointed to the large color ad on the wall, pretty enough to set her mouth salivating. "The chocolate-meringue pie is killer here."

"Better stick with the coffee." On her short frame, any extra pounds showed way too fast. She'd gained several since Dylan's death. She needed to stop trying to eat her grief.

"So what was that in there with Missy Nasher?" Kenny asked with an easy smile.

Oh, God, he'd noticed that, had he?

She gave a dismissive shake of her head. "She never really liked me. It doesn't matter. Old high-school rivalry."

Kenny drew up an eyebrow. "People who stick their noses in the air like that usually fall flat on their faces sooner or later."

The support felt nice. "Thanks."

But the truth was, even beyond Missy, she'd never been one of the popular people in town. She had never told anyone who Logan's father's was, which had started a rumor that he was a married man. It made most married women hate her on sight, because they wondered if it was their husband she'd slept with. And of course, married men went out of their way to avoid her so as not to fall under the cloud of suspicion.

Some of the single guys had come around, thinking she was an easy conquest. When she turned them down, they got offended and spread false rumors to pay her back for the rejection.

"Hullett is a small town with small-town morals. People have little to do for entertainment but gossip about their neighbors," Kenny was saying. "Move to Pebble Creek."

"Because that's, what, five hundred heads bigger?" she teased.

"All right, then just ignore the idiots here."

Easier said than done. With Dylan's death, the gossip mill was running full force again. But she nodded.

"Must be difficult out there alone," he said after the waitress filled their mugs.

She took a sip, the coffee burning the tip of her tongue. She set the mug down. "I'll manage."

He shook his head. "Having to go through Dylan's things can't be easy."

She closed her eyes for a second. "I haven't done it yet."

He leaned forward in his seat. "If you need help—"

She shook her head. "Not ready for that yet. But thank you." She could handle only so much at once. Someday she would deal with all that, but for now she was still grieving.

"You ever think about selling?"

She forced a smile. "Are you buying?"

He gave a white-toothed smile. "I wish I had the money. It's a fine piece of land."

She nodded. The farm had been in her family for generations.

"I have the animals," she said. "And I like it there. It's

the only place I've ever lived." The only place her son had ever lived, too.

And it would stay that way if she got her wish. She wasn't exactly a big fan of change. Change always brought trouble.

Kenny stirred his coffee. "Still, out there, alone…"

"I have the dogs." Who weren't exactly guard dogs, admittedly. She took another sip, more carefully than the first time. Her ranch wasn't in Kenny's jurisdiction, but he was so nice to her, while Shane was such a… "I think someone's been in one of the outbuildings last night," she blurted.

Kenny sat up straighter, his full attention on her. "What happened? Did they take anything?"

"Nothing's missing. It's weird." She told him about the scratches on the floorboards and the rest. Then she told him about her tires.

"You should be careful. Illegal crossings have slowed to a trickle, with the economy as it is, but there's still smuggling. Those are not people you want to tangle with."

That he believed her and didn't brush her off like Shane felt nice. Kenny was a good guy. He'd always been a good friend to Dylan. "I'm always careful."

"Maybe you should move into Dylan's apartment in Hullett," he suggested. "I'd be happy to help you. In the meantime, I'll make sure to drive by the ranch when I'm on the night shift. It's not my jurisdiction, but—" He shrugged. "Helping friends is what it's about, right?"

Was he her friend? She felt grateful for the sentiment. She didn't have too many friends these days. So she nodded and thanked him, then asked about that horse that needed boarding. A little bit of extra money always came in handy. And even beyond that, she was happy to help Kenny out if she could.

Making a friend was exactly what she needed.

"If anything else happens, you come to me," he told her. "It might be even better not to involve Shane at all."

"He's just upset over Dylan."

Kenny shrugged. "If Dylan was framed, we have no way of knowing right now who framed him." He grimaced, as if having said more than he'd meant to say.

She leaned forward, her mind buzzing suddenly. "You mean Shane could be involved?" She had a hard time believing that. She'd known Shane forever.

Kenny made a dismissive gesture. "Maybe not Shane, but somebody from his office. A couple of times a year, we bust someone either on the police force or at CBP for selling out to the smugglers."

His face turned serious. "If you find out anything about Dylan and all the bad business that went down, you come to me. Promise me, Molly."

"I promise."

SINCE SHE WASN'T HOME, Mo walked around the house and the outbuildings. He wasn't sure if he was doing it to check that everything was okay and she was safe, or because he was trying to find evidence that she'd been in cahoots with her brother.

He didn't like the ambiguity. It hadn't happened to him often. He'd always been able to keep his professional and personal lives separate.

The dogs followed him around, tails wagging, tongues lolling, a goofy bunch. He sincerely hoped she wasn't counting on them for protection. He checked the outbuildings, since she kept them all unlocked. Everything looked fine. Until he stepped into the shed. He didn't like what he found there.

He had worked himself into a right dark mood by the time her red pickup rolled down the road and pulled into the driveway.

"Someone's been here, searching your place," he said in the way of greeting as he strode forward to meet her. "Any idea who that might have been?"

She stood by her vehicle, her posture stiff. "What are you doing here?"

The jean shorts and pink tank top she wore kicked his heart rate up a notch. "Checking on you."

He lusted after her body. So there, he admitted it. He appreciated her curves, her loyalty to her brother and her dedication to her son, and was drawn by that hint of vulnerability in her eyes. She wasn't tough the way Grace Cordero was or some of the women he'd worked with on overseas missions. Yet she was plenty strong in her own way. She intrigued him.

He pushed all that out of his mind. "Somebody was out here, looking for something."

"I know. Last night."

"Who?"

"Maybe someone headed north, looking for food."

"Under floorboards?"

She stayed silent.

"The same week that someone slashed your tires?" He shook his head. "Too much of a coincidence for my taste. It could be one of your brother's smuggling partners looking for something."

"My brother had no smuggling partners, because he wasn't smuggling anything. Just as nobody was trying to send me a message with those tires. This has nothing to do with Dylan." She emphasized the last words, saying them slowly, as if she thought he had trouble understanding.

Part of him wanted to let her have the fantasies that she clung to. But with the situation she was in, denial could be dangerous. He didn't want her in danger.

He looked her straight in the eye. "You need to accept the truth so you can start dealing with it."

She stuck out her chin, her spine ramrod straight. "If I want free life-management advice, I'll tune in to Dr. Phil. I do own a television," she said in an icy tone, instead of telling him to go to hell. Oh, but she wanted to. Her eyes flashed with fire.

She had plenty of restraint, but underneath all that she hid heat and passion. Not that he needed to be intrigued any further by Molly Rogers. He filled his lungs. He was here for a reason.

He cleared his throat. "Do you know a Garcia Cruz?"

Her eyes narrowed. "Who?"

"Have you ever heard the name before? Maybe from your brother?"

She shook her head. "Who is he?"

"Are you aware of any links between your brother and the local gangs?"

She rolled her eyes at him. "There are no gangs in Hullett."

He nearly rolled his eyes back at her. "How about we let go of the delusion that small towns are paradises untouched by crime and that bad things happen only in the inner cities?" She needed a reality check, and he was the man to give it to her. "Who do you think handles the drugs and the guns and all the other illegal activity?"

She stared at him.

Could she be that naive? Maybe she was, living out here in the middle of nowhere, her life revolving around the ranch and her son. But oblivious was a dangerous way to be in today's world.

He didn't like the thought of her out here alone with only an eight-year-old for company. "You should stay in town for a while in your brother's apartment."

"I have animals."

"You can drive out twice a day to do what needs to be done. You don't need to spend the nights out here."

"The apartment hasn't been released yet."

"Still?" That seemed odd. It had been searched, everything cataloged. It wasn't a crime scene. He wondered what the holdup was. "I'll see what I can do about that. I don't want you here alone at night."

"I don't want to move." She turned her back to him, signaling that was her final word on the subject, then went around to the passenger side of the pickup to grab some groceries. He helped her, even though it only earned him a glare.

"Where is Logan?" he asked.

"In school."

"Any more trouble?"

She shook her head.

"He must miss your brother."

She stared for a moment, then blinked hard. She turned away and began walking toward the house. "I don't think he can even fully comprehend that Dylan is gone forever. I'm not sure I can. Sometimes I still almost call him to check when he'll be home for dinner."

She wasn't one of those stick women a man was afraid to look at for fear of breaking, but there was an aura of fragility to her as she walked away from him, and he suddenly had to fight the urge to comfort her. "I'll stop by as often as I can."

"I'd prefer it if you didn't."

"It'd be good for whoever is messing with you to see that you're not alone."

"Nobody is messing with me," she said over her shoulder. "It's all just random stuff. Bored teenagers."

She was in denial through and through, about too many things. He wanted her to be careful, to be safe, but for that, she first had to admit that she was in danger.

So when they were inside and the grocery bags were sitting on the table, he reached for her and turned her to him before she could bustle away. His palms tingled on her bare skin. In addition to tingles in other places.

He let his hands fall. He seriously needed to get over whatever crazy attraction he felt for her. So he focused on the trouble she was in. "I'd appreciate it if you kept what I'm about to say between us. It's part of our investigation."

She stepped back from him but nodded.

"The same knife that was used to slash your tires was also used in a vicious gang murder. The people who are coming around here, they are the wrong kind of people, Molly."

Chapter Three

"Almost done," Molly said, patting Nelly's flank as she finished up the evening milking. The smell of hay and fresh milk filled the barn, but her thoughts were only partially on what she was doing. They kept returning to Moses Mann, as they had all through the day.

He had told her she should stay away from the ranch at night for a while. Kenny had said the same thing.

"I don't want to go anywhere," she told Nelly and the other cows.

But she wouldn't put her son in danger just because she wasn't good with change. So if things got worse… "I can do it if I have to."

Nelly's gaze was doubtful, but the other cows nodded in silent support as they chewed their cud.

The first step was to have the apartment released, then she would have an option, at least, whether or not she decided to take it. Grace could do it. She'd move anywhere in the blink of an eye. She'd traveled the world with the Army. If Grace could go someplace where people were shooting at her, Molly thought, then she could go to Hullett, for heaven's sake.

She set the milk pails out of kicking distance from Nelly, her most ornery cow, then pulled out her phone and called the police station again. Margie May answered.

"It's Molly. Is Shane in yet?"

"Just went out on another call."

"I would really like access to my brother's apartment. I need to know when I can come in to pick up the keys. Could you have him call me back?"

"Sure, hon."

"That's what you said before," she said without accusation. Shane was avoiding her, and they both knew it.

A moment of silence passed between them. "Listen. I think, and I shouldn't be telling you this…" Margie May paused. "Since Shane missed the whole thing that was going on with Dylan, he wants to score some points in the rest of the investigation. So he's going through everything with a fine-tooth comb. All the reports, the apartment, your brother's truck. It might be a while yet."

"He is doing all that?" Relief washed over her. "Thanks."

If Shane was giving the case his full attention, he would realize sooner or later that Dylan had been framed. She wanted that, first and foremost. Maybe an official announcement of Dylan's innocence would get whoever was harassing her to quit. If people thought Dylan had drugs and Lord knew what else stashed around the ranch…

Mo's ominous announcement about gang connections sent chills running down her spine every time she thought of it. The knife that had slashed her tires had been used in a murder. That was creepy and scary.

And it didn't make any sense whatsoever.

The gang murder had happened in San Antonio, according to Mo. She barely knew anyone in the city, certainly no criminals.

She grabbed the milk pails, said good-night to the cows and closed up the barn. Then she glanced at the light in Logan's window.

He'd already had his dinner and bath and was in bed,

playing "Calvin Cat Counting" on his handheld player. The game taught kids math without them realizing they were learning. Logan loved the action; she loved the A's he brought home.

Learning was a big thing in the house; she'd made sure of that. And so was eating healthy and running around outside in fresh air. She tried to make up for her son not having a father and was raising him to the best of her abilities.

She took the milk to the old farm kitchen at the back of the house where she processed everything she sold. A car came up the driveway as she reached the door. A police cruiser. Kenny. She stopped and waited for him.

The dogs ran to check him out then dashed back to her, not nearly as excited about the visitor as they usually were about Mo. As much as Mo annoyed her, her animals and Logan seemed to like him. Logan had asked if he could go on a ride in his fancy car with him. Probably just wanted to push the siren button.

Kenny waved at her then walked back to where she waited for him. "Thought I'd make sure everything is all right out here."

"Pretty good so far." Aside from Mo's startling revelation, which she couldn't talk about. "Are you bringing the horse this weekend?"

"Charlie. He's a good one. In a couple of days."

She walked into the processing room and he came in after her. The dogs stopped outside the door. They knew they weren't allowed in there. She didn't want dog hair in the milk she sold.

"Night shift?" she asked as she screened the milk through cheesecloth, making sure it didn't have any stray pieces of hay.

He shook his head. "Just coming off shift. Long day.

Had a couple of speed traps up today. Weekend comes and people start driving like they're on a racetrack."

"Hand out any tickets?"

He gave a smug smile. "Filled up the tiller."

She tidied up. "I better close up for the night."

He followed her out and took his time looking around the shed, but said nothing about the break-in, just shook his head. She was tempted to ask his advice on the gang angle, the words on her lips a couple of times, but each time she held back, as Mo had asked.

The chickens were in their coop already, had gone in on their own once it started getting dark. All her animals knew the schedule. All she had to do was bar the doors so no stray coyote could get in. "You think I should put up padlocks?"

He thought about that for a second or two before he nodded. "I have a few extras at home. I can bring those over when I bring Charlie."

"Thanks."

"So coffee was nice the other day," Kenny said when they were finished. "How about we do it again? I would like to take you to dinner."

A second passed before full comprehension came. *A date.*

Wow. Okay.

She shifted from one foot to the other. It had been a while since she'd been asked out.

Kenny was…nice. She didn't feel any sparks, but so what? Her grandmother had always told her love grew with time. It started with respect. And she did respect Kenny. He was here trying to help, while most people would rather gossip about her and her brother.

She didn't want to offend him or alienate him. If she alienated any more people in her life, she'd have nobody left.

"Okay. Sure."

A confident smile spread across his face, as if he'd fully expected that answer. And why wouldn't he? He was a pretty good catch, young with a steady job and good looks, a good standing in the community.

"Tomorrow night?" he suggested.

"How about tomorrow afternoon? Maybe four-ish? Logan will be at the annual library treasure hunt from four to six." She could drop her son off, then pick him up later, have dinner in between.

"I'll come out to get you."

"I'll be in town anyway. Let's meet at the restaurant."

"I was thinking Gordie's?"

Gordie's served Tex-Mex cuisine, a nice place, but not so fancy that she would be uncomfortable. She nodded, trying not to think how fast they would set all the gossiping tongues wagging.

"Have a good night, then. See you tomorrow." Kenny flashed her another smile before he walked back to his car.

She looked after him as his dust-covered police cruiser pulled down the driveway.

Skipper came to lick her hand.

"I'm dating again. Okay, one date, but still, how weird is that?" she asked her, but if the dog thought it was weird, she kept it to herself. She just gave a goofy, lolling grin.

"I'm dating the Pebble Creek sheriff," Molly said experimentally. Yep, definitely sounded weird.

She went inside the house, letting the dogs in, picked up her yellow notepad from the windowsill where she'd left it earlier, and took it upstairs with her. She was working on a list of people she could ask for character references about Dylan, to submit to Shane. She wanted Shane to move the investigation in a new direction, help her figure out why and how her brother had been framed.

Maybe Kenny would help her.

She wished she was on speaking terms with Grace so she could call her friend and tell her all about that development. She hated the rift between them. But if she was against Dylan… No matter how good friends they'd been once, family came first.

At least Kenny was on her side.

As she got ready for bed, she tried to think of all the things she knew about him. He'd been one of the jocks back in high school, like her brother. Now he was a decent sheriff with a good record. He supported all kinds of fund-raisers, was behind the department getting new cruisers a few years back. His department in Pebble Creek wasn't laying off like Shane's here in Hullett.

She wondered what Logan would think of him.

But even as she thought about Kenny while falling asleep, her dreams were filled with Moses Mann. Oddly, in her dreams, he didn't come to accuse or frame her. He came to protect her.

ANOTHER DAY, another interrogation room. This one, at the Hullett jail, was bigger than the one at the office trailer Mo's team used, but the furnishings were older and pretty banged up. Obviously, the place had seen a lot of use over the years.

Mo rolled his shoulders. He missed Molly Rogers. How stupid was that? He looked across the desk at Mikey Metzner, owner of the Hullett Wire Mill, Dylan Rogers's partner in crime in human trafficking. He was in his early thirties, a trust-fund yuppie who'd inherited his father's business. Obviously, he hadn't been satisfied with all that easy money. Maybe he was an adrenaline junkie.

He looked pretty confident still, after nearly a week be-hind bars, two fancy Dallas lawyers flanking him. He'd been questioned before and denied everything. He held the firm belief that his money was going to save him.

Mo was here to convince him of the error of his thinking.

"How long have you been in the smuggling business, Mr. Metzner?" He didn't mince words. He wasn't in the best of moods. He hated starting his Sunday morning by having to talk to jackasses like the one before him.

"You don't have to answer that," one of the lawyers said.

"I had no idea something so atrocious was going on at my mill. I'm as shocked as you are," Metzner said straight-faced, wearing his best pious expression. "I can't tell you how terrible I feel that somebody would use my mill for something so completely reprehensible."

Give the man a golden statue, Mo thought morosely as he leaned forward in his seat. "Your hired men are out-doing each other confessing, blaming everything on you, hoping for a plea bargain."

Unfortunately, they had nothing valuable. The handful of underlings his team had caught only knew their own tasks.

He fixed Mikey with a flat look. "Who else was involved in running things on this side of the border beyond you and Dylan Rogers?"

"I have no idea what you're talking about."

"We have multiple, signed confessions from your goons, naming you the head of the operation in Hullett. Do you really want to take the rap for this?"

"I was head of nothing." The man's shoulders stiffened as he looked from one lawyer to the other, then back at Mo. "You can't believe anything those people say. They are the ones responsible. I'll testify against them."

Mo shrugged. "We already have all we need for a conviction. We caught them red-handed."

The bastard's face paled. Cold sweat broke out on his forehead. "What do you want from me?"

"A name. Who is the third partner?"

One of the lawyers coughed.

Mikey straightened and started talking stiffly, as if repeating a prerecorded message. "I wasn't involved in any smuggling. Whatever was going on in the basement at the mill, it had nothing to do with me. I'm a respectable businessman. I provide several hundred jobs in this community. The public is not going to be happy if those jobs disappear."

Mo shrugged again. "Public patience is running out with all the dirty dealings on the border. Local elections are coming up. Results need to be demonstrated. Somebody is going to be made an example of. The higher up in the chain of command in the smuggling ring, the better. So far, you're the highest we have."

He ignored the lawyers and pinned Metzner with a hard look. "Multiple counts of kidnapping, moving persons across international borders, child exploitation, human trafficking." He paused. "I could go on, but I'm in a hurry."

He pushed his chair back and stood. "Better get used to the idea of a maximum sentence. I have two words for you, Mikey—federal prison."

Metzner's Adam's apple bobbed. "There's no way I'm going to prison. You can't scare me. This is police intimidation. This is harassment."

Mo held the man's gaze. "You want harassment, wait till you're behind bars. You've gone soft from office work, Mikey. Life in prison's not gonna be pretty."

The man stared at him, radiating hate. A few seconds of silence passed before he said, "Look, I was brought in because I had the mill and it has a lot of room. Nobody notices a couple of extra Mexicans coming and going. None of this was my idea."

"Yeah, sure. Practically a victim," Mo said dispassionately. He didn't move toward the door, but neither did he sit back down. "Give me a name."

"I don't know anything."

"Give me a name."

"Look." His head snapped up. "I know Dylan was working with someone in town, but I don't know who. My only contact was Dylan. I swear."

Threatening him hadn't worked before, and it didn't look as if it would work now. He was too full of himself to truly believe he couldn't beat the charges.

Which gave Mo an idea. Maybe playing on the man's ego would work better.

"I understand. They didn't trust you. They didn't think you could handle it. They played you because they figured you weren't smart enough to know that you were being played."

"I'm plenty smart. Smarter than them."

"How do you figure?"

"Dylan is dead and I'm alive," he said, smug-faced.

"Yet you have nothing to give me to make your life easier."

Metzner rubbed his fingertips together. "If you drop the charges..."

Mo watched him carefully. So there *was* something. "Not going to happen. You tell me what you have, and it'll be taken into consideration at your sentencing."

Metzner looked at his lawyers. They were scowling, but the older one nodded again.

"Coyote," Metzner said in a low tone. "I overheard Dylan a few months ago talking on the phone to someone. He was saying something about the Coyote being pissed because too many of his mules were getting busted lately."

Now they were getting somewhere. He grabbed the back

of his chair and leaned on it. "You think this Coyote was Dylan's other friend who handles the smuggling around here?"

Mikey shook his head. "Coyote is the one who's sending the mules."

The big boss on the other side of the border? Hell, if they could identify him, it would be the biggest break they'd caught so far.

But no matter how many questions Mo asked after that, that single name was the only thing Metzner could give him. He headed back into the office more frustrated than when he'd left it earlier that morning.

He was beginning to hate this op. When they were sent in for an overseas mission, there was usually a clear-cut enemy. They were generally in some jungle or on some Afghan mountainside, or in the desert where they could maneuver without fear of civilian casualties. They did rescues, assassinations or intelligence gathering.

Now they were in small-town America, pussyfooting around fellow citizens who were too stupid to realize that by violating the border, they were weakening national security. He was a low-key guy. He had a pretty good rein on his temper for the most. But he seriously wanted to beat Mikey Metzner's head into the damned desk back there. He couldn't stand it when someone was messing with his country.

"Anything?" Ray, a big chunk of Viking wearing a leg cast, asked as soon as Mo walked through the door. He and Jamie were working from the office that morning, comparing satellite images and analyzing CBP data, looking for likely crossing points across the Rio Grande.

The team had already discovered two tunnels. Both discoveries had been compromised, unfortunately. One of the tunnels had blown up, injuring Ray. The transfer would happen someplace else. The key was to find out where and let no one know that they knew the location. They wanted the transfer to go ahead as planned so they could apprehend those terrorists and their weapons.

"Not much," he answered Ray. "Yet. But we'll get them."

"We're gonna kick terrorist ass." Ray grinned. "That's what we do."

The sooner, the better. "This small-town business is more like detective work," Mo grumbled. "Having to treat dirtbags like Metzner with kid gloves while the tangos are getting a step closer to crossing the border rubs me the wrong way."

He'd been made for action, not for investigative detail.

"Prepare for more of this when you transfer to the CIA," Jamie put in. "It's not all fancy gadgets and pretty women like in the movies."

He knew that. He wanted it anyway. His foster father, the man who'd pretty much saved his life, had tried out for the agency. He didn't pass the test because of an old war injury from his Marine days. But it had been his dream. He had been through some bad breaks, had lost close friends in his platoon due to bad intelligence. He'd wanted to do something about that, bring combat experience to the agency.

He had tried to direct his sons that way, too, but none of them had an interest in the military, let alone intelligence services. Except Mo. He wanted to make the man proud, wanted to make that dream come true. It was such a small thing compared to what his foster father had done for him.

"Anyway, I did get one thing from Metzner," Mo said as he headed for the coffee. "A nickname. Coyote."

Ray swore. "Could be anyone."

"Guy is smart. You have to be to run a billion-dollar business. Still," Jamie said. "It's something we didn't have before. Could be a starting point. We can ask around."

Shep strode in just then, coming off border patrol.

"Anything?" Mo asked, hoping his teammate had better luck this morning.

"Interviewed a dozen ranchers near the border, border agents, even bird watchers." He shrugged. "Everybody says the same thing. Barely anyone is crossing these days. They think it's because of the economy."

"Or because the bastard in charge is having everyone lie low while he gets ready for his big move," Mo thought out loud.

Jamie pushed to his feet. "I better head out. All we need is one lucky break, catching one guy who knows something."

He had been hired as operations coordinator. Technically, he didn't have to leave the office. But he'd insisted on being put on the rotation, even though walking around with his prosthetic legs had to be exhausting, possibly painful. He never used that as an excuse. If anything, he pushed himself harder than anyone else. If Mo knew one thing, it was this: when they all fell down, Jamie Cassidy would still be standing.

He had the hardest eyes Mo had ever seen and very few emotions. He had a legendary record within the SDDU, not that he ever talked about past missions. Especially not about the one that had taken his legs. And everybody respected that.

"Mo got a name from Mikey Metzner," he told Shep. "Coyote."

"Sounds like it could be a gang name," Shep said as he dropped into his chair and turned on his computer.

"Makes sense. The man could have started out in the gangs then risen in the ranks." The gangs were connected to the smuggling, the smuggling was connected to Dylan Rogers, and Dylan Rogers was connected to whoever the third man was that controlled illegal activity in this specific area. The very man they needed. Even if he didn't know the Coyote's true identity, he would know how to get in touch with him.

Mo thought about that for another minute before his thoughts switched to something else. "Did you go by the Rogers Ranch on your way in?"

"Yeah," Shep said. "Just the red pickup in the driveway."

"Had a police cruiser out last night. The sheriff from Pebble Creek. Forgot to tell you," Ray added.

Kenny Davis, Mo recalled. He pushed to his feet. "What time?"

"Around eight."

He didn't like it. Molly hadn't called for help. They monitored the emergency services channels. "Wonder what he wanted."

Jamie shrugged. "Maybe he's investigating her brother's dealings, too."

Mo frowned. "It's not his jurisdiction."

Keith was watching him closely. "You seem very interested in this woman."

Mo put on his best poker face. "She's closely tied to the smuggling. Her brother played an integral part."

"So you think she's involved?"

"No," he admitted after a long second.

Ray raised an eyebrow and grinned. "She's pretty. Fine curves."

Mo shot the big Viking a look. "She's got a kid."

"So?"

"Keep your dirty eyes off her."

Ray laughed out loud. "It's like that, huh?"

Now Jamie, too, was grinning.

"It's not like anything." He just didn't want any harm

to come to her or Logan. The idea of those two in danger because of her idiot brother bothered him.

"Hey," Ray said to Jamie. "If Molly Rogers and Mo hooked up, would their celebrity nickname be Mo-Mo?"

Jamie gave a bark of a laugh. "How about just Moo?"

Mo stepped forward. "How about I knock your heads together?" he offered without heat. They ribbed each other all the time, pretty much part of the op. It allowed for letting off some steam.

Ray lifted his hands in a defensive gesture. "Listen, we're nothing if not supportive."

Jamie's grin widened.

Mo gave them a disgusted look, made sure he had his gun and his wallet, and headed for the door. "I'm heading into Hullett. Want to look at Dylan Rogers's apartment again." Wanted to talk to the Hullett sheriff about that, too. Why the place hadn't been released to Molly yet. Maybe the sheriff had found something he wasn't sharing.

He was at his car when his cell phone rang. Keith, the youngest guy on the team, was calling in. He'd been gathering intelligence on the other side of the border. The gun, drug and human smuggling in the area all seemed to be connected.

"Picking up bits and pieces of clues here and there. Not nearly enough." Frustration laced Keith's voice. "The human trafficking was set up for Hullett, with the help of the wire mill. But so far everything I have says the drugs are coming through Pebble Creek and distributed from there. I think different crews are running those two businesses."

"Makes sense. If one is busted, the other is still running. Probably a third crew runs the guns. Anyone mention the name Coyote?"

"No. Who is he?"

"Might be the big boss on that side."

"I'll see what I can find out."

They talked for another minute before hanging up. Mo drove by the Rogers ranch on his way to town. Nothing suspicious out there. The driveway stood empty.

Since it was nearly four o'clock by the time he reached Hullett and he hadn't had lunch yet, he drove down Main Street, considering popping into the diner and grabbing a quick meal. But as he parked, he spotted Molly going into Gordie's across the street.

Wearing a pretty blue summer dress.

Two young guys turned after her, checking her out, but she was oblivious to her admirers, just smoothed her dress down and walked inside, looking a little nervous.

Mo crossed the road and went in after her. Might as well ask her if she had any trouble last night, why the Pebble Creek sheriff was over at her place. He wanted to make sure she was okay. But as he stepped into the restaurant, he spotted the man in question getting up from a table in the back and greeting Molly with a big smile.

For a moment, Mo stood and stared.

They're on a damned date.

Man, he felt stupid. And then he knew at once what Kenny had been doing at her place last night.

His jaw clenched, even as a perky blonde waitress hurried over to him.

She flashed a toothy smile. "How many are in your party?"

"I was just looking for someone. Thanks. They're not here." He turned on his heel and stalked out. The sight of the sheriff with Molly twisted his insides as if he'd swallowed poison. What the hell was wrong with him?

SAYING YES TO KENNY had been a mistake. She knew it five minutes into dinner, but at that point, it would have been

inexcusably rude to get up and walk away. She appreciated all Kenny was doing for her, but whatever her grandmother had said about love growing over time, she knew
at a gut level that nothing whatsoever was ever going to
grow between them. Even the least spark of chemistry was
completely missing.

She had more chemistry with Moses Mann, for heaven's
sake, and that man thought she was a criminal.

"I can probably find a buyer for Dylan's truck," Kenny
was saying as they walked out of the restaurant after dinner. They'd talked more about her brother than anything
else. "After the police release it."

"That would be great." Whatever money she got for
that she would immediately put into the new mortgage on
the ranch.

A pink convertible pulled up in front of the diner next
to them. Four women about her age got out, laughing and
teasing each other. They had matching tattoos on their
shoulders, maybe some sort of a sorority symbol. They
joked about their cross-country drive that sounded like a
grand adventure.

They looked wild and free, and she felt a sudden pang
of envy. She'd done everything possible in the past eight
years not to raise any eyebrows, to become a respectable
mother, someone people didn't whisper about. She didn't
want Logan to have to struggle with that in school like she
had to with her mother's reputation back in the day.

Her wild side scared her. She'd given in to it once and
ended up with the wrong man. She'd had to pay for that
every day since. She'd learned her lesson. Safe was always best.

Kenny looked safe enough. He was a sheriff.

Why couldn't she feel some attraction toward him?

He was looking her over, his interest clear in his gaze. "Wish I could drive you home."

She was flattered. She really was. But she wasn't interested.

"Got the pickup right here." She stepped toward her car. "Have to go get Logan from the library."

Kenny leaned forward, probably to kiss her on the cheek. She headed him off by lifting her hand for a quick wave and stepping back at the same time. Then she turned to search for her car keys in her purse. She didn't look up until she found them.

"Thank you for dinner. It was really nice to catch up." Was it too late to start pretending that the past hour and a half had been just a friendly meeting?

Kenny watched her for a second. "I'll see you around, then. I have the night shift tonight. I'll be driving by to make sure everything is all right out your way."

"Thanks," she said sincerely. Kenny wouldn't work as a boyfriend, but she was more than grateful to have him as a friend. Maybe she could pay him back in some small measure with a basket of goodies from her garden. And by taking extra-special care of his horse. Not that she didn't pretty much spoil all her animals rotten.

She drove over to the library, wishing once again that she had Grace to discuss her date with. Maybe Grace would talk her into trying harder. Heaven knew she was pitifully lonely these days. Somebody to share her life with would be nice.

She kept thinking about that as she drove to pick up her son, not liking at all that for some reason Moses Mann kept popping into her head.

"Look what I won, Mom!" Dylan held up a bag of books, his face radiating joy.

"I'm so proud of you. How about I take you for ice cream?"

"Ice cream!" He was hopping on one foot in excitement all the way to the car, then chatted on the drive to the ice-cream shop, filling her in on everything that had happened at the treasure hunt.

All right, so a boyfriend would have been nice, she thought, but as long as she had Logan, she was more than okay. The most important thing was that her son was happy.

They had ice cream, drove home singing to country songs on the radio, did their evening chores. After dinner, they moved on to their bedtime routine. Then she did some more work, washing glass jars, getting ready for the last of the canning. Eleven o'clock rolled by before she fell into bed, exhausted. But her rest was short-lived.

Shortly after midnight, she woke to the dogs barking outside.

Probably a coyote, she thought, fuzzy-brained. She turned onto her other side and tried to go back to sleep, but the dogs wouldn't give up. Then she came awake enough to remember the shed and all her recent problems with people prowling her property. Her heart rate picked up as she slipped from the bed.

She left the lights off so she could look outside and not be seen. Plenty of moonlight filtered into the room to make sure that she wouldn't trip on anything, so she shuffled to the nearest window.

The door on one of the outbuildings hung open. Had she forgotten to close the latch? No, she couldn't have. She'd been paying extra attention to make sure everything was closed up tight.

She tried to see the dogs but couldn't. One of them cried out, the long whine cutting through the night. She hurried downstairs and jumped into her boots. Then she stopped in her tracks when she thought about Mo's revelation that the knife used to slash her tires had also been used in a murder.

The dog whined again. She wasn't going to hide in here while one of her animals suffered, dammit. Who knew if Mo was even telling the truth? Could be he was just trying to scare her into spilling her brother's supposed secrets. She grabbed one of Dylan's rifles to be on the safe side and reached for the door, but then froze in her tracks as she put her hand on the doorknob.

She could see through the glass as a shadow, a human shadow, slipped from the outbuilding and ran around it, the dogs in close pursuit.

She opened the door and whistled for the dogs.

She had to whistle repeatedly before they came at last. She ordered them inside then locked the door and the doggie door. Then she went around to make sure all the other doors and windows were locked tight, too. And then she dialed Kenny. Shane and the Hullett police couldn't care less about her.

The phone rang and rang, but Kenny didn't pick up.

Her gaze fell on the card Mo left on her fridge. Okay, so it was possible he'd been right. Maybe someone *was* out there trying to do her harm.

Mo refused to believe that Dylan was innocent, but at least he cared about her and her son's safety. She dialed his number.

He picked up on the first ring. "Are you okay?" he asked before she could even say her name.

She had to raise her voice to be heard over the barking dogs that were jumping on the door, wanting to be let out. "There's someone outside."

"Go upstairs." His voice snapped tight. "Barricade yourself in one of the bedrooms with Logan and the dogs. I'll be right there. You have a gun with you?"

"Yes."

"If you need to use it, use it," he said before he hung up.

She had to practically drag the dogs upstairs with her. They wanted to go back outside, barking their heads off.

Waking up Logan, too.

"What happened, Mom?" he asked, sleepy-eyed, as she dragged the dogs into his room and locked the door behind them.

"Probably an armadillo."

His eyes closed. Then opened again. "Can I have pancakes for breakfast?"

"Sure. But it's not morning yet. You go back to sleep."

He drifted off again as the dogs jumped onto the bed and settled down around him in a protective circle.

An eternity passed before she heard a car pulling up her driveway. Which set the dogs barking again. She was pretty sure it was Mo, but since she couldn't see the front from Logan's room, she stayed put, hanging on to the gun.

Whoever it was didn't try to come into the house. But soon she did see Mo going around back, walking from outbuilding to outbuilding, checking everything. For the first time, she found his bulk and the determined way he moved reassuring. And she relaxed. Which was so stupid. She shouldn't relax around Mo. His presence shouldn't make her feel safe.

He wanted to pin multiple murders on her brother. He was scarcely her friend. And yet, she did feel better for having him here.

He spent half an hour doing a thorough job of checking every building before he came to the back door and knocked. "It's me."

"Coming." She padded downstairs to let him in. The dogs saw their chance and rushed out as soon as the door opened, this time ignoring her calls to get back inside.

He pretty much filled the doorway as he stood on the threshold, looking her over. "Are you and Logan okay?"

And there came that sense of safety again. As if everything was fine now just because he was here. She wanted to throw herself into his arms in relief. Which was an impulse beyond crazy, and very distracting.

He had to repeat his question before it finally reached her brain and she nodded.

"Did you see who it was?"

"Just a shadow."

"One person or more?"

"I only saw one." She reached for the kitchen light.

He put his large hand over hers. "In case somebody is out there still, let's not give them a target."

"You looked."

"Around the buildings. You can pick someone off with a good rifle from a fair distance."

Her stomach tightened at the thought. "Why would anyone want to hurt me?"

He seemed distracted. Kind of staring at her. And as she looked down, she realized she was standing in a shaft of moonlight, wearing nothing but her skimpy summer nightgown.

"Molly." His voice was low and thick.

Her gaze flew up and met his, and she found his eyes filled with hunger.

Tension ratcheted up and up between them. And then heat. All the heat that she'd been missing with Kenny.

Chapter Four

He'd been doing commando work long enough to have a sixth sense for knowing when trouble was coming.

Molly Rogers was trouble.

And the need that pulsed through his body as he took in her curves in the lavender silk gown was the least of it.

She stepped around him to the peg board by the back door, grabbed a summer cardigan and wrapped it around herself. He only registered disappointment where he should have felt relief. He didn't need the distraction.

He liked too many things about her. Her loyalty to her brother. Her devotion to her son. That she dealt with whatever came her way, worked the ranch, took care of everything with dignity and without complaint.

He'd asked around town about her. Found the town gossip at the diner. Mrs. Martin had called Molly "loose," not the kind of woman a decent man would get tangled with. But when Mo went after specifics...

"So she's in town and in and out of bars every night?" he'd asked.

"Well, no. She doesn't really do bars," the woman admitted with some reluctance.

"With a different man, then, every week, flaunting her boyfriends around town?"

"Not like that."

"Men go visit her at the ranch?"

"Probably. Just like her mother. It's in the blood. Women like her draw men to sin."

Okay, that he could picture. She certainly inspired sinful thoughts in him.

"You know any of the men?"

"She was here with a *sheriff* the other day. And I'm sure there are many others." Then came a meaningful look. "She never told anyone who her son's father is, you know. There has to be a reason for *that*."

At the end, he found out nothing new about Molly, but had felt dirtier for the gossip.

He had no trouble talking to her in the interrogation room, but he had no idea what to tell her now, in the middle of the night in her dark kitchen, with her standing there semi-naked. He wasn't exactly a ladies' man like some of the guys on his team.

He wanted her. He couldn't tell her that. For one, he had no business wanting her. He was here on an op, an op that was tied to her brother, even if she *was* innocent like he was believing more and more with every passing day.

"I hope Logan didn't get scared," he said. There, her son should be a safe subject.

She looked toward the stairs. "Barely woke up. Went right back to sleep." She turned from him and walked to the fridge. "I'm sorry for bothering you in the middle of the night. Thank you for coming out. Would you like a cold drink?"

"No bother. And a drink would be great."

She poured him sweet tea. "Sun-made." She filled a glass for herself then sat at the kitchen table by the window and looked out.

He followed her gaze to keep his eyes from sliding to

her bare legs. On second thought… He sat across the table from her. Better have something tangible between them.

Moonlight bathed the outbuildings in a silver glow, the stars bright in the sky. With very little pollution out here in the country, every star in the whole universe seemed visible from where they were sitting.

He liked sitting with her in the night, drinking her sweet tea and looking at the stars. He liked it too much. Being with her somehow made him feel as if he'd been lonely all his life, until now. Which was ridiculous. With back-to-back ops, he'd never had time to be lonely.

He shifted in his seat and tried to focus on things he should be focusing on. "Anything you can tell me about your brother will only help."

She drew back, her face hardening in a split second. A different kind of tension filled the air. "Who would it help? Not him. He's dead. Killed by one of the men you work with."

"If we had some answers, it would help you and Logan. Too many things are going on at the ranch. All the smuggling we discovered so far is not a good thing. And it might be just the tip of the iceberg." That was as much as he could tell her.

"Dylan was not a smuggler."

"You're not going to be able to move on until you face the truth. And you're not going to be safe until we figure out who his partners were and what exactly they were doing with him. They clearly want something from you. Your best chance at staying safe is if you help me take these men out of circulation."

Her lips flattened. "The truth is, my brother was framed. And the ranch is perfectly safe. The man…was probably just some drifter. It happens."

He looked at her for a long time. "You're a smart woman.

You've faced hardship before, but you made it work. You're raising your son just fine. You're handling the ranch…"

She cut him off. "I'm not in denial, if that's what you're getting at."

"Dylan—"

"Dylan can't be the bad guy." She shook her head stubbornly. "You don't understand. Dylan was always the perfect child in the family, the small-town football hero, then the successful businessman. I am the family goof-up."

She had plenty of conviction in her voice to tell him she fully believed that. Apparently, she saw herself in a completely different light than he saw her.

"I get it. Your brother was a very important part of your life. When people who are supposed to care about us do bad things, it's not an easy thing to face."

She shot to her feet, her hand grasping the back of her chair. "What would you know about that? I'm sure you grew up in a perfect family. I'm sure your father never drank, your mother never ran off with a stranger, you never had to—" She bit her lower lip.

A long moment of silence stretched between them.

"You think I have the perfect life?" He laughed out loud at that.

But she wouldn't give up. "You're strong. Whatever happens, you can defend yourself. You have all kinds of power, working for whoever you're working for. You're not at the mercy of anyone or anything. You have everything together."

He watched her. "And you?"

She let go of her chair and wrapped her arms around herself. "I have nothing together. I just lost my brother. People think he was a criminal. My son is getting into fights defending him. I can barely pay my bills. And strangers are coming to the ranch in the middle of the night for God knows what reason."

She sank back into her seat. "I'm a single mother. Half the time, I'm petrified of doing something wrong, not being able to protect my son, people being mean to him because of my mistakes." She shook her head. "I have nothing together. I'm just pretending that I do for Logan's sake."

They sat in the quiet of the night for a while after the confession ended, her gaze on the table. She was probably embarrassed that she'd told him all that.

He wished he knew what to say.

In combat, he was a well-trained fighting machine and pretty damned effective. With women, he was a bumbling idiot through and through. But she was in distress, and he hated the thought of that, wanted to say something to make it better if he could. He went with the stark truth, something he rarely, if ever, shared.

He stretched his legs out in front of him. "When I was born, my parents put me into a gym bag and dropped me into the Mississippi River from a bridge."

Her head snapped up. She stared at him. "I'm so sorry."

"Nothing to be sorry about. A Good Samaritan saw and fished me out. I went to foster care. Eventually ended up with the best family anyone could have wished for. Marine sergeant father, four older brothers, a mom who was kind and loving. They made me what I am today."

She sat silently for a long time. "What happened to your birth parents? It's just… It's unimaginable."

"It's unimaginable to you because you're a good mother. They were never identified."

"Are you still close to your foster family?"

"My mother and my father are gone. I keep in touch with my brothers." He didn't like the pity that sat on her face. "You might know one of them, actually. He's Calvin in 'Calvin Cat Counting.'"

"What?" Her eyes went wide. "Logan plays that game. Your brother is Calvin Mann? The guy who built an empire in educational software?"

"It's not that big of a deal. It's just a company."

Her eyes went wide. "Oh, my God. You're Mo."

He grinned. "I hope so. Otherwise, I'll have to have all new business cards printed."

"I mean, you're Mo the teddy bear, Calvin's best friend in the game."

He shook his head. "He did that without consulting me."

"Wait till Logan finds out." She laughed.

He couldn't help staring. She was pretty even under the worst circumstances, but when she laughed, she was dazzling. She should always be like that, happy and carefree.

But even as he thought that, she grew serious again. "Your name, Moses. Is it because…"

"Because I was pulled from water. The social worker who named me was a churchgoing woman." He finished his drink.

Molly watched him quietly, folding her hands together on the table in front of her. She opened her mouth, then closed it again. Then she finally said, "I want to tell you something, but I don't want you to make a big deal out of it."

His instincts prickled. She had his full attention. "Okay."

"Dylan took out a mortgage on the ranch," she said after a long minute. Then quickly added, "It doesn't mean he's a criminal. He could have needed the money for one of his businesses."

He chewed on the new piece of information for a few seconds. "Were you aware that he was having financial difficulties?"

She shook her head. "Maybe he wanted to expand the dealership."

"But he didn't say anything to you about it?"

"He had so many things going on. He was always running around. Sometimes he didn't even have time to stop in for dinner." She watched him. "Is there anything I could say to convince you that he was a good man?"

Moonlight glinted off her soft hair, for once loose and not up in a ponytail, the silky strands spilling over her shoulders. The silver light accentuated the wistful expression on her face. Every cell in his body responded to her. He didn't want to hurt her, but as far as her brother went…

"I believe he was good to you and Logan." He wanted to go around the table and pull her into his arms, offer her comfort he had no right offering. He pushed to his feet. "You get some sleep. I'm going back outside to check around again, walk in a wider circle."

She stiffened as she glanced to the window. "You think that man is still here?"

"It never hurts to be cautious. When the sun comes up, I'll find his tracks and take some tire molds. Maybe we can identify his vehicle."

She walked him to the door.

He stepped outside into the night. "Lock it behind me."

She looked worried. The urge to touch her, to smooth the furrows from her forehead, came on pretty strong. He wished he were more comfortable with women, more of a charmer, someone who could make a woman like her look differently at him.

But he wasn't. And she was dating the Pebble Creek sheriff.

So he walked away.

AFTER MOLLY PUT LOGAN on the school bus Monday morning, she paid her bills online, then looked Moses Mann up on Google while she had her second cup of coffee. Max and Cocoa were somewhere outside. Only Skipper lazed around in the kitchen, lying on the doormat by the back door. The old gal probably tuckered herself out running around outside half the night.

Molly scrolled down the list of hits, a very short list. The few things she found, articles in various newspapers, were mostly about Mo's brother Calvin Mann. Mo only got a sentence or two, about his role in his brother's business. He was a silent partner, according to one report.

Apparently, he'd been on active duty with the military when Calvin had started the software company in the family basement. Mo had fronted the money for the entire operation from his combat pay.

The "Calvin Cat Counting" game was a huge hit among elementary-school-age children, one of the top-rated educational games in the country. And they followed up with dozens of others from K–12 education to SAT- and college-prep software. Which meant both Mo and his brother had to be multimillionaires.

So why wasn't he sitting on some tropical island, sipping margaritas?

Even as the question popped into her head, it made her smile. She couldn't really imagine Mo as a surfer dude. Granted, he could be laid-back, but…there was also an intensity inside him, a drive. For a moment she couldn't pin it down, and then she did: he had a soldier's heart.

He would spend all day in over hundred-degree heat patrolling the border. He would rush to her house in the middle of the night when she was in trouble.

He would make a fierce enemy—she wasn't going to forget that interrogation anytime soon. But she had a feeling he also made the most loyal friend.

What kind of lover would he make?

She squeezed her eyes shut. She couldn't believe she'd just thought that.

To distract herself, she went back to her computer search. He had no Twitter or Facebook accounts, no social-media presence of any kind.

Maybe because he worked for the government. He was a consultant on border protection. Did that require some kind of security clearance and secrecy? She had no idea about these things.

Skipper gave a pitiful moan.

"Tired?" She offered some sympathy as she shut down the laptop. "Me, too. Maybe we'll get a little more sleep tonight. Want to go for a walk? I need to check on the garden."

As she walked to the door, Skipper struggled to her feet, and once she stood, she swayed.

"What is it, girl? Is your back hurting again?"

The dog gave another pitiful whine and threw up all over the doormat.

She rushed to her, grabbing a roll of paper towels in the process. "What did you eat out there last night?"

Skipper was notorious for eating anything she came across. She'd once eaten half of a two-by-four in the garage before Molly had noticed. And a cell phone. Several shoes. A dead mouse from the mousetrap in the barn. With the trap. Food that was left out... Forget it. Although she did do her level best to keep anything remotely tempting out of the dog's way.

She cleaned up, gave the poor dog some cold water. "You'll feel better now that it's out. What do I always tell you about eating only what I put in your dish?" She ran her fingers through the dog's fur and scratched behind her ear.

She didn't like how Skipper's brown eyes were glazed over. Or the way her muscles suddenly began to shake.

"All right. We're going to the doc." She grabbed her purse and walked out, really worried now. "Come on."

Skipper staggered after her. She didn't make it to the pickup. For the last couple of yards, Molly had to carry her.

She called the other dogs and they came running. They seemed fine, no signs of any sickness. Didn't look as if they'd eaten whatever Skipper had.

"When you recover from this, you're going on a diet." She struggled to get the dog onto the passenger seat.

All Skipper did was give her a pitiful look and an even more pitiful whimper.

"You'll be fine, okay? Just relax. We'll fix this," she said once she was in the driver's seat. But her heart was racing.

Nothing could happen to Skipper. She'd been a graduation present from Dylan. She'd been with Molly most of her adult life. She was Logan's favorite, the most faithful dog in the universe.

She called the vet from the road, got the receptionist. "I'm bringing Skipper in."

"We have a substitute today. Won't be in until this afternoon. Dr. Miller is off."

"It's an emergency. Can I go out to his place?" She'd done that before. Dr. Miller didn't keep strict hours.

"He's at a conference in San Antonio. The sub will be in by noon."

Skipper couldn't wait a couple of hours. And Molly did know another vet, someone who had just recently passed her last exam and got her license.

Grace Cordero, her once best friend.

"I'll figure something out," she told the receptionist and hung up, then took the turn that would lead her to the Cordero ranch.

Whatever their differences were these days, she was

willing to set them aside when Skipper's life hung in the balance.

But would Grace? For some reason Grace thought Dylan had tried to hurt her. Cold panic tingled down Molly's spine. If Grace didn't help…

They hadn't talked since the night Dylan died. When Grace had finally spread her own brother's ashes a few days later, Molly hadn't gone to the funeral. And Grace hadn't come to Dylan's. Nobody had.

Molly hadn't put an obituary in the paper. People were calling him a criminal, for heaven's sake. She had kept the funeral private. All she wanted in the paper was an official apology from the sheriff's department.

The drive to the Cordero ranch didn't take long. By the time she pulled up the driveway, Skipper's shaking had quieted. Grace's car was there. A good sign. Molly beeped the horn.

Grace opened the front door, took one look at her face through the windshield and came running. "What is it? Is it Logan?"

"Skipper," Molly said as she opened the door and jumped from the car, relieved to see only concern on Grace's face instead of any kind of resentment.

She was right there helping. A good thing, since it took the two of them to carry the listless dog into the house.

Grace lay Skipper right on the living-room floor and ran her hands all over the dog. "Muscle spasms. What happened? Snake bite?"

"I think she ate something again."

"Vomited?"

"Yes."

Grace probed the dog's belly with her fingers. Skipper squirmed and gave a humanlike moan.

"Did she have any shakes worse than this?"

"Yes." And just as she said that, the dog started shaking harder again.

Grace looked into her mouth, at her tongue, then ran to the laundry room and came back with her medical bag, measured out some medicine and dribbled the liquid into Skipper's mouth little by little. She kept examining the dog while Molly shifted on her feet.

"So how are *you* doing?" Grace asked without turning around, probably to distract her from the panic that was filling her chest.

What was a safe topic? "I think I kind of went on a date."

That earned a look and a tentative smile. "Mo?"

"Kenny," she said quickly.

"Oh. Ryder said Mo was kind of keeping an eye on your place. I thought…" Grace hesitated, as if wanting to say something about him, but then seemed to change her mind and only said, "I'm glad you're getting out. It's about time you stopped punishing yourself for the past."

Her defenses, barely lowered, went right back up. "I wasn't punishing myself for anything."

"You deserve love. How many guys have you turned down over the years?"

She shrugged. "I was busy with Logan and the ranch." But part of her, deep down, thought she didn't deserve some fairy-tale happily ever after.

She'd messed up when she'd been young. And worse than that, she was responsible for her family's falling apart, for her father's death. Just because nobody knew her darkest secrets, it didn't mean she didn't carry that guilt.

Grace was running her probing fingers over Skipper's abdomen again. "You keep any heavy-duty pesticides lying around?"

"No." She wouldn't dare have poison with Skipper getting into everything. And her gardening was strictly organic, her biggest selling point.

Grace gave her a quiet look. "Have any enemies?"

A chill ran through her. "You think she was poisoned?"

"I'm pretty sure. I'd like to keep her for a few days."

Dismay and anger filled her chest. "Why would somebody hurt her?"

"Maybe Dylan—" Grace started to say, then stopped. No way could they discuss her brother.

Molly stood. "How much do I owe you?"

"Don't be ridiculous."

And then they had nothing to say. The night of Dylan's death stood like an unbreachable stone wall between them once again.

She thanked Grace for the help and drove home, worrying about Skipper, trying to figure out what this all meant. So people believed the lies and thought Dylan had turned bad. But why take it out on her? And even if someone was doing just that, what had Skipper ever done to anyone? She was the best dog in the universe.

She was still worrying about the dog when she reached home and spotted a pickup and trailer in her driveway. Looked as if Kenny had brought his horse. He was coming from the stable, talking on his phone.

Bum date or not, she was happy to see him. The two-hundred-dollar boarding fee was a welcome addition to the ranch's budget. Knowing she had that little extra money would make her sleep easier.

He ended the call and put the phone away when she pulled up. "I put Charlie in the stall you made ready for him. Much obliged. Missed your call last night. By the time I saw it, I didn't want to call you back. I figured you'd be asleep."

"I had someone sniffing around." She told him about

the man in her backyard, about the possibility that Skipper might have been poisoned. "At least *you* believe that Dylan was innocent. I really appreciate that."

"Whatever you need from me. I want to be there for you." He stepped closer. "I mean it."

"Thanks. And I'll take good care of Charlie. I promise. I'll have him out in the back corral. I'm going to keep him separated from the others for a couple of days, until they all get used to each other." They should be fine. She didn't have another stallion, just a gelding and a couple of mares, and her mares weren't in heat.

"I'll be stopping in to check on him. Want to make sure I ride him. He needs the exercise."

"Come and go as you please. If I'm not here and you want to ride, just go straight back. I'll probably be putting padlocks on the outbuildings, but I'll give you a key."

He shook his head with an apologetic smile. "I was supposed to bring those locks, wasn't I? Don't know where my mind is these days. Next time I come out, I'll have them. I promise."

"Thanks, Kenny."

"You need to be safe."

"I need to find a way to prove that Dylan was framed and had nothing to do with smuggling. Whoever is coming around probably believes Dylan was guilty, and the idiot is trying to mete out some vigilante justice. Or they figure there may be some drugs or whatever other contraband hidden on the property, left over from the smuggling—easy pickings."

Once Dylan was exonerated, people would no longer have a reason to bother her. So that was what she had to achieve and in a hurry.

Kenny reached out to take her hand, a sympathetic expression on his face. "Listen—"

Her stomach sank. She pulled her hands away. "Don't tell me they talked you into this idiocy. Dylan was framed."

"Of course he was. But I was thinking, too, and…he might have had some link to something. Maybe he didn't even know it was bad. Somebody asking him for a favor. You know how he was."

"He would help anyone if they asked him."

"The wrong kind of people could take advantage of someone with a big heart like he had."

"Exactly."

"If someone asked him to store something for them for a while…"

She stilled. "Like drugs?"

"That man here last night." Kenny patted her hand again. "Sure sounds like he was looking for something. And…" He looked uncomfortable again.

"What?"

"I don't want you to be offended. I'm not accusing Dylan of anything."

"What is it?"

"I heard something through the grapevine this morning. An old informant called in."

Cold spread through her chest. "About Dylan?"

"No. But this guy says the local drug runners are looking for a missing shipment."

"My brother was no drug runner."

"Of course not. I'm just saying someone could have asked him to store something and he might not even have known what it was."

"But there's nothing like that here. I would know."

He tilted his head. "Would you?"

She thought of the bags and bags of feed, hay bales, the unused haylofts she hadn't climbed in ages, the covered-up grease pit in the garage. It was probably full of rattlers. "Maybe not," she admitted reluctantly.

Kenny gave a slow nod. "We got time. How about I help you look around? If we find something, I'll take care of it. I'll take it in. Your name or your brother's name doesn't have to come up."

Gratitude filled her. "You really are a good friend, Kenny."

Chapter Five

Mo squinted against the sun as he drove down the road, coming in from border surveillance, deciding to drop by the Rogers ranch. He was talking on the phone with Jamie, who was at the office, and turned up the Bluetooth so he could hear him better.

"Tell me you're doing something exciting and I can be there in ten minutes. Tell me you busted someone."

They were all itching for action.

"Barely any movement. The shipments are definitely on hold."

"The big boss probably figured out surveillance was stepped up. We did take two tunnels out of commission."

Right. They'd covered that ground before. It made sense. Except… Mo tapped his fingers on the steering wheel as he rethought their theory.

"CBP does raids and surges all the time. The smugglers just move to another method. When border surveillance is stepped up, they switch to transporting contraband hidden in trucks, right through the checkpoints. When checkpoints get extra agents, they switch to swimming the river. When the river is monitored, they go to the tunnels. They don't just stop everything all at once."

"Okay," Jamie said on the other end. "So why the moratorium now?" He paused and spoke to someone in the office, away from the phone, for a second before getting back to Mo. "So, um, Ryder's in. He says Grace says Molly Rogers's dog was poisoned last night. He thought you might want to know."

Cold filled his stomach. "Thanks. I'll talk to you when I get in." He hung up and pushed down harder on the gas pedal.

He pulled up to the house, wrestled with the greeting committee, two dogs only, when he got out of his SUV, then went looking for Molly.

She was in the garden, harvesting summer squash, her curves encased in jeans shorts, the heels of her cowboy boots and her cowboy hat giving her an extra couple of inches in height. She was okay.

The tension in his stomach relaxed. She was better than okay. The top two buttons of her short-sleeved shirt were unbuttoned in deference to the heat, the bottom of the shirt tied in a knot at her waist.

He tried not to stare at her bare midriff. Nothing motherly about her today. With all her curves, she looked like a pinup girl.

She straightened, buttoned up the shirt one button and let the bottom down to cover her skin as she watched him approach. He wished she hadn't. *Focus on the business at hand.*

A flash of anger replaced the worry inside him. "Skipper was poisoned. Why didn't you call me?"

She pushed her hat out of her eyes.

Even as his fingers itched to reach for a stray strand of hair. He didn't.

"You're not a vet," she said. "There was nothing you could have done to help."

"Anything happens here, I want to know about it."

"I'm not involved in smuggling." Her full lips pressed into a scowl. "I thought we were past that."

"We are. I know you're not involved. But you're still linked to it through your brother." That sounded more official than saying that the thought of her coming to harm put a lead ball in his stomach. "You're still part of the investigation."

Fire came into her eyes as always when he brought up that subject. She picked up her bushel of squash and came out of the garden, closed the gate behind her. She marched up to the house, went in through the back door, leaving it open for him.

She set the bushel down just inside the door, then stepped out of her boots and took off her hat. "Kenny says whoever was out here last night might have been looking for drugs or something. Dylan had a lot of friends. One of them could have given him a package or whatever to keep. If that's what happened, Dylan wouldn't even have known what was in it." She blew the hair out of her eyes. "I checked around."

"Find anything?"

Her shoulders fell. "Nothing. And I looked hard. Kenny helped me, too. We looked for hours."

Kenny the ever-helpful.

He shifted closer. She smelled like sunshine and her lemon-verbena shampoo, the two of them standing barely two feet from each other in the narrow back entryway. He wanted to reach out and pull her to him.

"So Kenny and you…" He left the sentence hanging.

"Kenny went to school with Dylan," she said as she turned and walked away from him. "He's boarding his horse here now."

He waited, but she said nothing more, nothing about them seeing each other socially. He wasn't going to ask.

It was none of his business. "Are you seeing him?" The words snuck out anyway.

She stopped by the fridge and opened the door, but turned back. "He's a friend."

She looked into his eyes as she said that. He didn't think she was lying. Still, she might think Kenny was her friend, but Kenny wanted more. The way the sheriff had looked at her at Gordie's… The thought tightened the muscles in Mo's jaw.

Kenny seemed to be spending a lot of time here lately, he thought as he walked over to the kitchen table where she set out a glass of sun-brewed iced tea for him.

He liked sitting in her kitchen and drinking sweet tea. He could easily imagine doing a lot more of that. Doing other things, too.

Except, when his op was over, he would be out of here. He'd be going to Washington to work for the CIA, then probably out of the country on his first assignment.

To start something with Molly under the circumstances wouldn't be right. Despite the gossip, he knew what kind of woman she was—the family kind. She wasn't out looking for a temporary lover. She deserved nothing less than a husband, and a father to Logan, someone who would stick by her, help her run the ranch.

And Mo couldn't give her that. He had a schedule. CIA first, while he was young enough to do active duty overseas—another ten years, he figured. Then he would be transferred to desk duty in the States. That was the time when he would be looking to settle down and start a family.

Molly was great, but he wasn't there yet, wasn't ready. Which was why he needed to get the idea of kissing her out of his head.

If only it was that easy.

HE HAD THE KIND of presence that filled up a place. Mo in her kitchen drinking her iced tea and making appreciative noises created tingles in her stomach. She wished Kenny could do that—Kenny, whom she'd known forever, who was actually interested in her.

Kenny believed in her brother's innocence. Kenny would still be around next year and the next and the next. Kenny was a normal person, not part-owner of a multimillion-dollar company like Mo.

She'd done the "most eligible bachelor" thing. She'd fallen in love with the son of the richest man in town, let herself be blinded by her teenage crush and be thoroughly seduced by him.

When she'd told him she was pregnant, he refused to believe he was the father. He refused to have anything to do with her. He'd threatened to take her son away if she ever breathed his name in connection with paternity. And he had enough money to hire all the lawyers he needed to get the job done.

Rich people lived by a different set of rules than the rest of the world. They got what they wanted, any way they wanted it. Smartest thing to do was to stay out of their path. When you hooked up with someone like that, they had all the power. She would never let that happen again. She was not an impressionable seventeen-year-old anymore.

Whatever attraction she felt for Mo, she was more than capable of resisting it. She would never be more than a temporary plaything to him, to fill his time while here on assignment. When this job ended, he would go away and leave her heartbroken. She needed that like a rattler in her boots.

"Listen, I should—" She was trying to politely tell him that she needed to get back to work—these little moments in her kitchen had to end—but the phone rang before she could finish the sentence. She stepped over to the counter to pick it up.

"Hi, is this Ms. Rogers? I'm Betty from the principal's office."

Her whole body tightened in an instant. "Did something happen to Logan?"

"He's okay, but he was in a fight a little earlier. Mr. Talbot would like you to come in."

Not again. She squeezed her eyes shut for a second. "I'll be right there." She hung up then turned to Mo. "Sorry, I have to go."

He emptied his glass as he stood. "What happened?"

"Logan got in trouble at school for fighting." She glanced down at her clothes. Other than one minor smudge of dirt from the garden, they were passable. She hurried to the pegs by the back door and grabbed her purse.

"I'll go with you." Mo was right behind her.

"It's not necessary. It's—"

"Why don't I just come anyway?"

She didn't have time to argue with him. She pulled on her summer sandals and rushed through the door. He drove.

She didn't mind that. She was distracted—all the things that had been happening at the ranch, then Skipper and now Logan... "He's a good kid." Her tone came out defensive.

"I know."

"He's taking Dylan's death really hard."

Mo nodded, his SUV gobbling up the miles. He drove faster than she would have normally been comfortable with, but under the circumstances, she didn't mind.

They sat in silence as she worried.

"Find any tire tracks from the other night?" she asked eventually. "I keep forgetting to ask."

He nodded. "They led east for half a mile then cut back

to the road. I took some casts. Generic tires you can buy at any gas station. Not much of a lead."

She filled her lungs. "I just want everything to go back to normal."

"Give it time. Things will settle down." He slowed as they reached the school and pulled into the visitors' parking lot right by the front door.

She was unbuckling the seat belt even before he shut off the engine. "Thanks. You don't have to come in."

"I don't mind." He followed her to the principal's office.

Mr. Talbot was waiting for them. Logan, with a split lip, sat in the corner, his head hanging.

She wanted to rush up to him and ask if he was okay. She didn't. He had behaved badly, and he knew it. She wasn't about to coddle him. Positive reinforcement had to be reserved for positive behavior. Parenting was hard business.

He hung his head even deeper as the door closed behind them. "I'm sorry, Mom."

"Ms. Rogers." The principal stood, then looked at Mo.

"Moses Mann," Mo introduced himself. "Friend of the family. What happened?"

"A fight in the bathroom, apparently. The other child involved has already been sent home. Both boys are receiving suspensions for the rest of the week."

Molly bit her lip. "I'm so sorry. It's not like Logan at all. He's been having a hard time lately." They were going to have a long talk about this. Again.

"I know," Mr. Talbot agreed. "And from what I hear, he didn't start the fight. Regardless, we don't condone violence."

Logan stood and shuffled over to her. While she didn't approve of his actions, she hated the crushed look on his little face. She put her hand on his shoulder, wanting nothing more than to get out of there.

But Mo said, "Do you condone bullying?"

The principal frowned. "Of course not."

"Were you aware that Logan has been bullied on multiple occasions over his uncle's death?"

"Mr. Mann—"

"Would you mind sharing with us what steps have been taken so far to stop it?"

The principal swallowed. He was a head shorter than Mo and probably a hundred pounds lighter. And it wasn't just Mo's physique that was impressive. He could turn his voice into tempered steel, his eyes hard and cold in a way that really made you want to not mess with him. She knew that voice and look, had the bad luck to experience it in the interrogation room.

He kept on pushing. "Do you think it's wise to allow bullying to go on in your school and then punish the victim? Have you thought about what kind of message you're sending to the children? To their parents? Do you take the safety of your students seriously, Mr. Talbot?"

"Well, Mr. Mann—"

"The law does allow for self-defense."

"Of course."

"So there should be no reason at all for Logan's suspension. Seeing how he didn't start the fight."

A strained silence stretched between them.

"Yes. I think you're correct." Mr. Talbot adjusted his tie then looked at her. "You can, of course, still take him home for the rest of the day."

Since Logan did look as if he could use a little cleaning up, she said, "Thank you. I will." And watched as her son stared at Mo as if he was some hero straight out of the comic books, an expression very similar to the one he used to regard Dylan with.

She hoped she was controlling her own expression a

little better. She couldn't remember the last time someone, other than her, had stood up for her son. The look on his smudged face told her how much that meant to him.

They stepped out of the principal's office just as the bell rang, kids filling the hallway. More than a few curious glances were directed toward Mo and his commando swagger. He put a friendly smile on his face, then a hand on Logan's shoulder as they walked out.

The kids pulled back respectfully. Logan seemed to grow several inches.

She glanced at his split lip. "Are you okay?" That her son had been cornered in the bathroom broke her heart. Maybe Mo was right and it wasn't always possible to walk away from trouble. She didn't want Logan hurt.

"No big deal." He shrugged, playing the tough guy.

But he shouldn't have to. He shouldn't have to suck up a beating, and she shouldn't have to worry about sending him to school.

"If the offer still stands," she told Mo as they walked out, "maybe you could teach him just a little bit about how to defend himself."

"I'd be happy to. Hope you don't mind that I spoke up in there. Punishing Logan didn't seem right or fair."

She shook her head. Honestly, she could have kissed him.

"ANYTHING INTERESTING so far?" Mo asked Jamie over the radio the next morning.

The air shimmered in the heat, the ground nothing but dust. What few bushes and grass still clung to life weren't terribly impressive. His SUV left a pretty big dust cloud behind as he drove over the landscape. He was probably visible from miles away. He doubted he'd be catching anyone today.

CBP had their own patrols, few and far between, due to budget restrictions. Mo's team had been set up to provide a more comprehensive coverage for the section they were interested in.

"Caught a handful of people crossing this morning, all at separate locations. Just swam for it. Didn't look like part of the smuggling operation. They had no guides," Jamie told him.

"Mules?"

"They didn't carry anything. Swam across with the clothes on their backs."

Customs and Border Protection could deal with them, Mo thought and kept driving, keeping an eye out for anything out of the ordinary.

He was looking for floating devices hid in the bushes or signs that trucks had gone through here. They were looking for a bigger operation, an organized one, people who transported massive amounts of illegal cargo, the ones who would be bringing those terrorists and their weapons of mass destruction over.

He drove up an incline, and when he reached the top, the land stretched in front of him all the way to the Rio Grande. He parked the SUV next to Jamie's and they both pulled out their binoculars, Mo scanning the land to the left and Jamie to the right.

His attention was on the job, but he still had Molly on his brain. He had Molly Rogers way too much on his brain lately. He hoped she was doing all right. And Logan, too. The kid deserved a break.

"I think I see something," Jamie said after a minute. "Straight west. There's something in that gully."

Mo looked and saw a boxy shape, a glint of metal. "A car?" Hard to tell from here. He set his binoculars down and drove in that direction.

Once they were closer, he could make out a small truck. Bingo.

Mo checked his gun, called the find in to Ray, who was on office duty, giving his leg a rest so the cast could come off eventually.

The closer they got, the slower he drove. No signs of movement around the truck; the lettering on the side advertised flower delivery. On a regular road, nobody would look at it twice. Out here, however, there were no flowers and nobody to deliver to.

"Flat tire," Jamie said when they were only a hundred feet away.

That explained why the truck was sitting in the gully, the coolest spot around. The motor was running, probably for the air-conditioning in the cab.

"I sure hope there are no people in the back." The truck didn't have any cooling back there, from what he could see, no outside vent units. Mo stopped his car. "You go left. I go right." He checked his gun again before getting out.

Even at six in the morning, the heat was intense. Any hotter and the dirt would start melting. They sucked up the heat and rushed the truck from the back, one on each side.

The driver must have seen them in his side mirrors because he rolled his window down and started shooting.

"Drop your weapon!"

Mo shot back and kept running forward, dodging bullets as he went. He reached the door the same time as Jamie did on the other side. They both aimed their weapons at the man's head.

"Hands up! Throw out your weapon and get out of the cab!"

The man had no way to escape and he knew it. He only hesitated a second before complying. He swore up a storm in Spanish as he opened the door and dropped to the ground, then onto his knees.

His clothes were wrinkled and lived-in, his face unshaven. He smelled like beer. He shot a murderous look at Mo, but put his hands on the back of his head without having to be prompted.

"He knows the drill," Jamie said, coming around.

Right. Sure looked as if he'd run into trouble with law enforcement before.

"Who are you?" Mo asked in English first, then in Spanish, holding his gun on the guy while Jamie patted him down for hidden weapons. He came up empty.

The man kept quiet, looking straight in front of him. He was probably more scared of the people he worked for than the border patrol.

As Mo cuffed the driver, Jamie shot off the lock from the back of the truck. The gate creaked as it opened. "Empty," he called.

Mo dragged the man to his feet, took him over to his SUV and locked him in the back. Jamie was climbing into the back of the truck. Nothing but a couple of empty water bottles and a rag in the far corner. He headed for that, kicked it.

"Anything interesting?"

"Just a dirty shirt." He came back and jumped to the ground.

"Human cargo. He brought them over the border then let them off when the truck broke down."

Jamie nodded and scanned the ground, too stony for footprints here. He walked a few yards away and kept looking.

Mo pulled out his cell phone and called in the find, asked Ray to let CBP know to be on the lookout for illegals. A daylong hike could be deadly in this heat.

He walked up to the cab as he hung up, turned off the engine, found nothing but snacks and more empty water bottles. No registration papers for the truck or any other documentation in the glove compartment. He was willing to bet they weren't going to find ID on the driver, either.

He checked the GPS unit and hit pay dirt. "Last address entered was the Hullett sheriff's office," he called out to Jamie. "You take the driver in. I'm going to drive over and see Sheriff Shane."

He lucked out, caught the sheriff right in his office.

The man received him with a smarmy smile and an assurance of his full cooperation with whatever Mo's problem was, and listened as Mo filled him in on the truck. "Any idea why the GPS would be programmed for this office?"

"Now, don't you start on that." The sheriff glared at him, taking a toothpick from his mouth and shoving it into his shirt pocket. "Just because you can't do your job and now you're getting desperate, don't think you're gonna go after my people." It was pretty clear he was tired of outsiders meddling in what he thought of as his business.

"I'm just here to see if you might know what that GPS is all about." No sense pissing off the local law until he knew something for sure. But if the sheriff and/or his staff was dirty, he was going after them with a vengeance. "All I'm asking is your opinion."

The sheriff flashed him a hard look. "My guess is they were coming to someplace in town. Put the station in the GPS so if they get caught nobody is the wiser about their true destination."

Mo thought about that for a second. *Maybe.* "I wouldn't mind seeing whatever files you have on smuggling cases you've had over the years."

The sheriff's face darkened another shade. Not that surprising. Nobody liked it when strangers messed with their business.

Better put a positive spin on it. "I'm putting together some statistics for the budget recommendations we're writing up. Who knows, maybe Hullett will get a chunk of federal money."

The man didn't look overly excited, but he did nod after a second. "I'll have my secretary gather up what we have."

Mo slid his card across the desk. "She can email me the files. I'd really appreciate it."

He left the Hullett sheriff, thinking about the exchange, about what the chances were that the man was involved. He hated to think that someone sworn to uphold the law would trample his oath into the mud like that. Then another silver star caught his eye. The Pebble Creek sheriff going past the receptionist with a nod. A professional visit?

An annoyed frown crossed Kenny's face as he spotted Mo. "Moses Mann." He even said the name with derision.

"Sheriff Davis."

"I hear you've been spending time at the Rogers ranch."

Okay, he hadn't planned on bringing up the subject, but as long as the sheriff had… Mo gave the man a level look. "I hear you've been doing the same."

"Molly is a friend. I don't like the idea of her out there alone," the man said easily, but his gaze hardened. "I don't like the idea of her being harassed, either."

"My concern exactly," Mo countered.

"I thought you were supposed to be watching the border."

"That and the people who cross it with bad intentions."

"And how long is this assignment of yours?"

"As long as it's necessary."

"Is it? Necessary? I'd hate to see taxpayer money

wasted. I'm sure whatever you're investigating, Molly is not connected."

"Just keeping an eye on her to make sure she's safe."

"How about you let me worry about that?" The sheriff's gaze hardened.

Getting into a confrontation with him would serve no purpose. So, as much as it burned him, Mo simply nodded and walked away from the man.

He had to go back to the office, but he decided to go out to the ranch and check on Molly when he was finished. He hadn't seen her yet today. He wanted to make sure Logan had been okay going back to school.

That some bully would mess with the kid ticked him off.

He was going to offer support to Logan. He was absolutely not going to think about kissing Molly. He had no business starting something he couldn't finish. Sooner or later, he'd be leaving. Kenny had been right about that.

Chapter Six

Molly went around finishing up her evening chores, trying not to stare at Mo in her backyard as he trained with Logan.

"Okay. So if someone grabs you from behind—" he demonstrated "—you do what?"

Logan flawlessly executed the move he'd been taught.

"And if the kid comes from the front, kicking?"

Once again, Logan was quick to block.

"Punching?" Mo's impressive muscles flexed under his black T-shirt as he demonstrated the attack in slow motion.

She felt her temperature rise a degree or two as she watched him. Who looked like that in a simple T-shirt? *Seriously.*

Logan whooped with glee as he deflected the punch.

The dogs watched them with interest, too. Max from a safe distance, Cocoa doing her best to get in the way.

Mo was teaching self-defense moves only, not to attack, just to deflect blows.

"The goal is not to hurt your opponent. Just to let him know that you can and will defend yourself. You use as little force as absolutely necessary. They'll get the message, believe me."

Logan beamed. "Yes, sir."

"How about you call me Mo? All right, let's try the

moves a little faster," she heard him say as she went into the barn to do the milking.

She started with Nellie, since she was the fussiest one. She had a tendency to kick over the milk bucket when she was in a temper. But she did all right this time, looking back toward the door as if listening for Mo's voice outside.

He did have a nice voice, deep-timbered and masculine. His tone could cut in the interrogation room, but she was beginning to wonder if that was a learned skill. He hadn't talked like that to her since, and he was extra gentle with Logan.

She moved her milking stool over to Holly, disinfected her udder then went on with the milking. By the time she finished with all the cows, Mo and Logan were coming into the barn.

Logan was grinning from ear to ear, eyes wide with excitement. "Mom, want to attack me from the front?"

"Ah, how about a little later?"

"Why don't we give her a hand first?" Mo reached for the pails.

They processed the milk then Mo helped with the rest of her evening chores.

"You don't have to do that," she told him as he collected the eggs with Logan. "Although I do appreciate the help."

She was used to doing it alone. Dylan had too many businesses to give a hand with the day-to-day operations at the ranch.

"Actually," Mo said as they walked inside through the back door. He waited until Logan rushed off to the laundry room to wash his hands, before continuing, "I didn't just stop by to quickly check on you. I'd like to do a stakeout at the ranch tonight, if you don't mind."

A stakeout? "Did something happen today?"

Logan ran back. Mo stayed silent.

"Sure," she said after a moment. She wanted him to catch the bad guys so Dylan's name would finally be cleared. "Thanks."

"I'll be around, then." He turned to leave.

"Would you like to have dinner with us?" she asked on impulse as she moved to the sink to clean up. He had helped her so much today. And not just today, really.

"You don't have to feed me." But he was smiling.

He was sexy when he smiled. She used to think his torn eyebrow made him look fierce and threatening. Now she thought it just made him look interesting. Added character.

"It's just a couple of burgers. And we have plenty." Why was she nervous all of a sudden? It wasn't as if she was asking him on a date.

"Love a good burger. Thanks."

Her fingertips tingled from nerves. Okay, this was way crazy. He was helping her out, and she was feeding him in exchange. No big deal.

Since she didn't want him to see how flustered she was, she turned from him and busied herself with making dinner.

He came to help.

He sure had a way of filling up the kitchen.

"So how did you lose that eyebrow, anyway?" she asked, then couldn't believe she had.

He ran his finger over the uneven skin. "I can't really talk about that. Sorry."

"No, I shouldn't have pried," she apologized. Then wondered just what kind of work he did. But she didn't bring up the subject again, not in front of Logan. And there wasn't really another moment of silence for a long time anyway.

During dinner, Logan entertained Mo with stories of the animals around the ranch. And how once, when he was little, he'd found a lizard in the yard, was afraid the chickens would get it while he had to take his nap, so he put it in his pocket, then hid it in the microwave.

Mo paid rapt attention and laughed at all the right places in the story, melting her heart little by little.

Then they discussed video games at length. Pretty much sounded like another language to her. The only thing she understood was that her son was way impressed with Mo's gaming knowledge.

When Logan asked if he could read to Mo instead of her before bed, she wasn't even surprised. They were rereading Harry Potter in the evenings, had switched to Logan reading to her a while back, instead of the other way around, so he could practice his reading skills. He also read to the dogs on occasion, which they oddly liked, but that was another story.

She had cleaned up and put away the last of the dishes by the time Mo came back down, his large frame filling the old house's narrow staircase. Twilight settled outside. They were alone in the small kitchen, the scene suddenly oddly intimate.

If she ever had a husband, she imagined this might be the part when he would pull her into his arms, kiss her and then they would go upstairs together. She swallowed.

"Thanks again for dinner," Mo said.

He really was a lot more handsome than scary. His size no longer intimidated her, not when she saw how gentle he was with Logan and with the animals around the ranch.

"You're welcome." Her gaze fell to his masculine lips and something deep inside her tingled. "Does this mean you'll cut me some slack the next time you come to arrest me?" She'd blurted the first stupid question that came to her mind out of nowhere.

He did have the decency to look chagrined. "I didn't arrest you. I took you in for questioning. For what it's worth,

I don't think you had anything to do with smuggling in the area. I haven't for a while. Nobody is coming to arrest you."

"Good to know," she said inanely, then winced. *Oh, great. Shoot me now.* A sparkling conversationalist she was not. "Thank you for what you did for Logan," she added, suddenly unable to stop talking. "I want him to have a good childhood. I want him to grow up and be able to reach his dreams."

He watched her for a quiet second. "What are your dreams?"

The images that pushed into her mind were too unrealistic so she pushed them away. "For Logan to be happy and for Dylan to be exonerated."

"Nothing for you specifically?"

She didn't want to go there, so she went on the defensive. "How about you?"

He shrugged. "Getting on the next team, the next level up."

She had no idea what that would be. "CIA? FBI?"

He gave her a half smile that was full of mystery. Right. If he were preparing to be some grand spymaster, he couldn't exactly tell her, could he?

So his current assignment was a stepping stone for him. "Do you know when you'll be leaving?"

"Molly…" He stepped forward and was suddenly too close. His gaze bored into hers.

She stood there wide-eyed, frozen like an armadillo in the headlights. The whole world seemed to stop for a moment.

She was pretty sure he was going to kiss her, and the thought nearly made her jump out of her skin.

But instead, after another moment, he shifted from one foot to the other, then turned and walked away. "I'll be out there if you need me. Just call my cell."

Then he was gone, and she felt a sudden wave of dizziness. Probably because she hadn't remembered to breathe in the past five minutes.

OKAY, THAT WAS CLOSE. That couldn't happen again. She was alone and in possible danger and no way in hell was he going to take advantage of her like that. Even if he really liked her.

The ranch was growing on him, too. Odd for a city kid, Mo thought as he walked around outside. But Molly's place had a lot of old-country charm, everything as neat as a pin, the house filled with warmth. He couldn't not feel comfortable sitting at that kitchen table.

Even the outbuildings were— He caught himself and shook his head. Right. Because he kept coming back due to his extreme fondness for the outbuildings. *Not.*

The dogs came running up from the back to walk with him.

"I even like you two goofballs," he admitted as they stared at him, tongues lolling.

But most of all, he really, really liked Molly. Truth was, he was developing an extreme fondness for Molly Rogers. Maybe even more than simple liking. He wanted her, that was for sure. His body was clear on that every time they were in the same room together.

And when they weren't together, he kept thinking about her. That was new. He wasn't the type to obsess over a woman. But she was different, had a different effect on him than the women he'd dated. Not that he'd had a great many relationships. His job didn't leave much time for that.

He'd always wanted family, just never thought it was time yet. Not for another ten years, according to the master plan.

Not that he knew how he would go about it once the time

did come. His experience with family had been his foster father and four brothers. His foster mother had died early on of cancer. The father, a retired Marine, ran the house like boot camp after that. The five boys definitely needed the discipline. He'd raised them well. But something had always been missing, and not until now had Mo realized what it was.

Motherly softness.

What Molly had here at the ranch, her gentle care of her son and even the animals, of which every single one had a name, down to the last scrawny chicken, was special. There was something here that drew him irresistibly, and it went beyond the fact that her amazing curves made his palms itch or that her kissable lips made him space out midthought, or that Logan was a great kid, one he wouldn't have minded spending more time with.

Of course, she probably couldn't wait to get rid of him. All she wanted was for her life to go back to normal. She'd said as much more than once.

Mo checked the outbuildings, walked through the stables, patted the horses. Sonoma, a young bay, snorted at him in greeting. The animals were starting to get to know him. He looked in at the new horse in the back. That one had to be Kenny's. He patted him, too. That he didn't like his owner had nothing to do with the animal.

He checked every stall then moved outside, Max and Cocoa escorting him all the way to his pickup. Skipper was getting better, according to Ryder, who visited Grace Cordero pretty much every day. Looked as if Ryder and Grace had something good, something real.

Mo squashed the beginning of some weird longing that thought awakened inside him. Ryder was ready for that next step. Good for him. Mo wasn't. He wanted to make it to the CIA. He wanted to make his father proud.

He started the engine and drove toward the fields instead of the main road. He pulled into the nearest mesquite grove, shut down the car and pulled out his binoculars. He could see the whole ranch from there, making it the perfect surveillance point. He scanned the house and the yard—everything was quiet.

Only one light was on in the house, Molly's bedroom. A shadow crossed behind the curtains. Stopped. She reached to the top button on her shirt and Mo swallowed hard. Then she stepped out of sight, and he didn't know whether to be relieved or disappointed.

He trained his binoculars elsewhere in case she came back to the window. She had no idea he was in the mesquite grove, in straight line of sight. He didn't want to invade her privacy.

He scanned the yard again, the outbuildings. Nothing but the two dogs moved. According to Molly, unless there was lightning and thunder, they preferred to sleep outside.

She'd kept them inside since Skipper had been poisoned, but he'd asked her to let them out tonight. If someone was sneaking around, they would signal. And this time, he was here to make sure nothing bad would happen to them.

But the dogs seemed relaxed, Max settling in to sleep, Cocoa patrolling the grounds.

Mo settled in for a long night, too. Some of his teammates hated surveillance. He didn't mind it. He liked quiet. He was comfortable being alone with his thoughts.

Except, this time, his thoughts kept returning to Molly Rogers.

A little after midnight, the light came on in her window. Maybe she was going to the bathroom. Then the light came on in Logan's bedroom. And stayed that way.

Mo glanced at his phone on the passenger seat next to him. If she was in trouble, she would call.

Unless she couldn't…

Someone could have gotten in through the front.

No. The dogs would signal.

Except it wasn't impossible to get by two dogs who were sleeping in the backyard. Cocoa and Max were stretched out next to each other.

Mo quietly slipped from the pickup, making sure he had his phone and his gun. If someone was out there, he didn't want to tip the guy off by turning on the motor or the lights. So he ran forward on foot, keeping to what little shadows the landscape provided.

The dogs woke up as he neared, came to check him out. He pushed them away and stole to the back door. It took less than thirty seconds to pop the old lock with the help of his knife.

He was just inching through the kitchen when Molly came down the stairs in that lavender silk nightgown that played a starring role in his dreams lately.

First she screamed, then she threw a heavy water glass at his head. He ducked just in time.

"It's me," he said quickly. "Are you all right?"

"Mom?" Logan called from upstairs.

"Spider," she called to him, then whispered to Mo, "What are you doing in here?"

"Saw your light come on." He picked up the glass that had luckily landed on the cushioned window seat. "You got a good arm."

"How did you get in?"

He shrugged. "I know a few useful tricks." He held out the empty glass. "What happened?"

"He had a nightmare. He's settled down now. I just wanted a cold drink."

But when she turned, he could see at last that she was more shaken than she'd let on, her eyes filled with worry.

"A dream about bullies?"

She shook her head as she walked to the fridge. "He dreamed he was out in the fields, far from the house, lost and alone." She filled her glass and held out the tea pitcher. "I think it's because of Dylan's death."

He picked another glass from the dish drainer and held it out for her to fill. "I think you're right."

He'd had those dreams, different variations, when he'd first found out he'd been abandoned by his parents as a baby, and then when his foster mother had died. He kept having dreams that his foster father would somehow disappear, too, and he would be alone in the world. He used to wake up in a dark terror, shaking.

"Do you see why it's so important for me to clear Dylan's name? I want to at least give Logan that."

He wished that was possible. But both she and Logan needed to somehow deal with Dylan's death, and the truth. Because his name wasn't going to be cleared. He wanted to fix this for her somehow, hated that he couldn't.

The shaft of moonlight that fell across her face revealed the desperation in her eyes.

He was here to protect her, Mo reminded himself. Touching her, in any way, would be plain stupid and completely inappropriate, even if the protection detail wasn't official. But no matter what he told himself, nothing seemed to work.

He sat his glass down and pulled her into his arms.

SHE COULDN'T REMEMBER the last time anything felt half as good as it did to be held by Moses Mann.

He was big and strong and made her feel protected. Nothing was going to get through him to get to her. She felt safe in his arms and comforted.

And not alone.

She'd felt so alone since her brother's death.

Logan was the light of her life, but Logan was different. She was responsible for Logan. Dylan had been another adult, more of a partner in life's small troubles. It really was nice to have another adult around again.

A week ago, she couldn't wait to see the last of Moses Mann. Now she dreaded the day when he would leave. It seemed impossible that she could come to trust him this fast. And her growing attachment to him, too, was disconcerting. She normally had better self-control than this.

She looked up and found him looking down at her. Even in the semi-darkness she could see the heat in his eyes. He wasn't touching her in any sexual way, offered nothing but comfort, but the heat was there between them anyway.

She didn't look away.

And then, in the blink of an eye, somehow everything changed. Slowly, giving her plenty of time to protest, he lowered his lips and brushed them over hers.

Oh, wow. Was this really happening?

That Moses Mann would be kissing her seemed surreal on some level. He was so…strong and brave and a millionaire and worldly—everything she wasn't. She was just a plain country girl.

They were so completely wrong for each other. Unfortunately, her hormones didn't give a damn. Need punched into her like never before, something big and scary and overpowering and completely unexpected.

For a second, she was too startled to do anything.

Then it was too late to resist, the flood of need washing over her completely. As if a dam had broken, she responded to the kiss with every fiber of her being. A low moan escaped her throat, her hands dug into his arms, her lips parted under his.

She burrowed against him, needing, wanting.

He tasted like the sweet tea he'd just drank. Like sunshine and, at the same time, the opposite—something dark and excitingly male. He tasted just right, frankly, after years of sexual repression and frustration.

So she wasn't dead below the neck like she'd told herself all these years, she thought, dazed, and as his tongue slow danced with hers, she swam with the pleasure.

Chapter Seven

She filled his senses. Her curves pressed to him, woke up his body and then some. The passion that exploded from her damn near took Mo's breath away. This was it, his instincts said, the real Molly, the one she took great pains to hide.

The grounded country girl, the good mother, the loyal sister he respected and was attracted to. The passionate woman he couldn't resist.

And, with everything he was, he wanted her.

But she pulled away suddenly, her hands pressed to her cheeks, her eyes round with embarrassment.

"I'm so sorry," she muttered. "I don't know why I did that. I'm really sorry." Then she turned on her heel and ran up the stairs, leaving him standing and staring in the middle of her kitchen.

He felt as if a tank had run him over.

He wanted to go after her, wanted to convince her that they both needed more of what they'd just shared. But he was pretty sure her speedy retreat upstairs meant no. And his foster father's many lessons included one on situations like this. When a lady said no, a real man accepted it and walked away. No pushing.

Even if it killed him. Even if in every other area of his life he'd been trained to push until he achieved his objective.

He ran his fingers through his crew-cut hair, considering dumping his remaining iced tea over his head. He could have used a little cooling off. But gaining perspective wasn't an easy thing with just a few steps separating them.

Steps he shouldn't take.

Their situation was pretty tricky. She was in trouble. He'd come to protect her, not to seduce her. Better put a little space between them right now.

He went outside, locking the doggie door to keep Max and Cocoa inside. They could guard the house while Mo took on the rest of the property.

He checked the outbuildings again and wouldn't let himself think about that kiss. No signs of anyone sneaking around while he'd been inside. All the animals were peaceful, all the doors closed and barred as he'd left them.

He didn't go back to his truck. He climbed up to the barn's hayloft. The old boards had enough gaps between them that he could see out in every direction, aided by the moonlight. An easy job, really, lying in the hay. It beat walking the border and having to worry about stepping on rattlers or being ambushed by smugglers.

Half his team was on patrol duty tonight, the other half on break. Even commando soldiers needed sleep. He was on break. Technically. But he didn't like leaving Molly alone at night. He wished she'd move into Hullett already.

He wished they were still in her kitchen, kissing. As much as he didn't want to think about that, he did, quite a bit, as he waited. Dawn was about ready to break when he heard some noise from down below that didn't come from the cows.

He listened more carefully to the slight scratching. A mouse?

No, something bigger. He eased toward the ladder, taking each step slowly so as not to rustle the hay. The scratching stopped. One of the cows, Nellie, turned to look at him and flicked some flies off her back with her tail.

He stood still in the shadows and waited. A minute or so later, the scraping sound returned. He could hear it better now, well enough to be able to tell where it was coming from: the small equipment room in the back where Molly kept her barn tools.

He stayed in the shadows as he moved forward, pulling his gun, ready.

The door, which had been closed before, now stood open. He eased his way over, saw a man inside with his back to the door, tapping the floorboards.

Mo stuck his gun behind his back, into his waistband. Better to take the bastard down by hand than shoot him. Dead men didn't talk, and he needed information. They needed to know who he was, who he worked for and what exactly he was looking for here.

He vaulted forward and crashed into the guy with his full weight. They slammed against the wall then went down, the both of them groaning.

Fist to the chin.

Grab the man's gun.

Toss it.

So far so good.

The intruder had plenty of muscle and knew how to use it, but Mo had managed to startle him. They grunted in unison as Mo tried to flip the man, get his hands behind his back so he could snap on the plastic cuffs he always carried.

Damned if the bastard didn't twist away at the last second. He put up a good fight, cursing alternatively in Spanish and English, both of them breathing hard once they'd rolled around a couple of times, smacking into the wall and various pieces of furniture, rolling over a pitchfork that nearly took out Mo's eye.

He had to put all his combat skills into play before he finally got the upper hand. With his knee in the middle of the guy's back, he used his whole weight to keep the man down while he twisted his arms back and finally snapped on the plastic cuffs. Just as he heard a footstep behind him.

He twisted, reaching for his gun. Too late.

The newcomer already had his weapon drawn.

THE DOGS WERE going mad at the back door, waking her from a perfectly good dream, in which she had a perfectly good man in her bedroom. Perfectly naked. Molly couldn't see his shadowed face, but his wide shoulders and massive build looked suspiciously like Mo's.

She opened her eyes and groaned at the ceiling in protest as she came awake. The dogs' barking grew more frenetic. Then she remembered that Mo was out there tonight.

Oh, God. Had they really kissed? She'd thrown herself at him like a starving woman. Embarrassment and heat filled her at the memory, in equal measure. Then worry, as the dogs kept barking.

She reached for her cell phone on the nightstand and dialed his number.

He didn't answer. And suddenly all sorts of bad premonitions filled her. She yanked on her bathrobe and ran downstairs. Grabbed her rifle from the gun cabinet. Pushed back the dogs, who were fighting to get out the back door as soon as she opened it.

"You stay here. Go to Logan," she told Cocoa as she went outside with Max. She locked the door behind her. Her dogs were sweet, but if anyone went after her or Logan, she was pretty sure they would have something to say about it, would probably give their lives to protect their humans. Max had gone up against an ocelot a couple of years ago to protect her and her horse when she'd been out riding.

The dog ran straight to the barn, still barking, so she followed, a little more carefully, keeping to cover.

"Mo?" she called out from the door.

Max had gone into the back room and stayed in there, quiet.

"Mo!" She raised her voice, clutching her weapon. She didn't dare turn on the lights, wasn't sure who might be in there, waiting for a chance to take a shot at her.

Then Mo called "In here" from the back.

She flipped on the lights then, but saw nobody save the cows. She ran to Mo.

He was sitting in the middle of the floor, rubbing his chest, looking dazed. Max was licking his face, doing the whole "I'll lick you back to health and happiness" routine dogs did so well.

Mo's face was bruised, his clothes scuffed.

"What happened?"

"There were two men." He groaned as he pushed to his feet. Patted Max. "Got me with a Taser."

"What?" She swung back toward the open barn, keeping her rifle ready. "When?"

He rubbed his chest again. "I think I blacked out a little." He looked at her rifle. Frowned. "You should have stayed inside."

She braced a hand on her hip. "Because you're the big bad man and I'm just a little helpless woman?"

He glared. "Have you ever shot anything bigger than a rattler?"

Okay, not really. But she didn't want to seem totally incompetent. "The bigger they are, the easier to hit, right?"

"The bigger they are, the worse they fight back." He pulled out his cell phone and dialed. "I'm going to call in my team to take some fingerprints."

She felt terrible that he'd gotten hurt on her property

and wanted to help, but she was at a loss as to how to do that. He wasn't like Logan, who could be set to rights with a hug and a kiss and some ice cream.

Yet she wanted to go up to him anyway, up real close…

She backed away. "I need to go back inside. Logan's in there alone."

"I'm coming with you." He followed her as he talked to someone on the other end, reporting in.

He went inside the house first, looked around while she made sure Max came back with them. He checked every door and window, every room upstairs, while she looked in on Logan, then plodded back down the stairs.

"Doesn't look like anyone tried to get in here," he told her.

"Logan is sleeping." She sank into one of the kitchen chairs. "Why do they keep coming?"

He thought for a long second. "They think you have something they want."

"I don't have anything."

"Maybe you don't know you have something."

Her jaw muscles tightened. "We've been over this with Kenny. Dylan wasn't hiding any contraband. He wouldn't. He wasn't into smuggling. And even if he was, he would never bring anything here and put Logan and me in danger."

"Wish I knew what it was," he said. "Searching for it would go easier if we knew we're looking for a truckload of weapons or a suitcase full of money."

She shook her head. None of this made any sense. Dylan didn't have a suitcase full of money. If he had, he wouldn't have mortgaged the ranch.

Mo rubbed his thumb over his damaged eyebrow, looking deep in thought, then he raised his head and considered her for a few seconds before he spoke. "I don't want you to stay here. For the time being. Especially at night. I can't be here every night, and you shouldn't be alone out in the middle of nowhere with Logan."

"I'm not going anywhere," she said on reflex, even if she knew he was right.

"How about we consider this for a minute?" he said patiently.

"Fine." She glared at him. "Be completely reasonable in an emotional moment. Just like a man."

The corner of his mouth tilted up.

She so didn't want to leave. She loved the ranch. It was the only thing she knew. But as much as she hated the idea of moving, for her son's safety she would. She would do anything for Logan.

She nodded with reluctance. "I'll be getting Dylan's apartment the day after tomorrow. Kenny talked to Shane about it. He's going to get me the keys."

He seemed to weigh her words. Then he said, "I've seen the apartment. Not exactly high security."

"I can't afford Secret Service detail." She couldn't afford to rent the apartment, either, and Dylan only had the rent paid until the end of the month. "You could stay at my place," Mo said carefully. "You can still come back here during the day to take care of the animals. I can make sure someone from the team is here when you come."

She stared at him. *His place.*

Okay. What did that mean? As a friend? As more? They *had* kissed. Or was he offering safety in an official capacity?

She could just barely picture herself leaving the ranch. Moving in with Mo… She needed to know what he meant by it. "I'm guessing you don't offer room and board to every person you interrogate."

A wry smile stretched his masculine lips. "Pretty much

never. I haven't even had the guys on the team over." He shrugged. "I'm not exactly a social butterfly. More of a loner, actually."

"Sounds like you like your private life private." She did, too. She liked living out here in the middle of nowhere. She'd never lived anyplace else.

Since she'd had Logan right after high school, she had never gone away to college. She'd received her agricultural-management degree through one of those low-residency programs where she only had to go on campus twice a year to take her exams. And the college had day care for young mothers during those residencies.

Her dream had been to create a preservation education operation, growing and preserving rare and heirloom fruits and vegetables and allowing various colleges to hold open-air lectures on her land. But Dylan had said it couldn't be done. They simply didn't have the resources.

She could have applied for grants, but he'd gotten upset when she'd mentioned that. He was proud that way, didn't like the idea of his sister going around begging, hat in hand.

And it was fine. She loved her animals, loved her garden, had a lot more time to spend with Logan than if she was running a serious operation. As long as she was on the ranch, she was happy.

Living at Mo's place…

The passionate kiss they'd shared earlier filled her mind, making her lips tingle. She felt awkward just sitting with him in her kitchen. What would it be like to spend serious time together? Could she pretend that she didn't like him as much as she really did?

"I'm on duty almost around the clock," he said, as if reading her thoughts. "And I'll come by at night as much as I can. I want to catch those men if they come back. You would pretty much have the place to yourself."

Odd how something could set a person more at ease while being disappointing at the same time. So, going to Mo's place... What choice did she have? Not much if she wanted to keep her son safe.

"I don't want harm to come to you or Logan," he said, underscoring her thoughts.

Which meant what? That they meant something to him? Her insides began tingling again.

"Okay." She closed her eyes for a second. "Thank you."

His shoulders relaxed, the smile on his face widened. He looked pleased as punch, while she worked hard to hide her misgivings. He was about to say something, but then the dogs barked and soon they heard the sound of a car coming up her driveway.

He went to the window and looked out. "It's Jamie and Shep. I'll go talk to them. You stay here."

She watched from the window as he led his friends to the barn and they disappeared inside. She fed the dogs breakfast to keep them quiet, but Logan woke up anyway and plodded down the stairs, bringing his handheld "Calvin Cat Counting" game with him.

He was even more obsessed with the games now that he knew Mo's connection. He was quickly developing some hero worship for Mo that had started after the school incident and martial-arts training. It worried her a little. She didn't want Logan to fall for Mo so completely, not when she knew Mo wouldn't be staying.

A worry for another day. She had plenty of other things on her plate today. She put a big smile on her face. "Hey, you. How about breakfast?"

He sat in his chair and yawned as he nodded, looked toward the window and saw the men in the backyard. "Mom? Who is that?"

"Some of Mo's friends. They're working in the barn."

She didn't want to scare her son with details. "Guess what?" She widened her smile as she got out the bowl to make pancakes. "Mo invited us to visit with him."

He brightened immediately. "I bet he has a lot of video games."

"I bet he does. And it's not just any visit. It's a sleepover. Probably for a few days."

Logan jumped from his chair, looking as if someone had just told him Santa Claus was coming early. "I'm not going to school?"

"I'm pretty sure the school bus stops there, too." She shook her head.

His enthusiasm waned a little, but not by much. "Can I pack now?"

She laughed as she stirred the pancake mix. "I think packing can wait until after breakfast."

So they ate together and Logan talked about nothing but going to Mo's place. They rarely went away, mostly because they had little family to visit, and also because somebody had to be here for the animals.

Since it was admin day, no school, they did go upstairs to pack. Logan finished first. She spent an eternity agonizing over which clothes to take. She didn't want to look like a country bumpkin in front of Mo. Stupid vanity, she told herself and nearly packed her rattiest work clothes. But at the last minute, she folded her nicer dresses into the suitcase instead.

The extra SUV was gone from the driveway by the time she came downstairs. Mo was just coming in.

"Everything's taken care of. I'll help you do morning chores before we leave."

And he did. And, Lord, that was nice, not just the help but the company. He was a quiet man, didn't talk her ear off like Kenny. Quiet, but strong and efficient. He figured out everything right quick, too. She didn't need to explain a thing.

As he mucked out the stalls, nobody would have guessed that he was some gaming-empire millionaire. She stared at him, just a little, before she caught herself. She'd been worried about Logan, but was she falling just as fast for Mo?

"Done here." He leaned the pitchfork against the wall. "I'll just wheel this out back." He grabbed the wheelbarrow.

"Thanks." She looked after him as he went, then busied herself with the cows, even as her thoughts kept lingering on Mo.

He seemed to be the type of man who could fit in anywhere, do anything and be good at it because he paid attention and gave top effort. He didn't put on airs. He could have been dressed all in Armani, but wore simple clothes and didn't mind getting them dirty.

By the time the chores were done, she nearly talked herself into the fantasy that they weren't so different after all, that maybe some relationship between them could be possible while he was here.

That thought went right out the window when they finally arrived at his apartment in Hullett an hour later.

Logan walked around wide-eyed, touching everything, exclaiming over something every second. She felt the same, although held herself back. But only just. She was more than a little shell-shocked.

"You, um, have a very nice place."

The understatement of the year. He rented in the fanciest building in town, a historical hotel on Main Street once owned by an oil baron. The whole top floor had been the baron's private living space. Now Mo was staying there.

"Sit," she ordered her dogs and pointed to a corner, hoping they wouldn't mess up anything. Thank God they weren't chewers. She couldn't afford to replace as much as a doormat here.

"They'll be fine." Mo was smiling at her.

"This is very fancy," she said weakly.

"Didn't want it, didn't need it." He set down her suitcase and raised his hands palms out, in a defensive gesture. "I came to rent something small. Turns out the manager is somewhat of a gaming buff. He gets every gaming magazine. My name was familiar to him and he asked. I didn't want to lie to his face. All he had to do was look it up on Google."

Of course, in the gaming circles the Mann name was probably famous. And the manager would insist that Mo take the penthouse apartment, the best they had.

She couldn't imagine who else would ever have money to rent the place. Visiting politicians? The pope?

He moved farther in, seemingly oblivious to all the fanciness. "Let me show you around so you and Logan can get settled in."

He led her through the large living room, where the furniture was modern and well made. "At least it came furnished," he said. "Otherwise, I'd be probably sleeping in a sleeping bag on the floor."

Logan stared at the longhorn armchairs, actually made with cattle horns. The leather couch was as big as Texas. It looked like something from one of those high-end home-design magazines she couldn't afford to read.

The place had a full kitchen with top-of-the-line appliances, although they were so fancy she wasn't sure she'd know how to operate them. She drew a hand over the smooth granite countertops, pure luxury.

"The place came with two guest bedrooms all set up." Mo led them forward.

She followed him hesitantly, already overwhelmed,

while Logan plowed ahead. The first bedroom had a flat-screen TV of immense proportions. In front of the TV stood some sort of a console, a leather armchair with a dashboard built in. Looked like the captain's chair from the USS *Enterprise*.

"My brother sent it over last week. Some new game he wants to put out. Space cowboys." He shrugged. "Not exactly my area of expertise. He's the programming genius. But from the beginning he insisted that I get a vote on everything. So I'm supposed to evaluate the *experience*." He shook his head. "Maybe Logan could help?"

"Mom," Logan squealed. "Can I have this room? Please?" He actually had his hands clutched together in front of him, his eyes as big as Ping-Pong balls.

"Sure," she said weakly. She had no idea how they were ever going to repay Mo for all this.

She backed out of the room. Logan stayed behind, diving for the game console. And where she wouldn't have had any idea how to even turn the thing on, he had a game going in less than thirty seconds.

Mo moved down the hallway, stopped in front of the next room. "This could be your room, if it's acceptable."

A four-poster bed dominated the space, the room decorated in grays and earth tones, sumptuous and sophisticated at the same time. So unlike her. And yet she was completely in love with it. She felt like a kid at the state fair and had an idea that she probably looked just as amazed and wide-eyed as Logan.

Mo stepped aside so she could walk into the room. "Do you need anything? All you have to do is push the number-one button on the phone for concierge."

Concierge. "I think we'll be fine."

"Bathroom is right next door."

She stayed where she was. She didn't want to see the

bathroom. It probably had a marble Jacuzzi or something. She could only deal with so much at once.

"I'll leave you to settle in. I'm going to go into the office for a while. My hours aren't exactly regular," Mo said with a smile that said he was happy to have her here and, at the same time, that he'd be happy to have her.

Heat crept up her neck.

"Call me if you need anything."

What else could she possibly need? The suite had everything but a private butler. She'd never seen anyplace like it. That Mo lived here boggled her mind more than a little. The gap between them suddenly widened to a giant gorge. She nodded and watched him leave.

They were so not in the same league.

He strode to the front door, but then suddenly stopped and came back. "One more thing."

Her heart leaped. God, don't let him kiss her. She was so overwhelmed, she wasn't sure she could resist.

But instead of trying to make a move on her, he hurried around the apartment, reached under furniture, behind sofa pillows, into a kitchen cabinet and gathered up half a dozen guns of all sizes. He carried them to an abstract painting on the wall that turned out to be a safe and locked them in there.

"I don't want these within reach with Logan here," he said as he moved to leave again. Then stopped again.

He reached into his pocket and handed her a key. "I'll get another one for myself from downstairs. Make yourselves at home. Feel free to use the room service."

And then he kissed her, a lingering brush of his lips over hers before he strode out the door, leaving her staring after him.

She was pitiful. And he was…

Room service. Just like that. Was that how he ate? On

a daily basis? A day of that probably cost more than her weekly grocery bill.

"Mom, it has alien cowboys! Want to see?" Logan called from his room.

"In a second, honey."

She took in the place, more carefully this time, feeling more overwhelmed by the minute.

She and Mo were from different worlds. The kiss had meant nothing. She sank into the nearest chair as dismay filled her. Girls like her were nothing but playthings to men like him.

She'd learned that lesson early and wasn't likely to forget. She'd fallen in love, let herself be seduced, then had been cast aside the day she'd found out she was pregnant. Rich men wanted women for entertainment. Mo wouldn't want more than that from her.

Oh, God, she thought, feeling sick to her stomach. She'd done this before. Mikey had dazzled her with his money and extravagant gifts. He'd told her how much he'd cared for her. But all of that had been a setup.

And she'd almost fallen for it again. She felt so disappointed, she nearly choked on the feeling. Then she gathered herself and stood. She wasn't an impressionable young girl anymore, ripe for the plucking.

"All right. Let's see how those aliens fight." She headed back to Logan, thinking about her own battles.

She might have moved into Mo's apartment, but if he thought she was just going to waltz straight into his bed, too, he had another think coming.

Chapter Eight

Mo filed his reports and was on his way out of the office to stop by the jail again, this time to talk to the driver they'd caught by the border, when Ryder came in.

"Can I see you for a sec?" Mo gestured with his head toward the interrogation room, the only room in the office that had a door. The rest was open space with enough desks for the six-man team.

"Sure." Ryder followed him.

He was looking at Mo with expectation. "Everything okay?"

Mo scratched the back of his neck, not entirely comfortable. "So, about Molly Rogers."

"You got something on her?"

"She has nothing to do with anything. Thing is…" He paused, then bit the bullet. "I moved her and her son to my place at the hotel."

Ryder's eyebrows slid up his forehead.

Mo thought how to best word his explanation. "She keeps getting night visitors. She has an eight-year-old son. They're out there alone."

"She could have gotten her own room at the hotel."

Mo cleared his throat. "She's not that well-off financially."

"She has to have some friends."

She probably did. Although some of the people in town looked down on her, there were plenty of nice folks in Hullett. "If whoever keeps searching her place decides that whatever he's looking for is not there, they could come after her. She's safest at my place."

Ryder raised an eyebrow. "With you?"

Right. Slippery ground. "I'm never at the apartment. I'm either here or looking for crossing points on the border. For the next few days, I'm going to spend as many nights as I can at the Rogers ranch, see if I can catch whoever keeps going back there."

Ryder rubbed the bridge of his nose. "I know there's a certain irony here, considering Grace and me, but I have to ask…do you have an interest in Molly Rogers beyond the professional?"

Mo shoved his hands into his pockets. He wasn't used to talking about stuff like this. But Ryder was team leader and he had a right to know where this was going, if it would distract from the mission. Oh, hell. He filled his lungs.

"I don't really know. I want her and her son to be safe. And then—" He shook his head. "I have no idea what she wants."

Maybe Ryder could give him some tips. Ryder had managed to win Grace over, and Grace Cordero was one tough cookie.

But all he gave Mo was a sympathetic look. "Rather go into armed combat myself than try to figure out a woman."

Mo nodded. At least Grace was a soldier. She and Ryder had that in common.

Molly Rogers seemed like a whole different world to Mo. He was pretty much a killing machine, usually surrounded by violence on a daily basis. She was a mother, surrounded by chickens.

What did he know about women anyway? His birth

mother had tried to drown him. His foster mother had died when he'd been a kid. He never had sisters.

But he knew enough to know that Molly was special. She would be worth any effort to win. If only the timing of all this didn't suck so much. But maybe he could work on the timing. They had weeks before the planned terrorist crossing, if their intel was right. And even after the capture, more weeks would pass while they wrapped up everything here.

They needed to run down every last person involved, to make sure something like this couldn't happen again. His team was determined to secure the hundred-mile section of the border that they'd been trusted with.

"Is this going to be a problem?" He didn't define what "this" was. He had no idea what to call the instant attraction—at least on his part—between them, and those spectacular kisses, which he hoped would soon be repeated. "She's no longer a person of interest."

Ryder thought that over. "We're hunting criminals here. Terrorists. If someone figures out who we are, if they come after us, everyone connected to us could be in danger. Which is why I'm keeping my relationship with Grace under wraps as much as possible."

And Grace, after several tours overseas as an Army medic, could defend herself. Molly, on the other hand...

Mo rolled his shoulders. He hadn't thought about that. "I don't want Molly and her son in danger."

Ryder's face grew somber. "Then don't put her in any."

Easier said than done. "She's fine at my place. I secured it when I moved in. Reinforced the door with Kevlar. Nobody comes through that door unless they're let in. But while Logan is at school, she'll be at the ranch, taking care of her garden and her animals. I want some sort of protection for her."

"She'll get it. We'll make sure someone is out there with her while she's working. Her ranch is connected to our investigation. I can justify expanding some manpower there."

"I appreciate that."

Ryder shook his head. "Grace is worried about her, too."

They talked for another minute or two, then went about their business. Ryder needed to plan the schedules for the following week. Mo headed over to the county jail. After that, he'd take Molly and Logan out so she could do her evening chores at the ranch, then take them back to the hotel. Then he would return to the ranch to lie in wait, should any bad guys stop by during the night.

"I'll be back in the morning," he told Jamie and Shep, who were working on their computers.

"Another stakeout?" Jamie asked.

"Ready for more electroshock therapy so soon?" Shep ribbed him. "Hoping it'll curl your hair?"

"Very funny. Want to see how you'd like a couple of hundred volts between your ribs?" he offered.

The friendly taunting didn't really bother him. Not when Ryder had as good as given his approval. Molly would get team protection, too. And she was living at his place. He knew a grin was spreading across his face but didn't care.

He walked through the office then outside into the heat. He pushed Molly out of his mind and organized his thoughts around what he needed to do next. He needed to get the truck driver talking. They needed the name of Dylan Rogers's partner. They needed the man to give up the Coyote's true identity. They needed the exact location of the planned border breach, and they needed the day.

The drive to the jail was long and hot, the visit a complete bust. The truck driver had hanged himself in his cell just minutes before Mo had gotten there. He called in the news to the office.

They'd had nothing but bad luck on this mission so far. Too much bad luck. The enemy always seemed one step ahead. His instincts prickled. There was something here they weren't seeing. Maybe Sheriff Shane *was* involved. It sure seemed as if the bad guys were getting some help from somewhere. Except, Ryder had looked into Sheriff Shane, and the man had come up squeaky clean. He thought about that as he headed off to the hotel to pick up Molly and Logan.

He wanted to greet her with a kiss, but couldn't in front of her son. How they handled that would have to be her decision.

"Did you find everything okay?" he asked as they were headed down in the elevator.

"Yes, thank you. And I want you to know that we will pay you back for everything."

There was a coolness to her tone that he hadn't heard since the first time he'd met her, when he'd been interrogating her. He winced at the memory.

"That's not necessary."

"Yes, it is."

The elevator stopped and Logan darted out. Mo tried to take her hand, but she pulled away.

Okay. What was that about?

He didn't get the chance to ask on the ride out to her place. And they didn't have much privacy while taking care of the evening chores, either, with Logan always within hearing distance.

He gave up trying, and while she did the milking, a chore that proved him a complete klutz and no help whatsoever, he took Logan to the backyard for some extra self-defense training.

"Hey, Mo, watch this!" Logan executed a pretty good punch to his solar plexus.

"Not that hard, remember? You want to show them that you can defend yourself. The goal is to prevent a real fight, so nobody gets hurt."

"What if somebody punches me hard?"

"You fight back just enough to make them stop. You won't respond blindly. You gain control of the situation."

The kid nodded solemnly.

"You can train with me as hard as you like. But only with me, okay?" Now that the kid would be cooped up in the apartment all day instead of running around the ranch, he needed a little extra exercise.

"So what do you do when someone tries to grab you from the front?" Mo stepped forward and reached out.

Logan deflected.

"What if they grab you by the foot?"

They kept on training. And he thought of his talk with Ryder, how being connected to them could put Molly and Logan in more danger. He would make sure that didn't happen. But being prepared was the key.

"What if they have a weapon?"

Logan's eyes went round. "I'm in elementary school."

"Right. I meant like a stick or something." He showed the kid a twist kick, just the right place to hit the wrist to send a weapon flying.

And then he turned and caught Molly watching.

"You shouldn't take up so much of Mo's time," she told her son. And then to Mo, "I'm done. We're ready to leave."

Logan talked about some of the games he'd been playing on the console, all the way home. Molly barely said anything. She looked almost relieved when Mo left them at the hotel. The only thing she told him was to make sure he ate something from her fridge and didn't go hungry.

Why did women have to be like that? Did they know how much they confused men? Did they do it on purpose?

He drove back to the ranch and pulled up the driveway. He missed the dogs running to greet him. He got out of the car and walked around, checked the buildings to make sure nobody had come by while he'd been gone.

Nelly gave him her evil look as he walked through the barn.

"Don't think I'm going to go close enough for a kick. I've taken enough abuse already in this barn." He could swear the cow grinned at him.

Mo looked in on the horses next. Paulie, the half-blind gelding, turned his good eye toward him and gave him a mournful expression.

"You're not fooling me, buddy. I know you're just milking this for everything it's worth." But he had an apple for the horse, and for Sid and Gypsy, too, and one for Kenny Davis's Charlie.

He closed everything up behind him, then walked up to the house, went in with the key Molly had given him. Didn't look as if anyone had been in there or tried to get in.

He opened the fridge for some tea. The leftover lasagna on the top shelf looked like heaven. *Later.*

He drank then went back outside. A couple of things about last night bothered him. The Taser for one. Not standard smuggler ammo. The people who smuggled contraband across the border were usually armed with more serious weapons and wouldn't hesitate to shoot anyone, even each other, right in the face at the slightest sign of trouble.

So what was up with the Taser here?

He hoped the bastards would come back. Of course, now they knew that Molly wasn't entirely defenseless and alone out here, they would be more careful. Not that they hadn't been careful last night.

They'd come after the lights in the house were turned off. After Mo's pickup had disappeared from the driveway.

Which meant they probably kept an eye on the place. Probably drove by a few times first, checked things out.

He sat in the deepest shadows of the porch, the scent of her yellow roses all around him, and watched the cars on the road. Traffic was sparse this time of the night. None of the cars that passed the house slowed. From where he was sitting, he had no way of telling whether any of the drivers were checking out her place.

He got his SUV out of the garage and drove to the end of the road then set up a one-man roadblock. Ten minutes passed before the first pickup rolled along. Mo stuck a CBP badge on his shirt, flagged the car down with his flashlight and asked for license and registration.

"Anything wrong?" the seventysomething man asked, pushing back his cowboy hat, his face leathered with old age. He squinted from the flashlight as Mo scanned the cab.

"Standard vehicle check. We've had some extra activity in the past week. More illegal shipments than we normally see." Mo handed the papers back, making sure to remember the name. In the morning, he would run everyone through the system back at the office, see if anything popped up.

"Good luck," the man said and drove away.

Mo checked the next car and the next. A pickup had two rifles on the gun rack in the back, but just regular hunting rifles. Almost everyone had at least one of those around here. No Tasers in sight and no serious firearms, either, nothing that would be used by professional smugglers.

Midnight passed by the time the first car rolled by that seemed out of place—a fancy SUV, close to the hundred-grand price tag. Mexican license plates. An Asian guy sat behind the wheel. He almost didn't stop, but at the last moment seemed to decide not to drive around Mo. A very lucky decision on his part, since Mo wasn't in the best of moods by that point.

He was tired and getting hungry. And frustrated because his mind kept returning to Molly and he had no idea why she was giving him the cold shoulder. And doubly frustrated because he was getting nothing out of the roadblock, dammit, nothing that looked suspicious or seemed like any kind of a lead.

"License and registration," he said as he stepped up to the driver's side window.

"I left my wallet at hotel." The man frowned. "What is this? I'm in a hurry. I have business meetings in morning."

Mo looked him over dispassionately, not the least impressed by the fancy car, fancy suit and tone of superiority. He panned the inside of the car with his flashlight. "You have no ID?"

"I'm Yo Tee. You call mayor about me. He tell you who I am."

Mo glanced at his watch—almost one in the morning. "I don't think we'll be calling the mayor. Why don't you get out of the car, sir."

"I have no time. I am important person. Everyone know who I am." He reached for the shift to put the car in Drive.

Mo reached inside and clamped his wrist. "I wouldn't try that."

He opened the door and pulled the guy out, pushed him against the vehicle and patted him down as he protested and yelled about racial profiling.

He wasn't carrying a weapon, but Mo did notice a pretty fancy semiautomatic in a holster behind the passenger seat, which he'd missed earlier because it was blocked by the door frame. Since the weapon was now in plain sight, it was fair game.

"I own factory in Mexico. You make big mistake." The

man swore at him first in Chinese and then in Spanish as Mo cuffed him and put him in the back of his SUV.

Then he called Jamie. "I got someone here. Armed, without papers. Money to burn from the looks of it."

The region was pretty hard hit by the economic downturn. Not many people ran around in cars like his. Some of the ones who did made their fortunes in illegal smuggling.

"He claims to be some big-time businessman."

"Legal or illegal?"

"Exactly. I wouldn't mind having prints run through the system, if you could come get him."

"On my way."

While he waited for Jamie, he pulled over another couple of cars. He hit pay dirt when he shone his flashlight into a beaten-up green pickup.

The driver handed over his papers with his left hand, then turned his swarthy face from the light, his right hand in his lap.

His driver's license said Garcia Cruz. Same name as the guy killed with the knife that had slashed Molly's tires. Then again, there had to be probably a hundred Garcia Cruzes in the state. It was a common name. Still...

"Hands on the steering wheel where I can see them." Mo didn't want him to try to go for a weapon.

The guy put his hands up, trying to cover one with the other.

What was he trying to hide?

Mo went for his gun. "Step out of the vehicle, sir."

And then, as the man did, Mo saw the bandages.

"What happened to your hand?"

The man shrugged, looking at his feet. He wore scuffed work boots, dirty jeans and a sweaty muscle shirt. "Fingers got cut in the reaper."

"How many?"

"Three."

A man who just happened to be missing three fingers. What were the chances? They'd need a DNA test to match him up to the fingers found on the border, but Mo was pretty sure they'd found their guy. That put him in a much better mood.

By the time Jamie got there, he was damn near smiling. Progress was a beautiful thing.

Jamie took in Garcia and Yo Tee, who was still yelling for his cell phone and his lawyer. Mo stayed the whole night, stopped every car that went through. They were mostly locals, but he did catch two illegal border crossers, teens, with nearly forty pounds of weed. Looked like an amateur operation, small-time fish swimming way below the notice of the big-time smugglers.

Jamie came for the entrepreneurial teens, too. Everyone who was taken in would get printed, questioned, then turned over to Customs and Border Protection when Mo's team was done with them.

Keith called him at seven, just as he'd headed inside Molly's house to get some coffee and breakfast. He was pretty much starving by that point. Molly's lasagna tasted even better than it looked. Not being the type to cut corners, she packed all the wholesome goodness into it that she could.

The house seemed empty without her. The ranch missed her. Oh, hell, *he* missed her. He had to figure out why she was mad at him.

"Just got back," Keith was saying. "Got nothing. Everyone's sitting tight. Want me to go out to the ranch and stay with the Rogers woman while she does her thing? I can do that before I turn in."

"I'm out here already. Thanks." He needed to go back

to his place for a shower and a clean set of clothes. Might as well bring Molly back with him.

He finished his breakfast, locked up, then drove into Hullett.

He ran into her in the lobby.

"Where's Logan?"

"I just put him on the school bus." Her smile was strained. "It's a different bus for him. Different driver. Different students. That's a big deal for kids."

"Was he nervous?"

She looked away. "I was. He thought it was great to be picked up at a fancy hotel. And he couldn't wait to tell the other kids about your gaming setup."

They went up in the elevator together. She smelled like his shampoo. He wanted to pull her closer, but she definitely kept her distance.

"Long night?" she asked as they got off on the top floor. "Any trouble?"

"I don't mind trouble."

She stared at him as if he was crazy.

"Looking for trouble is my job, kind of."

She nodded. "I'll be out at the ranch for a while. You can have your place to yourself to get some rest."

"I'll just shower and change," he said. "I'll take you back and stick around while you finish up."

For a second she looked as if she would protest, but then she simply nodded and thanked him.

By the time he'd showered—trying hard not to think that she had been in his shower already this morning, naked— she had breakfast ready for him in the kitchen. And he found he was hungry again. Hey, how often did he have someone cook for him?

Might as well take advantage of it while he could. He pretty much inhaled the bacon and eggs, slowed down for the pancakes that were covered in something red and gooey and tasted like heaven.

"What's that?"

She looked up from the counter, where she was writing something in a notebook. "Prickly pear jelly. I make a few dozen jars every year. I brought some over. Logan likes it."

He licked his lips. "I appreciate this. Best breakfast I've had in a long time." Then he added, "The lasagna was great, too." He could definitely get used to eating like that on a regular basis.

He went around her to rinse his plate and put it in the dishwasher, turned around just as she turned back to reach for something. He knocked her off balance and wrapped her in his arms so she wouldn't be knocked against the counter. "Sorry."

Their gazes locked.

Under the scent of the soap, he could smell her soft skin.

He'd wanted her from the moment he'd first seen her, and had spent half of last night thinking about her.

He wanted to taste her lips so badly he thought he'd go cross-eyed from desire. He needed to romance her. That was what women wanted, wasn't it? He knew he should say something, compliment her on her hair or her clothes or whatever.

"Listen, I—" But then he just pressed his lips against hers.

This time, the wave of blinding need didn't catch him by surprise as it had at their first kiss. This time he knew what to expect, and yet the sensation still nearly knocked him off his feet.

They had some instant chemistry that made him want to pick her up and carry her off to his bed like a caveman. As bad as he was around women, even he knew that wasn't acceptable. Women needed courting. And sweet words.

Romance, he thought again. The very word struck fear into the heart of most every man. God help him.

So he kept on kissing her before she could start missing any of that.

"This is not wrong," he said when they came up for air.

His body grew hard. He didn't want to scare her, so he tried to move back a little. Instead, he somehow ended up pushing her against the counter.

SHE HAD ABOUT as much brain as a weather vane. She'd done this before, allowed herself to become a rich man's plaything. It had ended badly. "Yes, it is." And yet she couldn't make herself push Mo away when he leaned in for another kiss.

The first words out of his mouth when he'd come through the door downstairs had been to ask after her son. He always did that. And each time he did, it melted a little bit of her heart.

He was probably faking interest in her and her son just to get into her pants. Other men had done that before. She was such a terrible judge of men, just really bad at making big decisions altogether.

If she were smart, she would run right now.

Instead, she let him lift her up onto the counter.

Instead of protesting, she opened her knees so he could get closer. His hardness pressed against her, and she reveled in his thorough kiss, in his obvious need for her.

Heaven knew she wanted him. He woke up every one of her dormant desires.

Stop. You can still stop. Stop now, a small voice of sanity said in her head.

He ran his fingers up her arms, his touch on her naked skin sending delicious shivers through her. Heat grew inside and flooded her body. Need pulsed in her blood.

"Beautiful," he whispered as he trailed kisses down her neck.

She felt safe with him. She really, really liked him—the way he was nice to Logan, that he cared about her safety and her animals, down to the last scrawny chicken.

The temptation to fall headfirst into something here was overpowering. But as her eyes fluttered half-open, her gaze caught on the granite countertop and the ten-thousand-dollar stove.

And she couldn't ignore the stark truth, that she didn't belong in this place, with this man.

She pulled back. "I shouldn't be doing this. None of this is real."

"Why?"

"Because life is unfair. Why couldn't you be a plain cowboy? Why do you have to be a millionaire playboy G.I. Joe or whatever you are?" She held up a hand. "Please don't protest. You and your team are definitely not some desk-jockey administrators."

A smile hovered over his sexy lips. "Millionaire playboy G.I. Joe?"

"Seriously, how many of those are running around in the average Texas small town? And I have to hook up with one? I don't have to do this just because I like it so much. I like chocolate, too, and I don't eat it for breakfast, lunch and dinner"

"So you like it?"

"More than chocolate," she said on a sigh.

He grinned and brushed his lips over hers again, and she lost all ability to protest.

Her luck was nothing if not rotten.

Even if right now, this part seemed okay. Better than okay. Pretty good. *Great*.

He cupped the back of her neck with one hand and her

breast with the other as he deepened the kiss. Pleasure shot through her, straight to her toes. She'd gone without passion for so long. What was wrong with taking a little of this? Just once?

After an eternity, he pulled back, banked fires burning in his gaze. "I didn't plan this."

"I know. It's okay." She closed the distance between their lips. She needed just one more kiss.

She expected nothing from him, was fully aware that this could go no further. She would be his temporary entertainment. As long as she kept that fixed firmly in her head, she would be okay.

She was no starry-eyed schoolgirl. She no longer believed in happily ever after. When Mo walked away, she wouldn't be heartbroken like before. And she wouldn't be left pregnant. He had to have a maxi-pack of condoms somewhere in this apartment. He was rich and sexy. He probably had women in his life who were classy and sophisticated.

And they probably had lots of fabulous, even scandalous, sex, things she didn't even know how to do. Self-doubt tore into her suddenly. Because she was just a country bumpkin pretty much. She had to face it.

And that was as far as she got with thinking.

His thumb flicked over her nipple and it drew into a tight bud. Moisture gathered between her legs.

She gave up trying to form coherent thoughts and gave herself over to the pleasure of being seduced by Moses Mann. If he thought she was hopelessly unsophisticated and inexperienced, let that be his problem.

He reached for the top button on her shirt. Fumbled. Ha!

She found it incredibly flattering that he was as affected as she. That he wanted her so badly his fingers trembled.

Her knees were so week, if she was standing, she would have probably folded.

The top button yielded at last.

Then the next.

His warm, seeking lips moved down her neck, leaving a tingling trail of desire.

She shrugged out of the shirt before he was half-done with the buttons. He gave an appreciative sound in the back of his throat as he took in her simple cotton bra.

Then he looked pained. "I don't know what to say."

Who wanted to talk? She reached to the back to unclasp the bra. Heat flared in his eyes. He put his hands on her and drew the flimsy material away inch by inch, revealing her breasts with agonizing slowness.

"I want—" he started, but then just dipped his head and drew a nipple between his lips.

As pleasure spiraled through her, for a second she thought she was going to go over the edge right then and there.

Modest country girl, mother and all that.

Having sex in a fancy hotel, on the kitchen counter!

She was wicked, wicked, wicked.

He took her other nipple, drew on it gently, and her body shivered in delight. A strangled sound escaped her throat, halfway between a sob and a moan.

He pulled back. "Did I hurt you?"

She couldn't answer. She just shook her head.

"I want you." He held her gaze. "I wish I knew some romantic way to say that."

He looked concerned, as if he was afraid that what he did say wouldn't be enough.

She felt a smile stretch her lips. "I like plain and honest. I'm not exactly a big-time player."

"I want to pick you up and carry you back to the bedroom."

She slid an inch forward.

His lips tightened. "I don't have protection. I don't suppose you're…"

She stared at him. The millionaire playboy G.I. Joe didn't have protection?

She could have cried as she shook her head. Her entire body ached to finish what they had started. A few long seconds passed before the haze cleared from her mind.

And then she drew her shirt closed and took a deep breath.

Maybe tomorrow she'd be happy that nothing happened between them, but right now, she was awash in disappointment. She tried to remind herself that they weren't in the same league. That he was just playing here.

"Probably for the best," she forced herself to say. She avoided his gaze as she slid off the counter. "My animals are waiting. I usually feed them pretty early."

He let her go. "I need to grab something from the bedroom." His voice sounded a little rough as he said the words.

She straightened her clothing as he walked away. Then, needing something to do, she went back to her notebook and stuffed it into her purse.

Mo was coming back already. "What's that?"

She glanced at the notebook that stuck out of her bag. "I'm making a list of the people I'll need to contact to get Dylan's name cleared. I want something publicly said. In the paper."

"Molly—"

"No." She held up a hand. She didn't want him to say anything bad about her brother right now. She couldn't handle it, not after what they'd just shared, what they had almost done.

Something they shouldn't have done, really. It wasn't as if they were a couple or anything, or as if he even believed her about Dylan.

"Can we—" She glanced toward the counter. "Could we please just forget that this happened?"

His answer was a long time coming. But then he said, "Sure."

She didn't dare look up into his face.

The elevator ride down was awkward, the car ride to the ranch spent in silence. She ran from him the second she slipped out of the car, keeping away from him as she did her chores, pretty much the way she had the night before.

He knew what needed to be done at this stage, so he helped without asking anything, without following her, for which she was grateful. She needed time to recover.

When they were done, she went inside to clean up and water her plants. He was waiting for her in his car when she came out.

She slid into the passenger seat. "Thank you for bringing me here."

"We're doing everything we can to figure out what's going on so you can return home," he said, back in his official persona, his tone impersonal.

He drove down the driveway and turned right instead of turning left, toward Hullett. Maybe he wanted to drive around her land. She wasn't about to complain. It wasn't as if she needed to be anywhere in a hurry.

She leaned back in her seat, more than a little sleepy. She'd had a restless night. As luxurious as her room was, she wasn't used to sleeping in a strange bed.

She was up half the night, walking around. And once

she stopped being blinded by all that opulence, she realized how sterile it all seemed. Just a hotel suite, really.

Not one personal item graced the living room, nothing that said warmth or family. No pictures, no memories, no favorite mug with #1 Uncle on it or anything like that. Everything was decorated in just the standard white the hotel provided. All the luxuries didn't make the place a home. In some sense, she had so much more out at the ranch than he had in his big fancy hotel.

She was so lost in her thoughts she wasn't paying any attention to where he was driving, so she was surprised when they pulled over in front of an old cabin. "Where are we?"

But he was already getting out.

She followed him to the cabin and then inside. "What's this?"

"We're on the Cordero ranch. This is the cabin where Dylan shot and killed four of his accomplices."

Denial sprung to her lips, but died there as she spotted the rust-colored stains on the floor—blood that had seeped into the floorboards. Her stomach rolled. One by one, she noticed the holes where bullets had been pried out of the logs, probably by Mo's team.

"It can't—" Her voice broke.

"It happened. You need to somehow be able to accept that."

"You don't know—"

"I was here. I helped clean up the bodies."

"You were only here after," she whispered. "You don't know what happened."

"Grace Cordero was here during the shooting. Are you saying she's an unreliable witness?"

Grace.

The truth came crashing down on her so hard she couldn't breathe. The carnage here…the bloodbath…and

Grace had been in the middle of it. She could have been killed.

Molly turned and ran outside, ran behind Mo's car then fell to her knees and gave back her breakfast.

She heard his car door open and close, then he was there, gently helping her up, handing her a bottle of water.

"Just because Dylan did something bad here, it doesn't reflect on you or Logan," he said.

She couldn't talk. She rinsed her mouth, then walked to the passenger side and got in. She felt as if she'd just eaten poison.

He took his seat, too, and watched her with concern. "I'm sorry. I shouldn't have brought you here."

"No." She closed her eyes and leaned her head against the headrest, couldn't bear looking at the cabin. "The truth is always good, even if it hurts."

He started the car and drove away.

Minutes passed before she could open her eyes. She still couldn't look at him. She was so hurt and so ashamed.

Oh, Dylan, what have you done?

How had she not known that her brother had gotten involved in smuggling? If they'd talked more, if she'd asked more questions…

"I can't tell Logan," she said at last, horror filling her at the thought. Logan would be devastated.

"Then don't."

"I don't want to lie to him, either. At some point he will have to face the truth, too." That was the right way to go, not her denial. Mo had been right to take her to the cabin, even if it was ripping her apart right now.

"He'll have to accept this, yes, but it doesn't have to happen when he's eight years old. You can give him some of the truth. I don't think details would be necessary at this stage."

She nodded, feeling numb. "What will he think? I don't want him to feel bad about himself because of this."

"Just keep telling him you love him." He paused. Cleared his throat. "When I first found out about being dumped by my parents…" He shook his head. "They tried to drown their own kid. What the hell kind of person does that? And those are my genes. I think I went into the armed forces right out of high school because I wanted to be under close supervision, in case somehow the 'evil' broke out."

She turned to stare at him. "There's nothing evil about you. You're not your parents."

He held on to the wheel with one hand and took her hand with the other, gave a gentle squeeze. "And you're not your brother. And neither is Logan."

She looked away. "I can't talk to you about this."

TEARS BRIMMED IN HER EYES, the first one spilling over, rolling down her face. He felt like a jerk. She needed comfort, but he had no idea how to give it to her, not when she didn't want anything to do with him at the moment.

Mo couldn't blame her. He'd brought her here. He'd brought her this pain. And yet, being pushed away both frustrated and hurt him.

His phone rang. He glanced at it. Jamie. He had to take the call.

"There's movement on the border. The rest of the team is there. I'm heading out right now. Multiple breaches at multiple points." He gave GPS coordinates.

"I'll be right there."

"Try to avoid Ryder. The Chinese guy you got the other night, Yo Tee, he's the real deal. Big-money business guy. Lawyers filed a complaint and everything. Ryder isn't happy. Way to go not bringing attention to the op."

"He looked suspicious."

"Everyone who comes within a mile of Molly Rogers seems suspicious to you these days."

Maybe Jamie was right. Maybe he was losing his objectivity. He wasn't sure there was anything he could do about it. Molly was becoming more and more important to him. "I'll see you in a bit," he said, then ended the call, not feeling like making explanations to Jamie.

"Just take me back to the ranch." Molly still wouldn't look at him.

"You're not going to hang out at your place alone." He turned the car and sped down the dirt road that led to the Cordero ranch.

He might not have been able to help Molly right now, but he knew who could. And he would make sure she was in good hands before he left her. He hoped Grace Cordero was home.

Chapter Nine

Tension tightened Molly's shoulders as Mo pulled up in front of Grace's place.

"I think you should talk to her," he said. "But it's your choice." He waited.

Then Skipper came running, and for a moment she forgot about everything else and jumped from the car, caught the dog up into her arms. The unconditional love and support felt incredibly good.

She scratched behind the dog's ear before giving her another big hug and a kiss.

The front door of the house creaked open.

"Hey." Grace stepped outside. "I was just about to call you. She can go home whenever you're ready."

"I have to go," Mo told them from behind the wheel. "Can you take Molly back to the hotel when she's ready?"

As soon as Grace nodded, he drove away, with one last look at Molly, conflicting emotions darkening his face.

Grace tilted her head. "What's going on? What hotel is he talking about?"

Molly stood, but kept her hand on the dog's head. "I'm… Logan and I are not at the ranch right now. We're in Hullett."

"Everything okay?"

She hesitated. She had so much to say. And she didn't know where to start.

"Why don't we go inside?" Grace suggested. "How about a cold drink?"

She was being nice, a good hostess, but there was a wariness in her tone. Molly couldn't blame her.

She followed Grace inside and sat at the kitchen table, hugged Skipper. The dog stuck to her like glue.

Twinkie, a stray cat Grace had rescued a few weeks back, sauntered in from the direction of the laundry room.

"I hope Skipper was okay with Twinkie and the kittens." Grace had adopted a boxful of barn kittens, too, from a nearby ranch when their mother had disappeared.

"Very gentle." Grace poured two glasses of lemonade then set the pitcher between them.

And then they were out of neutral topics of conversation. Molly drew a deep breath. "We need to talk about Dylan."

Grace's face grew somber as she pulled back a little. She probably expected an argument.

Molly folded her hands on her lap, not sure how to start. "I'm sorry." She was, and it had to be said.

"You haven't done anything." Absolution came quickly and without hesitation.

Her eyes burned. "Mo took me out to the cabin." A tear spilled over. Pain filled her chest. "Dylan... I don't understand. How could he? He was a good brother. He really was. He loved Logan." Another tear broke loose. "How can he have had this monster inside him? How did I not know this?"

"None of it was your fault." Grace came around the table and folded her into a group hug with Skipper, who'd jumped up on Molly to lick her face, needing to be in the middle of everything, as usual.

Molly hugged them back as warmth spread inside her chest. "Can you ever forgive me? I'm so glad you didn't get hurt. I'm so sorry, Grace. We were like sisters back in high school."

"We're still sisters." Grace smiled as she returned to her chair.

Molly blew her nose and dried her face. "Sorry," she said again, unable to think of anything else to say. The vivid image of the blood-splattered cabin loomed large in her head. "You should have never had to go through something like that."

"You have nothing to apologize for. Mo shouldn't have taken you to the cabin. You really didn't need to see that place."

Protectiveness instead of blame. They'd been best friends once. Was it possible that the damage wasn't irreparable?

"He was right. I needed to face the truth. Denial is not healthy."

Grace nodded slowly. "How is Logan?"

"Getting into fights at school." She shook her head. "Mo is… He's teaching him how to stand up for himself, how to avoid violence and how to defend himself if he can't avoid it."

"So Mo is spending a lot of time with you two?" A glint of interest came into Grace's eyes. "He used to scare me. He's so big and rough-looking. But I'm pretty sure he's a gentle giant. He came to Tommy's funeral. All of Ryder's friends did."

"I'm sorry I didn't." The funeral had been right after Dylan's death when she'd been drowning in grief, blaming everyone around her.

"I shouldn't have brought that up. I didn't mean it as a

reproach." Grace winced. "You had a lot to deal with. We both lost brothers we love. I understand."

Except Grace had lost a brother who was a war hero, while Molly had lost a brother who was apparently the town villain. She pushed the bitterness back, determined not to let it get a toehold. "Yes," she agreed.

"I'm glad Mo is spending time with Logan. Whatever else Dylan did, he was a good uncle."

Tears burned Molly's eyes all over again. "Thank you for understanding that."

Grace tilted her head. "So what's this with Mo? I thought you were dating Kenny."

"Temporary insanity." She bit her lip. "We are kind of living at Mo's place."

A smile teased Grace's lips. "You want to tell me something?"

Definitely not that little incident on the kitchen counter. She felt herself flush. The way she'd just abandoned all sense… Not like her at all. Thank goodness she was sane now. Nothing like that was going to happen between her and Mo again.

"He's very helpful," she said.

Grace raised an eyebrow. "I'll bet." Then her mouth curved into a smile. "Have you seen the rest of his team?"

"Some of them."

She fanned herself with her hand. "Lord have mercy."

And then they giggled like two schoolgirls, just like back in the good old days, their friendship mending.

That mended link went a long way toward her feeling better, Molly thought on her way back to the hotel with Grace. Just the two of them. Grace agreed to keep Skipper a little longer. Three dogs in the presidential suite might have been a little too much for hotel management.

"I need to pick up something at the strip mall for Ryder's birthday," Grace said. "Do you mind if we stop in?"

Molly shook her head. She wasn't in a hurry. "What is he getting?"

"Lingerie." Grace grinned.

Molly grinned back. And then it was like two best friends out on the town, and it felt amazing.

So while Grace shopped, Molly picked up a personalized coffee mug made for Mo with his name on it and a super-muscled arm for the handle. MO COFFEE. She hoped he would get a kick out of that.

She picked him up a pretty country pitcher perfect for sweet tea. She bought ingredients so she could make a few dinners, and some plastic storage containers to freeze single portions so he could have some homemade food now and then. He seemed to enjoy her cooking. She was in the checkout line when she ran back and grabbed everything she needed to bake some cookies, as well.

She started cooking as soon as Grace dropped her off at the hotel. Then when Logan came home from school, they baked up a storm together.

Then waited for Mo.

But Mo never came.

THE BORDER OP was a bust—half a dozen people who were carrying nothing. They were first-timers, looking for work. They confessed as soon as they were apprehended. They'd been told to cross and were shown the right spot for free.

A test.

Whoever was running the smuggling rings wanted to know how closely the border was watched. They sent over some decoys, then probably watched from the other side of the river with binoculars as the decoys were caught.

Mo staked out the ranch again that night, actually slept

some on her sofa. He needed to catch up on rest or he'd start making mistakes. Like kissing her in the kitchen.

He'd gotten carried away. She was living at his place. When he'd offered his apartment, he'd meant it to be a sanctuary. She should be able to live there in peace, without being harassed by him because he couldn't control his lust.

But every time he saw her, he wanted her. So maybe the key was to stay away from her, at least for the time being.

Toward dawn he set up another roadblock. He stopped a couple of cowboys going to work early. They weren't thrilled with the harassment. He wasn't thrilled with his lack of progress. He needed a new plan.

He called Jamie. "I'm heading in. Can you drive out here and stick around while Molly takes care of her morning chores?"

Time to get out of here. Even if he did want to see her. Even if he wanted to do way more than just see her. Well, especially because of that.

SINCE THEY ALL DROVE the same model black SUV, Molly couldn't tell who'd be helping her today until Jamie walked out of the barn as she pulled into her driveway.

She'd been hoping for Mo, wondered why he hadn't come home last night.

"Is Mo okay?" The words flew from her mouth before she remembered her manners. "Good morning."

"Good morning. He's at the office. He was out here all night."

She wished he'd stuck around, but tried not to show her disappointment.

"Where are we starting today?" Jamie asked.

"I need to do the milking."

He nodded. "How about if I let out the chickens?"

He was a nice guy, handsome, mild, although that mildness hid plenty of restrained power. He didn't smile much, or ever, really. There were walls all around him that were nearly palpable. She wondered what had happened to him, but she didn't dare ask.

Instead, she headed off to get her buckets, then headed to the barn and greeted the cows.

She didn't mind being at Mo's place as much as she thought she would, and Logan treated it like a vacation, glued to the video games. He thought the whirlpool tub was great and the fancy electronics still made him go wide-eyed.

But Molly missed her house.

She did her chores and Jamie helped, although she insisted he shouldn't. He was supposed to be here to make sure she was safe. He could have sat in his air-conditioned car; he didn't need to be stepping in chicken droppings for her sake. But, of course, he wouldn't hear of it. Like Mo, he had an inner sense of honor and chivalry.

The cowboy code, some people around here called it. Except none of the men on Mo's team were cowboys, although some of them had adopted the local dress code of jeans and cowboy boots to fit in better.

Jamie pulled out of the driveway first, Molly right behind him, just stopping to get the mail out of the mailbox. She sat there, the car idling while she went through the stack of envelopes, hoping for no surprise bills. She had Dylan's mail, too, from the apartment, forwarded here, so she had a handful to go through.

Kenny's cruiser was coming down the road toward her place. Probably coming to check on his horse.

Jamie rolled his window down, his cell phone pressed to his ear. "Are we good here?"

"If you need to go someplace, go," she told him. "I'll be fine here with Kenny."

She set the organic-heirloom-seed catalogs on the passenger seat as Jamie pulled away. Then came a magazine on sustainable farming. Then a bunch of flyers. A credit-card solicitation. Then something that did look like a bill, from the Hullett Storage Park. She tore open the envelope. Huh. Dylan was renting some storage.

For what? They had plenty of room at the ranch for anything he would have needed to store.

Unless it was something he didn't want her to know about…

Her head snapped up and she reached for the horn, but Jamie had already disappeared down the road. She drew a deep breath. Might not be anything important, in any case.

Then she caught herself. She had to stop making excuses for Dylan. She had to accept that he was capable of doing wrong. She reached for her purse on the floor to call Mo, but by the time she dug her cell phone out from the bottom, Kenny's patrol car was pulling up next to her.

He didn't look like his usual spiffy self. His hair was mussed. Dark circles ringed his eyes. "Everything okay? I've been by a couple of times. Your pickup wasn't here."

Right. She'd forgotten to tell him. "Mo thought I shouldn't be out here alone with Logan at night. We're staying in Hullett."

His eyebrows slid up his forehead. "I thought Dylan's apartment wasn't released yet."

"Mo rents a place he doesn't really use. He let us have it."

"You're staying with Moses Mann?" Kenny's forehead pulled together into a scowl.

"Not with him. Just at his place. He only stops in for a change of clothes."

Kenny's lips flattened. "Isn't he a dedicated government employee?" He watched her for a second. "When are they gonna be done with their budget recommendations?"

"I'm not sure. He doesn't really talk about his job."

"Bunch of idiot pencil pushers flown in from D.C. Think they can drive around the border for a few weeks, have everything figured out. I've lived here all my life, worked here since I got my badge. You'd think CBP would be asking people like me if they needed help."

She wasn't sure what exactly Mo was, but she was pretty sure he wasn't a pencil pusher. The way he moved, the way he was built... All she could think of was the commando soldiers she'd seen in movies.

"They do work pretty hard," she said, defending the team. They put in some serious hours. They wanted to figure out what was going on at the border, and they gave the task their all. While taking time to protect her. "You look tired," she said to change the subject.

"Been pulling some double shifts." Kenny tilted his head. "So this Mo and his super team still blame your brother for everything?"

She closed her eyes for a second. "I— It looks like Dylan might have somehow gotten involved in something he shouldn't have." It hurt just saying the words.

"They know that for a fact?" Kenny leaned forward. "They have any idea who he might have been working with?"

"I don't know. I just..." She lifted the bill on her lap. "Got a bill for a storage unit he was renting in Hullett."

He stared at the envelope, an unreadable expression on his face. "Could be nothing." He reached a hand out the open window toward her. "Let me see it."

She handed the bill over and waited while Kenny scanned the contents then handed the envelope back to her.

"You shouldn't go out there. Don't put your fingerprints

on anything. Moses Mann and those yahoos are desperate to pin all their problems on someone. Make sure it's not you. You don't want them to take you in for another interrogation."

He was right about that. But she didn't think Mo's team were a bunch of yahoos. Still. "I'm not planning on going anywhere near that storage unit."

"If you want, I can go check it out after my shift is over tonight. Nobody has to know about it until then."

She nodded. "Thanks, Kenny."

"You'd probably do best if you stayed away from those outsiders. They think they're hotshots, know everything better, look down on us country folk. They're not like you and me, Molly."

That Kenny would think that didn't surprise her. Hullett and Pebble Creek were small towns, filled with people whose ancestors had lived on the borderlands for generations. They were fiercely proud of that and protective of their heritage. Newcomers were often greeted with suspicion. They usually came to take.

She exchanged a few more words with Kenny before parting ways. She wanted to deliver her vegetables before they completely wilted in the back.

She was almost in town when Mo called to check on her.

Kenny had said nobody had to know about the storage unit. But Mo…

"I just got a bill from the storage park in Hullett. It looks like Dylan was renting a unit," she told him on impulse, then wondered if she'd done the right thing.

Mo HAD BEEN OUT by the border investigating a rope line across the river that had gone up overnight, either to help people cross or to pull contraband. He got in his car as soon as Molly told him about the storage unit, but it took him an hour to reach Hullett. The GPS led him straight to the storage park. He marched into the office, flashed his CBP badge and asked for the locker number assigned to Dylan Rogers.

"And I'll need a lock cutter, too. I'm sure you have one of those back there somewhere," he told the twentysomething clerk behind the desk who was covered in tattoos from head to toe.

"I don't know, dude. Do you have, like, a search warrant?" The kid chewed his wad of gum, patting his greasy goatee.

Mo had a Beretta in his holster, good enough for a padlock, he figured. He didn't have time to play here. "Never mind. Just point me to the locker."

The kid shook his head. "You can't just bust into somebody's locker, man."

To hell with him. Mo strode out of the office and straight into the maze of lockers, followed the signs and numbers until he reached 763. The clerk caught up with him, protesting.

Then gaped at the sight that greeted them.

The lock had been busted off the unit, the space empty save for some some packing peanuts scattered around on the floor.

Mo glanced up at the security camera. Broken. Chunks of plastic lay on the ground. Still, it might have caught something before it connected with a baseball bat or whatever.

"I'm going to need the security footage."

The kid backed away. "You're gonna need a search warrant, man."

He didn't have time for a search warrant. This was their best lead in weeks and it was fresh. He'd be damned if he was going to waste it. He looked the kid over, considered a bullet in his kneecap.

He'd been on plenty of missions where interrogations had been conducted like that. But he believed that senseless violence was never an intelligent man's first weapon. So he asked nicely. While pulling himself to full height and putting on his meanest face.

"How about I just look at the footage on your screen? I won't ask for the tape."

The clerk's Adam's apple bobbed up and down a few times. "Um…I suppose that would be okay."

But the tape proved to be no help whatsoever. It didn't show a damned thing. Whoever had taken out the camera had snuck up to it from behind. Since the unit was in the last row, near the employee entrance, no other cameras caught the guy, either. Looked as if he'd come in through the back. Mo was willing to bet that lock, too, would be busted.

The only clue he got was the time. The security footage stopped thirty minutes ago.

He thanked the clerk and called Molly on his way out. He needed to find out if she'd told anyone else about the storage bill.

But he couldn't reach her.

Chapter Ten

Molly tried not to think of the worst while she waited on the line to be transferred to the school office. The apartment was silent around her, the dogs sleeping in Logan's bedroom. Where Logan should have been right now, doing homework, but wasn't.

Maybe he'd gotten into another fight and was serving detention. That he hadn't come home on the school bus didn't have to mean anything worse than that.

She let out a pent-up sigh. They would definitely have to have another talk about fighting.

"Mrs. Langton," said the school secretary on the other end at last.

"Hi, this is Molly Rogers. Logan wasn't on the school bus. Could you please see what happened to him? Did he get detention?"

"Oh, are you okay?"

"Yes. Do you know where he is?"

"Sheriff Davis took him. Kenny said you were unavailable." An uncomfortable silence followed the last word.

"When?" Her phone beeped, an incoming call. She ignored it.

"Just as the buses were pulling out. Are you sure everything is okay? I thought—"

Mrs. Langton didn't have to finish. Molly knew what

she thought. That Molly had been arrested in connection with her brother's crimes, that Kenny was taking Logan to Social Services.

"Thanks. I'm sure it's just a misunderstanding." She hung up, confused and worried. She glanced at the phone. Mo had called. She was about to call him back and beg for his help when another call came in: Kenny.

"Why did you take Logan?"

"I haven't been completely honest with you, honey." A pause followed the words, then, "Your brother and I were kind of business partners. He took delivery of a considerable amount of merchandise. Then he died before we could have passed on the goods. Well, I thought he had, but as it turns out he hadn't. The people on the other side of the border want their money."

A sense of betrayal washed over her, sending a chill down her spine. She couldn't have cared less about money or merchandise or any of that stupid business. "Where is Logan?"

"Logan will be safe as long as you cooperate. I've been given an ultimatum over here, you understand. I would have rather done this the nice way. I had plans for you and me. But time is running out."

Her heart gave a long, hard squeeze. "What do you want?"

"The drugs. Looks like Dylan only used the storage locker as a temporary place. Or maybe he ran his distribution from there. There was nothing in it. I have twenty-four hours to come up with the full shipment. I'd rather not find out what will happen if I can't produce the goods. So it's the boy for the drugs. That's how simple it is. Nothing to worry about. You give me what I want, and the boy comes home."

Was he nuts? Cold fear spread through her, desperation constricting her throat. "I have no idea where any drugs are."

"You probably just don't know that you know. Nobody knew Dylan half as well as you did. I'm sure there's some clue in that house or in that pretty little head of yours that will lead us to the rest. You just have to want to find it. Twenty-four hours."

She was so upset, she couldn't talk.

"I'll be calling. And, in the meanwhile, I wouldn't tell anyone about this, especially your devoted friend, Moses Mann, and his team, if you know what's good for your kid," Kenny added. "If you tell anyone, I'll know it. If you want the kid back, the most important thing you can do is to keep this between us, honey."

SHE WASN'T AT THE HOTEL.

The dogs were happy to see him, though, jumping all over Mo as he strode in.

"Where is everybody?"

Max and Cocoa licked his face, but that was it. No information was forthcoming.

He looked through the apartment carefully, checking for any signs of forced entry or struggle. Everything seemed in its place.

Maybe Molly took Logan shopping. Although, it looked as if she'd already shopped. He noted the soft blanket folded over the back of the couch and the throw pillow that would make taking a nap there actually comfortable. He went for a drink and saw the sweet tea in a brand-new pitcher.

Okay, his place did lack the niceties. He mostly came here to sleep. She was making herself more comfortable, he thought, then noticed the coffee mug. MO COFFEE. And a dog-shaped cookie jar on the counter. He opened it and smiled. Cookies.

Warmth spread through him as he realized that she was trying to make life nicer for him.

And she had. Just her presence in his apartment had somehow transformed it. Molly and Logan made the place a home instead of a hotel suite.

He pulled out his phone and dialed her again. He'd tried several times already, but she wasn't picking up. This time the robot voice said the number was unavailable. Her phone was either turned off or her battery was dead.

Was she avoiding him again?

Too bad. He had to talk to her. He needed to know who else she told about the storage locker.

He called Jamie. "Was everything okay with Molly when you were out at the ranch with her this morning?"

"Fine. Why?"

"She's not at the hotel, and I can't reach her on the phone."

"I had to run off to follow up on a lead, but we were done by then, leaving. The Pebble Creek sheriff was coming to see his horse."

"Okay. I'll go out there. Maybe she went out early for the evening feeding." She really shouldn't have done that. She knew it wasn't safe.

He hung up then checked his weapons and hurried down to his car, pretty much ignoring the speed limit as he drove through town. He didn't relax until he was turning down her road and could see her pickup sitting in the driveway.

When he walked into the house, she was just coming down the stairs, her chestnut hair tied up in a haphazard bun. A dust streak stretched across her face. Looked as if she'd been cleaning.

"You shouldn't be here alone." Relief and frustration shot through him in a tangled mix. "You're going to risk your life for dust bunnies?"

"I've really been neglecting the place," she said apologetically without meeting his eyes.

"You still should have waited for me." He drew a slow breath. He hadn't come here to yell at her.

She gave a strained smile, the house silent around them. Too silent.

He looked around. "Where's Logan?"

She turned from him, her hands fidgeting over things as she tidied up the kitchen, her movements stiff and jerky. "He's at a friend's house."

"Everything okay?"

She nodded without turning around. "Just tired. I never sleep well in a strange place."

She wanted to come home. Of course. Thing was, he'd gotten used to her and Logan being there when he popped in for this and that. He liked it.

"Thanks for the mug," he said. "And all the rest, too." For the first time, the apartment actually looked lived-in. There were books and toys lying about. He wished he had the right words to tell her how he felt about that, how he felt about having her and Logan in his life. Instead, he turned to business. "I called you earlier."

"My battery is probably dead. I'll charge it when we get back to the hotel." She stood at the sink with her back to him.

"I need to ask you something. Have you told anyone else about the storage locker?"

Her shoulders tensed even more. "No." She didn't turn to face him. "I should go take care of the animals. After I finish up outside, I'll need to come back in here and gather up some things. You can leave if you have to go back to work. I should be okay."

Was she mad at him? It was as if she couldn't even stand

to look at him. But if she were mad, then what were the cookies and the mug and all the other stuff about?

God, women were confusing.

Maybe all those things were her way of paying him back for their stay. She didn't want to be beholden to him or some such nonsense. Completely unnecessary. He would have given her whatever she asked, everything he had.

Or maybe the cookies and all were Logan's idea. He loved the apartment and the game console.

"I'll walk around the outbuildings, see if I can find any tire tracks or some sign that people have been out here lately."

She nodded as she put something in the fridge.

It was plain that she wanted him gone.

So he obliged her by walking away.

MOLLY RUSHED BACK upstairs to Dylan's room as soon as Mo went outside. She needed to stay away from him. She'd almost told him about Logan a half-dozen times. But if Kenny found out she told... Kenny was a sheriff. He was listening to all the law-enforcement channels. He would know the second Mo passed the news on to his team.

Kenny... Oh, God. She searched through Dylan's dresser frantically, looking at every piece of paper in the bottom drawer. Most turned out to be old receipts for farm equipment, warranties and catalogs. She shoved the drawer shut, desperation washing over her as she stood.

There had been nothing in Dylan's desk, nothing under his mattress, either. Where else would he hide something? Of course, she had no idea what she was looking for. Receipts for another storage unit?

She went downstairs for the largest knife she had, then back up to test the floorboards to see if there might be some hidden nook where her brother had kept information.

One board did come up, and as it did, a spring shot off a rubber band that smacked her in the nose. One of Dylan's early booby traps. She looked at the empty vodka bottle in the hole as she rubbed her nose. Probably left over from Dylan's teenage years.

Where were the damn drugs?

How could Dylan get involved in something like this? How could Kenny? Kenny was a sheriff, for heaven's sake. He should have been on the side of good, steering her brother right, not dragging him into dirty business.

She couldn't trust anyone.

Her brother hadn't been who she thought he was. Kenny, a sheriff, had his own share of secrets. She wanted to trust Mo, she really did. But her judgment was so obviously terrible.

What if Mo, too, had his own secret agenda?

Maybe he'd only offered her the apartment to keep a closer eye on her. Maybe he didn't care about her one bit, only cared about his mission. He'd said as much before.

If she told him about Logan, would he and his team charge ahead to catch Kenny, not caring what happened to her son? Would they think one little kid was an acceptable casualty when they had border security at risk?

She desperately needed a friend in all this, but there was too much at stake. She couldn't talk to anyone, not even Grace. Grace could tell Ryder.

She gave up on Dylan's room and went through all the others, feeling more desperate and more alone than she'd ever felt in her life. She knew only one thing: she would do anything to save her son. She would sacrifice anything. If she found any drugs, or any indication of where they were hidden, she would hand them over to Kenny in the blink of an eye. Even if it meant she had to go to prison afterward.

But she found nothing.

She went back down to the kitchen and happened to glance at the answering machine. The light was blinking. She hadn't seen that earlier. She had four messages, three from telemarketers, one from the agent for Brandsom Mining. She deleted them all.

Even if she eventually got desperate enough to call Brandsom, she had the agent's card. He'd sent it in the mail, along with various offers. Several times.

The thought that things might come to that further twisted her heart. Dylan had always been very adamant about not letting anyone near the old mine shafts.

She froze where she stood.

The old mine shafts.

Some had collapsed, while others had been blown in on purpose to make sure local teens didn't go in there to do whatever teens did when they were hiding from their parents. The shafts were way too dangerous. All the openings had been boarded up. But what if…

If there was a spot on the ranch where multiple crates of something could be hidden, those old mine shafts would be it.

She looked outside, into the approaching darkness. She had only a vague idea where the openings were. She would never find them in the dark. She'd be lucky to find them in the daylight.

The thought that she would have to wait brought tears of frustration into her eyes. She wanted her son back and she wanted him now. She blinked away the tears. She couldn't afford to break down. Best thing was to keep busy.

She went outside and hurried through her chores, trying her best to avoid Mo as much as possible. She didn't want him to realize that she was upset. She didn't want to chance him guessing that something was wrong.

He was cleaning off his boots when she finished up and came out of the barn, closing it up behind her for the night.

"Thank you." She did her best to put on a smile. "You probably have to go back to work. I'm going to head over to Grace's place for a little while."

But he said, "I don't think Grace is home. She was going to help Ryder with something tonight."

"Oh. Well." She tried not to look as frustrated as she felt. "I suppose I'll go to the feed store, then." She waited for him to leave.

"I'll go with you."

Great. "I shouldn't take up all your time."

"I don't mind. I have the night off."

And true to his word, he stuck by her. So she was forced to go to the feed store, pick up things she didn't really need, drop them off at the barn, then head back to Hullett with him.

All the while worrying about her son, petrified that she wouldn't be able to save him.

"When is Logan coming home?" Mo asked over dinner. He was glad he'd taken the night off. Something was wrong with Molly. He needed to figure out what.

"Tomorrow," she said ashen-faced without looking up from her plate.

The dogs lay at her feet. They didn't beg for food. They were pretty well behaved.

"It's good that he has close friends. He's a pretty special little kid. You raised him well."

She ate, but without true appreciation. Were her eyes glistening?

Looked as if all the stress was really getting to her. He felt guilty as hell. She'd lost her brother, her only support, had some financial issues at the ranch, was accused of being involved in smuggling and had been interrogated. And then he'd taken her to that damn cabin.

Which might not have been the best decision he'd ever made. She clearly needed something to hang on to, and some false ideal of Dylan had been it. Now that he'd taken that away from her, she had nothing.

He was wired differently. He needed the truth. He would take any truth, no matter how harsh, and then he could deal with it. He liked to know where he stood. He didn't believe in clinging to fantasies.

"You're a strong woman. You will work through this," he told her, reaching for her hand across the table.

She pulled away. "I'm not strong. Not like you are," she said miserably.

"You might not be jumping in front of bullets on a daily basis, but what you do day after day, running the ranch, raising your son, takes strength."

The sight of a tear rolling down her face twisted his gut.

"Hey." He reached across the table again and brushed away the tear with his thumb.

She pushed her seat back so fast she nearly knocked it over. "Better get started on the dishes."

He stood. "I'll do that."

But she was already standing by the sink.

"How about you wash, I dry," he said, offering a compromise. She accepted.

They worked in silence for a while, their movements strangely harmonized as if they'd done this often. She looked at him a couple of times, as if on the verge of saying something, but each time she changed her mind and turned away.

"How about some TV?" he suggested when they were done. She looked as if she could use some distraction.

She looked toward her bedroom, then nodded. "Sure."

He flipped through the channels, found a sappy romantic comedy. Supposedly women liked that kind of thing. He tried to think what else he could do to cheer her up. Flowers. Women usually found flowers comforting. He glanced around the apartment. She'd brought him some sort of potted herb. The pot stood behind them on the sofa table. He put his arm over the back of the sofa as unobtrusively as he could and pushed the plant closer to her.

She looked up at him, a moment of confusion on her face.

Right. Because it looked as if he had his arm up there to kind of drop it over her shoulders. As if he was making a move.

He acted as though he was just stretching, then pulled back and stared straight ahead at the TV, where a pair of rambunctious dogs were wrapping their owners together with their leashes.

Max padded in, barked at the screen, then, after Molly patted him, he went back out to the kitchen. He liked lying on the tile floor. It was probably colder.

The movie went on. Minutes ticked by.

She looked straight ahead, but he wasn't sure she was really watching. Her shoulders were still tight, the look on her face still unhappy.

He hated that he couldn't help her, watched the movie without registering much of it, thinking mostly about Molly beside him. Truth was, he wanted to pull her into his arms and distract her from her troubles in the most ancient way. By making love to her.

He wasn't proud of himself for the thought. What kind of man would use a woman's temporary distress to seduce her?

In the movie, the heroine was going through her troubles alone, consoling herself with copious amounts of ice cream.

He wished he had some of that in the freezer. Or chocolate. He tried to think what he had in his half-empty cabinets. Then cheered up a little when he thought of something.

"How about some beef jerky?"

She drew her eyebrows together. "Are you hungry? We just ate."

"I meant for…" He almost said *female upset* but finished lamely with "dessert."

A dubious look flashed across her face. "We have cookies," she reminded him. "Maybe later. But thank you," she said politely, then went back to watching the movie.

He tried to think of something that might work to relax her. Maybe a bubble bath. Women liked that, didn't they?

The image of her naked in his tub resulted in a predictable response from his body. He shifted in his seat. But his condition only worsened when the star-crossed couple on the screen finally made up and had their hot-and-heavy love scene.

Molly didn't seem to enjoy it. Her eyes glistened, in fact, almost as if she were close to tears. Definitely not the same response that the scene was getting from him.

Women were complicated.

Men were simple. They saw a woman they liked, they wanted sex. They watched sex, they wanted sex.

He glanced at her from the corner of his eye again.

She was beautiful and strong—no matter what she thought—and a great mother, honest, hardworking, sexy. He was mostly focused on the sexy part at the moment. Every cell of his body wanted her.

He couldn't take any more of the writhing bodies and throaty moaning on the TV. He got to his feet and retreated to the kitchen. He needed something cold. "Want a drink?"

"Sure. Thanks."

He stood in front of the open fridge door for a while,

letting the frigid air hit him, then grabbed the sweet-tea pitcher, poured two glasses and added ice. He also turned up the air-conditioning while he was walking by the thermostat.

She stood as she took the glass from him. "I think I'll go to bed early if you don't mind. I'm a little tired today."

Upset, she meant. He wished she would confide in him. She tried so damned hard to be strong. Too hard.

He set his glass on the sofa table and slowly pulled her into his arms. "What is it?"

"Just having a rough day." She put the glass down.

"I don't like seeing you sad."

"Mo…" She hesitated. "I should…"

"What?" He held her loosely, not wanting to scare her, not wanting to seem too pushy.

"Logan and I should probably move back home tomorrow."

Not what he wanted to hear. "Not yet. I like it when you're here," he admitted.

And that softened her face a little.

He reached up to brush the hair back from her eyes. Then rested his lips against her forehead, just savoring the feel of her in his arms. He wanted to keep her there forever, keep her safe from her troubles. "You know if there's anything I can help you with, I would, right? Whatever it is."

SHE WAS SO TEMPTED to tell him. But Kenny had said if she told anyone, her son would die. And that was a risk she wasn't willing to take.

If she told Mo, he would tell his team. His team would set up some kind of op. Her only experience with those was what she'd seen on TV shows. There'd be a shoot-out, probably.

There had been a shoot-out the night Dylan had died.

Her heart constricted.

She could deal with Kenny. Kenny wanted the drugs. She wanted Logan back. It would be a simple exchange. No fancy team of outsiders needed. The more people involved, the better chance that something could go wrong, someone could make a mistake.

She trusted Mo. She really did. To a point. She wanted to trust him all the way, but when her son was involved... she just couldn't make that final leap.

So she let him comfort her and kept quiet.

She leaned against him and soaked up his calm, self-assured energy. His steady heartbeat against her palm felt incredibly reassuring. He was a solid wall of strength.

"If you were in any kind of trouble, you would tell me, right?"

She nodded, unable to say the lie out loud.

He gathered her closer. Kissed her eyebrow.

She let him. Because when Mo found out that she had lied to him, that she helped Kenny, he would hate her.

The thought broke her heart. Because she'd been falling for him.

Starting tomorrow, she would be the enemy again, an accomplice in smuggling, for real this time. Back in the interrogation room without a doubt. But Logan would be safe from Kenny. Even if she got arrested, Grace would take care of her son. Logan would be safe. And that was worth whatever sacrifice Molly had to make.

So she said goodbye to Mo, silently, as he lowered his head and gently kissed her lips.

So unfair. They could have had something, she realized too late. He was different from all the other men she'd met. Images of what could have been flashed across her mind and took her breath away. Except, tomorrow he would hate her.

But she could have something, a little, tonight, a small voice said in her head. So she leaned into the kiss.

A low rumble sounded in his throat, a primal sound of passion that sent heat through her. He lifted her into his arms and headed straight to his bedroom with her. She didn't protest, just let him keep on kissing her.

He lay her on top of the covers as softly as if he thought she might break. Then he pulled his shirt over his head.

She sucked in a breath.

He was incredibly built. Action-movie stars had to paint on muscles to look like him. While he was fairly large, he didn't have an ounce of fat on his body, reminding her that she had curves sticking out every which way that she wished were much smaller.

She was a farm girl and she ate farm food, not designer protein shakes.

He stopped. "What's wrong?"

"I'm rethinking some of those pancake breakfasts."

"Don't," he said with a slow grin. "I'm pretty much crazy about your body."

That was news to her. "You are?"

He gave a strangled laugh as he lowered himself onto the giant bed next to her. "I can barely think every time I look at you. I wanted you while I was interrogating you." He covered his face with a hand as he lay on his back next to her. "How professional is that?"

Maybe not professional, but it was incredibly flattering.

"You never said anything."

He turned to his side and came up on one elbow. "You're a good woman. A mother. That needs to be respected."

A man who wanted her *and* respected her. And she was going to lose him tomorrow. She looked at the wall across from the bed and considered getting up to bang her head against it.

Instead, she reached up and pulled him down, fitting her mouth against his with a boldness she didn't know she possessed.

That was all the hint he needed.

He kissed her gently at first, tasting her lips. Then she opened for him and he accepted the invitation with enthusiasm. Hot need flooded her in an instant, pleasure surging through her.

The way he kissed her…almost reverently, but with so much heat and restrained passion. The sensations spreading through her made her head spin.

She was nearing thirty and she'd never truly been kissed. Not like this. The realization stunned her. And even scared her a little. Because she knew she was never again going to meet anyone like Mo.

She lifted her hands to his bare chest, her fingers gliding over the smooth skin that covered all those muscles.

His hand ran down her arm and up her belly, tugging her shirt upward. She wanted to feel his fingers on her bare skin. And then she did. His large hand covered half her abdomen, his heat burning through her skin. He caressed her gently, moving up inch by slow inch, stopping just under her breast.

Then his hand cupped her at last, and she arched into his touch. When he pulled his hand back, she almost protested before she realized he only pulled back to undo her shirt buttons so he could bare her to his gaze.

"I wish I knew just what to say," he said in a raspy whisper. "But you take my breath away."

Which was exactly the right thing to say.

Her shirt opened at last. She wished she owned something fancier than her simple white cotton bra. But he didn't seem to mind. He seemed mesmerized by it.

She lifted away from the bed a little so he could remove

the shirt, then held herself still while he fumbled with her bra clasp in the back.

"Not too good at this. Fingers too big," he said apologetically.

But she loved that he wasn't some skilled seducer, loved it that he wanted her so much it made his fingers tremble. He was Mo, exactly the man she wanted, needed.

Then she was naked to the waist and his eyes narrowed. Her nipples pebbled under his burning gaze. His head moved toward them as if drawn by a string.

The first touch of his lips against her hard nipple sent a hot flash of desire slicing through her. When he laved that nipple, heat pooled at the V of her thighs. Suddenly, she wanted things she didn't even know existed until now.

He was a steady man, one who liked to think things through, pay close attention to every step of the process. He brought those same skills to his lovemaking, leaving not a square inch of skin untouched, unkissed, driving her out of her mind with need.

She wished she'd met him before, not when everything was falling apart. She wished Dylan hadn't done what he'd done. She wished her life wasn't this complicated, that they could hold on to what they had here, that she didn't have to lie to him.

Then she pushed those thoughts away. If they were given only this night, she wasn't going to borrow trouble from tomorrow and poison what little time they had together.

Chapter Eleven

She was perfect. And for this moment, she was his.

What she made him feel…

He was old enough to know this kind of thing didn't come around all the time. Never before for him, in fact. And now that he had it, he didn't want to let her go. The only solution was to make her his forever. Starting right now, right here.

"A man could get used to this." Her soft skin felt like silk under his fingertips. She had enough curves to fill even his large hands, making him senseless with want. She fitted to him perfectly, as if she had been made for him.

She was passionate, responding to his every touch, arching her back, her eyes fluttering closed when he kissed her, then flying wide open when he touched her in her most intimate places. He reveled in that responsiveness, in the fact that he could make her feel that way.

He grinned at her. "You're good for me, you know that?"

For a second, her eyes cleared and something he couldn't identify flashed across them. Then she pulled his head down and kissed him silly again.

He had condoms in the nightstand drawer this time. He'd learned his lesson from the other day. He hadn't expected this to happen, but he'd been hoping.

He removed the rest of his clothing, and for a moment

they lay against each other, skin to skin. If that moment lasted a year, it wouldn't have been enough.

Then she parted her legs and drew her knee up over his hip, and the moment gained a sense of urgency.

He reached back, tore open a foil wrapper and sheathed himself then rolled her under him. "What have I done to deserve this?"

She tipped her head back and closed her eyes.

He moved to her opening, waited, for a moment finding it hard to believe this was happening, that she was giving herself to him like this. Then she lifted herself, welcoming him inside her body.

His eyes about rolled back in his head from the sharp pleasure. She was tight and wet for him. Moving.

Sweat broke out on his forehead.

"Molly." Her name came out in a strangled whisper.

And then he pushed, inch by slow inch, until he filled her to the hilt.

He could run twenty miles in full battle gear, but he was breathing hard now from that last little push. His heart beat against his ribs. He drew back, pushed in again, the friction increasing, his world spiraling out of control pretty damned rapidly.

He supported himself on his elbows as he dipped his head to kiss her, claiming those glorious lips again and again, their bodies rocking against each other, heat and pleasure building.

Then her body went taut and she gave a small cry, and the next thing he knew her muscles were contracting around him, pulsating, squeezing, sending him over the edge.

She blew his mind just absolutely, completely. When they lay side by side later, panting, all he could think was that he wanted to do this again as soon as possible.

He almost told her that, but somehow he wasn't sure if it would be romantic or just plain selfish, so he said nothing.

HER BONES MELTED. She'd never known sex could be like this. Wow. "Did that just happen?"

"And then some." He chuckled, sounding sated.

She'd always thought romantic movies and romance novels exaggerated. They had a product to sell, right?

But no. What they'd shared here, in Mo's bedroom, was all that and more, way beyond her wildest fantasies. He was a great guy. Her son liked him and looked up to him. And sex with him was out-of-this-world phenomenal.

And this was the end. She pressed closer.

Tomorrow he would hate her for lying to him.

The thought about killed her.

He drew her into his arms and kissed the top of her head.

His gentleness brought tears to her eyes. She hated lying to him. She had to press her lips together so the truth about Logan wouldn't burst out. So she stayed quiet and stayed close to him, soaking up the feeling while she could.

When he finally slept, she pulled away so she wouldn't disturb him with her tossing and turning and worrying about her son. She tried to remember the few times she'd been out to the mines. Could she find the right place?

Her grandfather had taken her out a few times, on horseback, to talk about the family's glory days. His grandfather and grand uncle had come to the area as poor miners. Between the two of them, they somehow scrimped together enough to buy partial stake in a small mine, eventually. They were successful for a while. Then they found out that the deposits weren't nearly as vast as advertised. They lost most of their money, bought land with what they had left and started ranching.

She thought about those old mine shafts, getting Logan back, losing Mo.

She passed out from sheer exhaustion toward dawn, but woke again a little while later. She slipped from the bed at first light, grabbed her clothes and dressed in the bathroom. She shut down all emotion, left a note for Mo on the kitchen counter, then sneaked away.

Couldn't sleep. Went out to the ranch. I'll ask Grace to come over with me.

MO READ THE NOTE over for the second time.

Grace Cordero, an army vet, was definitely good enough for bodyguard duty. But he would have liked to spend the morning with Molly.

Did she have second thoughts about what had happened last night? He hoped not. He'd liked every minute and wanted more. And not just the sex. He wanted more of her. All of her.

But it seemed she wanted space.

Okay. Fine. Whatever she needed. He was in this for the long haul. So he drank his coffee, got dressed and went into the office.

SHE DIDN'T CALL GRACE. She didn't want anyone else involved in her lies. She didn't need a bodyguard. She knew now who sent the men who'd searched her ranch: Kenny. And he was waiting for word from her on the whereabouts of the drugs. She took care of her animals in record time. They seemed agitated.

The horizon was a threatening shade of purplish-gray when she came out of the barn with her milk pails. Looked as if a storm was coming, she thought as she finished up.

A bad storm could wipe out half her gardens. She

couldn't worry about that now. She only cared about Logan today and his well-being. "I'm coming, baby," she muttered under her breath, trying not to let desperation get the better of her.

She hurried to her pickup and rode out on the dirt road that wound its way through the fields.

She knew the mine openings were to the east of the house. She sort of knew where they were in relation to each other. Once she found one, she was pretty sure she could find the rest.

Heat shimmered over the land, the vegetation dry, dust blowing from the bare patches. A dust devil rose up on the road right in front of her. She drove around it and scanned the land, followed her memories and, after some false starts, found the first opening.

She pulled up next to the pile of rocks that had some old two-by-fours and rebar sticking out. Rubble covered the ground, some scraggly weeds growing in the dirt the winds had deposited between the rocks over the years. Didn't look as if anybody had been here since the shaft had been blown in.

At least she was in the general area. "Hang in there, Logan," she whispered into the wind. "I'm coming."

She drove around in expanding circles, looking for another entry. She found one half an hour later, looking the same as the first. Then another one that obviously hadn't been disturbed in ages, either. Doubt began to fill her, cold panic spreading through her limbs.

The mines *had* to be the answer. This had to be it, because she had no other ideas, and her son's life depended on her locating the stupid drugs Kenny wanted.

She had trouble finding the next shaft, maybe because she was becoming more and more frazzled. She was praying out loud as she drove and almost missed the spot. The opening was covered with dry brush. She only recognized the place because of the car-size rocks by a nearby mesquite grove. She recalled trips with her grandfather, sitting on those rocks in the shade and drinking water out of his canteen, eating homemade beef jerky.

The dry brush, carried here from someplace else, gave her hope. It certainly looked as if someone had tried to camouflage the spot.

She jumped out of her pickup and began dragging those dead bushes away. Under the brush, a faded brown tarp covered a rusty set of metal doors, the kind people used for outside basement entries. She zeroed in on the padlock. New.

Every instinct she had screamed that this was it.

A small voice inside said it wasn't too late to call Mo. She almost did. But no, she shoved her cell phone back into her pocket.

She was so close. She could do it. Her son's safety was the most important thing here, and if Kenny thought she brought anyone in, who knew what he would do. She would have never thought he could hurt a kid, but then again, she would have never thought he could be involved in smuggling, either.

She kicked the padlock in frustration. A lock cutter would have been nice. She didn't have that, but she did have a tire iron in the back of the pickup. So she ran to get that and used it to bust the lock, grunting and sweating in the heat, but refusing to give up until the metal gave.

Then she threw open the rusty doors and looked into the darkness. A makeshift wooden ramp led down, a flashlight conveniently sitting on the top step. She left it there. She had no idea how good the battery was. She had a newly charged flashlight in her glove compartment and she went to get that.

She turned on the flashlight then followed the ramp.

Fist-size spiders hung on the walls and above her head. She could hear something scurrying up ahead, then nearly stepped on a rattlesnake.

"Easy. I'm not here to hurt you." She backed around it carefully, grateful that it had sounded its rattle to warn her.

She wiped her forehead with her free hand, moving forward even more carefully, especially when she remembered how fond Dylan had been of booby traps. She felt as if she was in an Indiana Jones movie, half expected poisoned darts to shoot out of the walls, or the ceiling to start pressing down on her. She really hated dark, ominous places.

She moved forward anyway. She found no traps, just discarded beer cans here and there. Budweiser. Her brother's favorite. Disappointment choked her.

"Dammit, Dylan." She kicked a can that bounced far ahead, the sound echoing off the walls. She followed after it.

She only had to go in a few hundred feet before she saw the two crates, the wood slats new, unlike the blackened supports of the old mine shaft. These crates had been a recent addition to the place, and she knew what they held without having to pry one open. She'd let Kenny do that.

She walked back out of the mine shaft so she could get reception for her phone, then called him, giving him directions on how to find her.

"I knew you could do this, darling. You just stay where you are, now. I'm bringing the boy," he promised.

Mo spent his morning on the border, but when he had to head into Hullett to check on something and had to drive close by the Rogers ranch on his way into town, he decided to stop in. He was willing to give Molly the space she needed to think, but he wanted to make sure she was okay.

Her pickup wasn't in the driveway, but he got out and checked around the buildings anyway. The chickens were out, all the animals fed and watered. She'd gotten an early start and had probably finished early. Made sense. She was most likely back in Hullett by now.

He drove into town and decided to swing by his place, but only the dogs greeted him.

"Hey, are you here?" He walked through the empty living room and kitchen, back to her room. Knocked on her door. "Are you in there?"

No answer.

He knocked again then pushed the door in. Her room stood empty. Maybe she'd gone to pick up Logan from his sleepover. He grabbed a cookie and a cold drink then headed over to the sheriff's office.

Ryder called just as Mo pulled out of the underground parking garage. "Hey, I caught up with the informant we have on the other side of the border."

"Yeah?" he asked absentmindedly, weaving through traffic, thinking about Molly.

"He says the Pebble Creek sheriff is over there a lot. He likes cockfights."

That had Mo sitting up and paying attention. "If he has a gambling problem—if some criminal has him in his debt—"

"They might be able to call in some favors," Ryder finished for him. "At the very least, get him to turn a blind eye."

Mo rubbed the back of his neck. "I don't like the guy. I can see him being up to no good. He's shifty."

"Maybe. Don't go convicting the sheriff yet just because the man is sweet on Molly Rogers."

Mo coughed. "I don't know what you're talking about. I'm not the jealous type."

"Sure. That's why your head turned blue the other day when Keith told you the sheriff's car was in her driveway."

He didn't want to go there. But talking about Molly... He hesitated for a second before he asked, "Have you seen Grace today yet?"

"Sure."

"She didn't mention anything about Molly being upset this morning, did she?"

"Why would Molly Rogers be upset?"

He didn't want to go there, either. "Just thought, you know, since Grace helped her at the ranch this morning, she might have mentioned something to you."

"Grace didn't go to the Rogers ranch this morning."

"Early. Maybe before you stopped by her place. Around six."

A moment of silence passed. "Grace was with me at six. And before six, too."

Meaning that he'd spent the night with Grace. Unease skittered down Mo's spine.

"Is something wrong?" Ryder asked.

"I don't think so. Just got our wires crossed, probably."

But as soon as he hung up with Ryder, he dialed Molly. He should have called her sooner, but didn't want to crowed her if she needed a little time to process what had happened between them last night. He didn't want her to think he was pushing her into anything.

The call rang out, but she didn't pick up. Which didn't necessarily mean trouble. Could be she was just ignoring him. He was almost hoping that was the case.

He sure didn't like the alternative.

SHE DIDN'T TAKE Mo's call. She didn't want to lie to him again. It was almost over.

She kept her eyes on the approaching black van in the

distance and the dust cloud that followed it. She slid off the rock she used to sit on as a kid and left the shade of the mesquite grove, hurried over to the pickup, reached in through the open window and beeped her horn to guide Kenny in the right direction.

Endless, agonizing seconds passed before he reached close enough so she could see Logan in the passenger seat. Then she could fully fill her lungs for the first time since he hadn't stepped off the school bus yesterday.

Logan was here. He looked okay. Everything would be fine now.

She ran to the van as soon as Kenny stopped, got her son out and grabbed him up into her arms, kissing him silly. "Are you okay?"

He held on to her neck for all he was worth, didn't protest about being a big boy or any of that.

She never wanted to let him out of her arms again. "Did anyone hurt you?"

He shook his head, keeping a brave face, but there were smudged tear tracks on his little cheeks. "Can we go home, Mom?"

"Yes, we can." She set him down, took his hand and walked toward her pickup with him when Kenny said, "I'd like to see what you have here first."

"It's down there." She pointed at the open metal doors.

"I'd rather that you came with me." Then he added, "The kid, too."

He might not have brought his police cruiser, but he did bring his service revolver. He glanced at the gun in the holster at his side, then at her, without saying anything.

Her pickup waited a few steps away. If they ran… But they'd be sitting ducks while they got in and she started the engine. She didn't want to give Kenny a reason to do something stupid. She would do whatever it took to stop the situation from escalating into violence.

So she held her son's hand and walked to the dark hole. "It's fine. Almost done." She did her best to reassure him, holding on to him as they went down together.

Kenny followed right behind them, picking up the extra flashlight.

She skirted around the snake, keeping herself between it and Logan, trying not to make a big deal of the move, hoping Kenny would step right on the rattler. But he was paying attention, pulled his gun and blew the snake's head clear off.

The sound was deafening in the tunnel. Logan held on to her tightly. "Mom?"

"It's okay. Just a snake, honey." She led Kenny to the two crates, panned them with the flashlight, ready to turn and leave.

But Kenny said, "Where is the rest?"

Her stomach sank. This couldn't be happening. "What rest?"

"I'm looking for a lot more than this. I need the full shipment."

The shaft stretched in front of them, breaking off into several corridors up ahead. Would Dylan leave these two crates here as a decoy? Maybe for the authorities, in case they found his hiding place? Then he would hide the bulk of his hoard in a place more difficult to reach. Possibly.

"Maybe the rest are farther in," she suggested, just as Kenny's light went out.

He banged it against the heel of his hand, but nothing happened. He tossed it aside and grabbed hers then strode forward. "Let's find the damned things."

"You don't need us for this. Please let us go. It's all yours now, Kenny."

But he gestured for her to walk ahead of him. "Just to make sure you delivered what you promised."

For a second the beam of the flashlight hit his face and she saw his expression, regret mixed with determination.

"Go ahead. And make sure the kid sticks close to you."

The kid. He hadn't called Logan by name once. He hadn't called her by name, either, not on the phone, not since he'd gotten here.

Because he is distancing himself. A chill ran down her spine.

"Just let us go. All I want is Logan. I won't ever say a word about this to anyone. I swear."

His gaze fell on her son. "We'll find the crates together."

Fear sliced through her when she understood at last. Kenny didn't plan on letting Logan and her leave.

"Go," he snapped, getting impatient.

Panic filled her as she stumbled forward, her finger-tips going numb. Why hadn't she thought of this before? Of course he wouldn't let them go. She was a witness. She knew that the Pebble Creek sheriff was involved in smuggling. He couldn't risk that she would tell someone about it. And even if he thought she could keep her mouth shut, there was Logan. He wouldn't trust a kid to keep his secret.

God, she'd been an idiot.

She'd been so focused on getting Logan back. And Kenny had been her brother's friend. She'd known the man all her life. She simply hadn't thought he would cross that line. Harming anyone, let alone a kid, was so unimaginable to her, she had trouble believing someone she knew would do something like that.

A naive and dangerous way to be.

Dylan had been ready to shoot Grace. She no longer doubted that Grace was telling the truth about that. Bitterness rose in her throat. This was what money and greed did to people—turned them into something you no longer recognized.

"Kenny, you can't—"

"Keep going."

She should have trusted Mo. She squeezed her eyes shut for a second. She should have told him what was going on. Mo would have helped her.

She shoved her free hand into her pocket. If she could get off a text message to Mo without Kenny noticing… She glanced at the display. She had zero reception down here.

No calls going out, no calls coming in.

It was too late.

MO LOOKED AT the finger-challenged gangbanger in the interrogation room then shoved the table aside. The man had been questioned by both Shep and CBP but had refused to talk. Gang code or whatever.

Jose Caballo. He was the one who'd stabbed Garcia Cruz to death, as it turned out. He'd been using his victim's ID as a joke.

"I'm only going to ask one more time. Why did you slash Molly Rogers's tires? What were you doing there?"

The man flashed him a dispassionate look.

Mo slammed the bastard against the wall, shoving his thumb into just the right spot between the man's vertebrae.

Jose gave a shout of pain.

"How is the bottom half of your body feeling?" Mo whispered into the man's ear. "Feel anything?" He waited as the man moaned. "I didn't think so." He pushed harder. "I can make it so you'll never have feeling down there again."

Sweat rolled down the man's face.

"Kiss the chicas goodbye, amigo," Mo went on. "Then again, women aren't going to be a big problem for you any-

way, not when you're going to federal prison for murder.
Plenty of gangs there. And you in a wheelchair. Hell, I sure
wouldn't want to be defenseless like that."

Jose's lips were turning white.

"What were you looking for at the Rogers ranch?" Mo
asked.

And for the first time, the man spoke. "Drugs."

"Who sent you? Who told you to scare her?"

"Nobody. I got my fingers chopped for that. I was just
supposed to find the drugs. She wasn't supposed to know.
I got angry when I didn't find anything."

She wasn't supposed to know. Just like the other men
in the barn, using a Taser instead of a gun. As if whoever
sent them made sure to tell them Molly shouldn't get hurt.

In the back of his mind, puzzle pieces shuffled and revealed a picture he didn't like. He needed to know for sure
if he was right. "Who do you work for? Is it Sheriff Davis?"

The man squeezed his eyes shut and pressed his lips together. The pain had to be close to unbearable.

Molly was missing.

Mo pushed harder.

"Yes." The man bit out the words then dropped at Mo's
feet.

He left him, strode past a couple of cops in the hallway.
"He passed out. Probably low blood pressure. Might want
to give him a cup of water."

Then he drove to the office for extra guns and ammo
and a quick powwow with his team.

"Something kept pricking my instincts about him, but I
thought it was just because the man was putting moves on
Molly." He'd called already, but Kenny was off duty and
couldn't be reached. Same as Molly. He swore, frustration
and worry filling him.

"She could be at the hairdresser or whatever, with her phone turned off," Jamie suggested.

Mo shook his head. Molly was in trouble. He could feel it in his bones, and it drove him crazy.

Ryder's face darkened. "Hey, we've all been working in this field long enough to respect instinct. If you say something's wrong, something's wrong. What do you want to do?"

"Track her cell phone." It was the best idea he could come up with during the ride back from Hullett. "I'd like to know where she is. If her car is parked in front of some hair salon…" But he knew it wouldn't be.

"What's her number?" Shep asked, bringing up the satellite log-in.

Mo rattled it off.

Shep entered it. "It's going to take a couple of minutes."

"We can track Kenny Davis's car, too. All the police cruisers have trackers," Jamie said. "That might go faster."

Shep worked his keyboard for a few interminably long minutes. "Okay, got the tracking code for the car." He typed something into the keyboard. Waited, then looked up, his face grim. "The sheriff's cruiser is parked in front of the police station. He's using another vehicle."

"Want me to call in Keith and Ray?" Ryder offered.

Mo shook his head. "Let's see first if we have anything." But he knew they did. He checked the pistol he normally carried, then grabbed his two backup weapons from his desk drawer and holstered up.

"Last known location is her ranch, right?" Jamie asked. "Any sign of struggle there?"

"No."

"All right. Satellite response. Here's Molly." Shep turned his screen around, and Mo leaned closer. The image showed the borderlands with a red dot in the middle of nowhere.

"That's on the Rogers ranch." Mo recognized the section of the map immediately. He'd studied it enough in the past few weeks. "Can you tell how long she's been there?"

"Actually, that's not a current reading. It's from about an hour ago."

"What about now?"

"Nothing. The signal disappeared."

"Pretty close to the border," Shep observed. "If she is involved in something…"

The Rio Grande, a dark line snaking through the landscape, rolled just a little to the south.

"No." Mo entered the coordinates into his phone's GPS then strode for the door. "She's in trouble. I don't know what's going on, but there's something wrong about this."

Ryder kicked his chair back, reaching for his weapon on his desk. "Don't think you're going to have all the fun."

They all followed after him, each going to his own SUV. His team, Mo thought. It was the darndest thing. They'd only been a team for a few months. He barely knew them. Other than a security detail once or twice here in the U.S. under special circumstances, he'd done lone-wolf operations, mostly overseas, for most of his career.

He didn't figure himself for a team guy. He'd never even played team sports. In high school, he'd done weight lifting. The funny feeling that caught him now, as the others all lined up to follow him on a hunch, caught him unexpectedly.

"I appreciate this," he called out as they all jumped into their SUVs.

They didn't dillydally on the road, either. They were on the Rogers ranch in record time, then off-roading it to the GPS coordinates. A storm gathered, dark clouds rolling across the sky.

Dammit, Molly. He'd sensed that something wasn't quite

right last night, but had let lust carry him away instead of pushing her for answers. And that note this morning… He should have called her sooner. He wished she could have trusted him enough to ask for his help.

He'd thought they were closer.

But obviously she didn't share the feeling. Which bothered him for a number of reasons.

He spotted her pickup and headed straight for it, worried about the van parked just a few feet away. No windows in the back, license plate smeared with dirt, nondescript dark color. The type of car used by people who didn't want to be noticed. Because they were up to no good. *Hell.*

He pulled up hard, jumped out, then the others were there, too, half a minute later. That he didn't know what was going on just about killed him.

"What's this?" Jamie hurried forward, toward the hole in the ground, catching up with Mo.

Mo's muscles tightened. "Old mine shaft." The county was riddled with them. Most of them were completely unsafe, nothing but death traps. Which was why they were kept blocked off, usually.

"You knew about this?" Ryder wanted to know.

He shook his head. "Whatever is going on here, Molly is not a willing participant."

Jamie looked at the sky. "It's going to rain soon," he observed casually. "Getting trapped underground in torrential rains wouldn't be the smartest thing."

Ryder called in Keith and Ray for backup, but nobody was about to wait for them.

"Better get her up and out of here fast." Mo drew his gun and went down the ramp first, pulled the standard military-issue flashlight off his belt. He saw a dead snake that had recently met with a bullet. He kicked it aside. A little farther in, two wooden crates stood in the middle of the path. Beyond that, the shaft went on for a few hundred feet before branching off in several directions.

"Looks like we found our drugs," Ryder said.

Mo passed by the crates without looking at them twice. "Now let's find Molly. And keep an eye out for her son, too," he added on instinct. He could only think of one reason why Molly would be down here, with crates of drugs.

He'd bet his Cat Counting company shares Logan was in trouble.

They hurried forward, stopped at the intersection of tunnels, four shafts for the four of them. They didn't waste time arguing over whether to stick together or split up. They were tough commando soldiers; each could handle pretty much anything on their own.

Mo took the shaft that went straight forward, gun in one hand, flashlight in the other.

Thunder sounded above and the earth shook as lightning struck. Dirt snowed on his head, underscoring the fact that the old structure wasn't exactly stable. He just hoped it held long enough to rescue Molly and Logan.

Chapter Twelve

They had precious little light to see by. The surrounding darkness was oppressive, a heavy presence pushing down on them. The air smelled musty. The deeper they went, the more the temperature dropped. *Cold as a grave.* Molly shook off the thought. She had to keep it together. She had to figure out a way to escape or they'd be killed.

"Faster," Kenny ordered. "I have other things to do today."

"I can barely see where I'm going." She had no intention of hurrying. She needed time to think.

As soon as they found the rest of the crates, he would shoot them, like he had shot the snake, she thought as they passed yet another shaft, this one going straight down. When Kenny shined the light into the hole, she could see water about seven or eight feet below.

This part of her ranch lay higher than the lands a little farther south, where the Rio Grande rushed to the east, but was still low enough for her to wonder if the rain that threatened would come and when. She had plans to escape from Kenny, and she didn't plan on drowning.

"Not down there, I'm guessing," Kenny said as he passed by the hole. "Keep moving."

Then they reached another central spot that led to multiple shafts. A giant mass loomed up ahead in one of them, a dark shadow that reached from the floor to the ceiling. They found the rest of the crates.

"Good," Kenny said with a dose of relief. "We lost too much money in the factory raid. Your brother ponied up for that. If this got lost, I'd have to pay for it."

Pain bubbled up in her heart. Dylan... She shook her head. Was that why he'd mortgaged the ranch? Didn't matter now. She couldn't worry about that at the moment. She had to figure out a way to survive this.

As Kenny panned the crates with the flashlight, she caught the glint of a thin wire a few feet in front of them. Only because she'd been looking, because she'd been expecting it. Kenny didn't seem to notice the booby trap. So Dylan *had* protected his treasure.

She had a split second to make a decision. She gave Logan's hand a squeeze, a silent warning. Then she spun around and kicked the flashlight from Kenny's hand, doing her best to copy the move she'd seen Mo teach Logan.

Miraculously, she hit her target. The next second they were plunged into darkness.

"Quick!" She dragged her son down a shaft, away from the crates, running forward in the pitch dark and praying they didn't fall. Her only goal was to get as far from Kenny and that wire as possible.

"Get back here!" Kenny shouted, swearing after them.

Then he found the flashlight and shone the light around. She saw another shaft to her left. She dragged Logan into it, into the darkness and out of Kenny's line of sight.

With a little luck, he would want to check the crates first. She ran forward, stumbling, catching herself. "Hurry!"

Logan didn't have to be told twice. He ran as fast as his little legs could carry him. Soccer practice paid off, obviously. He ran just as fast as she did.

She only wished she could see better. She was completely disoriented in the dark, hoping the tunnel was straight so she wouldn't run face first into a wall. She kept a step in front of Logan, so at least she could save him from injury. If she crashed, she would just have to pick herself up and keep going.

They were both breathing hard, wheezing for air that was musty and humid this deep inside the shaft.

The explosion, when it came, knocked her off her feet.

THE GROUND-SHAKING boom didn't come from lightning above. This was an explosion, underground, and it scared the spit out of Mo. He'd seen plenty of explosions in his life, had been the cause of a number of them.

But this time, Molly's life was at stake, and possibly Logan's.

At least the sound told him in what direction to run. He picked up speed, ready for anything, panning the light over the ground then on the ceiling to make sure he wasn't running headfirst into a tunnel that was collapsing.

Then, after an eternity, he spotted another light up ahead and soon made out the form of a man sitting, heard him cough from the dust that filled the air. Behind him, the tunnel was filled with rubble.

Mo pushed forward. "Sheriff?"

Only then did the man notice him, looking up with a startled expression on his face. But before Mo could ask where Molly was, the Pebble Creek sheriff swung his arm around and opened fire.

Bam. Bam. Bam. The acrid smell of gun smoke filled the dusty air.

Mo tossed his flashlight that did nothing at this stage but make him a target, then returned fire. Kenny was smart enough to turn off his own light the next instant. The two of them shot at each other blindly, bullets ricocheting off the rock walls.

God, this was stupid.

"Molly?" Mo called out in the dark. Just because he hadn't seen her didn't mean she hadn't been back there somewhere in the shadows. He didn't want to hit her accidently.

But no response came.

Shots peppered the air for about another minute. Then nothing. Looked as if they ran out of bullets at the same time.

He shoved his empty gun into the back of his waistband and lurched forward, groping for Kenny. Beams creaked above them, an ominous sound. But even over that, he could hear the bastard's wheezing.

That led him to the man, and Mo grabbed him by the shoulders, from the feel of it. "Where is she?"

"Go to hell." Kenny kicked out, bringing them to the stone-covered ground.

Rolling on that didn't feel too good, as sharp shards shredded Mo's skin. He tried to keep on top of Kenny as much as possible. The sheriff was in pretty good shape and trained in hand-to-hand combat, putting up a damned good fight. He was lighter than Mo and quicker. But in the end Mo's sheer muscle-mass advantage got the better of him.

"Where is she?" He slammed the man into the ground and felt something wet on the back of his hands. Probably blood. Couldn't tell which one of them was bleeding.

Kenny coughed. "Ran into a tunnel."

"Which one?"

Kenny only laughed at that.

"Where is she?" Mo demanded again and shook him harder, but the man's body went slack.

This time Kenny didn't cough, just wheezed. He didn't

fight back, either. Maybe he'd caught a bullet. "Don't know. Got away."

He'd find her. "Who sends the drugs over?" Mo asked next.

This was the closest his team had gotten to something real. Dylan Rogers had died before he could have been questioned. "Who is Coyote?"

Kenny wheezed.

"Tell me how I find the guy, and I'll get you out of here," Mo promised. "Or I'm leaving and you can bleed out in this hellhole, wondering if the rats or the collapsing ceiling will get to you first."

The beams groaned, underscoring his words.

Kenny gave a weak cough, his body completely limp now. "Coyote," he said, his hand coming up to grab Mo's wrist.

"Who is he?"

But Kenny's hand fell away, each breath shallower than the one before it.

"Don't you die, you damned traitor." Mo swore.

"Needed the money." Kenny gasped. "Doesn't hurt anybody. If I don't do it, someone else will."

"Bringing terrorists into the country doesn't hurt anybody?"

"Just drugs and guns. Some illegals."

Mo shook him again, running out of patience. "What do you know about the terrorists?"

"Nobody's coming in." He took a break to wheeze. "It's all on hold."

They already knew that. But now something new occurred to Mo. Once Coyote let his dogs loose, they'd rush to make up for the lost income. A sudden influx of contraband would keep CBP busy. Busy enough so that someplace unexpected, a small group of terrorists could be sneaked across the border. Sure looked as if all this was part of a grand plan.

He gripped the man's shoulders. "Until when is everything on hold? When can you start up again?"

But the sheriff seemed past talking.

Mo let the man go and searched for his flashlight, found it after a few minutes of mad groping. "Talk to me, dammit." He aimed the light at Kenny.

A gunshot wound bloomed in the middle of the man's chest.

"When?" he demanded.

For a second, Kenny's eyes slid open. "Help," he gasped. "I'm dying."

"At least don't die a traitor." But he wasn't sure the bastard heard him. His eyes closed again.

Mo shook him. Nothing. The sheriff was completely out of it, dammit. There'd be no answers coming from him.

Mo gritted his teeth while the mine rumbled around them as cracks ran through the tunnels, the shock waves from the explosion destabilizing the entire structure.

He needed to get to Molly. A half-dozen shafts opened from the main tunnel he'd followed here. No time to make mistakes. Which one to take?

A scraping sound came from behind him.

He swung the flashlight that way. "Molly?"

Skipper bounded out of the darkness, giving an anxious bark.

"How did you get here?"

He knew the answer before Skipper jumped up on him, barking, licking his face. Ryder had called Grace, and she had come with the dog. Thank God.

He ruffled Skipper's fur. "Find Molly. Come on, girl. Where's Logan?"

The dog's intelligent eyes glistened in the semidarkness. She sniffed around then darted down the closest shaft.

Mo ran after her. "Molly!"

And somewhere, far ahead, he heard a scream.

The sound cut right through his heart. He ran. Then he ran harder. He was running for the woman he was falling in love with, dammit.

The few minutes until he found her seemed an eternity. They huddled in the dark a hundred feet ahead of him, looking like statues, covered in gray dust. Skipper was whining and prodding them with her nose. And then the tangle of limbs moved. His heart dared beat again.

"Are you two okay?" He held his breath for the answer.

"Some of the dirt came down. I thought it would bury us." She shook dust from her head, then ruffled Logan's hair to clean him off.

He helped them stand. They could move. Okay. Good. Nothing looked broken. He pulled them up into his arms, held them tight, Skipper muscling her way into the middle. "Did Kenny have anyone with him?"

"He was alone." Molly's voice was more than a little shaky. "What are you doing here with Skipper? How did you find us?"

"Long story. I'll tell you later."

The mine groaned and creaked all around them, an ominous boom sounding in the distance.

"Run!" He grabbed for her hand. She tugged Logan after her, and they moved as fast as was possible under the circumstances, the dog running ahead, barking.

When they reached Kenny, Mo panned the light over the man. He *had* promised to take him out. But Kenny was no longer breathing. His eyes gazed off into nothing.

Then Mo caught something in the dust next to him. Some scribbles: *10 1.* His mind registered the numbers before Skipper walked all over the writing and erased it. She sniffed Kenny, nudged him with her nose a couple of times, then walked back to Logan.

October first.

But what did the date mean? They needed the information Kenny could have given them. Too late. And no time to worry over it. Mo kept moving.

He had to focus on what could still be saved. "We have to hurry."

Except, somehow the force of the explosion traveled through certain layers of rock and collapsed the tunnel ahead of them, too, he realized as he panned ahead with his flashlight. They were in some kind of a pocket, held up as if by a miracle.

They stared at the pile of rocks that blocked their way, only a small hole open on top. And that not for long, Mo saw. The entire structure was unstable. The rest would come down if any of them tried to climb up there.

Molly stepped forward. "We can push through." Panic tinged her voice.

"No." He held her back. Then gave her the truth straight-out, because she deserved to know. "This whole level is collapsing."

COLD FEAR PARALYZED HER. "We have to get out," she begged, her gaze fixed on that little hole. They could squeeze through there. She knew they could. It was the way they had come in. They needed to get out. *Now.*

But Mo pulled her back again. "Not that way."

"There's no other way!"

"There was a shaft going down, to a lower level."

That hole with the water at the bottom? That made no sense. She didn't want to go down, deeper into the earth. She wanted to go up. Her panic and every instinct she had pushed her toward that small gap in the rubble. If they could crawl through there...

Skipper could help with the digging. She was a great digger. "Come on, Skipper."

But Skipper was backing away.

"Listen to me," Mo said in that steady voice of his. "Trust me."

Trust? Oh, God, now? She was nearly blind with fear, ready to bolt like a scared animal.

Yet on some level... She closed her eyes for a second. Drew a deep breath. *This is Mo,* she thought. *This is Mo.* He wanted to protect her. She didn't doubt that. Did she trust him to know what he was doing?

She wanted to trust him. She swallowed hard. "Okay."

And then she let him lead her and her son back, to the hole that freaked her out completely.

The ceiling shook above them. Water glistened below. Just above the level of the water, an opening gaped in the side of the vertical drop, the entry to another horizontal tunnel, parallel to theirs. The remains of a wooden ladder clung to the wall of the down shaft, pretty thoroughly rotted. No way could they step on that.

"So we just drop? Then what?"

"We don't drop. There could be something in that water, a sharp beam. Don't want anyone to get skewered." He lay on the ground and leaned in, panned the hole with his flashlight. "I'll lower you down. Come on. You first. Logan? Can you hold the flashlight, buddy?"

Logan stared at her, too shaken to move.

"It's like the next level in a video game," Mo told him, his voice steady and gentle. "That's the level that takes us out of here. Then we win."

Logan nodded at last and took the flashlight from him, angled it at the hole below them.

Mo took her hands, lowered her, swung her toward the opening. She lunged for her target, landed on her knees, probably lost some skin, but it was the least of her worries. An inch or two of water covered the bottom. Other than that, she couldn't see much of the shaft.

"Ready?" His voice came from above.

She moved back to the opening, caught the flashlight Mo tossed her and set it down so it illuminated the entry and he would know what to aim for. "Yes." And then she caught Logan as Mo swung him.

He came next, lowering himself handhold by handhold while beams fell above.

"Come on, Skipper. Jump!" He held out his arms as soon as his feet were on solid ground.

Skipper whined above.

"Jump!" Logan shouted.

And the dog lunged into the hole while Molly held her breath.

Mo caught her, dragged her into the shaft with them.

And then the mine shuddered around them once again. It felt like an earthquake. Rocks fell down the drop they'd just come down. Dust filled the space as the upper level collapsed, everything shaking.

They held their breaths, Mo sheltering them from the falling debris with his great body. But that was all, just some earth and small rocks. Their level held.

"Let's get out of here," he said as soon as the tremors stopped.

Skipper led them, and they followed her, coughing up dust, sloshing through rising water. Must be raining up on top, on the surface. It didn't look good. In fact, it didn't look as if they were going to make it.

She squeezed her son's hand. "Good job. I love you."

Logan looked up to her. "I love you, too, Mom."

She bit her lip as she turned to Mo. "I'm sorry I didn't tell you about Kenny. I'm sorry about everything."

It needed to be said. She had never been as happy as when she heard Mo's voice calling for her back there. "I know you're mad at me, but I can explain—"

"I'm not mad at you." He took her hand and held it. "Are you okay there, buddy? You're not scared, are you?" he asked Logan.

"It's like a video game, right?" Logan asked with a measure of uncertainty, but he held it together.

Skipper stuck to him like glue. That probably helped a lot.

"It's exactly like that," Mo reassured her son with full confidence. "And guess what? We're definitely winning."

"We are?"

"Do I know about video games or what?"

And then Logan gave a little smile, and Molly's heart melted. Whether they were really winning or not, he took her son's fear away and that was a big thing.

They slogged forward for what seemed an eternity, found other tunnels. Mo moved forward without hesitation each time. Now and then, he let Skipper guide them.

"How do you know which way to go?" Logan asked.

"I have a pretty good sense of direction. And so does your dog. If there's fresh air coming in anywhere up ahead, she can smell it."

Molly gave thanks for that. Maybe they did have a slim chance. If they could outrun the water.

"How many entrances to the mine?" Mo asked her.

"Half dozen, but other than the one we came through, the rest are sealed."

"They can be unsealed. We have backup. If we can't find a way up, they'll come for us. Very likely most of the shafts are connected."

Okay. That made her feel better.

He stopped when they reached air that wasn't so filled with dust. It seemed the explosion hadn't shaken this section. He pulled out his phone.

"No reception down here," she told him.

"That's fine. I'm activating an emergency beacon."

"Will that work?"

"You bet. It's new technology we just started testing. A new generation of the technology they use in black boxes in airplanes."

That sounded encouraging. Authorities could find black boxes all the way on the bottom of the ocean after planes crashed. They should be able to find them here. A little more hope came to life inside her.

"I'd appreciate it if you didn't mention this to anyone," Mo said to the both of them. "It's still experimental and kind of a government secret."

"Sure," she promised.

While Logan said, "It's like a spy video game," looking wide-eyed and impressed.

Truth be told, she was no less excited about the gadget. But as they moved on, it occurred to her how strange it was that he would have something like that. Why would a policy-recommendation team test top technology such as this? *Secret* technology.

Not for the first time, she had the sneaky suspicion his team was more than what they seemed. Not a topic to bring up in front of Logan, obviously.

They'd been sloshing through water that was an inch or two deep, but suddenly it was reaching to midcalf, rising rapidly now. Either the tunnel slanted down or rain was coming down pretty hard above. She tightened her hold on Mo's hand.

He looked back at her, then at the water and squeezed

back as if saying *It's fine.* He had noticed her apprehension. She should have known. He missed little.

He kept on moving forward, and she followed, instead of backing up to higher ground. She had decided she would trust him, and so she would. She would trust him with her life and with her son's, because he'd earned her trust and because she was in love with him.

The admission shook her as hard as the explosion had.

But she was jarred out of her daze when his cell phone pinged.

"What's that?" Logan asked as Skipper let out a woof.

"A sign that the rescue team is coming for us." Mo looked at the screen. "From that direction." He pointed straight ahead. "Might as well meet them halfway, if you can keep going."

"Yep," Logan said.

"We're fine," Molly added. The sooner they were above ground, the better.

But the going was slow over the uneven ground. Here and there they had to crawl over old rubble. Nearly an hour passed before they met the rescue detail, Ryder and Shep. By then, the water was up to their knees.

Ryder scooped up Logan.

Mo scooped up Molly.

And then the going got quite a bit faster. The men moved like a well-oiled machine.

They reached a shaft that led up, a rope hanging down, Jamie looking down on them from above. Ryder climbed easily with Logan on his back. Shep tossed a squirming Skipper across his shoulders and Skipper lay flat, if whining a little.

Mo put Molly down and turned his back to her. "Piggy-back ride. Get on."

She hesitated.

"We don't have time for this," he reminded her gently.

The water reached midthigh.

She set aside her pride and climbed on, her arms around his neck, but not too tight. He took them up without effort and didn't put her down when they reached the top, just started running with her.

As the light of his flashlight wobbled in front of them, she could see why. Several support beams had fallen. The tunnel could collapse at any second.

And then it did, just as Mo dived through the opening with her, out into the night lit up by car beams all around them.

Rain lashed at her face as they lay side by side, gasping for air. Hands reached for them, Logan plowing into her before she had a chance to stand, knocking the both of them into the mud. Mo pulled them up.

Grace was there somewhere, asking how they were, what she could do to help. Skipper was licking Logan's face.

"I got them," Mo said, his voice rough.

Grace got in a hug anyway. "Friends don't give friends gray hair," she groused before she stepped away, her eyes brimming with relief.

Molly could barely breathe. She was covered in mud and bruises. So was her son. She hugged him tight as rain lashed them.

Mo put a hand on her shoulder. "Better get into the car. I'm going to take you over to the hospital."

She nodded and followed him. She was fine, but she wanted to make sure Logan was all right. She sat in the back of the SUV with Logan, not wanting to let go of him.

"I'm sorry." She apologized to Mo again once Logan fell asleep, exhausted from his ordeal.

Skipper snored on the seat next to them, her head on

Logan's lap, smelling like wet dog. She didn't mind in the least. She could have hugged her. She'd saved their lives.

"You did what you thought was best in order to save your son." His gaze cut to hers in the rearview mirror. "But don't ever do it again. If you are in any kind of trouble, you call me first."

"Yes." She'd learned her lesson. "I wanted to trust you. I do trust you…" She bit her lip.

"What is it?"

"I'm a terrible decision maker. I've done so many stupid things over the years."

"I doubt that," he said mildly.

"You barely know anything about me."

"You have deep, dark secrets?" He sounded skeptical.

If only he knew… She squeezed her eyes together for a second. "My mother had affairs. A lot of them."

"You're not your mother."

"My father drank. I blamed her. We had a big fight one day. I told her we'd all be better off without her. She left. Instead of getting better, my father drank himself to death."

"Not your fault. He was the adult. You were the kid."

Oh, but he didn't know all of it. "Then I was…stupid with a guy a few years older than me. Got pregnant." She drew a deep breath, about to tell him something she'd never told anyone. "Mikey Metzner is Logan's father."

He'd been the most eligible bachelor in town, son of the owner of the wire mill. Now in jail for trafficking. She winced. A long silence stretched between them before she continued.

"I thought he'd be happy with the baby. I thought we'd be getting married. First he told me he didn't believe me that he was the father. Then he told me that if I repeated my dirty lies to anyone, he would make sure the baby was taken away from me. He has money to burn. He could hire every lawyer in the county."

Even now, if he ever decided he wanted a son. Even with him in prison, he could petition that custody be given to his mother. Grandparents had rights. With all his money, he could take Logan away from her, a fear she'd lived with for the past eight years.

"You were what, a teenager?" Mo asked, his tone clipped.

"Seventeen."

It sounded as if he was swearing under his breath, but she wasn't sure.

She didn't even want to know what he was thinking of her. That she was the village idiot, probably.

Which was so unfair. Because he was great, and she was completely in love with him.

Pitiful, really.

Epilogue

One week later

"If you want me to come get you, just give me a call," Molly said into the phone, standing in the middle of her foyer, looking out at the front yard where her three dogs were wrestling.

"No way, Mom," Logan said on the other end. "Aunt Grace needs me."

Yes, she was sure Grace made her son feel wanted. It was nice of her to offer to have him over for the birth of a foal that was coming into the world tonight. Logan was a tough little kid, but the kidnapping and escape from the mine had rattled him. He needed some new happy memories to push the bad ones away.

He'd been sticking to her like glue since the mine incident, even missed a day or two of school. And she'd been sticking to him, truth be told, not wanting to let him out of her sight. But she had to.

Even if she would be lonely tonight.

Or not, she thought as she saw Mo's SUV pull up her driveway. Her heart leaped.

"All right. Be very gentle and do whatever Grace tells you," she told Logan.

"Okay, Mom."

"I love you bunches."

"I love you, too."

Even if he thought he was too old to hold hands, he still thought saying *I love you* was okay. That was something. She was determined to enjoy what she could get before he reached the surly teenage years.

She hung up then went to let Mo in. She'd been locking her doors, a newfound habit.

They hadn't seen each other since the rescue. The team was working around the clock to track down a new clue Kenny provided them with, although Mo wouldn't tell her what it was.

He had asked whether Dylan had a friend named Coyote, but he wouldn't tell her who Coyote was, either. If her brother had known anyone like that, she knew nothing about it. Still, he did mention progress, which was nice to hear. She had a feeling his team was working on something big and it had nothing to do with policy recommendations.

"Hi." Mo came through the door, looking handsome and smelling like soap, probably fresh out of the shower.

The dogs were jumping all over him. He was handing out squeaky toys left and right. "I got some mighty big bones, too, in the car. Skipper gets double."

She'd missed him. Stupid. He was probably only here to read her the riot act over her stunt with Kenny. He'd said he'd understood, but then he hadn't come out to the ranch since.

She'd broken his trust. Of course, he was about to break her heart. She'd fallen for him and he would be leaving for the next step in his career as soon as his project here was finished.

She tried not to show how much the thought of that killed her. "How is work?" she asked as the dogs ran off with their toys.

"We're moving forward. Not as fast as we'd like, but it's something." He reached out and took her hand, sending her temperature up a notch.

It was ridiculous that all he had to do was touch her to make her go weak in the knees. He meant nothing by it. He'd seen her at her worst. He couldn't possibly want her.

So they'd had great sex. He'd probably had that with a lot of women. He probably wasn't dreaming of her every night, as she was dreaming of him.

"Sweet tea?" she asked by way of a distraction.

"Later," he said and kissed her.

Thank God was all she could think.

He tasted like prickly pear jelly.

He pulled away too soon. "I'm sorry I haven't come sooner. I missed you." He glanced toward the stairs. "Where's Logan?"

"Spending the night with Grace."

The grin that spread across his face was downright devilish. It sent her heart racing.

He dipped his head and this time kissed her deeper, claiming her. A blissful eternity passed before he pulled away again, with a satisfied look, and reached into his back pocket, pulledout an envelope and handed it to her. "A gift for you."

What? All she could think about was that kiss. She tore into the envelope impatiently then unfolded the papers, thumbed through them, stunned, her throat tightening.

Termination of parental rights. Signed by Mikey Metzner.

Mikey gave up his parental rights to Logan, forever and irrevocably. Logan was hers, only hers, and nobody could ever take her son away from her.

Moisture flooded her eyes. "How did you do this?"

"Offered him a nicer prison than the one where he was headed."

She flew into Mo's arms, and he gathered her against him, claimed her lips all over again. He explored her mouth, her face framed by his large hands, then kissed her eyes, planted more kisses down the line of her nose. He nudged her ear and nibbled his way down her neck, too.

When he backed her toward the kitchen counter, heat pooled at the V of her thighs. And she cringed.

"What is it?" he asked immediately.

She hung her head. "I'm embarrassed."

A puzzled look came over his face.

"I'm just like people say I am. Wanton and out of control." Her voice weakened as she admitted, "I've thought about this."

"And?"

"And I wanted it," she whispered.

He looked as pleased as peaches.

She swatted at his wide shoulder. "It's not normal. In the kitchen!"

"So you thought about the two of us? More than once?" He was watching her closely.

She gave a sheepish nod. "I'm a mother. I'm not supposed to think about naked men."

"How do you think people get the second and third kid?" His gaze searched her face. "So because of a few idiots who couldn't mind their own business, you locked your sensuality away."

It sounded kind of silly when he said it. Yet… "I'm completely out of control. I thought about you *a lot*. In worse places than the kitchen."

His eyes darkened with heat. "Go on. You thought about us where?"

She couldn't look at him. "Under the stars. Who does that? Maybe teenagers."

"The woman I love, that's who," he said and left her speechless. "Does that four-wheeler out in the garage have gas in it?"

"Sure."

He lifted her off the counter and took her hand. "Where are the keys?"

"What?" She felt the blood run out her face. Then it returned in a rush. And her body was suddenly tingling all over.

He didn't leave her time to hesitate, but drew her after him. He glanced at the keys by the back door, grabbed the right one.

They were in the middle of the fields by the time she half recovered, hardly able to believe that this was happening. He drove as if he was in a hurry. She had her arms tightly around his body, as much to hang on as because she liked the feel of him in her arms.

He finally stopped. They'd reached a high spot from where she could see her rolling fields in the moonlight, the stars bright above.

He shut down the engine then did some super move so he ended up with his back to the dashboard and her straddling him. She could feel his hardness through his jeans.

"You can't be serious."

But he did look serious. Very. "I want you."

She nodded weakly.

"I love you."

She had a hard time accepting that. "How do you know? It's too soon."

"When you know something is right, you don't have to think about it too much."

And she kind of understood what he was talking about,

because she felt the same way, as if Mo was right for her, just right, perfect.

But *she* wasn't perfect. Never had been.

Getting pregnant as a teenager was the least of it. She'd done worse things than that, much worse. She bit her lower lip. "I broke up my parents' marriage. I'm responsible for my father's death."

He took her hands. "How about you let them take some of that responsibility? I think you've punished yourself long enough."

She shook her head. "You sound like Grace."

"You have some damn smart people in your life. You should start listening to them," he said, making her smile.

A moment of silence passed between them.

"Have you ever heard from your mother?" He reached under her chin and lifted it.

She couldn't bear looking at him as she confessed, "A few years later she was beaten to death by a violent boyfriend." She swallowed hard. "If I didn't run her off—"

"No." He shook his head. "Your parents made their own choices. None of it was your fault. You were a kid."

His complete lack of judgment lightened some of the old heaviness inside her.

He rubbed his thumbs over her hands in a comforting gesture, then gave her a searching look, as if measuring her up for something. "I'm moving out to the ranch. I don't want you out here alone."

"Grace is alone."

"Ryder is with her as much as he can be. And Grace is an Army veteran. I want to be with you, and not just for your protection. But make no mistake, I will be protecting you. I don't think you're helpless, but I can't see you and Logan in danger. I'm just not made that way."

She stared at him.

"And I'm not coming just to protect you. I want to be with you."

Her heart turned over in her chest. "People will think I'm a total hussy if I shack up with you after barely knowing each other."

"People will extend us all courtesy, I believe."

Ha! "Why would they?"

"I'm about to become the town's favorite son. You'll be hosting social functions at my side. Can you handle the society pages?"

She had a hard time picturing herself anyplace else but in the gossip column at best. "I don't understand."

"I just talked my brother into building his new factory in Hullett. The town is about to see some seriously improved employment, I believe."

Her chin dropped. "You did that? Why?"

"I told you, I love you. I want to settle down here. What do you have to say about that?"

She swallowed. "The mind boggles."

HE GRINNED AT HER. "Not exactly what I wanted to hear. Let's try this again. I love you, Molly Rogers. What do you have to say about that?"

"I love you back," she said at last.

Warmth spread through his chest.

"Much better." He leaned forward and pulled her head to his.

But she held back. "What happens when you leave? I don't even know how long you'll be staying."

"I'm not going anywhere."

Hope filled her eyes. "What about that next level, the career move you wanted?"

"My father's dream. Here is the thing…" He rubbed his chin. "I see how you are with Logan. You just want him to be happy. When it comes right down to it, I think my father would have wanted that for me, too." He'd wanted to join the CIA to make his father's dream come true. While his father, if he was alive, would probably have wanted Mo's dream to come true.

And Mo's dream was Molly and a life with her and her son. "All I want is right here," he said. And then came the tricky part. "What I do… What if I can't really ever tell you about it?" Secrets could kill a relationship. He'd seen that in his line of business.

"Then I'll trust you that you have a good reason."

"Just like that?"

"I know you're working to stop people like Kenny. That's enough for me."

"You liked him. I'm sorry he betrayed you."

"He was only nice to me to be able to come and go at the ranch. He was hoping he could find the drugs without having to resort to drastic measures."

"You went on a date with him." A wave of cold jealousy washed over him even as he said the words.

"Worst date ever. I was thinking about you the whole time."

He kissed her.

If he lived to a hundred he wouldn't get tired of kissing her lips. He savored her thoroughly, distracted her from everything else. She might have fantasized about this, but it still made her nervous. First he made sure she was comfortable, then worked his way up to mindless passion.

He began unbuttoning her shirt, button by button, claiming with his lips every newly discovered inch of skin. Then the shirt disappeared. Her simple cotton bra made him smile. She wasn't given to vanity. But she was mind-blowingly sexy even without accessories.

Right now, even the cotton bra seemed like too much,

in fact. He reached around and unhooked it with more finesse than the last time, then bared her to his hungry gaze.

He covered one amazing breast with his hand, the other with his mouth. Her head dipped back, her lips slightly parting from pleasure. *Nothing* in the whole world was better than this.

She reached out to unbutton his shirt, timidly at first, then more boldly. Her fingers splayed over his chest. She seemed to enjoy touching him. Good. Because he suddenly felt as if he'd die if she took her hands away.

She stroked his heated skin gently, then more insistently, her soft core rocking against his hardness as she straddled him. He wanted to drag out the moment, the pleasure that nearly bordered on pain, and he did, but only for a few minutes before he reached the point where he needed more, where he needed it all.

He reached for the button on her jeans and she reached for his. A flurry of activity followed, which left them both breathing hard and naked. When he grabbed a foil pocket from his back pocket and took care of that, he drew her onto his lap again so she straddled him like before, but then he stayed still, letting her lower herself onto him when she was ready, wanting to let her set the pace even if it killed him.

When her moist opening touched against him, the searing pleasure stole his breath. But yet he held still. She braced her hands on his shoulders, her slim fingers kneading his flesh. Her perfect breasts, the most tempting fruit in the world, jutted forward inches from his face, the nipples hard pebbles.

She lowered herself slow inch by slow inch, while all he could do was hang on to her hips and drown in the pleasure she was gifting him. When he was fully sheathed, she stopped, looked into his eyes, hers wide with wonder. And then he gently rocked against her, smiling when her breath caught from the sensation.

He felt it, too, the building pressure.

She moved a little faster. So did he.

Then her hands tightened on his shoulders, her head falling back, a low, sexy groan escaping her throat. He leaned forward and took her hard nipple into his mouth, drew on it sharply while rolling her other nipple between his thumb and forefinger. He had no idea where he got that kind of coordination. His brain was pretty much melted.

But she appreciated the effort and with a cry went over the edge, tightening and pulsing around him. Which sent him flying.

Later, when they were trying to catch their breath, leaning against each other, he pushed the hair back from her face and kissed her.

"You're right," he said. "If I move to the ranch, town tongues will be wagging. I have a solution."

"You do?" she asked weakly, her face still glowing with pleasure, the most beautiful sight he'd ever seen.

He brushed his lips over her swollen mouth gently, then whispered the question in her ear. "Molly Rogers, would you marry me?"

* * * * *

HQ: TEXAS *is just heating up!*
Look for Dana Marton's next book, MY SPY,
on sale in October 2013. You'll find it
wherever Intrigue books are sold!

Wrap up warm this winter with Sarah Morgan…

Sleigh Bells in the Snow

Kayla Green loves business and hates Christmas.

So when Jackson O'Neil invites her to Snow Crystal Resort to discuss their business proposal… the last thing she's expecting is to stay for Christmas dinner. As the snowflakes continue to fall, will the woman who doesn't believe in the magic of Christmas finally fall under its spell…?

4th October

www.millsandboon.co.uk/sarahmorgan

She's loved and lost — will she ever learn to open her heart again?

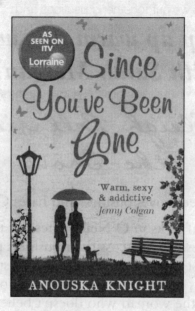

From the winner of ITV Lorraine's Racy Reads, Anouska Knight, comes a heart-warming tale of love, loss and confectionery.

'The perfect summer read — warm, sexy and addictive!'
—Jenny Colgan

For exclusive content visit:
www.millsandboon.co.uk/anouskaknight

0813/MB438

Special Offers

Every month we put together collections and longer reads written by your favourite authors.

Here are some of next month's highlights— and don't miss our fabulous discount online!

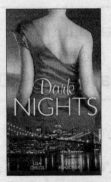

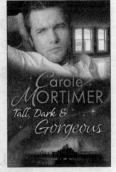

On sale 20th September   On sale 4th October   On sale 4th October

Save 20%
on all Special Releases

The World of Mills & Boon®

There's a Mills & Boon® series that's perfect for you. We publish ten series and, with new titles every month, you never have to wait long for your favourite to come along.

Blaze.

Scorching hot, sexy reads
4 new stories every month

By Request

Relive the romance with the best of the best
9 new stories every month

Cherish™

Romance to melt the heart every time
12 new stories every month

Desire™

Passionate and dramatic love stories
8 new stories every month

Visit us Online